FORD MADOX FORD

The Good Soldier

Edited by DAVID BRADSHAW

PENGUIN BOOKS

PENGUIN CLASSICS

Published by the Penguin Group
Penguin Books Ltd, 80 Strand, London WC2R ORL, England
Penguin Group (USA) Inc., 375 Hudson Street, New York, New York 10014, USA
Penguin Group (Canada), 90 Eglinton Avenue East, Suite 700, Toronto, Ontario, Canada M4P 2Y3
(a division of Pearson Penguin Canada Inc.)
Penguin Ireland, 25 St Stephen's Green, Dublin 2, Ireland
(a division of Penguin Books Ltd)
Penguin Group (Australia), 250 Camberwell Road, Camberwell, Victoria 3124, Australia
(a division of Pearson Australia Group Pty Ltd)
Penguin Books India Pvt Ltd, 11 Community Centre, Panchsheel Park, New Delhi – 110 017, India
Penguin Group (NZ), 67 Apollo Drive, Rosedale, North Shore 0632, New Zealand
(a division of Pearson New Zealand Ltd)
Penguin Books (South Africa) (Pty) Ltd, 24 Sturdee Avenue, Rosebank, Johannesburg 2196, South Africa

Penguin Books Ltd, Registered Offices: 80 Strand, London WC2R ORL, England

www.penguin.com

First published by The Bodley Head 1915
Published in Penguin Books 1946
Reprinted with Introduction and Notes in Penguin Classics 2002
012

Introduction and editorial material copyright © David Bradshaw, 2002
All rights reserved

The moral right of the author has been asserted

Set in 10/12.5 pt PostScript Monotype Dante
Typeset by Rowland Phototypesetting Ltd, Bury St Edmunds, Suffolk
Printed in England by Clays Ltd, St Ives plc

978–0–141–44184–9

www.greenpenguin.co.uk

MIX
Paper from
responsible sources
FSC™ C018179

Penguin Books is committed to a sustainable
future for our business, our readers and our planet.
This book is made from Forest Stewardship
Council™ certified paper.

PENGUIN CLASSICS

THE GOOD SOLDIER

FORD MADDOX FORD was born Ford Hermann Hueffer in Surrey in 1873. He married Elsie Martindale in 1894. His first published works were fairy stories. In 1898 he met Joseph Conrad and they collaborated on several works including the novels *The Inheritors* and *Romance*. Ford published over eighty books in total, *The Fifth Queen* appearing in three parts during the period 1906–8. In 1915 he published *The Good Soldier*, which he regarded as his finest achievement. In the same year he enlisted in the army and served as an infantry officer. *Parade's End*, the culmination of his experiences during the First World War, was published in four parts between 1924 and 1928. Ford moved to Paris in 1922 and two years later founded the *Transatlantic Review*, whose contributors included, among others, James Joyce, Ezra Pound and Gertrude Stein. In his later years he divided his time between France and America. Ford also published several volumes of autobiography and reminiscence, including *Return to Yesterday* (1931) and *It Was the Nightingale* (1934). A final characteristically personal and ambitious volume of criticism, *The March of Literature*, appeared in 1939, the year he died.

Educated at Newcastle University and the University of Oxford, David Bradshaw is Hawthornden Fellow and Tutor in English Literature at Worcester College, Oxford. He has edited *The Hidden Huxley* (1994), *Brave New World* (1994) and Oxford World's Classics editions of *The White Peacock* (1997), *Women in Love* (1998), *Mrs Dalloway* (2000) and *The Mark on the Wall and Other Short Fiction* (2001) by Virginia Woolf. In addition he has edited Evelyn Waugh's *Decline and Fall* for Penguin Classics (2001), a volume on *Modernism* for Blackwell (2002) and has published articles on Bloomsbury, Conrad, T. S. Eliot, Huxley, Woolf, Yeats and various aspects of literature and politics in the 1930s. He is an Editor of the *Review of English Studies* and a Fellow of the English Association.

Contents

Introduction

This may or may not be 'the saddest story' *you* will ever hear, but it will certainly be one of the best. As a tale of the 'broken, tumultuous, agonized, and unromantic' human condition it has few equals and it spellbinds from the beginning. Ford once said that he and his friend and collaborator Joseph Conrad (whom he first met in 1898) strove for *progression d'effet* in their novels, where 'every word set on paper – *every* word set on paper – must carry the story forward, and, that as the story progressed, the story must be carried forward faster and faster and with more and more intensity',[1] and *The Good Soldier*, with its tortuous retreat from the farthest reaches of the Empire and the cosmopolitan watering-places of Europe to a loose box in a Hampshire stable (by way of two suicides, one fatality and one mental collapse), achieves *progression d'effet* of rare degree. It is universally regarded as one of the masterworks of modernist literature, a novel which explores tensions between light and darkness (epistemological, moral and narrative), speech and silence, desire and restraint, order and chaos with an ever-tightening power. Sadness is one of its many attributes; humour, oddly enough, is another.

But, if there is one mood which dominates the novel, it is doubt: *The Good Soldier*, like Conrad's *Heart of Darkness* (1902) and F. Scott Fitzgerald's *The Great Gatsby* (1925), is orchestrated by an unreliable narrator, in this case John Dowell. One of the richest sources of pleasure for readers is in pitting themselves against Dowell, attempting to figure out the stories behind his story, trying to make sense of his peculiarities, obsessions, tonal shifts and evasions. It is not easy, since there is no aspect of the novel which is not either shaded by or shot through with uncertainty.

One thing, however, seems clear: Captain Edward Ashburnham was not just a good soldier, but a very fine soldier indeed. A holder of both the Distinguished Service Order and the 'Royal Humane Society's medal with a clasp' for having twice jumped from a troopship to rescue 'Tommies', Ashburnham, even more impressively, has been twice recommended for the Victoria Cross, the highest honour conferrable on a member of the British armed forces for conspicuous bravery in battle, 'and, although owing to some technicalities he had never received that . . . order, he had some special place about his sovereign at the coronation [of Edward VII in 1901]'. It is small wonder Ashburnham's troop had 'loved him beyond the love of men'. Of course, by the time the Dowells meet the Ashburnhams in August 1904, the good soldier has resigned his commission, but being 'tall, handsome, [and] blond', and with a moustache 'as stiff as a toothbrush', Ashburnham still looks the consummate cavalry officer, even though his demeanour, like so many other aspects of this enthralling and challenging book, is deceptive.

As Ford mentions in his 'Dedicatory Letter to Stella Ford', he had wanted to call the novel *The Saddest Story*, and had only offered an alternative as a joke when his publisher insisted that his preferred title would render the book 'unsaleable' following the outbreak of the First World War. Ford 'never ceased to regret' yielding to this importunity, and, as he anticipated, the title was something critics latched on to when the novel first appeared on 17 March 1915. The *Observer*'s reviewer, for example, saw it as indicative of 'a desire to catch that public that does not want to hear of any other kind of excellence but military excellence',[2] although readers who did buy it for this reason would have been surprised, if not disappointed, to find Prussia treated sympathetically (apart from one passing slight) and the War unmentioned (though there are two oblique references to its build-up: in Part Four, Ashburnham attends a meeting of an imaginary 'National Reserve Committee' and a little further on he expresses his eagerness to get 'the numbers of the Hampshire territorials up to the proper standard'). But it was the title's moral thrust, with its apparent stress on Ashburnham's goodness as a man rather than on the calibre of his soldiering, which provoked most of the critical flak. One reviewer thought it unthinkable that 'an officer and a gentleman . . . should have behaved as in close on three hundred pages of brilliant writing Mr Hueffer tells us he did behave',[3] while another maintained, with full-chested pomposity, that 'good soldiers soon escape the fumes and do not descend so readily to the inferno of caddishness'.[4]

Nevertheless, while Ashburnham's conduct as a husband leaves much to be desired, 'along at least the lines of his public functions' his goodness seems incontrovertible. Though his soldierly prowess is a thing of the past by 1904, he remains an altruistic 'county magnate' with a highly developed sense of *noblesse oblige* until the day he dies, granting 'his tenants very high rebates', allowing a hard-pressed man named Mumford to pay no rent at all, giving 'an oldish horse to a young fellow called Selmes . . . [whose] father had been ruined by a fraudulent solicitor', and, just before his death, spending two hundred pounds on the defence of 'the daughter of one of his tenants, who had been accused of murdering her baby'. Time and time again, from the beginning of the novel to the end, Ashburnham's unwavering goodness and decency are amplified by Dowell:

He was, according to [his wife] Leonora, always remitting his tenants' rents and giving the tenants to understand that the reduction would be permanent; he was always redeeming drunkards who came before his magisterial bench; he was always trying to put prostitutes into respectable places – and he was a perfect maniac about children.

Dowell goes on to tell us he has no idea 'how many ill-used people [Ashburnham] did not pick up and provide with careers – Leonora has told me, but I daresay she exaggerated and the figure seems so preposterous that I will not put it down. All these things, and the continuance of them seemed to him to be his duty – along with impossible subscriptions to hospitals and Boy Scouts and to provide prizes at cattle shows and anti-vivisection societies'. Ashburnham is even responsible for 'a thousand little acts of kindliness, of thoughtfulness for his inferiors . . . on the Continent', coming to the assistance, for example, of Hessian paupers and the Hotel Excelsior's deserted head waiter. In fact, apart from his all-too-public lapse with the Kilsyte girl, 'the public side of his record' is spotless, as Dowell is ever ready to attest. He describes Ashburnham as 'the cleanest-looking sort of chap; an excellent magistrate, a first-rate soldier, one of the best landlords, so they said, in Hampshire' and he is so unequivocal about the virtues of 'Teddy Ashburnham', and lists his merits and accomplishments so regularly, that his adulation of his friend is possibly the only consistent element of his story. Indeed, his reverence of the man who cuckolds him is hardly less ardent than that of Nancy Rufford, Ashburnham's infatuated ward. 'Have I conveyed to you the splendid fellow that he was – the fine soldier, the excellent landlord, the extraordinarily kind, careful and industrious magistrate, the upright, honest, fair-dealing, fair-thinking, public character?' Dowell asks anxiously at one point. 'It is impossible of me to think of Edward Ashburnham as anything but straight, upright and honourable,' he confesses at another.

Yet the more fulsomely Dowell praises Ashburnham and affirms that he possessed 'all the virtues that are usually accounted English' and that he believed 'constancy was the finest of the virtues', the more the reader feels inclined to respond to his words with puzzlement, if not amazement. As the novel unfolds, we become increasingly conscious of the discrepancy between Ashburnham's almost saintly 'public character' and the shabbiness of his private life. It is true that Dowell regards himself as a poor judge of his fellow men, but this deficiency alone cannot fully explain the slippage between the paragon whom the narrator exalts and the libertine whose affairs he chronicles. Dowell represents Ashburnham as a 'sentimentalist' and an incurable romantic, but from a less sentimental viewpoint he is an incurable philanderer, 'a rake impregnated with lachrymose sensibility', as the *Athenaeum*'s critic put it in 1915.[5] In his roles as feudal squire, county magistrate and cavalry officer, Ashburnham personifies loyalty and integrity; in his extra-marital relationships with La Dolciquita, Mrs Basil, Mrs Maidan and Mrs Dowell, he more obviously embodies the absence of those virtues.

Ashburnham is most certainly a bit of a mystery, but Dowell is English literature's most fascinating enigma. Paradoxically, the more gushingly he idolizes the errant ex-soldier and the more contradictory his appraisals of the other main characters turn out to be, the more urgently we feel the need to fathom not them but him. Whether

Leonora is at heart a frigid and malevolent harpy or whether her humanity has dwindled with her marriage will be for the reader to decide; and whether the wayward Florence Dowell, admittedly a bit of a 'riddle', is really a scheming temptress or simply an opportunist who exploits Dowell's perverse determination to marry her in order to resume her affair with the Europe-bound Jimmy, is similarly open to question. But coming to terms with Dowell himself is far more exacting. 'I don't know that analysis of my own psychology matters at all to this story,' he remarks at the beginning of Part Three, but he could not be more mistaken. Ultimately, depending on how Dowell's relationships with Florence, Leonora, Nancy and Ashburnham are configured; on how the reader interprets the various relationships amongst these last four and, above all, on whether the reader sees Dowell as 'an American millionaire of exaggerated density'[6] or a more switched-on and manipulative story-teller, seemingly intent on hiding rather than revealing the truth, 'analysis of [his] . . . psychology' is probably the *only* reliable angle from which the novel may be approached. So much so, that some critics have recommended that we subject Dowell not only to the closest scrutiny, but that we 'assume an unrelievedly critical attitude toward everything he tells us and keep our eye on him at every moment, or the story gets away from us'.[7] To focus on Dowell is not to lose sight of other aspects of the text but to accept that without him there would be no other aspects of the text.

It is rich, in a novel powered forward by perfidy, passion and lies, that four of the five main characters – Ashburnham, Leonora, Florence and Nancy – have blue eyes: traditionally, blue has symbolized truth, loyalty, constancy, chastity, piety and fidelity.[8] And while it is appropriate that the righteous Leonora has always looked at her best 'in a blue tailor-made', it is thumpingly ironic that the only dress of Florence's that Dowell can remember is 'a very simple one of blue figured silk'. The narrator, we should remember, favours ties of a 'special shade of blue', but whether his preferred colour is apt or not is more difficult to say, not least because his ironizing self-consciousness makes it almost impossible, at times, to decide where, if anywhere, his honesty and sincerity lie. We never discover the colour of Dowell's eyes, and the only thing we do know about his appearance is that he is on the short side. We sit opposite him, as he imagines, but we can't see him. Like T. S. Eliot's J. Alfred Prufrock (who also made his debut before the reading public in 1915), Dowell is 'Natty, precise, well-brushed', conscious of his lack of stature, and faceless.

Nor is it any easier to hold his story with confidence, and more than one critic, confronted with the task of trying to make sense of the text's many complexities and confusions, has laid the blame squarely at the feet of Dowell the dodo. *The Good Soldier*, the argument goes, narrated by a 'leisured American' of the *belle époque*, is a slow-paced tale, punctuated with longeurs, recapitulations, inconsistencies, errors and corrections, and that, for the most part, is because the narrator is slow. He *must* be formidably dense and dull-witted, readers have argued, because how else is it possible to be the odd man out in a close foursome for *nine* years? How could he know the other three with 'extreme intimacy', be an integral part of 'an acquaintanceship . . . as close as a good glove's with your hand', and yet not realize that two of the quartet (one his wife) are having an affair? 'Don't you see?' Leonora roars at him during the fateful excursion to Marburg, 'Don't you see what's going on?', to which Dowell responds feebly, 'No! What's the matter? Whatever's the matter?' And if Dowell is as stupid as he appears to be, then his projection of Ashburnham as a wellnigh godly hero requires no further investigation. When he is not lamenting his ignorance, he's regretting his gullibility – 'But think of the fool that I was' – and in conceding that Florence 'had the seeing eye', Dowell tells us (with redundant candour) that he has not. He only learns of Florence's relationship with Ashburnham through a chance remark of Leonora's soon after her husband's funeral. Dowell also discovers that rather than dying of a strained heart, Florence committed suicide. 'It had never entered my head. You may think that I had been singularly lacking in suspiciousness; you may consider me even to have been an imbecile. But consider my position.' It is absolutely crucial that the reader does exactly that from the splendidly catchy outset of this novel to its unbelievably nonchalant end.

It should not amaze anyone that a man who appears to be so switched off from reality should be such an apparently inept narrator. 'It is so difficult to keep all these people going', Dowell complains near the end of the book, but he has not helped himself by narrating his tale in a disjointed and misleading fashion. For instance, we are led to believe that Ashburnham's pigskin travelling cases, all stamped 'EFA', epitomize his fastidious, old-world, slightly foppish, perfect-country-gentleman persona, but we subsequently discover that 'they were Leonora's manifestations', given to him by the character whom we have otherwise been urged to identify only with the relentless enforcement of 'economies'. Likewise, in Part Three, Chapter 4, Dowell tells us that Ashburnham's 'love-affairs, until the very end, were sandwiched in at odd moments or took place during the social evenings, the dances and dinners. But I guess I have made it hard for you, O silent listener, to get that impression.' He also remarks with some pride in this same section that 'I have generally found that my first impressions were correct enough,' but this, pointedly, is only true 'as far as waiters and chambermaids were concerned'. When faced with making sense of his own close circle or the world at large, Dowell is a good deal less reliable and has to apologize more than once for having conveyed the wrong impression. 'I see that I have unintentionally misled you when I said that Florence was never out of my sight,' he observes, for example, in Part Two, Chapter 1. 'Yet that was the impression that I really had until just now. When I come to think of it, she was out of my sight most of the time.' Similarly, any reader who does 'gather' from Dowell's 'statement' on the first page of the novel that the reason for his wife's death was her 'heart' will absorb the wrong impression along with an ironic take on the truth. In Part One, Chapter 4, the narrator brings to mind an American city where 'the blocks are all square and the streets all numbered, so that you can go perfectly easily from Twenty-fourth to Thirtieth', but the layout of his own story is altogether more obstructive. In fact, it is more like a labyrinth: with every page we turn, another dark passage lies before us. Some readers will regard Dowell's narrative technique as perfectly suited to his gradual reconstruction of an imbroglio from which he was excluded; others will consider his mode of story-telling obfuscatory and entangling.

Dowell certainly makes it difficult for the reader to follow his tale, not only by failing to tell it chronologically, but also by digressing from it and loading it with a welter of geographical, topographical, cultural and personal asides. For instance, if his 'anecdote' in Part One, Chapter 2 about old Mr Hurlbird dispensing Californian oranges about the globe is briefly diverting in both senses of the word, to follow on from the tense 'Protest' scene with information about his 'appetites' (helpings of caviare at a typical table d'hôte are insufficient, he complains), his 'impatiences' (he cites the Belgian State Railway's scandalous treatment of French trains), and other miscellaneous issues, seems nothing less than a goad to the reader, a deliberate holding back of the story. A little earlier, Dowell has shared with us his fondness for catching the 2.40 train from Nauheim to Marburg and the sights one can see on the journey, and earlier still he has told us the story of Peire Vidal. 'Is all this digression or isn't it digression?' he muses in Part One, Chapter 2, and it is a question which hovers around in the reader's mind, not least in Part Three, Chapter 4, when Dowell goes on at some length about his brief and uneventful business career in Philadelphia. 'Perhaps all these reflections are a nuisance,' Dowell acknowledges in Part Four, Chapter 2, 'but they crowd on me. I will try to tell the story.'

If the narrator draws attention to his unfitness for his task throughout the novel, he also spotlights himself in more intriguing ways. Most obviously, though Dowell carries the 'title deeds of [his] farm' around in his pocket and expresses pride in his Quaker roots, 'his account of his background', in the words of the American critic Grover Smith, 'does not hold up well: he calls his country the "United States of North America" . . . [and] boasts that he came of a family originally English, the first Dowell having "left Farnham in Surrey in company with [the Quaker leader] William Penn" (there are no Penn associations at Farnham . . .)'. Most curious of all, according to Smith, is Dowell's assertion that he 'learned "Pennsylvania Duitsch" (*sic*) in childhood. In general, American probabilities are so foreign to him that . . . we might suspect him to be bogus.' Smith emphasizes that Ford (who was born in 1873 to an English mother and a German father and christened 'Ford Hermann Hueffer'):

could not have been guilty of this howler, for he of all people would have known that Pennsylvania *Deutsch* is not Holland *Dutch*. Dowell is marked as ignorant and pretentious – and, in some sense which, even so, is not quite the literal one, as an imposter. He has touched up and tinted his own photograph.[9]

The bath attendants at Nauheim have an unfailing 'air of authority', but the narrator, emphatically, does not.

As with every aspect of this text, however, things are not quite so black and white as they seem. It is probable, for instance, that rather than drawing attention to his ignorance, pretentiousness and bogusness, Dowell's use of 'Duitsch' is an orthographic detail intended by Ford to *accentuate* his genuineness. *Duitsch* is a variant of *Deutsch* in *Plattdeutsch*, the Low German dialect spoken by immigrants from rural north Germany, otherwise known as 'Pennsylvania Dutch': the Amish and other Pennsylvanian communities still speak it today. It is quite conceivable that Dowell would have picked up the spelling with the 'Pennsylvania Duitsch' he absorbed from his German immigrant school friends, or, more likely, the Dowell family's German immigrant servants. It is not a 'howler' at all.

But if Dowell is not quite the 'marked' American some critics have made him out to be, his handling of detail on this side of the Atlantic is at times just as iffy. At one point, for example, Dowell says the castle at Marburg is 'not a square castle like Windsor', which would be helpful were it not for the fact that Windsor Castle is nothing like a square and never has been. More strikingly, 'Bramshaw Teleragh', the nearest settlement to Bramshaw Manor, the Ashburnham family home, sounds almost more Irish than Hampshirish, half real place, half trumped-up location, while Leonora's maiden name, Powys, is a most singular and unaccountable Irish surname in that it is a well-known and long-standing Welsh place-name.[10] The surname Maidan arouses similar misgivings in that *maidan* is an Urdu word meaning 'an open space in or near a town; a parade-ground'.[11] It is the kind of word an officer's wife like Maisie Maidan would have heard and even used in India on a daily basis. And while it may sound like a name 'of country parsonage origin', it would normally be spelt 'Maiden' or 'Madin': 'Maidan' is unrecorded as an English surname.[12] Like a number of Dowell's American references, therefore, 'Bramshaw Teleragh', 'Powys', 'Maidan' and the Windsor Castle remark all seem designed to arouse the reader's suspicions – though it is also true, conversely, that 'Dowell' is a surname which in the late nineteenth century had a specific association with Philadelphia and nowhere else in the United States.[13] If Ford goes to the trouble of giving his narrator such an authentic Philadelphian surname, why does he also make him come across as an 'imposter' in some ways? And why do at least three of the novel's other proper nouns sound questionable? A 'dowel' (while the dictionary is to hand) is 'a headless wooden pin' used to hold together the components of a structure, but because of his dubious nomenclature and a host of other problems, Dowell's narrative does not hold together very tightly at all. Of course, whether this is because Dowell is constitutionally 'headless' and 'wooden', or because Ford was occasionally slapdash, is harder to say. But some of the elements of Dowell's story are so inexplicably baffling or strange, the likelihood is that they were planted on him by the author in order to further encourage the reader to study *everything* Dowell says with the utmost care and circumspection, and to make us think even harder about what he might be keeping back. Dowell calls his trust of his wife 'madness', but there is plenty to suggest that it would be just as crazy for the reader wholly to trust him.

Dowell's dubiousness is matched by his secretiveness. 'I have a taste for good cookery and a watering tooth at the mere sound of the names of certain comestibles,' he tells the reader. 'If Florence had discovered this secret of mine I should have found her knowledge of it so unbearable that I never could have supported all the other privations of the regime that she extracted from me. I am bound to say that Florence never discovered this secret.' And it is this same zest for concealment, presumably, which accounts for his reluctance to spell out the word 'Marburg' – there appears to be no other reason why he should refer to it as 'M—' throughout his tale – providing further evidence that a man who frequently laments his inability to communicate may well actually relish non-communication.

Furthermore, although Dowell does his best to portray himself as a thin-blooded and undemonstrative man, we glimpse other sides of his character that are more disturbing. For example, the supposedly timid and genteel narrator tells us that when his old black valet dropped Florence's 'grip' he attacked him: 'I saw red, I saw purple. I flew at Julius . . . I filled up one of his eyes; I threatened to strangle him.' Dowell has already admitted that he 'hate[d Florence] with the hatred of the adder' and that she lived in fear of him: 'For that was really the mainspring of her fantastic actions. She was afraid that I should murder her.' It is almost certainly this terror, Dowell is 'convinced', rather than the sight of Ashburnham kissing Nancy, which induces Florence to swallow prussic acid immediately after seeing her husband in conversation with Bagshawe, the man who once caught her leaving Jimmy's bedroom in the early hours of the morning they (and old Mr Hurlbird) were guests at Bagshawe's house in Herefordshire. It is, after all, in the event of this kind of exposure that she always has the prussic acid to hand. Dowell may wish to present himself as passionless, may even think of himself as passionless, but he is clearly a man with a great capacity for passion of one kind or another, a man more than capable of 'the maddest kind of rage'.

Thinking hard about the reliability of Dowell's narrative makes the reader chary of all acts of disclosure in the novel. Ashburnham's goodness as a soldier, for example, looks distinctly less clear-cut when we bear in mind that the principal source of Dowell's information is the awe-struck Nancy. '[C]hant[ing] Edward's praises to [Dowell]', Nancy glorifies her guardian to such a degree that he becomes, as Dowell sees it, a superhuman combination of Lohengrin, El Cid and the Chevalier Bayard, three heroes of legendary status. Nancy's transfiguration of Ashburnham from an exemplary soldier into an unexampled warrior is all the more noticeable because our only knowledge of his military service which does not appear to originate with her is the fact that he received the DSO and was promoted to the rank of brevet-major 'during the shuffling of troops' that happened as a result of the South African, or second Boer, War (1899–1902). To hold the Distinguished Service Order (awarded to officers for exceptional service) and be twice recommended for the Victoria Cross and yet remain at the rank of captain seems meagre reward for Ashburnham's outstanding gallantry and a soldiering career which must have lasted around fifteen years. When Dowell asks Ashburnham about his DSO, he dismisses the question with either an embarrassed or a cynical disclaimer. Has Ashburnham embroidered the truth in order to entertain himself at the expense of Nancy or to impress Dowell? Or has Nancy, or Dowell, made most of it up, inventing a heroic record of service in tribute to the hero they worship? It is impossible to say, of course, but the more closely we examine the matter, the less certain we can be that Ashburnham *was* a good soldier – and that is without taking into consideration his affairs with Mrs Basil and Mrs Maidan, the wives of 'injured brother officer[s]'. And what applies to Ashburnham's soldiering is applicable to the novel as a whole: the more intensively it is scrutinized, the more densely uncertainties proliferate. For this reason, it is crucial that the reader stays alert and open-minded at all times. If we too readily accept Dowell's characterization of Florence as a flirtatious 'Anglo-maniac' hell-bent on charming her way into the Hampshire rural gentry, for example, it will come as quite a shock to learn that she is 'of a line that had actually owned Bramshaw Teleragh for two centuries before the Ashburnhams came there'.

Nor would it be wise to dismiss Dowell as a booby too hastily. There are other ways of approaching his narrative which suggest he may be more ringmaster than clown. First and foremost, Dowell's narrative method, for all its apparent flaws, is closely modelled on Ford's own theory of story-telling. 'I have, I am aware,' Dowell admits at the beginning of Part Four,

told this story in a very rambling way so that it may be difficult for anyone to find their path through what may be a sort of maze. I cannot help it. I have stuck to my idea of being in a country cottage with a silent listener, hearing between the gusts of the wind and amidst the noises of the distant sea, the story as it comes. And, when one discusses an affair – a long, sad affair – one goes back, one goes forward. One remembers points that one has forgotten and one explains them all the more minutely since one recognizes that one has forgotten to mention them in their proper places and that one may have given, by omitting them, a false impression. I console myself with thinking that this is a real story and that, after all, real stories are probably told best in the way a person telling a story would tell them. They will then seem most real.

By the time Ford wrote *The Good Soldier*, he had come to exactly the same conclusion about the anti-realistic effect of a strictly chronological narrative structure. Indeed, in *Joseph Conrad: A Personal Remembrance*, Ford recalls how he and Conrad had decided that the whole problem of the British novel was that it went straight forward, whereas in your gradual making acquaintance with your fellows you never do go straight forward. You meet an English gentleman at your golf club. He is beefy, full of health, the moral of the boy from an English Public School of the finest type. You discover, gradually, that he is hopelessly neurasthenic, dishonest in matters of small change, but unexpectedly self-sacrificing, a dreadful liar but a most painfully careful student of lepidoptera and, finally, from the public prints, a bigamist who was once, under another name, hammered on the Stock Exchange . . . To get such a man in fiction you could not begin at his beginning and work his life chronologically to the end. You must first get him in with a strong impression, and then work backwards and forwards over his past.[14]

Which is exactly what Dowell does with Ashburnham, of course.

Vincent J. Cheng has usefully reconstructed 'a clear chronology (or as clear as possible) of the events of the story' and in doing so he, like other critics, has drawn attention to a number of inconsistencies in *The Good Soldier* – for example, an apparent confusion about the date of the first meeting of the Ashburnhams and Dowells at Nauheim, and the fact that Dowell appears to finish writing a novel published in 1915 at the beginning of 1916![15] – but while these 'problems' may point to Ford's imperfect workmanship, it is just as likely that they are integral to his representation of the lack of 'straight forward[ness]' in human experience and his belief that a discontinuous and inconsistent narrative structure is more true to life than one which is flawlessly chronological. In Part Three Dowell mentions that he is well aware of the distinction between 'a cheap novelist' and 'a very good novelist' and tells us that 'it's the business of a novelist to make you see things clearly'. Riddled with darkness and doubt though *The Good Soldier* may be, and notwithstanding Dowell's protestations of incompetence, the fact is that it, and he, successfully get across the messiness, 'unhappiness', bewilderment and isolation of what Dowell calls 'this sweltering hell of ours'. The truth is that Dowell is both tiresomely ineffectual and subtly effective as a narrator, often simultaneously, and the more the novel is re-read, the more his craftsmanship and his achievement may be appreciated. For 'an ageing American with very little knowledge of life', a man who freely confesses that he 'doesn't know much about human beings',

Dowell, especially in the second half of the book, writes almost with tragic insight.

The idea of a narrator addressing a 'silent listener' is also found in Ford's criticism. In writing of this figure in a two-part essay called 'On Impressionism' (1914), Ford discussed the literary artist's absolute need to 'capture' and 'hold' his 'silent listener's' attention:

You will do this by methods of surprise, of fatigue, by passages of sweetness in your language, by passages suggesting the sudden and brutal shock of suicide. You will give him passages of dullness, so that your bright effects may seem more bright; you will alternate, you will dwell for a long time upon an intimate point; you will seek to exasperate so that you may the better enchant. You will, in short, employ all the devices of the prostitute. If you are too proud for this you may be the better gentleman or the better lady, but you will be the worse artist.[16]

The 'silent listener' of *The Good Soldier*, though facing Dowell across a cosy cottage fire, is never permitted a cosy grasp of things, but Ford's credo suggests that our discomfort may well be intentional and that we must listen all the harder to what Dowell says in order to locate his meaning. As he remarks to the reader apropos of Edward and Leonora's quarrel about sending Nancy back to her father: 'I can't make out which of them was right. I leave it to you.'

Above all, Ford himself was an unreliable narrator, never averse to downplaying the truth in order to heighten an effect. 'This book . . . is full of inaccuracies as to facts', he wrote of *Ancient Lights* (1911), a volume of reminiscences dedicated to his daughters, 'but its accuracy as to impressions is absolute',[17] while in his preface to *Joseph Conrad* Ford declared:

Where the writer's memory has proved to be at fault over a detail afterwards out of curiosity looked up, the writer has allowed the fault to remain on the page; but as to the truth of the impression as a whole, the writer believes that no man would care – or dare – to impugn it.[18]

If we are prepared to read Dowell as a Fordian impressionist, rather than an unreliable narrator, the dependability of his narrative becomes less of a critical issue. The only problem then, as one critic puts it, is that

'Dowell is not merely an untrustworthy narrator but an untrustworthy impressionist'.[19]

But even if there were no parallels between Ford's narrative theory and Dowell's narrative practice, there is plenty to suggest that the American narrator knows exactly what he is doing, and that in writing his story he wants to show us he has more of a 'good' novelist in him than a 'cheap' one. For example, Carol Jacobs has examined the layered complexity of the incident on the journey from Nauheim to Marburg when Dowell looks out of the train window and sees 'a brown cow hitch its horns under the stomach of a black and white animal and the black and white one [is] thrown right into the middle of a narrow stream'. Jacobs addresses the way in which this 'apparently irrelevant interlude' actually 'operates as an inexorably precise, almost mechanical, if ultimately problematic, allegory' of what is about to happen to the party: the 'black and white' relationship between the two couples will be upended when Leonora discovers that she has been displaced by Florence, and at about this time, back at the Hotel Excelsior, 'Maisie Maidan is thrown into the middle of a portmanteau, with her feet in the air, like the black and white cow'.[20] Nor should such narrative flair surprise us, for Dowell is a well-read narrator who likes to show off his learning: telling us that Nancy saw Ashburnham as a compound of Lohengrin, El Cid and the Chevalier Bayard is a case in point. Just as Florence is keen to display how much she has read up on the cultural sites that the quartet visit, so Dowell, no less conspicuously, embroiders his tale with allusions to, among other texts, the Bible, John Dryden's *All for Love* (1678), Edmund Burke's *Reflections on the Revolution in France* (1790), Thomas Hardy's *Tess of the D'Urbervilles* (1891) and Conrad's *The Nigger of the 'Narcissus'* (1897) and *Heart of Darkness*, and borrows quotations from the poetry of Robert Herrick (1591–1674) and Algernon Charles Swinburne (1837–1909). And he is familiar (though 'an old-fashioned Philadelphia Quaker') with the Latin of the Roman Catholic Church.

Dowell's use of figurative language is also notable. In the first half of the book, he is drawn chiefly to nautical imagery, telling us, among other things, that he 'had never sounded the depths of an English heart. I had known the shallows'; that he is 'invisibly anchored' to Philadelphia, and that Leonora hated Ashburnham 'with an agony that was as bitter as the sea'. He portrays their foursome as a noble and seaworthy vessel: 'We were, if you will, one of those tall ships with the white sails upon a blue sea, one of those things that seem the proudest and the safest of all the beautiful and safe things that God has permitted the mind of men to frame.' These descriptions seem almost deliberately uninspired, as if Dowell, true to Ford's advice about narration, is lulling the reader into a false sense of his ability as a writer/narrator, not least because he goes on to show us that he can also use similes to good effect – for instance, when describing the Ashburnhams as being 'like fire-ships afloat on a lagoon'; when noting Edward's ability to enter a room and capture every woman's gaze 'as dextrously as a conjurer pockets billiard balls', and when describing the Englishman's desire for La Dolciquita arising 'like fire in dry corn'.

In addition, Dowell's metaphors occasionally take on such eye-catching boldness and obtrude with such a disconcerting extravagance that it is almost as if he is trying to make the reader laugh. Somewhat less than heart-rendingly, for example, Maisie Maidan's trunk ingests her (save for 'a small pair of feet in high-heeled shoes') 'like the jaws of a gigantic alligator', and when Leonora recovers Maisie's corpse she finds her 'smiling, as if she had just scored a goal in a hockey match'. In a similar vein, when Florence creeps up on Ashburnham and Nancy 'under the dark trees of the park', Dowell conjectures that Nancy, in her cream muslin dress, must have resembled 'a phosphorescent fish in a cupboard'. These comparisons are precisely wacky, memorably weird, as is Dowell's description, towards the end of the novel, of Leonora and Nancy persecuting Ashburnham 'like a couple of Sioux who had got hold of an Apache and had him well tied to a stake'. There seems to be a calculated flippancy in play here, an irreverent ingenuity which pushes against the tragic swell of the story. Other examples might include Dowell's description of himself going up and down the rope ladder to and from Florence's bedroom 'like a tranquil jumping jack'; Leonora glancing at Dowell 'as if for a moment a lighthouse had looked at [him]', and Dowell's use of this elaborately bizarre analogy to describe his role as Florence's 'sedulous, strained nurse': 'It was as if I had been given a thin-shelled pullet's egg to carry on my palm from Equatorial

Africa to Hoboken.' Once the reader tunes in to Dowell's apparent frivolity it can be very hard to tune out, and the more distinctly we catch his words, the more inviting it becomes to read his sideswipe at the Belgian State Railway and his other digressions and quips ('And then she stepped over the sill, as if she were stepping on board a boat. I suppose she had burnt hers!') as part of a pattern of cynical disengagement. This impression is only reinforced when Dowell says in response to the imagined question of the imaginary silent listener: 'You ask how it feels to be a deceived husband. Just Heavens, I do not know. It feels just nothing at all.'

Do we take these last words literally? Do they tell us that for Dowell, *qua* Florence's husband, this saddest of stories is not really that sad 'at all'? Or has the revelation of Florence's adultery and Ashburnham's affairs, their suicides and Nancy's mental collapse, disturbed Dowell to such a degree that his distress intermittently finds voice in his outlandish turns of phrase? Like other aspects of his narrative, Dowell's metaphors are unquestionably attention-seeking, and a key question for the reader is whether they betray a lack of nuance and control on Dowell's part, as some critics have argued, or whether they provide evidence of his ironic detachment from his tale. All the reader can be certain of is that Ford has provided Dowell with a stock of flamboyant comparisons which bring him even more prominently to the centre of the stage, where the reader may observe him all the more closely, and where Dowell, now and again, loves to ham it up for all he's worth:

You can't kill a *minuet de la cour*. You may shut up the music-book, close the harpsichord; in the cupboard and presses the rats may destroy the white satin favours. The mob may sack Versailles; the Trianon may fall, but surely the minuet – the minuet itself is dancing itself away into the furthest stars. Isn't there any heaven where old beautiful dances, old beautiful intimacies prolong themselves? Isn't there any Nirvana pervaded by the faint thrilling of instruments that have fallen into the dust of wormwood but that yet had frail, tremulous, and everlasting souls?

This overblown and actorly passage suggests that Nancy was more than justified in laughing at 'some old-fashionedness in [Dowell's] phraseology'; his assertion that, in future, all smoking-rooms will be 'peopled with incalculable simulacra amidst smoke wreaths' is a no less ornate but more succinct example of the same tendency.

Florence, Dowell maintains, wanted to appear 'like the heroine of a French comedy', but at times she must have felt as if she had landed a part in a good old British farce. Soon after Ashburnham first sets eyes on her, for example, he lets out 'an appreciative gurgle'. Like the 'sound that was very like a groan' which Leonora vents on hearing that her husband has exempted Mumford from paying his rent, Ashburnham's utterance may betoken the disruptive and 'tempestuous forces' which surge just below the starched surface of Edwardian decorum, but if the reader hears anything other than a strictly gruff note in his noise, it could well raise a smile. In a similar way, the image of Leonora and Maisie standing silently side by side in the hotel corridor with Leonora's gold key caught up in Maisie's hair and it having to be untangled by Florence, may strike the reader as more humorous than horrendous, and there are a number of other scenes in the novel which assume a comical aspect once we try to picture them. These include the dead of night, rope-ladder flitting of Florence and Dowell; Dowell standing by with his axe outside Florence's bedroom door in Paris 'in case she ever failed to answer my knock'; Leonora, towards the end, returning to her room 'like a lame duck' after a confrontation with Edward and 'stumbl[ing] over the familiar tiger skins in the dark hall'; Leonora, just ten days after her husband's suicide, looking out of the window and seeing rabbits on the lawn at Bramshaw, four-legged precursors of the rabbit-like Rodney Bayham who will soon take her husband's place, and, most comic of all (if it strikes us that way), the mute and vacant Nancy suddenly blurting out 'Shuttlecocks!' with 'her knife and fork . . . suspended in mid-air'.

As long ago as 1948, the critic Mark Schorer wrote an influential critique of *The Good Soldier* in which he hailed it as one of the 'great works of comic irony' and argued, among other things, that

perhaps the most astonishing achievement in this astonishing novel is the manner in which the author, while speaking through his simple, infatuated character, lets us know how to take his simplicity and his infatuation. This is comic genius. It shows, for example, in the characteristic figures, the rather simple-minded and, at the same time, grotesquely comic metaphors . . .[21]

Nowadays, few commentators would risk being so categorical about the design of the novel – especially since so much of its greatness is tied up with its elusiveness. *The Good Soldier* is both 'grotesquely comic' *and*, in places, almost unbearably tragic: few will complete it unmoved. In Dowell's opinion, it is a story which has neither 'elevation' nor 'nemesis' nor 'destiny' nor 'villain', but for most contemporary readers it will have more than enough tragic substance. What will surprise some readers, however, is to find themselves smiling here and there.

To sum up, Sondra J. Stang wrote with as much insight as gusto when she claimed that Dowell, far from being 'an ignorant fool', as he would have us believe,

> is a *faux-naif* of the most artful kind, a pretender to innocence, a master of obfuscation, a manipulator of every trick, the most unreliable of unreliable narrators. There are overstatements, understatements, denials, lies, evasions, contradictions, accusations, exaggerations, puns, apparent irrelevancies, logical fallacies, omitted links, digressions, sharp anticipations, delayed explanations, swings of mood, and explosions great and small. He embarrasses, bullies, confuses and tests the reader; he presumes on his credulity; he cloys, simpers, condescends; he writes of 'monstrous things' in a 'frivolous manner'. He spirals up and down, toward and away from his point, buries it, conceals it, flattens and misleads with false emphasis; he lurches from self-denigration to self-promotion and back; he suddenly varies the intensities and the volume and pushes himself into the story. And he repeats.[22]

Stang overstates her case, but nothing she asserts is untrue and many readers will find her placement of Dowell at the helm of the novel far more persuasive than the kind of interpretation which marginalizes him as a cack-handed tugboat pilot and a nincompoop to boot.

In his 'Dedicatory Letter', Ford says that he began writing *The Good Soldier* on his fortieth birthday, 17 December 1913. He thought it would be his last novel and that it would easily surpass the nineteen he had published to date. As a general rule, it is unwise to make too much of correlations between a writer's life and work, but in the case of this text it is practically irresistible. Ford's life was in disarray by 1913. Having married Elsie Martindale, his childhood sweetheart, in 1894, he seems to have fallen in love with her sister, Mary Martindale, at some point around 1903. Following the discovery of their relationship, Ford suffered a nervous breakdown in 1904. Early in August that year he went abroad to recuperate at a number of spas in Germany (but not at Nauheim on this occasion) and elsewhere on the Continent, and by the following year, 1905, he had made a reasonable recovery, though the after-effects of his breakdown, in particular agoraphobia, were to stay with him for the rest of his life. In 1909 he left his wife for Violet Hunt, a fashionable writer, whom he 'married' in 1911, though he was not divorced from Elsie. But further instability, both emotional and professional, followed, and by the time he sat down to write *The Good Soldier* in 1913 a young woman named Brigit Patmore (with whom he had also fallen in love) was on the point of rejecting him and he had become estranged from two of his closest male companions: temporarily from Conrad, and permanently from a Tory squire named Arthur Marwood, with whom he had been intimate, almost continuously, since they had first met in 1905. In the 'Dedicatory Letter' Ford says that he put *all* that I knew about writing' into *The Good Soldier*, and it seems certain that he also poured into it a great deal of the passion, disappointment and pain he had accumulated in his life to date. Just how much of his real life Ford imported into his novel is a question which has always intrigued its admirers. Graham Greene, one of the most avid, once wrote:

the impression which will be left most strongly on the reader is the sense of Ford's involvement. A novelist is not a vegetable absorbing nourishment mechanically from soil and air: material is not easily or painlessly gained, and one cannot help wondering what agonies of frustration and error lay behind [it].[23]

In an earlier work, *The Spirit of the People* (1907), Ford described how he had witnessed the actual event on which he based Ashburnham's parting from Nancy in Part Four of *The Good Soldier*. One summer he stayed at the house of a married couple – 'good people' – and a young woman, the husband's ward, was also resident. An 'attachment' had grown up between the husband and the ward and it was decided to send the young woman round the world with some friends. When the day came for the ward to depart, Ford, like Dowell, was asked to ride to a nearby railway station in a dogcart with the husband and his ward. As the young woman boarded her train Ford noticed that 'P–. never even shook her by the hand: touching the flap of his cloth cap sufficed for leave-taking . . . it was playing the game to the bitter end. It was, indeed, very much the bitter end, since Miss W–. died at Brindisi on the voyage out, and P–. spent the next three years at various places on the Continent where nerve cures are attempted.'[24] (It is from Brindisi, of course, that Nancy sends Ashburnham the jolly-hockey-sticks telegram which prompts him to slit his throat with his 'little neat penknife'.)

As Dowell recognizes on two occasions, there is a 'curious coincidence of dates' in his story, and this, too, may have a biographical explanation which has now been lost:

[Florence] had been born on the 4th of August [1874]; she had started to go round the world on the 4th of August [1899]; she had become a low fellow's mistress on the 4th August [1900]. On the same day of the year [ie, 4 August 1901] she had married me; on . . . 4th [August 1913] she had lost Edward's love, and Bagshawe had appeared like a sinister omen – like a grin on the face of Fate.

The afternoon excursion to Marburg also occurs on 4 August (1904) and precisely ten years later, on 4 August 1914, the 'sinister omen[s]' which had long portended the First World War were suddenly reified in the German invasion of Belgium. However, it seems there is no connection between the date of Germany's ominous move westwards and Ford's choice of date: he had fixed on 4 August many months before it achieved lasting notoriety in August 1914.[25] It is possible that Ford brought 4 August to even greater prominence in his novel after the outbreak of war, but he had already deployed it as a motif before hostilities commenced.

The list of casualties in this novel is worthy of a 'melodrama' (as are many of its scenes, such as Florence creeping up on Ashburnham and Nancy in the park; her sensational re-entry into the hotel lounge, and the sardonic 'happy ending with wedding bells and all'), but who bears most blame for its cumulative suffering and sadness? Who is the real 'villain of the piece'? At one point Dowell calls Florence a 'whore', and elsewhere he refers to her as 'a cold sensualist', a 'Tartar', 'a contaminating influence' and 'a common flirt', but is she the root cause of the tragedy? Florence is undoubtedly coquettish and unprincipled, but Dowell surely brings about his own misfortune through his mulish resolve to marry her. 'I just drifted in and wanted Florence', he states in Part One, Chapter 2. 'I determined with all the obstinacy of a possibly weak nature, if not to make her mine, at least to marry her', is how he puts it at the beginning of Part Two, and almost immediately afterwards, in another of his remarkably offhand similes, Dowell says that in his blinkered pursuit of Florence he was 'like a chicken that is determined to get across the road in front of an automobile'. The Misses Hurlbird try to talk him out of his plan, hinting that their niece is not quite the unsullied young maiden they would wish her to be, but Dowell concludes his interview with them by declaring: 'I don't care. If Florence has robbed a bank I am going to marry her and take her to Europe.' Even after a further interview, this time with Florence's Uncle John, Dowell still goes ahead and marries her, in the face of all reason and seemliness, at about four o'clock in the morning. 'I suppose it was my own fault, what followed', he ruminates. No less capricious is his conduct immediately before the ceremony. Florence receives him at the top of the ladder with 'an embrace of warmth':

Well, it was the first time I had ever been embraced by a woman – and it was the last when a woman's embrace has had in it any warmth for me . . . I fancy that, if I had shown any warmth then, she would have acted the proper wife to me, or would have put me back again. But, because I acted like a Philadelphia gentleman, she made me, I suppose, go through with the part of a male nurse.

If Dowell's idolization of Ashburnham is one salient feature of this novel, his vilification of Leonora is hardly less evident. Dowell says Ashburnham found her 'cold and unsympathetic' and tells us, near the end of Part Three, Chapter 3, that Ashburnham 'seemed to regard [Leonora] as being not only physically and mentally cold, but even as being actually wicked and mean'. 'She had no conversation with Edward for many years – none that went beyond the mere arrangements for taking trains or engaging servants', we read in Part One, Chapter 5, and on one occasion, when Ashburnham says to Leonora: 'By jove, you're the finest woman in the world. I wish we could be better friends', his wife just turns her back on him. At one point Leonora is glimpsed 'watching [Ashburnham] as a fierce cat watches an unconscious pigeon in a roadway' and at another she is observed 'watching Edward more intently and with more straining of ears than that which a cat bestows on a bird overhead'. By Part Four, Chapter 2, Leonora has become 'a cold fiend' who tells Nancy all about Ashburnham's extra-marital affairs and urges her to have a physical relationship with her husband, while two chapters further on, Dowell asserts, 'Leonora with her hunger, with her cruelty, had driven Edward to madness'. When Nancy is brought back to Bramshaw from Ceylon, Leonora does not even make the effort to drive over from her new home to see her.

Dowell even suggests at one point that Leonora was 'pimping for Edward', and it is true that she plays a strangely proactive role in his infidelities. For instance, if Ashburnham had not been travelling in a third-class railway carriage to save money, he would not have come across the Kilsyte girl: as Dowell puts it, 'It is part of the peculiar irony of things that Edward would certainly never have kissed that nursemaid if he had not been trying to please Leonora.' And it is Leonora's worldly priest who suggests that she should take her rather prudish husband to Monte Carlo in order that he may indulge in a 'touch of irresponsibility' (which he does, of course, with disastrous results). The same drive for economies which drives Ashburnham into the arms of the Kilsyte girl also takes him and his wife to India. By renting out Bramshaw Manor, Leonora straightens out the Ashburnham finances, but by moving to the subcontinent and going into retreat at Simla she abandons her husband to Mrs Basil. Lastly, it is Leonora's idea to bring Maisie Maidan to Nauheim, and it is Leonora who suggests that she and Edward sit next to the Dowells at dinner. She does so to outface Florence (who has cottoned on to the true state of the Ashburnhams' marriage when untangling Leonora's wrist from Maisie Maidan's hair earlier that day), but Leonora must have been aware that she was placing more temptation in her husband's path. And even if she didn't quite see it this way, Ashburnham's 'appreciative gurgle' should have sounded like a tocsin in her ears rather than occasioning nothing more than 'a slight hesitation' on her part. The next time Ashburnham gurgles that evening

Leonora shivers 'as if a goose had walked over her grave', a typically Dowellian trope that is both creepy and droll in equal measure.

Yet Leonora feels utterly betrayed by her husband and has suffered at his hands for many years. In Dowell's eyes Ashburnham is a 'sentimentalist', but in his wife's he is lecherous. For Dowell, Ashburnham is a noble and duty-bound traditionalist, but as far as Leonora is concerned his fling with La Dolciquita shows that he is careless of his inheritance in that he almost loses his house and land as a result of it. To Dowell, Ashburnham is generous; to Leonora, he is profligate. With hardly any clothes of her own, she buys the expensive travelling cases for Ashburnham as a sign of her devotion to him, and it is the depth of her love for her husband which accounts for the depth of her bitterness when she finds out she has been deceived. A convent girl and a woman of unbending faith, Leonora first realizes her husband and Florence are intimate when Florence touches his wrist over the glass case covering one of the most important documents of the Protestant Reformation. It is this which makes the revelation of his faithlessness almost unendurable. And while Leonora is a woman of principle, it is Ashburnham's rigidity, not hers, which leads to Nancy being sent back to her father, 'a violent madman of a fellow' who has previously smashed her mother to the floor, whose voice makes Nancy almost lose consciousness, and who once knocked her out for a full three days. According to Leonora, Ashburnham's determination to return Nancy to her father is 'the most atrocious thing' he has done in his 'atrocious life' and it's hard to disagree with her. That Nancy goes under mentally while crossing the same Red Sea from which Ashburnham has twice plucked 'Tommies' is one of the novel's more piercing ironies.

Dowell's attitude to Leonora is coloured in various ways. He is antagonistic to her religion; he is something of a misogynist who thinks all women are 'intolerably cruel to the beloved person', and, above all, in setting herself against Ashburnham and corrupting Nancy, Leonora harms 'the only two persons' whom Dowell says he 'ever really loved'. Indeed, when Dowell first sees Ashburnham, his enraptured tone is all the more noteworthy in that at no point does he direct the kind of language he uses then or at other times in the novel to his wife or to another woman: 'I never came across such a perfect expression before and I never shall again.' On one occasion he tells us he 'cannot think of

Edward without sighing' and at another he admits: 'I can't conceal from myself the fact that I loved Edward Ashburnham – and that I love him because he was just myself.' 'It would be merely glib to argue that Dowell's protestation of concealed love for Ashburnham reveals a homosexual impulse', Max Saunders has cautioned. 'But it would be slightly deceitful to deny that the thought crosses the reader's mind as Dowell makes his revelation.'[26] All we can say with any certainty is that in a novel packed tight with images of incarceration – Jimmy confined to Europe by Florence's uncle; the 'imprisonment' of Dowell and Florence on the same continent; Leonora's 'immense' blue eyes 'like a wall of blue that shut [Dowell] off from the rest of the world' and her gold circlet in which 'she locked up her heart and her feelings'; Leonora and her six sisters 'interned' in their convent and then immured 'behind the high walls of the manor-house that was almost more cloistral than any convent could have been'; 'the never-opened door between' Leonora's and Ashburnham's rooms; the two couples like 'a prison full of screaming hysterics' – the most imprisoned thing of all could be Dowell's love of Ashburnham. And if this is the case, then the fervour and frequency of his eulogies to Ashburnham's 'public side' may be explained, along with his flippant interpolations and his tone of ironic disengagement: as a secretive and deeply conventional 'gentleman', Dowell would indeed have a great secret to hide. Significantly, Dowell describes himself as 'a sort of convent', and one of the last glimpses we have of him is sitting in Ashburnham's gun-room in a state of solitary confinement: 'All day and all day in a house that is absolutely quiet. No one visits me, for I visit no one. No one is interested in me, for I have no interests.' As Martin Stannard has shown, Dowell even writes his story using the kind of hunting and equestrian terms which an accomplished horseman like Ashburnham would have used all the time.[27] By the last chapter of the novel there will be readers who feel authorized to construe Dowell's purchase of Ashburnham's place at Bramshaw Teleragh as the ultimate act of love in this 'Tale of Passion', but if the novel has taught us anything it has taught us to be wary of all 'black and white' readings of the text – or, indeed, of any 'black and white' image in the text, such as Dowell's vision, 'in black and white', of God's judgement on Leonora, Edward and Florence. To be dogmatic about Dowell's sexuality would be to lose touch with the spirit of a novel which generates questions rather than answers (to whom, for instance, does the epigraph refer?). But by the very end of the book, when Dowell tells us, almost as an afterthought, that Ashburnham has killed himself, his casualness barely holds back his passion. If 'Dowell's offhand manner is his defence against breaking down with grief', as one critic has argued,[28] then it is a glaringly vulnerable defence. The truth is that Ashburnham, the slightly priggish and very sentimental Tory Englishman, is everything Dowell, the slightly priggish and very sentimental conservative American of old English stock, desires to be.

Rather than trying to pin labels on Dowell and searching for consistency in his words, it is probably best to accept his fundamental slipperiness. During the course of the novel, for instance, he tells us on a number of occasions that he loathes Leonora and yet he also says, more than once, that he loves her. Even as he sits alone in Bramshaw Manor he states that he would 'very cheerfully lay down [his] life . . . in her service'. And it would be possible to assemble a whole dossier of statements in which Dowell's feelings for Nancy, Florence and Edward, and Edward's feelings for Florence, Nancy and Leonora, and Leonora's attitude to Dowell, Florence, Edward and Nancy could all be shown to be equally contradictory. But to make too much of this would be to read against the grain of the novel, because, as Max Saunders has argued:

Ambivalence becomes for [Dowell], as for Ford, a habit of sensibility: a mode of thinking about society, history, and morality. Above all, Dowell's tone embodies, and elicits, ambivalence about the very story he is telling. Fascinated by telling stories which were at once plausible and improbable, both compelling and outrageous, in *The Good Soldier* Ford invented a character, Ashburnham, at once sympathetic and outrageous, whose story is told by a narrator who is both convincing and ridiculous.[29]

It is fitting that a tale which registers the end of so many Edwardian certainties should have first appeared in *Blast*, the incendiary mouthpiece of the English Vorticist movement. Entitled 'The Saddest Story', Ford's ten-page excerpt from the beginning of the novel may have looked a little out of place in such an abrasively avant-garde publication, but as Robert Green has noted:

the image of the 'vortex' printed in the same issue of *Blast* and representing 'whirling concentrations of energy' framed by the 'stable and self-contained' – the basic Vorticist tenet of 'internal energy and external calm' – is suggestive of the novel's combination of phlegm and hysteria, the presence in *The Good Soldier* of anarchy, fission and incest within a rigid formal structure.[30]

This juxtaposition of 'internal energy and external calm' is particularly evident in the text's representations of the British Empire. The leisurely pursuits of a cavalry officer's life in India, for instance, such as an afternoon's polo or cricket, and the annual decampment of the raj to Simla, are offset by snipers on 'the Northwest Frontier', just as the Boers fight a guerilla war against the British in South Africa and in Ireland Leonora's father's tenants take 'pot-shots at him from behind a hedge'. While the 'Vorticist' theme is most obviously embodied in the two couples and their seemingly ultra-steady quartet, as well as the apparently 'quiet and ordered' life of Bramshaw Manor in Part Four of the novel, its 'calm pococurantism' masking all manner of passionate intensity, it is typified, as well, in the post-hockey match 'saturnalia' which disrupts the normally calm rituals of Nancy's convent school. It assumes a polite guise in the polo game involving Ashburnham and Count Baron von Lelöffel (where Anglo-German imperial rivalry quickens the sporting encounter) and it takes a potentially more volcanic form when Florence's disdain of Irish Catholics is met by Leonora's silent fury.

One way or another the old order is under attack from modernity on many fronts in the novel, whether it be in the form of the Kilsyte girl and her courtroom victory over a county squire or Ashburnham's 'Nonconformist adversaries' who seize on the case for political gain. The period leading up to the publication of *The Good Soldier* was one of serious political, industrial, social and cultural unrest in Britain – the suffragettes, for example, had been in full cry – and the novel's predominantly wistful mood reflects Dowell's nostalgia for the era of early-Edwardian high style which this period of disruption brought to an abrupt end. Dowell's sympathies clearly lie with the old order, but the old order, we see, is doomed, just as Nancy's 'stable and self-contained' view of marriage is sent into a spin by the 'whirling concentration of energy' which is released when she reads about the Brand divorce case.

With the exception of his *Fifth Queen* trilogy (*The Fifth Queen*, 1906; *Privy Seal*, 1907; and *The Fifth Queen Crowned*, 1908), Ford had not had much success as a novelist prior to the publication of *The Good Soldier*. He would go on to receive some acclaim for his post-War tetralogy, *Parade's End* (*Some Do Not*, 1924; *No More Parades*, 1925; *A Man Could Stand Up*, 1926; and *Last Post*, 1928), but it is *The Good Soldier* on which his reputation mainly rests. In 1915, however, while its artistry impressed some of the more astute reviewers, its subject matter dismayed many more. 'The portrayal of marital infidelity is dangerous enough even when delicately handled', the *Boston Transcript* intoned, 'and for the written page to linger upon the indecencies of intrigue – details to be expected from the reeking tongue of an alley-gossip – there is no excuse whatever. For all the author's clever manipulation of words, he has given his story nothing to compensate for its artistic feebleness or to clear its distorted, sex-morbid atmosphere.'[31]

Ford, on the other hand, needed no convincing that *The Good Soldier* was his 'best book' ('Dedicatory Letter'). Immediately before starting work on it he had completed his study of *Henry James* (1914), and with the publication of his novel Ford showed that he had absorbed the lessons of both James and Conrad and could produce a work of fiction as technically fine and as psychologically complex as, say, *What Maisie Knew* (1897) or *Heart of Darkness*. In addition to Graham Greene, writers as diverse as Conrad, Ezra Pound, May Sinclair and H. G. Wells all expressed their admiration of *The Good Soldier*'s technique and its capacity to hold the reader's attention. 'For the subject is,' Rebecca West wrote in 1915, 'one realizes when one has come to the end of this saddest story, much vaster than one had imagined that any story about well-bred people, who live in sunny houses, with deer in the park, and play polo, and go to Nauheim for the cure, could possibly contain.'[32] West also said, much later, that *The Good Soldier* 'set the pattern for perhaps half the novels which have been written since'.[33] Here she exaggerated, but quite understandably. For how can anyone *not* read on, stalk-eyed with curiosity, after an opening paragraph as engrossing yet ambiguous, as outspoken yet muted, as clear yet contradictory as the first paragraph of *The Good Soldier*?

NOTES

1. Ford Madox Ford, *Joseph Conrad: A Personal Remembrance* (London: Duckworth, 1924), 210.

2. *Observer* (28 March 1915), 5, rep. in Martin Stannard (ed.), Ford Madox Ford, *The Good Soldier* (New York and London: Norton, 1995), 221–2. Cited hereafter as 'Stannard'.

3. *Outlook* (17 April 1915), 507–8, rep. in Stannard, 226–7. *The Good Soldier* first appeared under the name 'Ford Madox Hueffer'. The author changed his name to Ford Madox Ford in 1919.

4. Thomas Seccombe, 'The Good Soldier', *New Witness* (3 June 1915), 113–14, rep. in Stannard, 229–30. For further information about the controversy caused by the title see Max Saunders, *Ford Madox Ford: A Dual Life* 2 vols (Oxford and New York: Oxford University Press, 1996), i, 418–19. Cited hereafter as 'Saunders'.

5. *Athenaeum* (10 April 1915), 334, rep. in Stannard, 225.

6. The phrase comes from a review in the *Independent* [USA], 81 (22 March 1915), 432, rep. in Stannard, 221.

7. Sondra J. Stang, *Ford Madox Ford* (New York: Frederick Ungar, 1977), 74.

8. J. C. Cooper, *An Illustrated Encyclopaedia of Traditional Symbols* (London: Thames and Hudson, 1978), 40.

9. Grover Smith, *Ford Madox Ford*, Columbia Essays on Modern Writers, No. 63 (New York: Columbia University Press, 1972), 28–9.

10. Bramshaw, situated on the edge of the New Forest about six miles west of Fordingbridge in Hampshire, appears in the *Domesday Book* (1086) as 'Brammesage', and means (appropriately, given the entanglements which come to light there) 'Bramble Wood' (Eilert Ekwall, *The Concise Oxford Dictionary of English Place-Names*, 4th ed. (Oxford: Clarendon Press, 1960), 60). 'Teleragh' is not listed in A. H. Smith's *English Place-Name Elements*, Part II (Cambridge: Cambridge University Press, 1956), but there is a 'Telleraught' (or 'Talleraght') in County Wexford in Ireland. 'Powys' is not recorded in Edward MacLysaght's *The Surnames of Ireland*, 6th ed. (Dublin: Irish Academic Press, 1985).

11. *New Shorter Oxford English Dictionary* (1993).

12. Charles Wareing Bardsley, *A Dictionary of English and Welsh Surnames with Special American Instances* (London: Oxford University Press, 1901), 506.

13. Bardsley, *A Dictionary of English and Welsh Surnames*, 250.

14. Ford, *Joseph Conrad*, 129–30.

15. Vincent J. Cheng, 'A Chronology of *The Good Soldier*', *English Language Notes*, 24 (September 1986). See also Thomas C. Moser, *The Life in the Fiction of Ford Madox Ford* (Princeton, New Jersey: Princeton University Press, 1980), 162–3.

16. Ford Madox Hueffer, 'On Impressionism', *Poetry and Drama*, 2, Nos. 6 and 8 (June and December 1914), 167–75, 323–34. Quote from p. 333.

17. Ford Madox Hueffer, 'Dedication to Christina and Katharine', *Ancient Lights and Certain New Reflections: Being the Memories of a Young Man* (London: Chapman and Hall, 1911), xv.

18. Ford, *Joseph Conrad*, 6.

19. Smith, *Ford Madox Ford*, 30.

20. Carol Jacobs, '*The* (too) *Good Soldier*: "a real story"', *Glyph*, 3 (1978), 32–51, rep. in *Telling Time: Lévi-Strauss, Ford, Lessing, Benjamin, de Man, Wordsworth, Rilke* (Baltimore and London: Johns Hopkins University Press, 1993), 75–94. Quote from pp. 84–5.

21. Mark Schorer, 'The Good Novelist in *The Good Soldier*,' *Princeton University Library Chronicle*, 9 (April 1948), 128–33. Quotes from pp. 128 and 132, rep. in Stannard, 305–10.

22. Stang, *Ford Madox Ford*, 72–3.

23. Graham Greene, 'Introduction', *The Bodley Head Ford Madox Ford*, 5 vols (London, Sydney, Toronto: The Bodley Head, 1962), i, 12.

24. Ford Madox Hueffer, *The Spirit of the People: An Analysis of the English Mind* (London: Alston Rivers, 1907), 148–50.

25. Martin Stannard has much of interest to say on the 'much-debated date of completion' of the novel and more specifically on Ford's use of 4 August as a motif. See Stannard, 182–3.

26. Saunders, i, 406.

27. See, for example, the footnotes to Stannard, 71, 81, 105, 159.

28. Saunders, i, 438.

29. Saunders, i, 455.

30. Robert Green, *Ford Madox Ford: Prose and Politics* (Cambridge: Cambridge University Press, 1981), 91. By 'incest', of course, Green alludes to Ashburnham's relationship with Nancy, an angle on the novel developed at length by Saunders, i, 420–27.

31. *Boston Transcript* [USA] (17 March 1915), 24, rep. in Stannard, 220–21.

32. *Daily News and Leader* (2 April 1915), 6, rep. in Stannard, 222–4.

33. Quoted in Saunders, i, v.

Selected Reading

WORKS BY FORD

The Correspondence of Ford Madox Ford and Stella Bowen, eds. Sondra J.
    Stang and Karen Cochran (1994).
Critical Essays, eds. Max Saunders and Richard Stang (2002).
Critical Writings, ed. Frank MacShane (1964).
The Fifth Queen (Trilogy, 1906–1908: *The Fifth Queen* (1906), *Privy Seal*
    (1907) and *The Fifth Queen Crowned* (1908)). Available as a one-
    volume Penguin edition.
The Ford Madox Ford Reader, ed. Sondra J. Stang (1986).
The Good Soldier, ed. Martin Stannard (1995). This Norton Critical
    Edition is the standard scholarly text of the novel, containing
    very important textual (pp. 175–216) and extremely useful critical
    (pp. 219–398) appendices.
Letters of Ford Madox Ford, ed. Richard M. Ludwig (1965).
Memories and Impressions, ed. Michael Killigrew (1971).
Parade's End (Tetralogy, 1924–1928: *Some Do Not* (1924), *No More Parades*
    (1925), *A Man Could Stand Up* (1926) and *Last Post* (1928)). Available
    as a one-volume Penguin edition.
*Pound/Ford, The Story of a Literary Friendship: The Correspondence between
    Ezra Pound and Ford Madox Ford and Their Writings about Each
    Other*, ed. Brita Lindberg-Seyersted (1983).
War Prose, ed. Max Saunders (1999).

CRITICISM

Paul B. Armstrong, *The Challenge of Bewilderment: Understanding and Representation in James, Conrad, and Ford* (1987).

Todd K. Bender, *Literary Impressionism in Jean Rhys, Ford Madox Ford, Joseph Conrad and Charlotte Brontë* (1997).

Richard A. Cassell (ed.), *Critical Essays on Ford Madox Ford* (1987).

——, *Ford Madox Ford: A Study of his Novels* (1961).

Nicholas Delbanco, *Group Portrait: Joseph Conrad, Stephen Crane, Ford Madox Ford, Henry James, and H. G. Wells* (1982).

Ambrose Gordon Jr., *The Invisible Tent: The War Novels of Ford Madox Ford* (1964).

Robert Green, *Ford Madox Ford: Prose and Politics* (1981).

Sara Haslam, *Fragmenting Modernism: Ford Madox Ford, the Novel and the Great War* (2002).

Samuel Hynes, *Edwardian Occasions: Essays on English Writing in the Early Twentieth Century* (1972). There are three fine essays on Ford and 'The Epistemology of *The Good Soldier*' (pp. 54–63), first published in the *Sewanee Review*, 69 (Spring 1961), 225–35, is the best of them.

Carol Jacobs, 'The (too) *Good Soldier*: "a real story"', in *Telling Time: Lévi-Strauss, Ford, Lessing, Benjamin, de Man, Wordsworth, Rilke* (Baltimore and London: Johns Hopkins University Press, 1993), 75–94.

Alan Judd, *Ford Madox Ford* (1990).

Michael Levenson, *Modernism and the Fate of Individuality: Character and Novelistic Form from Conrad to Woolf* (1991).

Richard Wald Lid, *Ford Madox Ford: The Essence of His Art* (1964).

David H. Lynn, *The Hero's Tale: Narrative in the Early Modern Novel* (1989).

Frank MacShane (ed.), *Ford Madox Ford: The Critical Heritage* (1972; 1997).

——, *The Life and Work of Ford Madox Ford* (1965).

John A. Meixner, *Ford Madox Ford's Novels: A Critical Study* (1962).

Arthur Mizener, *The Saddest Story: A Biography of Ford Madox Ford* (1972).

Thomas C. Moser, *The Life in the Fiction of Ford Madox Ford* (1980).

Carol B. Ohmann, *Ford Madox Ford: From Apprentice to Craftsman* (1964).

C. Ruth Sabol and Todd K. Bender, *A Concordance to Ford Madox Ford's 'The Good Soldier'* (1981).

Max Saunders (ed.), Special Ford double issue of *Agenda*, 27, No. 4/28, No. 1 (Winter 1989–Spring 1990). See esp. the essays by Carol Jacobs on Ford's fictional theories (67–76) and by Wilbur Sanders on Ford's drama of narration (85–92).

Max Saunders, *Ford Madox Ford: A Dual Life*, 2 vols (1996). This standard critical biography of Ford contains the most exhaustive single essay on the novel.

Grover Smith, *Ford Madox Ford* (1972).

Ann Barr Snitow, *Ford Madox Ford and the Voice of Uncertainty* (1984).

Sondra J. Stang (ed.), *The Presence of Ford Madox Ford: A Memorial Volume of Essays, Poems, and Memoirs* (1981).

—— , *Ford Madox Ford* (1977).

Joseph Wiesenfarth (ed.), Special Ford issue ('Ford Madox Ford and the Arts') of *Contemporary Literature*, 30, No. 2 (Summer 1989). See esp. the article by Sondra J. Stang and Maryann De Julio on Ford's own translation into French of *The Good Soldier*, of which 37 manuscript pages have survived (263–79).

Paul L. Wiley, *Novelist of Three Worlds: Ford Madox Ford* (1962).

Note on the Text

The extant manuscripts of *The Good Soldier* are held by Cornell University Library's Division of Rare Books and Manuscript Collections. One manuscript comprises 376 pages of holograph and typescript, and a second, probably the printer's copy, consists of 305 pages of typescript.

Among other things, these manuscript sources reveal intriguing evidence of Ford's remodelling of Edward Ashburnham. By discarding material which projected him as an unregenerate libertine (and the father of a number of illegitimate children), Ford accentuated the tragic sentimentalist in Ashburnham and made him less obviously the principal cause of the novel's abundant suffering. For a full account of the various changes which Ford made, see *The Good Soldier* ed. Martin Stannard (New York and London: Norton, 1995), 179–216, and Charles G. Hoffmann, 'Ford's Manuscript Revisions of *The Good Soldier*', *English Literature in Transition*, 9, No. 4 (1966), 145–52.

The copy-text for this edition of *The Good Soldier* is the first English edition of the novel, published by John Lane on 17 March 1915 (which was also, almost certainly, the date of the first American edition). There is a reference to 'Waterbury, Ill.[inois]' in Part Four, Chapter 2 of the first edition, but no such place existed in 1915 (nor does it exist today). Ford obviously had in mind 'Waterbury, Conn.[ecticut]', and the text has been amended accordingly. Similarly, in Part One, Chapter 2, this edition changes the first edition's 'Frantz Hals' and 'Woovermans' to 'Frans Hals' and 'Wouwerman' on the grounds that the 1915 spellings were clearly unintentional errors.

Foreign words seem to have been italicized almost at random in the first edition: '*Schreibzimmer*' (writing-room), for example, was set in italics, whereas 'Reiseverkehrsbureau' (travel agency) was not. In this edition, an effort has been made to introduce consistent practice in this area, and all French, German, Italian, and Latin words and phrases, apart from proper names, have been italicized except where the word or phrase appears without italics in the *New Shorter Oxford English Dictionary* (1993).

By far the most important change this edition makes is to follow Martin Stannard's Norton Critical Edition in amending the first edition's 'Branshaw Teleragh' to 'Bramshaw Teleragh' throughout the text. In his 'Textual Appendices', Stannard notes that 'Bramshaw' was Ford's preferred spelling in the manuscript and that an error seems to have crept in between the typing up of the manuscript and the compositor's setting of the novel from the ensuing typescript. 'Although', Stannard writes, 'later consistently corrected in MS and TS to "Bramshaw Teleragh", the compositor takes the typist's first mistranscription as the standard and prints "Branshaw" throughout' (p. 197). 'One might argue that the corrupt forms [unlike this edition, Stannard also alters the name of one of Ashburnham's tenants from "Mumford" to "Mudford"] received Ford's tacit approval at proof stage,' Stannard acknowledges elsewhere, 'but it would have been wearisome (and costly) to go through the whole text altering the names . . . [and] there is a strong argument for removing textual corruption here as the product of external agency (the typist) and economic factors' (p. 192).

Stannard's argument is persuasive enough in its own right, but its strength is only fortified when we also take into account something he does not mention: that is, that Bramshaw (unlike 'Branshaw') is a real place in Hampshire. Parts of *The Good Soldier* are set in a specific area of that county, and Bramshaw is at the heart of the locality in question.

The Good Soldier

Dedicatory Letter to Stella Ford[1]

My Dear Stella,

I have always regarded this as my best book – at any rate as the best book of mine of a pre-war period; and between its writing and the appearance of my next novel nearly ten years must have elapsed, so that whatever I may have since written may be regarded as the work of a different man – as the work of *your* man. For it is certain that without the incentive to live that you offered me I should scarcely have survived the war-period and it is more certain still that without your spurring me again to write I should never have written again. And it happens that, by a queer chance, *The Good Soldier* is almost alone amongst my books in being dedicated to no one: Fate must have elected to let it wait the ten years that it waited – for this dedication.

What I am now I owe to you: what I was when I wrote *The Good Soldier* I owed to the concatenation of circumstances of a rather purposeless and wayward life. Until I sat down to write this book – on the 17th December 1913[2] – I had never attempted to extend myself, to use a phrase of racehorse training. Partly because I had always entertained very fixedly the idea that – whatever may be the case with other writers – I at least should not be able to write a novel by which I should care to stand before reaching the age of forty; partly because I very definitely did not want to come into competition with other writers whose claim or whose need for recognition and what recognitions bring were greater than my own. I had never really tried to put into any novel of mine *all* that I knew about writing. I had written rather desultorily a number of books – a great number – but they had all been in the nature of *pastiches*, of pieces of rather precious writing, or of *tours*

3

de force. But I have always been mad about writing – about the way writing should be done and partly alone, partly with the companionship of Conrad,[3] I had even at that date made exhaustive studies into how words should be handled and novels constructed.

So, on the day I was forty I sat down to show what I could do – and *The Good Soldier* resulted. I fully intended it to be my last book. I used to think – and I do not know that I do not think the same now – that one book was enough for any man to write, and, at the date when *The Good Soldier* was finished, London at least and possibly the world appeared to be passing under the dominion of writers newer and much more vivid. Those were the passionate days of the literary Cubists, Vorticists, *Imagistes* and the rest of the *tapageux* and riotous *Jeunes*[4] of that young decade. So I regarded myself as the Eel which, having reached the deep sea, brings forth its young and dies – or as the Great Auk I considered that, having reached my allotted, I had laid my one egg and might as well die.[5] So I took a formal farewell of Literature in the columns of a magazine called the *Thrush*[6] – which also, poor little auk that it was, died of the effort. Then I prepared to stand aside in favour of our good friends – yours and mine – Ezra, Eliot, Wyndham Lewis, H. D.,[7], and the rest of the clamorous young writers who were then knocking at the door.

But greater clamours beset London and the world which till then had seemed to lie at the proud feet of those conquerors; Cubism, Vorticism, Imagism and the rest never had their fair chance amid the voices of the cannon, and so I have come out of my hole again and beside your strong, delicate and beautiful works have taken heart to lay some work of my own.

The Good Soldier, however, remains my great auk's egg for me as being something of a race that will have no successors and as it was written so long ago I may not seem over-vain if I consider it for a moment or two. No author, I think, is deserving of much censure for vanity if, taking down one of his ten-year-old books, he exclaims: 'Great Heavens, did I write as well as that then?' for the implication always is that one does not any longer write so well and few are so envious as to censure the complacencies of an extinct volcano.

Be that as it may, I was lately forced into the rather close examination of this book, for I had to translate it into French,[8] that forcing me to give it much closer attention than would be the case in any reading however minute. And I will permit myself to say that I was astounded at the work I must have put into the construction of the book, at the intricate tangle of references and cross-references. Nor is that to be wondered at for, though I wrote it with comparative rapidity, I had it hatching within myself for fully another decade. That was because the story is a true story and because I had it from Edward Ashburnham himself and I could not write it till all the others were dead. So I carried it about with me all those years, thinking about it from time to time.

I had in those days an ambition: that was to do for the English novel what in *Fort comme la mort*, Maupassant had done for the French.[9] One day I had my reward, for I happened to be in a company where a fervent young admirer exclaimed: 'By Jove, *The Good Soldier* is the finest novel in the English language!' whereupon my friend Mr John Rodker[10] who has always had a properly tempered admiration for my work remarked in his clear, slow drawl: 'Ah yes. It is, but you have left out a word. It is the finest French novel in the English language!'

With that – which is my tribute to my masters and betters of France – I will leave the book to the reader. But I should like to say a word about the title. This book was originally called by me *The Saddest Story*, but since it did not appear till the darkest days of the war were upon us, Mr Lane[11] importuned me with letters and telegrams – I was by that time engaged in other pursuits! – to change the title which he said would at that date render the book unsaleable. One day, when I was on parade, I received a final wire of appeal from Mr Lane, and the telegraph being reply-paid I seized the reply-form and wrote in hasty irony : 'Dear Lane, Why not *The Good Soldier*?' . . . To my horror six months later the book appeared under that title.

I have never ceased to regret it but, since the War, I have received so much evidence that the book has been read under that name that I hesitate to make a change for fear of causing confusion. Had the chance occurred during the War I should not have hesitated to make the change, for I had only two evidences that anyone had ever heard of it. On one occasion I met the adjutant of my regiment just come off leave and looking extremely sick. I said: 'Great Heavens, man, what is the matter with you?' He replied: 'Well, the day before yesterday I got engaged to be married and today I have been reading *The Good Soldier*.'

On the other occasion I was on parade again, being examined in drill, on the Guards' Square at Chelsea. And, since I was petrified with nervousness, having to do it before a half-dozen elderly gentlemen with red hatbands,[12] I got my men about as hopelessly boxed as it is possible to do with the gentlemen privates of H.M. Coldstream Guards. Whilst I stood stiffly at attention one of the elderly red hatbands walked close behind by back and said distinctly in my ear, 'Did you say, *The Good Soldier*?' So no doubt Mr Lane was avenged. At any rate I have learned that irony may be a two-edged sword.

You, my dear Stella, will have heard me tell these stories a great many times. But the seas now divide us and I put them in this, your letter, which you will read before you see me in the hope that they may give you some pleasure with the illusion that you are hearing familiar – and very devoted – tones. And so I subscribe myself in all truth and in the hope that you will accept at once the particular dedication of this book and the general dedication of the edition.

Your
F. M. F.
New York,
January 9, 1927

NOTES

1. *Stella Ford* the Australian painter Esther Gwendolyn 'Stella' Bowen (1893–1947) was never actually married to Ford. Their relationship lasted from 1919–28 and it was with Bowen that Ford had his third daughter, Esther Julia, born in November 1920. The 'Dedicatory Letter' was specially written for the second American edition of the novel (1927) and was subsequently reprinted in the second British edition (1928).

2. *17th December 1913* was Ford's fortieth birthday. He was born in Merton, Surrey, in 1873 and christened 'Ford Hermann Hueffer'. He changed his name to Ford Madox Ford in 1919.

3. *the companionship of Conrad* the Polish-born novelist Joseph Conrad (1857–1924) was one of Ford's closest companions (especially between 1898 and 1909) and perhaps his chief literary inspiration. They collaborated on three novels, *The Inheritors* (1901), *Romance* (1903) and *The Nature of a Crime* (1924), and it is thought that Ford may have written part of Conrad's *Nostromo* (1904).

4. *literary Cubists, Vorticists, Imagistes . . . Jeunes* the Franco-Spanish Cubist movement began around 1907 (and petered out *c.*1914) with the multi-perspectival paintings and sculptures of Pablo Picasso (1881–1973) and Georges Braque (1882–1963), though who, precisely, Ford has in mind as 'the literary Cubists' of Britain is harder to determine. Vorticism was an iconoclastic art movement that flourished in London between 1912 and 1915. Influenced by both Cubism and Italian Futurism, its chief exponent was the writer, painter and polemicist Percy Wyndham Lewis (1882–1957). A 10-page excerpt from the beginning of *The Good Soldier* appeared in the first number of Vorticism's aggressively opinionated mouthpiece, the pink-covered *Blast*, edited by Lewis. *Imagisme* (or Imagism) was an Anglo-American literary movement inspired by the critical ideas of T. E. Hulme (1883–1917) which began in 1912. The *Imagistes* were dedicated to the concise expression of pure visual images, and an influential anthology, *Des Imagistes*, appeared in 1914. The French words *tapageur* (*-euse*) and *jeune* mean 'loud, showy or noisy' and 'young' respectively, so Ford has in mind riotous youth.

5. *Eel . . . might as well die* European and American freshwater eels swim to the Sargasso Sea to breed. The Great Auk (*Pinguinus impennis*) was a flightless seabird which was hunted to extinction in 1844.

6. *a formal farewell . . . the Thrush* Ford contributed an essay to the *Thrush*, an ephemeral poetry magazine that flourished between December 1909 and May 1910, but he actually announced his intention to abandon fiction in a magazine called *Poetry and Drama* soon after completing *The Good Soldier*: 'Writing up to my own standards is such an intolerable labour and such a thankless job . . . that for my part I am determined to drop creative writing for good and all.' ('On Impressionism: Second Article', *Poetry and Drama*, 2, No. 8 (December 1914), 323–34. Quote from p. 326.

7. *Ezra, Eliot . . . H. D.* the American poet Ezra Pound (1885–1972) was one of the father figures of Anglo-American modernist literature and, at the time Ford sat down to write *The Good Soldier*, the author of *A Lume Spento* (1908), *Personae* (1909), *Canzoni* (1911) and *Ripostes* (1912). Pound became a leading member of the *Imagiste* school of poetry along with the American poet, novelist and dramatist 'H. D.', the *nom de plume* of Hilda Doolittle (1886–1961). The American poet and critic T. S. Eliot (1888–1965) was a major force in Anglo-American

literature and criticism in the first half of the twentieth century. His first significant poem, 'The Love Song of J. Alfred Prufrock', appeared three months after *The Good Soldier* in June 1915.

8. *translate it into French* the first French translation of the novel to be published was by Jacques Papy (1953). Ford himself began a translation of the novel into French in 1916 but only 37 manuscript pages have survived. He called it '*Le bon soldat*': see the entry under 'Joseph Wiesenfarth' in the 'Selected Reading' section.

9. *Fort comme la mort . . . French* Ford greatly admired the work of Guy de Maupassant (1850–93), a pupil of Flaubert and the author of naturalist novels and short stories. *Fort comme la mort (Strong as Death)* was published in 1889.

10. *Mr John Rodker* John Rodker (1894–1955) was a writer, publisher and translator.

11. *Mr Lane* John Lane (1854–1925) was co-founder, in 1887, of the Bodley Head press, the firm that brought out *The Good Soldier* in 1915.

12. *the Guards' Square . . . red hatbands* designed by George Moore and built in 1861–2 to house foot guards, Chelsea Barracks (wherein is located 'the Guards' 'Square') on the Chelsea Bridge Road in London was completely rebuilt in 1900–1906. Ford enlisted in the army at the end of July 1915, four months after the publication of *The Good Soldier*. A 'red hatband' denotes a senior officer.

The Good Soldier

A TALE OF PASSION

'Beati Immaculati'[1]

Part One

I

This is the saddest story I have ever heard. We had known the Ashburnhams for nine seasons of the town of Nauheim[2] with an extreme intimacy – or, rather, with an acquaintanceship as loose and easy and yet as close as a good glove's with your hand. My wife and I knew Captain and Mrs Ashburnham as well as it was possible to know anybody, and yet, in another sense, we knew nothing at all about them. This is, I believe, a state of things only possible with English people of whom, till today, when I sit down to puzzle out what I know of this sad affair, I knew nothing whatever. Six months ago I had never been to England, and, certainly, I had never sounded the depths of an English heart. I had known the shallows.

I don't mean to say that we were not acquainted with many English people. Living, as we perforce lived, in Europe, and being, as we perforce were, leisured Americans, which is as much as to say that we were un-American, we were thrown very much into the society of the nicer English. Paris, you see, was our home. Somewhere between Nice and Bordighera provided yearly winter quarters for us, and Nauheim always received us from July to September. You will gather from this statement that one of us had, as the saying is, a 'heart', and, from the statement that my wife is dead, that she was the sufferer.

Captain Ashburnham also had a heart. But, whereas a yearly month or so at Nauheim tuned him up to exactly the right pitch for the rest of the twelvemonth, the two months or so were only just enough to keep poor Florence alive from year to year. The reason for his heart was, approximately, polo, or too much hard sportsmanship in his youth. The reason for poor Florence's broken years was a storm at sea upon our first crossing to Europe, and the immediate reasons for our imprisonment in that continent were doctor's orders. They said that even the short Channel crossing might well kill the poor thing.

When we all first met, Captain Ashburnham, home on sick leave from an India to which he was never to return, was thirty-three; Mrs Ashburnham – Leonora – was thirty-one. I was thirty-six and poor Florence thirty. Thus today Florence would have been thirty-nine and Captain Ashburnham forty-two; whereas I am forty-five and Leonora forty. You will perceive, therefore, that our friendship has been a young-middle-aged affair, since we were all of us of quite quiet dispositions, the Ashburnhams being more particularly what in England it is the custom to call 'quite good people'.

They were descended, as you will probably expect, from the Ashburnham who accompanied Charles I to the scaffold,[3] and, as you must also expect with this class of English people, you would never have noticed it. Mrs Ashburnham was a Powys; Florence was a Hurlbird of Stamford, Connecticut, where, as you know, they are more old-fashioned than even the inhabitants of Cranford,[4] England, could have been. I myself am a Dowell of Philadelphia, Pa., where, it is historically true, there are more old English families than you would find in any six English counties taken together. I carry about with me, indeed – as if it were the only thing that invisibly anchored me to any spot upon the globe – the title deeds of my farm, which once covered several blocks between Chestnut and Walnut Streets.[5] These title deeds are of wampum, the grant of an Indian chief to the first Dowell, who left Farnham in Surrey in company with William Penn.[6] Florence's people, as is so often the case with the inhabitants of Connecticut, came from the neighbourhood of Fordingbridge,[7] where the Ashburnhams' place is. From there, at this moment, I am actually writing.

You may well ask why I write. And yet my reasons are quite many. For it is not unusual in human beings who have witnessed the sack of a city or the falling to pieces of a people to desire to set down what they have witnessed for the benefit of unknown heirs or of generations infinitely remote; or, if you please, just to get the sight out of their heads.

Someone has said that the death of a mouse from cancer is the whole sack of Rome by the Goths,[8] and I swear to you that the breaking up of our little four-square coterie was such another unthinkable event.

Supposing that you should come upon us sitting together at one of the little tables in front of the club house, let us say, at Homburg,[9] taking tea of an afternoon and watching the miniature golf, you would have said that, as human affairs go, we were an extraordinarily safe castle. We were, if you will, one of those tall ships with the white sails upon a blue sea, one of those things that seem the proudest and the safest of all the beautiful and safe things that God has permitted the mind of men to frame. Where better could one take refuge? Where better?

Permanence? Stability? I can't believe it's gone. I can't believe that that long, tranquil life, which was just stepping a minuet, vanished in four crashing days at the end of nine years and six weeks. Upon my word, yes, our intimacy was like a minuet, simply because on every possible occasion and in every possible circumstance we knew where to go, where to sit, which table we unanimously should choose; and we could rise and go, all four together, without a signal from any one of us, always to the music of the *Kur* orchestra,[10] always in the temperate sunshine, or, if it rained, in discreet shelters. No indeed, it can't be gone. You can't kill a *minuet de la cour*.[11] You may shut up the music-book, close the harpsichord; in the cupboard and presses the rats may destroy the white satin favours. The mob may sack Versailles; the Trianon[12] may fall, but surely the minuet – the minuet itself is dancing itself away into the furthest stars, even as our minuet of the Hessian[13] bathing places must be stepping itself still. Isn't there any heaven where old beautiful dances, old beautiful intimacies prolong themselves? Isn't there any Nirvana pervaded by the faint thrilling of instruments that have fallen into the dust of wormwood but that yet had frail, tremulous, and everlasting souls?

No, by God, it is false! It wasn't a minuet that we stepped; it was a prison – a prison full of screaming hysterics, tied down so that they might not outsound the rolling of our carriage wheels as we went along the shaded avenues of the Taunus Wald.[14]

And yet I swear by the sacred name of my creator that it was true. It was true sunshine; the true music; the true splash of the fountains from the mouth of stone dolphins. For, if for me we were four people with the same tastes, with the same desires, acting – or, no, not acting – sitting here and there unanimously, isn't that the truth? If for nine years I have possessed a goodly apple that is rotten at the core and discover its rottenness only in nine years and six months less four days, isn't it true to say that for nine years I possessed a goodly apple? So it may well be with Edward Ashburnham, with Leonora his wife and with poor dear Florence. And, if you come to think of it, isn't it a little odd that the physical rottenness of at least two pillars of our foursquare house never presented itself to my mind as a menace to its security? It doesn't so present itself now though the two of them are actually dead. I don't know . . .

I know nothing – nothing in the world – of the hearts of men. I only know that I am alone – horribly alone. No hearthstone will ever again witness, for me, friendly intercourse. No smoking-room will ever be other than peopled with incalculable simulacra amidst smoke wreaths. Yet, in the name of God, what should I know if I don't know the life of the hearth and of the smoking-room, since my whole life has been passed in those places? The warm hearthside! – Well, there was Florence: I believe that for the twelve years her life lasted, after the storm that seemed irretrievably to have weakened her heart – I don't believe that for one minute she was out of my sight, except when she was safely tucked up in bed and I should be downstairs, talking to some good fellow or other in some lounge or smoking-room or taking my final turn with a cigar before going to bed. I don't, you understand, blame Florence. But how can she have known what she knew? How could she have got to know it? To know it so fully. Heavens! There doesn't seem to have been the actual time. It must have been when I was taking my baths, and my Swedish exercises,[15] being manicured. Leading the life I did, of the sedulous, strained nurse, I had to do something to keep myself fit. It must have been then! Yet even that can't have been enough time to get the tremendously long conversations full of worldly wisdom that Leonora has reported to me since their deaths. And is it possible to imagine that during our prescribed walks in Nauheim and the neighbourhood she found time to carry on the protracted negotiations which she did carry on between Edward Ashburnham and his wife? And isn't it incredible that during all that time Edward and Leonora never spoke a word to each other in private? What is one to think of humanity?

For I swear to you that they were the model couple. He was as devoted as it was possible to be without appearing fatuous. So well set up, with such honest blue eyes, such a touch of stupidity, such a warm goodheartedness! And she – so tall, so splendid in the saddle, so fair! Yes, Leonora was extraordinarily fair and so extraordinarily the real thing that she seemed too good to be true. You don't, I mean, as a rule, get it all so superlatively together. To be the county family, to look the county family, to be so appropriately and perfectly wealthy; to be so perfect in manner – even just to the saving touch of insolence that seems to be necessary. To have all that and to be all that! No, it was too good to be true. And yet, only this afternoon, talking over the whole matter she said to me: 'Once I tried to have a lover but I was so sick at the heart, so utterly worn out that I had to send him away.' That struck me as the most amazing thing I had ever heard. She said 'I was actually in a man's arms. Such a nice chap! Such a dear fellow! And I was saying to myself, fiercely, hissing it between my teeth, as they say in novels – and really clenching them together: I was saying to myself: "Now, I'm in for it and I'll really have a good time for once in my life – for once in my life!" It was in the dark, in a carriage, coming back from a hunt ball. Eleven miles we had to drive! And then suddenly the bitterness of the endless poverty, of the endless acting – it fell on me like a blight, it spoilt everything. Yes, I had to realize that I had been spoilt even for the good time when it came. And I burst out crying and I cried and I cried for the whole eleven miles. Just imagine *me* crying! And just imagine me making a fool of the poor dear chap like that. It certainly wasn't playing the game, was it now?'

I don't know; I don't know; was that last remark of hers the remark of a harlot, or is it what every decent woman, county family or not county family, thinks at the bottom of her heart? Or thinks all the time for the matter of that? Who knows?

Yet, if one doesn't know that at this hour and day, at this pitch of civilization to which we have attained, after all the preachings of all the moralists, and all the teachings of all the mothers to all the daughters *in saecula saeculorum*[16] . . . but perhaps that is what all mothers teach all daughters, not with lips but with the eyes, or with heart whispering to heart. And, if one doesn't know as much as that about the first thing in the world, what does one know and why is one here?

I asked Mrs Ashburnham whether she had told Florence that and what Florence had said and she answered: – 'Florence didn't offer any comment at all. What could she say? There wasn't anything to be said. With the grinding poverty we had to put up with to keep up appearances, and the way the poverty came about – *you* know what I mean – any woman would have been justified in taking a lover and presents too. Florence once said about a very similar position – she was a little too well-bred, too American, to talk about mine – that it was a case of perfectly open riding and the woman could just act on the spur of the moment. She said it in American of course, but that was the sense of it. I think her actual words were: "That it was up to her to take it or leave it . . ."'

I don't want you to think that I am writing Teddy Ashburnham down a brute. I don't believe he was. God knows, perhaps all men are like that. For as I've said what do I know even of the smoking-room? Fellows come in and tell the most extraordinarily gross stories – so gross that they will positively give you a pain. And yet they'd be offended if you suggested that they weren't the sort of person you could trust your wife alone with. And very likely they'd be quite properly offended – that is if you can trust anybody alone with anybody. But that sort of fellow obviously takes more delight in listening to or in telling gross stories – more delight than in anything else in the world. They'll hunt languidly and dress languidly and dine languidly and work without enthusiasm and find it a bore to carry on three minutes' conversation about anything whatever and yet, when the other sort of conversation begins, they'll laugh and wake up and throw themselves about in their chairs. Then, if they so delight in the narration, how is it possible that they can be offended – and properly offended – at the suggestion that they might make attempts upon your wife's honour? Or again: Edward Ashburnham was the cleanest looking sort of chap; – an excellent magistrate, a first rate soldier, one of the best landlords, so they said, in Hampshire, England. To the poor and to hopeless drunkards, as I myself have witnessed, he was like a painstaking guardian. And he never told a story that couldn't have gone into the columns of the *Field*[17] more than once or twice in all the nine years of my knowing him. He didn't even like hearing them; he would fidget and get up and go out to buy a cigar or something of that sort. You would have said that he was just exactly the sort of chap that you could have trusted your wife with. And I trusted mine and it was madness.

And yet again you have me. If poor Edward was dangerous because of the chastity of his expressions – and they say that is always the hall-mark of a libertine – what about myself? For I solemnly avow that not only have I never so much as hinted at an impropriety in my conversation in the whole of my days; and more than that, I will vouch for the cleanness of my thoughts and the absolute chastity of my life. At what, then, does it all work out? Is the whole thing a folly and a mockery? Am I no better than a eunuch or is the proper man – the man with the right to existence – a raging stallion forever neighing after his neighbour's womankind?

I don't know. And there is nothing to guide us. And if everything is so nebulous about a matter so elementary as the morals of sex, what is there to guide us in the more subtle morality of all other personal contacts, associations, and activities? Or are we meant to act on impulse alone? It is all a darkness.

II

I don't know how it is best to put this thing down – whether it would be better to try and tell the story from the beginning, as if it were a story; or whether to tell it from this distance of time, as it reached me from the lips of Leonora or from those of Edward himself.

So I shall just imagine myself for a fortnight or so at one side of the fireplace of a country cottage, with a sympathetic soul opposite me. And I shall go on talking, in a low voice while the sea sounds in the distance and overhead the great black flood of wind polishes the bright stars. From time to time we shall get up and go to the door and look out at the great moon and say: 'Why, it is nearly as bright as in Provence!' And then we shall come back to the fireside, with just the touch of a sigh because we are not in that Provence where even the saddest stories are gay. Consider the lamentable history of Peire Vidal.[18]

Two years ago Florence and I motored from Biarritz to Las Tours, which is in the Black Mountains. In the middle of a tortuous valley there rises up an immense pinnacle and on the pinnacle are four castles – Las Tours, the Towers. And the immense mistral[19] blew down that valley which was the way from France into Provence so that the silver grey olive leaves appeared like hair flying in the wind, and the tufts of rosemary crept into the iron rocks that they might not be torn up by the roots.

It was, of course, poor dear Florence who wanted to go to Las Tours. You are to imagine that, however much her bright personality came from Stamford, Connecticut, she was yet a graduate of Poughkeepsie.[20] I never could imagine how she did it – the queer, chattery person that she was. With the far-away look in her eyes – which wasn't, however, in the least romantic – I mean that she didn't look as if she were seeing poetic dreams, or looking through you, for she hardly ever did look at you! – holding up one hand as if she wished to silence any objection – or any comment for the matter of that – she would talk. She would talk about William the Silent, about Gustave the Loquacious, about Paris frocks, about how the poor dressed in 1337, about Fantin-Latour, about the Paris-Lyons-Mediterranée train-de-luxe, about whether it would be worth while to get off at Tarascon and go across the windswept suspension-bridge, over the Rhone to take another look at Beaucaire.[21]

We never did take another look at Beaucaire, of course – beautiful Beaucaire, with the high, triangular white tower, that looked as thin as a needle and as tall as the Flatiron, between Fifth and Broadway[22] – Beaucaire with the grey walls on the top of the pinnacle surrounding an acre and a half of blue irises, beneath the tallness of the stone pines. What a beautiful thing the stone pine is! . . .

No, we never did go back anywhere. Not to Heidelberg, not to Hamelin, not to Verona, not to Mont Majour – not so much as to Carcassonne itself.[23] We talked of it, of course, but I guess Florence got all she wanted out of one look at a place. She had the seeing eye.

I haven't, unfortunately, so that the world is full of places to which I want to return – towns with the blinding white sun upon them; stone pines against the blue of the sky; corners of gables, all carved and painted with stags and scarlet flowers and crowstepped gables with the little saint at the top; and grey and pink palazzi and walled towns a mile or so back from the sea on the Mediterranean, between Leghorn[24] and Naples. Not one of them did we see more than once, so that the whole world for me is like spots of colour in an immense canvas. Perhaps if it weren't so I should have something to catch hold of now.

Is all this digression or isn't it digression? Again I don't know. You, the listener, sit opposite me. But you are so silent. You don't tell me anything. I am, at any rate, trying to get you to see what sort of life it was I led with Florence and what Florence was like. Well, she was bright; and she danced. She seemed to dance over the floors of castles and over seas and over and over and over the salons of *modistes* and over the *plages*[25] of the Riviera like a gay tremulous beam, reflected from water upon a ceiling. And my function in life was to keep that bright thing in existence. And it was almost as difficult as trying to catch with your hand that dancing reflection. And the task lasted for years.

Florence's aunts used to say that I must be the laziest man in Philadelphia. They had never been to Philadelphia and they had the New England conscience. You see, the first thing they said to me when I called in on Florence in the little ancient, colonial, wooden house beneath the high, thin-leaved elms – the first question they asked me was not how I did but what did I do. And I did nothing. I suppose I ought to have done something, but I didn't see any call to do it. Why does one do things? I just drifted in and wanted Florence. First I had drifted in on Florence at a Browning tea,[26] or something of the sort in Fourteenth Street, which was then still residential. I don't know why I had gone to New York; I don't know why I had gone to the tea. I don't see why Florence should have gone to that sort of spelling bee.[27] It wasn't the place at which, even then, you expected to find a Poughkeepsie graduate. I guess Florence wanted to raise the culture of the Stuyvesant[28] crowd and did it as she might have gone in slumming. Intellectual slumming, that was what it was. She always wanted to leave the world a little more elevated than she found it. Poor dear thing, I have heard her lecture Teddy Ashburnham by the hour on the difference between a Frans Hals and a Wouwerman and why the Pre-Mycenaic[29] statues were cubical with knobs on the top. I wonder what he made of it? Perhaps he was thankful.

I know I was. For do you understand my whole attentions, my whole endeavours were to keep poor dear Florence on to topics like the finds at Cnossos and the mental spirituality of Walter Pater.[30] I had to keep her at it, you understand, or she might die. For I was solemnly informed that if she became excited over anything or if her emotions were really stirred her little heart might cease to beat. For twelve years I had to watch every word that any person uttered in any conversation and I had to head it off what the English call 'things'– off love, poverty, crime, religion and the rest of it. Yes, the first doctor that we had when she was carried off the ship at Havre assured me that this must be done. Good God, are all these fellows monstrous idiots, or is there a freemasonry between all of them from end to end of the earth? . . . That is what makes me think of that fellow Peire Vidal.

Because, of course, his story is culture and I had to head her towards culture and at the same time it's so funny and she hadn't got to laugh, and it's so full of love and she wasn't to think of love. Do you know the story? Las Tours of the Four Castles had for chatelaine Blanche Somebody-or-other who was called as a term of commendation, La Louve – the She-Wolf. And Peire Vidal the Troubadour paid his court to La Louve. And she wouldn't have anything to do with him. So, out of compliment to her – the things people do when they're in love! – he dressed himself up in wolfskins and went up into the Black Mountains. And the shepherds of the Montagne Noire and their dogs mistook him for a wolf and he was torn with the fangs and beaten with clubs. So they carried him back to Las Tours and La Louve wasn't at all impressed. They polished him up and her husband remonstrated seriously with her. Vidal was, you see, a great poet and it was not proper to treat a great poet with indifference.

So Peire Vidal declared himself Emperor of Jerusalem or somewhere and the husband had to kneel down and kiss his feet though La Louve wouldn't. And Peire set sail in a rowing boat with four companions to redeem the Holy Sepulchre. And they struck on a rock somewhere, and, at great expense, the husband had to fit out an expedition to fetch him back. And Peire Vidal fell all over the Lady's bed while the husband, who was a most ferocious warrior, remonstrated some more about the courtesy that is due to great poets. But I suppose La Louve was the more ferocious of the two. Anyhow, that is all that came of it. Isn't that a story?

You haven't an idea of the queer old-fashionedness of Florence's aunts – the Misses Hurlbird, nor yet of her uncle. An extraordinarily lovable man, that Uncle John. Thin, gentle, and with a 'heart' that made his life very much what Florence's afterwards became. He didn't reside at Stamford; his home was in Waterbury[31] where the watches come from. He had a factory there which, in our queer American way, would change its functions almost from year to year. For nine months or so it would manufacture buttons out of bone. Then it would suddenly produce brass buttons for coachmen's liveries. Then it would take a turn at embossed tin lids for candy boxes. The fact is that the poor old gentleman, with his weak and fluttering heart, didn't want his factory to manufacture anything at all. He wanted to retire. And he did retire when he was seventy. But he was so worried at having all the street boys in the town point after him and exclaim: 'There goes the laziest man in Waterbury!' that he tried taking a tour round the world. And Florence and a young man called Jimmy went with him. It appears from what Florence told me that Jimmy's function with Mr Hurlbird was to avoid exciting topics for him. He had to keep him, for instance, out of political discussions. For the poor old man was a violent Democrat in days when you might travel the world over without finding anything but a Republican.[32] Anyhow, they went round the world.

I think an anecdote is about the best way to give you an idea of what the old gentleman was like. For it is perhaps important that you should know what the old gentleman was; he had a great deal of influence in forming the character of my poor dear wife.

Just before they set out from San Francisco for the South Seas old Mr Hurlbird said he must take something with him to make little presents to people he met on the voyage. And it struck him that the things to take for that purpose were oranges – because California is the orange country – and comfortable folding chairs. So he bought I don't know how many cases of oranges – the great cool California oranges, and half-a-dozen folding chairs in a special case that he always kept in his cabin. There must have been half a cargo of fruit.

For, to every person on board the several steamers that they employed – to every person with whom he had so much as a nodding acquaintance, he gave an orange every morning. And they lasted him right round the girdle of this mighty globe of ours. When they were at North Cape,[33] even, he saw on the horizon, poor dear thin man that he was, a lighthouse. 'Hello,' says he to himself, 'these fellows must be very lonely. Let's take them some oranges.' So he had a boatload of his fruit out and had himself rowed to the lighthouse on the horizon. The folding chairs he lent to any lady that he came across and liked or who seemed tired and invalidish on the ship. And so, guarded against his heart and having his niece with him, he went round the world . . .

He wasn't obtrusive about his heart. You wouldn't have known he had one. He only left it to the physical laboratory at Waterbury for the benefit of science, since he considered it to be quite an extraordinary kind of heart. And the joke of the matter was that, when, at the age of eighty-four, just five days before poor Florence, he died of bronchitis there was found to be absolutely nothing the matter with that organ. It had certainly jumped or squeaked or something just sufficiently to take in the doctors, but it appears that that was because of an odd formation of the lungs. I don't much understand about these matters.

I inherited his money because Florence died five days after him. I wish I hadn't. It was a great worry. I had to go out to Waterbury just after Florence's death because the poor dear old fellow had left a good many charitable bequests and I had to appoint trustees. I didn't like the idea of their not being properly handled.

Yes, it was a great worry. And just as I had got things roughly settled I received the extraordinary cable from Ashburnham begging me to come back and have a talk with him. And immediately afterwards came one from Leonora saying, 'Yes, please do come. You could be so helpful.' It was as if he had sent the cable without consulting her and had afterwards told her. Indeed, that was pretty much what had happened, except that he had told the girl and the girl told the wife. I arrived, however, too late to be of any good if I could have been of any good. And then I had my first taste of English life. It was amazing. It was overwhelming. I never shall forget the polished cob that Edward, beside me, drove; the animal's action, its high-stepping, its skin that was like satin. And the peace! And the red cheeks! And the beautiful, beautiful old house.

Just near Bramshaw[34] Teleragh it was and we descended on it from the high, clear, windswept waste of the New Forest. I tell you it was amazing to arrive there from Waterbury. And it came into my head – for Teddy Ashburnham, you remember, had cabled to me to 'come and have a talk' with him – that it was unbelievable that anything essentially calamitous could happen to that place and those people. I tell you it was the very spirit of peace. And Leonora, beautiful and smiling, with her coils of yellow hair, stood on the top doorstep, with a butler and footman and a maid or so behind her. And she just said: 'So glad you've come,' as if I'd run down to lunch from a town ten miles away, instead of having come half the world over at the call of two urgent telegrams.

The girl was out with the hounds, I think.

And that poor devil beside me was in an agony. Absolute, hopeless, dumb agony such as passes the mind of man to imagine.

III

It was a very hot summer, in August, 1904; and Florence had already been taking the baths for a month. I don't know how it feels to be a patient at one of those places. I never was a patient anywhere. I daresay the patients get a home feeling and some sort of anchorage in the spot. They seem to like the bath attendants, with their cheerful faces, their air of authority, their white linen. But, for myself, to be at Nauheim gave me a sense – what shall I say? – a sense almost of nakedness – the nakedness that one feels on the seashore or in any great open space. I had no attachments, no accumulations. In one's own home it is as if little, innate sympathies draw one to particular chairs that seem to enfold one in an embrace, or take one along particular streets that seem friendly when others may be hostile. And, believe me, that feeling is a very important part of life. I know it well, that have been for so long a wanderer upon the face of public resorts. And one is too polished up.

Heaven knows I was never an untidy man. But the feeling that I had when, whilst poor Florence was taking her morning bath, I stood upon the carefully swept steps of the *Englischer Hof*,[35] looking at the carefully arranged trees in tubs upon the carefully arranged gravel whilst carefully arranged people walked past in carefully calculated gaiety, at the carefully calculated hour, the tall trees of the public gardens, going up to the right; the reddish stone of the baths – or were they white half-timber châlets? Upon my word I have forgotten, I who was there so often. That will give you the measure of how much I was in the landscape. I could find my way blindfolded to the hot rooms, to the douche rooms, to the fountain in the centre of the quadrangle where the rusty water gushes out. Yes, I could find my way blindfolded. I know the exact distances. From the Hotel Regina you took one hundred and eighty-seven paces, then, turning sharp, lefthanded, four hundred and twenty took you straight down to the fountain. From the *Englischer Hof*, starting on the sidewalk, it was ninety-seven paces and the same four hundred and twenty, but turning lefthanded this time.

And now you understand that, having nothing in the world to do – but nothing whatever! I fell into the habit of counting my footsteps. I would walk with Florence to the baths. And, of course, she entertained me with her conversation. It was, as I have said, wonderful what she could make conversation out of. She walked very lightly, and her hair was very nicely done, and she dressed beautifully and very expensively. Of course she had money of her own, but I shouldn't have minded. And yet you know I can't remember a single one of her dresses. Or I can remember just one, a very simple one of blue figured silk – a Chinese pattern – very full in the skirts and broadening out over the shoulders. And her hair was copper-coloured, and the heels of her shoes were exceedingly high, so that she tripped upon the points of her toes. And when she came to the door of the bathing place, and when it opened to receive her, she would look back at me with a little coquettish smile, so that her cheek appeared to be caressing her shoulder.

I seem to remember that, with that dress, she wore an immensely broad Leghorn hat – like the Chapeau de Paille of Rubens,[36] only very white. The hat would be tied with a lightly knotted scarf of the same stuff as her dress. She knew how to give value to her blue eyes.

And round her neck would be some simple pink, coral beads. And her complexion had a perfect clearness, a perfect smoothness . . .

Yes, that is how I most exactly remember her, in that dress, in that hat, looking over her shoulder at me so that the eyes flashed very blue – dark pebble blue . . .

And, what the devil! For whose benefit did she do it? For that of the bath attendant? of the passers-by? I don't know. Anyhow, it can't have been for me, for never, in all the years of her life, never on any possible occasion, or in any other place did she so smile to me, mockingly, invitingly. Ah, she was a riddle; but then, all other women are riddles. And it occurs to me that some way back I began a sentence that I have never finished . . . It was about the feeling that I had when I stood on the steps of my hotel every morning before starting out to fetch Florence back from the bath. Natty, precise, well-brushed, conscious of being rather small amongst the long English, the lank Americans, the rotund Germans, and the obese Russian Jewesses, I should stand there, tapping a cigarette on the outside of my case, surveying for a moment the world in the sunlight. But a day was to come when I was never to do it again alone. You can imagine, therefore, what the coming of the Ashburnhams meant to me.

I have forgotten the aspect of many things, but I shall never forget the aspect of the dining-room of the Hotel Excelsior[37] on that evening – and on so many other evenings. Whole castles have vanished from my memory, whole cities that I have never visited again, but that white room, festooned with papier-mâché fruits and flowers; the tall windows; the many tables; the black screen round the door with three golden cranes flying upward on each panel; the palm-tree in the centre of the room; the swish of the waiter's feet; the cold expensive elegance; the mien of the diners as they came in every evening – their air of earnestness as if they must go through a meal prescribed by the *Kur* authorities and their air of sobriety as if they must seek not by any means to enjoy their meals – those things I shall not easily forget. And then, one evening, in the twilight, I saw Edward Ashburnham lounge round the screen into the room. The head waiter, a man with a face all grey – in what subterranean nooks or corners do people cultivate those absolutely grey complexions? – went with the timorous patronage of these creatures

27

towards him and held out a grey ear to be whispered into. It was generally a disagreeable ordeal for newcomers but Edward Ashburnham bore it like an Englishman and a gentleman. I could see his lips form a word of three syllables – remember I had nothing in the world to do but to notice these niceties – and immediately I knew that he must be Edward Ashburnham, Captain, Fourteenth Hussars,[38] of Bramshaw Manor, Bramshaw Teleragh. I knew it because every evening just before dinner, whilst I waited in the hall, I used, by the courtesy of Monsieur Schontz, the proprietor, to inspect the little police reports that each guest was expected to sign upon taking a room.

The head waiter piloted him immediately to a vacant table, three away from my own – the table that the Grenfalls of Falls River, N.J.,[39] had just vacated. It struck me that that was not a very nice table for the newcomers, since the sunlight, low though it was, shone straight down upon it, and the same idea seemed to come at the same moment into Captain Ashburnham's head. His face hitherto had, in the wonderful English fashion, expressed nothing whatever. Nothing. There was in it neither joy nor despair; neither hope nor fear; neither boredom nor satisfaction. He seemed to perceive no soul in that crowded room; he might have been walking in a jungle. I never came across such a perfect expression before and I never shall again. It was insolence and not insolence; it was modesty and not modesty. His hair was fair, extraordinarily ordered in a wave, running from the left temple to the right; his face was a light brick-red, perfectly uniform in tint up to the roots of the hair itself; his yellow moustache was as stiff as a toothbrush and I verily believe that he had his black smoking jacket thickened a little over the shoulder-blades so as to give himself the air of the slightest possible stoop. It would be like him to do that; that was the sort of thing he thought about. Martingales, Chiffney bits,[40] boots; where you got the best soap, the best brandy, the name of the chap who rode a plater down the Khyber cliffs;[41] the spreading power of number three shot before a charge of number four powder . . . by heavens, I hardly ever heard him talk of anything else. Not in all the years that I knew him did I hear him talk of anything but these subjects. Oh, yes, once he told me that I could buy my special shade of blue ties cheaper from a firm in Burlington Arcade than from my own people in New York. And I have bought my ties from that firm ever since. Otherwise I should not remember the name of the Burlington Arcade.[42] I wonder what it looks like. I have never seen it. I imagine it to be two immense rows of pillars, like those of the Forum at Rome, with Edward Ashburnham striding down between them. But it probably isn't the least like that. Once also he advised me to buy Caledonian Deferred, since they were due to rise. And I did buy them and they did rise. But of how he got the knowledge I haven't the faintest idea. It seemed to drop out of the blue sky.

And that was absolutely all that I knew of him until a month ago – that and the profusion of his cases, all of pigskin and stamped with his initials, E.F.A. There were guncases, and collar cases, and shirt cases, and letter cases and cases each containing four bottles of medicine; and hat cases and helmet cases. It must have needed a whole herd of the Gadarene swine[43] to make up his outfit. And, if I ever penetrated into his private room it would be to see him standing, with his coat and waistcoat off and the immensely long line of his perfectly elegant trousers from waist to boot heel. And he would have a slightly reflective air and he would be just opening one kind of case and just closing another.

Good God, what did they all see in him; for I swear that was all there was of him, inside and out; though they said he was a good soldier. Yet Leonora adored him with a passion that was like an agony, and hated him with an agony that was as bitter as the sea. How could he arouse anything like a sentiment, in anybody?

What did he even talk to them about – when they were under four eyes? – Ah, well, suddenly, as if by a flash of inspiration, I know. For all good soldiers are sentimentalists – all good soldiers of that type. Their profession, for one thing, is full of the big words, courage, loyalty, honour, constancy. And I have given a wrong impression of Edward Ashburnham if I have made you think that literally never in the course of our nine years of intimacy did he discuss what he would have called 'the graver things'. Even before his final outburst to me, at times, very late at night, say, he has blurted out something that gave an insight into the sentimental view of the cosmos that was his. He would say how much the society of a good woman could do towards redeeming you, and he would say that constancy was the finest of the virtues. He said it very stiffly, of course, but still as if the statement admitted of no doubt.

Constancy! Isn't that the queer thought? And yet, I must add that poor dear Edward was a great reader – he would pass hours lost in novels of a sentimental type – novels in which typewriter girls married Marquises and governesses Earls. And in his books, as a rule, the course of true love ran as smooth as buttered honey. And he was fond of poetry, of a certain type – and he could even read a perfectly sad love story. I have seen his eyes filled with tears at reading of a hopeless parting. And he loved, with a sentimental yearning, all children, puppies, and the feeble generally . . .

So, you see, he would have plenty to gurgle about to a woman – with that and his sound common sense about martingales and his – still sentimental – experiences as a county magistrate; and with his intense, optimistic belief that the woman he was making love to at the moment was the one he was destined, at last, to be eternally constant to . . . Well, I fancy he could put up a pretty good deal of talk when there was no man around to make him feel shy. And I was quite astonished, during his final burst out to me – at the very end of things, when the poor girl was on her way to that fatal Brindisi[44] and he was trying to persuade himself and me that he had never really cared for her – I was quite astonished to observe how literary and how just his expressions were. He talked like quite a good book – a book not in the least cheaply sentimental. You see, I suppose he regarded me not so much as a man. I had to be regarded as a woman or a solicitor. Anyhow, it burst out of him on that horrible night. And then, next morning, he took me over to the Assizes and I saw how, in a perfectly calm and business-like way, he set to work to secure a verdict of not guilty for a poor girl, the daughter of one of his tenants, who had been accused of murdering her baby. He spent two hundred pounds on her defence . . . Well, that was Edward Ashburnham.

I had forgotten about his eyes. They were as blue as the sides of a certain type of box of matches. When you looked at them carefully you saw that they were perfectly honest, perfectly straightforward, perfectly, perfectly stupid. But the brick pink of his complexion, running perfectly level to the brick pink of his inner eyelids, gave them a curious, sinister expression – like a mosaic of blue porcelain set in pink china. And that chap, coming into a room, snapped up the gaze of every woman in it, as dexterously as a conjuror pockets billiard balls. It was most amazing. You know the man on the stage who throws up sixteen balls at once and they all drop into pockets all over his person, on his shoulders, on his heels, on the inner side of his sleeves; and he stands perfectly still and does nothing. Well, it was like that. He had rather a rough, hoarse voice.

And, there he was, standing by the table. I was looking at him, with my back to the screen. And suddenly, I saw two distinct expressions flicker across his immobile eyes. How the deuce did they do it, those unflinching blue eyes with the direct gaze? For the eyes themselves never moved, gazing over my shoulder towards the screen. And the gaze was perfectly level and perfectly direct and perfectly unchanging. I suppose that the lids really must have rounded themselves a little and perhaps the lips moved a little too, as if he should be saying: 'There you are, my dear.' At any rate, the expression was that of pride, of satisfaction, of the possessor. I saw him once afterwards, for a moment, gaze upon the sunny fields of Bramshaw and say: 'All this is my land!'

And then again, the gaze was perhaps more direct, harder if possible – hardy too. It was a measuring look; a challenging look. Once when we were at Wiesbaden watching him play in a polo match against the Bonner Hussaren[45] I saw the same look come into his eyes, balancing the possibilities, looking over the ground. The German Captain, Count Baron Idigon von Lelöffel[46] was right up by their goal posts, coming with the ball in an easy canter in that tricky German fashion. The rest of the field were just anywhere. It was only a scratch sort of affair. Ashburnham was quite close to the rails not five yards from us and I heard him saying to himself: 'Might just be done!' And he did it. Goodness! he swung that pony round with all its four legs spread out, like a cat dropping off a roof . . .

Well, it was just that look that I noticed in his eyes: 'It might,' I seem even now to hear him muttering to himself, 'just be done.'

I looked round over my shoulder and saw, tall, smiling brilliantly and buoyant – Leonora. And, little and fair, and as radiant as the track of sunlight along the sea – my wife.

That poor wretch! to think that he was at that moment in a perfect devil of a fix, and there he was, saying at the back of his mind: 'It might just be done.' It was like a chap in the middle of the eruption of a volcano, saying that he might just manage to bolt into the tumult and set fire to a haystack. Madness? Predestination? Who the devil knows?

Mrs Ashburnham exhibited at that moment more gaiety than I have ever since known her to show. There are certain classes of English people – the nicer ones when they have been to many spas, who seem to make a point of becoming much more than usually animated when they are introduced to my compatriots. I have noticed this often. Of course, they must first have accepted the Americans. But that once done, they seem to say to themselves: 'Hallo, these women are so bright. We aren't going to be outdone in brightness.' And for the time being they certainly aren't. But it wears off. So it was with Leonora – at least until she noticed me. She began, Leonora did – and perhaps it was that that gave me the idea of a touch of insolence in her character, for she never afterwards did any one single thing like it – she began by saying in quite a loud voice and from quite a distance:

'Don't stop over by that stuffy old table, Teddy. Come and sit by these nice people!'

And that was an extraordinary thing to say. Quite extraordinary. I couldn't for the life of me refer to total strangers as nice people. But, of course, she was taking a line of her own in which I at any rate – and no one else in the room, for she too had taken the trouble to read through the list of guests – counted any more than so many clean, bull terriers. And she sat down rather brilliantly at a vacant table, beside ours – one that was reserved for the Guggenheimers. And she just sat absolutely deaf to the remonstrances of the head waiter with his face like a grey ram's. That poor chap was doing his steadfast duty too. He knew that the Guggenheimers of Chicago, after they had stayed there a month and had worried the poor life out of him, would give him two dollars fifty and grumble at the tipping system. And he knew that Teddy Ashburnham and his wife would give him no trouble whatever except what the smiles of Leonora might cause in his apparently unimpressionable bosom – though you never can tell what may go on behind even a not quite spotless plastron! – And every week Edward Ashburnham would give him a solid, sound, golden English sovereign. Yet this stout fellow was intent on saving that table for the Guggenheimers of Chicago. It ended in Florence saying:

'Why shouldn't we all eat out of the same trough? – that's a nasty New York saying. But I'm sure we're all nice quiet people and there can be four seats at our table. It's round.'

Then came, as it were, an appreciative gurgle from the Captain and I was perfectly aware of a slight hesitation – a quick sharp motion in Mrs Ashburnham, as if her horse had checked. But she put it at the fence all right, rising from the seat she had taken and sitting down opposite me, as it were, all in one motion.

I never thought that Leonora looked her best in evening dress. She seemed to get it too clearly cut, there was no ruffling. She always affected black and her shoulders were too classical. She seemed to stand out of her corsage as a white marble bust might out of a black Wedgwood vase. I don't know.

I loved Leonora always and, today, I would very cheerfully lay down my life, what is left of it, in her service. But I am sure I never had the beginnings of a trace of what is called the sex instinct towards her. And I suppose – no I am certain that she never had it towards me. As far as I am concerned I think it was those white shoulders that did it. I seemed to feel when I looked at them that, if ever I should press my lips upon them that they would be slightly cold – not icily, not without a touch of human heat, but, as they say of baths, with the chill off. I seemed to feel chilled at the end of my lips when I looked at her . . .

No, Leonora always appeared to me at her best in a blue tailor-made. Then her glorious hair wasn't deadened by her white shoulders. Certain women's lines guide your eyes to their necks, their eyelashes, their lips, their breasts. But Leonora's seemed to conduct your gaze always to her wrist. And the wrist was at its best in a black or a dog-skin glove and there was always a gold circlet with a little chain supporting a very small golden key to a dispatch box. Perhaps it was that in which she locked up her heart and her feelings.

Anyhow, she sat down opposite me and then, for the first time, she paid any attention to my existence. She gave me, suddenly, yet deliberately, one long stare. Her eyes too were blue and dark and the eyelids were so arched that they gave you the whole round of the irises. And it was a most remarkable, a most moving glance, as if for a moment a lighthouse had looked at me. I seemed to perceive the swift questions

33

chasing each other through the brain that was behind them. I seemed to hear the brain ask and the eyes answer with all the simpleness of a woman who was a good hand at taking in qualities of a horse – as indeed she was. 'Stands well; has plenty of room for his oats behind the girth. Not so much in the way of shoulders,' and so on. And so her eyes asked: 'Is this man trustworthy in money matters; is he likely to try to play the lover; is he likely to let his women be troublesome? Is he, above all, likely to babble about my affairs?'

And, suddenly, into those cold, slightly defiant, almost defensive china blue orbs, there came a warmth, a tenderness, a friendly recognition . . . oh, it was very charming and very touching – and quite mortifying. It was the look of a mother to her son, of a sister to her brother. It implied trust; it implied the want of any necessity for barriers. By God, she looked at me as if I were an invalid – as any kind woman may look at a poor chap in a bath chair. And, yes, from that day forward she always treated me and not Florence as if I were the invalid. Why, she would run after me with a rug upon chilly days. I suppose, therefore, that her eyes had made a favourable answer. Or, perhaps, it wasn't a favourable answer. And then Florence said: 'And so the whole round table is begun.' Again Edward Ashburnham gurgled slightly in his throat; but Leonora shivered a little, as if a goose had walked over her grave. And I was passing her the nickel-silver basket of rolls. *Avanti!* . . .[47]

I V

So began those nine years of uninterrupted tranquillity. They were characterized by an extraordinary want of any communicativeness on the part of the Ashburnhams to which we, on our part, replied by leaving out quite as extraordinarily, and nearly as completely, the personal note. Indeed, you may take it that what characterized our relationship was an atmosphere of taking everything for granted. The given proposition was, that we were all 'good people'. We took for granted that we all liked beef underdone but not too underdone; that both men preferred a good liqueur brandy after lunch; that both women drank a very light Rhine wine qualified with Fachingen water[48] – that sort of thing. It was also taken for granted that we were both sufficiently well off to afford anything that we could reasonably want in the way of amusements fitting to our station – that we could take motor cars and carriages by the day; that we could give each other dinners and dine our friends and we could indulge if we liked in economy. Thus, Florence was in the habit of having the *Daily Telegraph* sent to her every day from London. She was always an Anglo-maniac, was Florence; the Paris edition of the New York *Herald* was always good enough for me. But when we discovered that the Ashburnhams' copy of the London paper followed them from England, Leonora and Florence decided between them to suppress one subscription one year and the other the next. Similarly it was the habit of the Grand Duke of Nassau Schwerin,[49] who came yearly to the baths, to dine once with about eighteen families of regular *Kur* guests. In return he would give a dinner to all the eighteen at once. And, since these dinners were rather expensive (you had to take the Grand Duke and a good many of his suite and any members of the diplomatic bodies that might be there) – Florence and Leonora, putting their heads together, didn't see why we shouldn't give the Grand Duke his dinner together. And so we did. I don't suppose the Serenity minded that economy, or even noticed it. At any rate, our joint dinner to the Royal Personage gradually assumed the aspect of a yearly function. Indeed, it grew larger and larger, until it became a sort of closing function for the season, at any rate as far as we were concerned.

I don't in the least mean to say that we were the sort of persons who aspired to mix 'with royalty'. We didn't; we hadn't any claims; we were just 'good people'. But the Grand Duke was a pleasant, affable sort of royalty, like the late King Edward VII, and it was pleasant to hear him talk about the races and, very occasionally, as a *bonne bouche*,[50] about his nephew, the Emperor,[51] or to have him pause for a moment in his walk to ask after the progress of our cures or to be benignantly interested in the amount of money we had put on Lelöffel's hunter for the Frankfurt Welter Stakes.

But upon my word, I don't know how we put in our time. How does one put in one's time? How is it possible to have achieved nine years and to have nothing whatever to show for it? Nothing whatever, you understand. Not so much as a bone penholder, carved to resemble a chessman and with a hole in the top through which you could see four views of Nauheim. And, as for experience, as for knowledge of one's fellow beings – nothing either. Upon my word, I couldn't tell you offhand whether the lady who sold the so expensive violets at the bottom of the road that leads to the station, was cheating me or no; I can't say whether the porter who carried our traps[52] across the station at Leghorn was a thief or no when he said that the regular tariff was a lira a parcel. The instances of honesty that one comes across in this world are just as amazing as the instances of dishonesty. After forty-five years of mixing with one's kind, one ought to have acquired the habit of being able to know something about one's fellow beings. But one doesn't.

I think the modern civilized habit – the modern English habit of taking every one for granted – is a good deal to blame for this. I have observed this matter long enough to know the queer, subtle thing that it is; to know how the faculty, for what it is worth, never lets you down.

Mind, I am not saying that this is not the most desirable type of life in the world; that it is not an almost unreasonably high standard. For it is really nauseating, when you detest it, to have to eat every day several slices of thin, tepid, pink india rubber, and it is disagreeable to have to drink brandy when you would prefer to be cheered up by warm, sweet Kümmel.[53] And it is nasty to have to take a cold bath in the morning when what you want is really a hot one at night. And it stirs a little of the faith of your fathers that is deep down within you to have to have it taken for granted that you are an Episcopalian when really you are an old-fashioned Philadelphia Quaker.[54]

But these things have to be done; it is the cock that the whole of this society owes to Aesculapius.[55]

And the odd, queer thing is that the whole collection of rules applies to anybody – to the anybodies that you meet in hotels, in railway trains, to a less degree, perhaps, in steamers, but even, in the end, upon steamers. You meet a man or a woman and, from tiny and intimate sounds, from the slightest of movements, you know at once whether you are concerned with good people or with those who won't do. You know, this is to say, whether they will go rigidly through with the whole programme from the underdone beef to the Anglicanism. It won't matter whether they be short or tall; whether the voice squeak like a marionette or rumble like a town bull's; it won't matter whether they are Germans, Austrians, French, Spanish, or even Brazilians – they will be the Germans or Brazilians who take a cold bath every morning and who move, roughly speaking, in diplomatic circles.

But the inconvenient – well, hang it all, I will say it – the damnable nuisance of the whole thing is, that with all the taking for granted, you never really get an inch deeper than the things I have catalogued.

I can give you a rather extraordinary instance of this. I can't remember whether it was in our first year – the first year of us four at Nauheim, because, of course, it would have been the fourth year of Florence and myself – but it must have been in the first or second year. And that gives the measure at once of the extraordinariness of our discussion and of the swiftness with which intimacy had grown up between us. On the one hand we seemed to start out on the expedition so naturally and with so little preparation, that it was as if we must have made many such excursions before; and our intimacy seemed so deep . . .

Yet the place to which we went was obviously one to which Florence at least would have wanted to take us quite early, so that you would almost think we should have gone there together at the beginning of our intimacy. Florence was singularly expert as a guide to archaeological expeditions and there was nothing she liked so much as taking people round ruins and showing you the window from which someone looked down upon the murder of someone else. She only did it once; but she did it quite magnificently. She could find her way, with the sole help of Baedeker,[56] as easily about any old monument as she could about any American city where the blocks are all square and the streets all numbered, so that you can go perfectly easily from Twenty-fourth to Thirtieth.

Now it happens that fifty minutes away from Nauheim, by a good train, is the ancient city of M—, upon a great pinnacle of basalt, girt with a triple road running sideways up its shoulder like a scarf. And at the top there is a castle – not a square castle like Windsor[57] but a castle all slate gables and high peaks with gilt weathercocks flashing bravely – the castle of St Elizabeth of Hungary.[58] It has the disadvantage of being in Prussia; and it is always disagreeable to go into that country,[59] but it is very old and there are many double-spired churches and it stands up like a pyramid out of the green valley of the Lahn.[60] I don't suppose the Ashburnhams wanted especially to go there and I didn't especially want to go there myself. But, you understand, there was no objection. It was part of the cure to make an excursion three or four times a week. So that we were all quite unanimous in being grateful to Florence for providing the motive power. Florence, of course, had a motive of her own. She was at that time engaged in educating Captain Ashburnham – oh, of course, quite *pour le bon motif!*[61] She used to say to Leonora: 'I simply can't understand how you can let him live by your side and be so ignorant!' Leonora herself always struck me as being remarkably well educated. At any rate, she knew beforehand all that Florence had to tell her. Perhaps she got it up out of Baedeker before Florence was up in the morning. I don't mean to say that you would ever have known that Leonora knew anything, but if Florence started to tell us how Ludwig the Courageous wanted to have three wives at once – in which he differed from Henry VIII, who wanted them one after the other[62] and this caused a good deal of trouble – if Florence started to tell us this, Leonora would just nod her head in a way that quite pleasantly rattled my poor wife.

She used to exclaim: 'Well, if you knew it, why haven't you told it all already to Captain Ashburnham? I'm sure he finds it interesting!' And Leonora would look reflectively at her husband and say: 'I have an idea that it might injure his hand – the hand, you know, used in connection with horses' mouths . . .' And poor Ashburnham would blush and mutter and would say: 'That's all right. Don't you bother about me.'

I fancy his wife's irony did quite alarm poor Teddy; because one evening he asked me seriously in the smoking-room if I thought that having too much in one's head would really interfere with one's quickness in polo. It struck him, he said, that brainy Johnnies generally were rather muffs when they got on to four legs. I reassured him as best I could. I told him that he wasn't likely to take in enough to upset his balance. At that time the Captain was quite evidently enjoying being educated by Florence. She used to do it about three or four times a week under the approving eyes of Leonora and myself. It wasn't, you understand, systematic. It came in bursts. It was Florence clearing up one of the dark places of the earth,[63] leaving the world a little lighter than she had found it. She would tell him the story of Hamlet; explain the form of a symphony, humming the first and second subjects to him, and so on; she would explain to him the difference between Arminians and Erastians,[64] or she would give him a short lecture on the early history of the United States. And it was done in a way well calculated to arrest a young attention. Did you ever read Mrs Markham?[65] Well, it was like that . . .

But our excursion to M— was a much larger, a much more full dress affair. You see, in the archives of the *Schloss*[66] in that city there was a document which Florence thought would finally give her the chance to educate the whole lot of us together. It really worried poor Florence that she couldn't, in matters of culture, ever get the better of Leonora. I don't know what Leonora knew or what she didn't know, but certainly she was always there whenever Florence brought out any information. And she gave, somehow, the impression of really knowing what poor Florence gave the impression of having only picked up. I can't exactly define it. It was almost something physical. Have you ever seen a retriever dashing in play after a greyhound? You see the two running over a green field, almost side by side, and suddenly the retriever makes a friendly snap at the other. And the greyhound simply isn't there. You haven't observed it quicken its speed or strain a limb; but there it is, just two yards in front of the retriever's outstretched muzzle. So it was with Florence and Leonora in matters of culture.

But on this occasion I knew that something was up. I found Florence some days before, reading books like Ranke's *History of the Popes,* Symonds' *Renaissance,* Motley's *Rise of the Dutch Republic* and Luther's *Table Talk.*[67]

I must say that, until the astonishment came, I got nothing but pleasure out of the little expedition. I like catching the two-forty; I like the slow, smooth roll of the great big trains – and they are the best trains in the world! I like being drawn through the green country and looking at it through the clear glass of the great windows. Though, of course, the country isn't really green. The sun shines, the earth is blood red and purple and red and green and red. And the oxen in the ploughlands are bright varnished brown and black and blackish purple; and the peasants are dressed in the black and white of magpies; and there are great flocks of magpies too. Or the peasants' dresses in another field where there are little mounds of hay that will be grey-green on the sunny side and purple in the shadows – the peasants' dresses are vermilion with emerald green ribbons and purple skirts and white shirts and black velvet stomachers. Still, the impression is that you are drawn through brilliant green meadows that run away on each side to the dark purple fir-woods; the basalt pinnacles; the immense forests. And there is meadowsweet at the edge of the streams, and cattle. Why, I remember on that afternoon I saw a brown cow hitch its horns under the stomach of a black and white animal and the black and white one was thrown right into the middle of a narrow stream. I burst out laughing. But Florence was imparting information so hard and Leonora was listening so intently that no one noticed me. As for me, I was pleased to be off duty; I was pleased to think that Florence for the moment was indubitably out of mischief – because she was talking about Ludwig the Courageous (I think it was Ludwig the Courageous but I am not an historian) about Ludwig the Courageous of Hessen who wanted to have three wives at once and patronized Luther – something like that! – I was so relieved to be off duty, because she couldn't possibly be doing anything to excite herself or set her poor heart a-fluttering – that the incident of the cow was a real joy to me. I chuckled over it from time to time for the whole rest of the day. Because it does look very funny, you know, to see a black and white cow land on its back in the middle of a stream. It is so just exactly what one doesn't expect of a cow.

I suppose I ought to have pitied the poor animal; but I just didn't. I was out for enjoyment. And I just enjoyed myself. It is so pleasant to be drawn along in front of the spectacular towns with the peaked castles and the many double spires. In the sunlight gleams come from the city – gleams from the glass of windows; from the gilt signs of apothecaries;

from the ensigns of the student corps high up in the mountains; from the helmets of the funny little soldiers moving their stiff little legs in white linen trousers. And it was pleasant to get out in the great big spectacular Prussian station with the hammered bronze ornaments and the paintings of peasants and flowers and cows; and to hear Florence bargain energetically with the driver of an ancient *Droschke*[68] drawn by two lean horses. Of course, I spoke German much more correctly than Florence, though I never could rid myself quite of the accent of the Pennsylvania Duitsch[69] of my childhood. Anyhow, we were drawn in a sort of triumph, for five marks without any *Trinkgeld*,[70] right up to the castle. And we were taken through the museum and saw the firebacks, the old glass, the old swords and the antique contraptions. And we went up winding corkscrew staircases and through the *Rittersaal*, the great painted hall where the Reformer[71] and his friends met for the first time under the protection of the gentleman that had three wives at once and formed an alliance with the gentleman that had six wives, one after the other (I'm not really interested in these facts but they have a bearing on my story). And we went through chapels, and music rooms, right up immensely high in the air to a large old chamber, full of presses, with heavily-shuttered windows all round. And Florence became positively electric. She told the tired, bored custodian what shutters to open; so that the bright sunlight streamed in palpable shafts into the dim old chamber. She explained that this was Luther's bedroom and that just where the sunlight fell had stood his bed. As a matter of fact, I believe that she was wrong and that Luther only stopped, as it were, for lunch, in order to evade pursuit. But, no doubt, it would have been his bedroom if he could have been persuaded to stop the night. And then, in spite of the protest of the custodian, she threw open another shutter and came tripping back to a large glass case.

'And there,' she exclaimed with an accent of gaiety, of triumph, and of audacity. She was pointing at a piece of paper, like the half-sheet of a letter with some faint pencil scrawls that might have been a jotting of the amounts we were spending during the day. And I was extremely happy at her gaiety, in her triumph, in her audacity. Captain Ashburnham had his hands upon the glass case. 'There it is – the Protest.' And then, as we all properly stage-managed our bewilderment, she continued: 'Don't you know that is why we were all called Protestants? That is the pencil draft of the Protest they drew up. You can see the signatures of Martin Luther, and Martin Bucer, and Zwingli, and Ludwig the Courageous . . .'[72]

I may have got some of the names wrong, but I know that Luther and Bucer were there. And her animation continued and I was glad. She was better and she was out of mischief. She continued, looking up into Captain Ashburnham's eyes: 'It's because of that piece of paper that you're honest, sober, industrious, provident, and clean-lived. If it weren't for that piece of paper you'd be like the Irish or the Italians or the Poles, but particularly the Irish . . .'

And she laid one finger upon Captain Ashburnham's wrist.

I was aware of something treacherous, something frightful, something evil in the day. I can't define it and can't find a simile for it. It wasn't as if a snake had looked out of a hole. No, it was as if my heart had missed a beat. It was as if we were going to run and cry out; all four of us in separate directions, averting our heads. In Ashburnham's face I know that there was absolute panic. I was horribly frightened and then I discovered that the pain in my left wrist was caused by Leonora's clutching it:

'I can't stand this,' she said with a most extraordinary passion; 'I must get out of this.'

I was horribly frightened. It came to me for a moment, though I hadn't time to think it, that she must be a madly jealous woman – jealous of Florence and Captain Ashburnham, of all people in the world! And it was a panic in which we fled! We went right down the winding stairs, across the immense *Rittersaal* to a little terrace that overlooks the Lahn, the broad valley and the immense plain into which it opens out.

'Don't you see?' she said, 'don't you see what's going on?' The panic again stopped my heart. I muttered, I stuttered – I don't know how I got the words out:

'No! What's the matter? Whatever's the matter?'

She looked me straight in the eyes; and for a moment I had the feeling that those two blue discs were immense, were overwhelming, were like a wall of blue that shut me off from the rest of the world. I know it sounds absurd; but that is what it did feel like.

'Don't you see,' she said, with a really horrible bitterness, with a really horrible lamentation in her voice, 'Don't you see that that's the cause of the whole miserable affair; of the whole sorrow of the world? And of the eternal damnation of you and me and them . . .'

I don't remember how she went on; I was too frightened; I was too amazed. I think I was thinking of running to fetch assistance – a doctor, perhaps, or Captain Ashburnham. Or possibly she needed Florence's tender care, though, of course, it would have been very bad for Florence's heart. But I know that when I came out of it she was saying: 'Oh, where are all the bright, happy, innocent beings in the world? Where's happiness? One reads of it in books!'

She ran her hand with a singular clawing motion upwards over her forehead. Her eyes were enormously distended; her face was exactly that of a person looking into the pit of hell and seeing horrors there. And then suddenly she stopped. She was, most amazingly, just Mrs Ashburnham again. Her face was perfectly clear, sharp and defined; her hair was glorious in its golden coils. Her nostrils twitched with a sort of contempt. She appeared to look with interest at a gypsy caravan that was coming over a little bridge far below us.

'Don't you know,' she said, in her clear hard voice, 'don't you know that I'm an Irish Catholic?'

V

Those words gave me the greatest relief that I have ever had in my life. They told me, I think, almost more than I have ever gathered at any one moment – about myself. I don't think that before that day I had ever wanted anything very much except Florence. I have, of course, had appetites, impatiences . . . Why, sometimes at a table d'hôte, when there would be, say, caviare handed round, I have been absolutely full of impatience for fear that when the dish came to me there should not be a satisfying portion left over by the other guests. I have been exceedingly impatient at missing trains. The Belgian State Railway has a trick of letting the French trains miss their connections at Brussels. That has always infuriated me. I have written about it letters to *The Times* that *The Times* never printed; those that I wrote to the Paris edition of the New York *Herald* were always printed, but they never seemed to satisfy me when I saw them. Well, that was a sort of frenzy with me.

It was a frenzy that now I can hardly realize. I can understand it intellectually. You see, in those days I was interested in people with 'hearts'. There was Florence, there was Edward Ashburnham – or, perhaps, it was Leonora that I was more interested in. I don't mean in the way of love. But, you see, we were both of the same profession – at any rate as I saw it. And the profession was that of keeping heart patients alive.

You have no idea how engrossing such a profession may become. Just as the blacksmith says: 'By hammer and hand all Art doth stand,' just as the baker thinks that all the solar system revolves around his morning delivery of rolls, as the postmaster-general believes that he alone is the preserver of society – and surely, surely, these delusions are necessary to keep us going – so did I and, as I believed, Leonora, imagine that the whole world ought to be arranged so as to ensure the keeping alive of heart patients. You have no idea how engrossing such a profession may become – how imbecile, in view of that engrossment, appear the ways of princes, of republics, of municipalities. A rough bit of road beneath the motor tyres, a couple of succeeding 'thank'ee-marms'[73] with their quick jolts would be enough to set me grumbling to Leonora against the Prince or the Grand Duke or the Free City[74] through whose territory we might be passing. I would grumble like a stockbroker whose conversations over the telephone are incommoded by the ringing of bells from a city church. I would talk about medieval survivals, about the taxes being surely high enough. The point, by the way, about the missing of the connections of the Calais boat trains at Brussels was that the shortest possible sea journey is frequently of great importance to sufferers from the heart. Now, on the Continent, there are two special heart cure places, Nauheim and Spa,[75] and to reach both of these baths from England if in order to ensure a short sea passage, you come by Calais – you have to make the connection at Brussels. And the Belgian train never waits by so much as the shade of a second for the one coming from Calais or from Paris. And even if the French trains are just on time, you have to run – imagine a heart patient running! – along the unfamiliar ways of the Brussels station and to scramble up the high steps of the moving train. Or, if you miss the connection, you have to wait five or six hours . . . I used to keep awake whole nights cursing that abuse.

My wife used to run – she never, in whatever else she may have misled me, tried to give me the impression that she was not a gallant soul. But, once in the German Express, she would lean back, with one hand to her side and her eyes closed. Well, she was a good actress. And I would be in hell. In hell, I tell you. For in Florence I had at once a wife and an unattained mistress – that is what it comes to – and in the retaining of her in this world I had my occupation, my career, my ambition. It is not often that these things are united in one body. Leonora was a good actress too. By Jove she was good! I tell you, she would listen to me by the hour, evolving my plans for a shock-proof world. It is true that, at times, I used to notice about her an air of inattention as if she were listening, a mother, to the child at her knee, or as if, precisely, I were myself the patient.

You understand that there was nothing the matter with Edward Ashburnham's heart – that he had thrown up his commission and had left India and come half the world over in order to follow a woman who had really had a 'heart' to Nauheim. That was the sort of sentimental ass he was. For, you understand, too, that they really needed to live in India, to economize, to let the house at Bramshaw Teleragh.

Of course, at that date, I had never heard of the Kilsyte case. Ashburnham had, you know, kissed a servant girl in a railway train, and it was only the grace of God, the prompt functioning of the communication cord and the ready sympathy of what I believe you call the Hampshire Bench, that kept the poor devil out of Winchester Gaol for years and years. I never heard of that case until the final stages of Leonora's revelations . . .

But just think of that poor wretch . . . I, who have surely the right, beg you to think of that poor wretch. Is it possible that such a luckless devil should be so tormented by blind and inscrutable destiny? For there is no other way to think of it. None. I have the right to say it, since for years he was my wife's lover, since he killed her, since he broke up all the pleasantnesses that there were in my life. There is no priest that has the right to tell me that I must not ask pity for him, from you, silent listener beyond the hearth-stone, from the world, or from the God who created in him those desires, those madnesses . . .

Of course I should not hear of the Kilsyte case. I knew none of their friends; they were for me just good people – fortunate people with broad and sunny acres in a southern county. Just good people! By heavens, I sometimes think that it would have been better for him, poor dear, if the case had been such a one that I must needs have heard of it – such a one as maids and couriers and other *Kur* guests whisper about for years after, until gradually it dies away in the pity that there is knocking about here and there in the world. Supposing he had spent his seven years in Winchester Gaol or whatever it is that inscrutable and blind justice allots to you for following your natural but ill-timed inclinations – there would have arrived a stage when nodding gossips on the *Kursaal* terrace would have said, 'Poor fellow,' thinking of his ruined career. He would have been the fine soldier with his back now bent . . . Better for him, poor devil, if his back had been prematurely bent.

Why, it would have been a thousand times better . . . For, of course, the Kilsyte case, which came at the very beginning of his finding Leonora cold and unsympathetic, gave him a nasty jar. He left servants alone after that.

It turned him, naturally, all the more loose amongst women of his own class. Why, Leonora told me that Mrs Maidan – the woman he followed from Burma[76] to Nauheim – assured her he awakened her attention by swearing that when he kissed the servant in the train he was driven to it. I daresay he was driven to it, by the mad passion to find an ultimately satisfying woman. I daresay he was sincere enough. Heaven help me, I daresay he was sincere enough in his love for Mrs Maidan. She was a nice little thing, a dear little dark woman with long lashes, of whom Florence grew quite fond. She had a lisp and a happy smile. We saw plenty of her for the first month of our acquaintance, then she died, quite quietly – of heart trouble.

But you know, poor little Mrs Maidan – she was so gentle, so young. She cannot have been more than twenty-three and she had a boy husband out in Chitral[77] not more than twenty-four, I believe. Such young things ought to have been left alone. Of course Ashburnham could not leave her alone. I do not believe that he could. Why, even I, at this distance of time am aware that I am a little in love with her memory. I can't help smiling when I think suddenly of her – as you might at the thought of something wrapped carefully away in lavender, in some drawer, in some old house that you have long left. She was so – so submissive. Why, even to me she had the air of being submissive – to me that not the youngest child will ever pay heed to. Yes, this is the saddest story . . .

No, I cannot help wishing that Florence had left her alone – with her playing with adultery. I suppose it was; though she was such a child that one has the impression that she would hardly have known how to spell such a word. No, it was just submissiveness – to the importunities, to the tempestuous forces that pushed that miserable fellow on to ruin. And I do not suppose that Florence really made much difference. If it had not been for her that Ashburnham left his allegiance for Mrs Maidan, then it would have been some other woman. But still, I do not know. Perhaps the poor young thing would have died – she was bound to die, anyhow, quite soon – but she would have died without having to soak her noonday pillow with tears whilst Florence, below the window, talked to Captain Ashburnham about the Constitution of the United States . . . Yes, it would have left a better taste in the mouth if Florence had let her die in peace . . .

Leonora behaved better in a sense. She just boxed Mrs Maidan's ears – yes, she hit her, in an uncontrollable access of rage, a hard blow on the side of the cheek, in the corridor of the hotel, outside Edward's rooms. It was that, you know, that accounted for the sudden, odd intimacy that sprang up between Florence and Mrs Ashburnham.

Because it was, of course, an odd intimacy. If you look at it from the outside nothing could have been more unlikely than that Leonora, who is the proudest creature on God's earth, would have struck up an acquaintanceship with two casual Yankees whom she could not really have regarded as being much more than a carpet beneath her feet. You may ask what she had to be proud of. Well, she was a Powys married to an Ashburnham – I suppose that gave her the right to despise casual Americans as long as she did it unostentatiously. I don't know what anyone has to be proud of. She might have taken pride in her patience, in her keeping her husband out of the bankruptcy court. Perhaps she did.

At any rate that was how Florence got to know her. She came round a screen at the corner of the hotel corridor and found Leonora with the gold key that hung from her wrist caught in Mrs Maidan's hair just before dinner. There was not a single word spoken. Little Mrs Maidan was very pale, with a red mark down her left cheek, and the key would not come out of her black hair. It was Florence who had to disentangle it, for Leonora was in such a state that she could not have brought herself to touch Mrs Maidan without growing sick.

And there was not a word spoken. You see, under those four eyes – her own and Mrs Maidan's – Leonora could just let herself go as far as to box Mrs Maidan's ears. But the moment a stranger came along she pulled herself wonderfully up. She was at first silent and then, the moment the key was disengaged by Florence she was in a state to say: 'So awkward of me . . . I was just trying to put the comb straight in Mrs Maidan's hair . . .'

Mrs Maidan, however, was not a Powys married to an Ashburnham; she was a poor little O'Flaherty whose husband was a boy of country parsonage origin. So there was no mistaking the sob she let go as she went desolately away along the corridor. But Leonora was still going to play up. She opened the door of Ashburnham's room quite ostentatiously, so that Florence should hear her address Edward in terms of intimacy and liking. 'Edward,' she called. But there was no Edward there.

You understand that there was no Edward there. It was then, for the only time of her career, that Leonora really compromised herself – She exclaimed . . . 'How frightful! . . . Poor little Maisie! . . .'

She caught herself up at that, but of course it was too late. It was a queer sort of affair . . .

I want to do Leonora every justice. I love her very dearly for one thing and in this matter, which was certainly the ruin of my small household cockle-shell, she certainly tripped up. I do not believe – and Leonora herself does not believe – that poor little Maisie Maidan was ever Edward's mistress. Her heart was really so bad that she would have succumbed to anything like an impassioned embrace. That is the plain English of it, and I suppose plain English is best. She was really what the other two, for reasons of their own, just pretended to be. Queer, isn't it? Like one of those sinister jokes that Providence plays upon one. Add to this that I do not suppose that Leonora would much have minded, at any other moment, if Mrs Maidan had been her husband's mistress. It might have been a relief from Edward's sentimental gurglings over the lady and from the lady's submissive acceptance of those sounds. No, she would not have minded.

But, in boxing Mrs Maidan's ears, Leonora was just striking the face of an intolerable universe. For, that afternoon she had had a frightfully painful scene with Edward.

As far as his letters went, she claimed the right to open them when she chose. She arrogated to herself the right because Edward's affairs were in such a frightful state and he lied so about them that she claimed the privilege of having his secrets at her disposal. There was not, indeed, any other way, for the poor fool was too ashamed of his lapses ever to make a clean breast of anything. She had to drag these things out of him.

It must have been a pretty elevating job for her. But that afternoon, Edward being on his bed for the hour and a half prescribed by the *Kur* authorities, she had opened a letter that she took to come from a Colonel Hervey. They were going to stay with him in Linlithgowshire[78] for the month of September and she did not know whether the date fixed would be the eleventh or the eighteenth. The address on this letter was, in handwriting, as like Colonel Hervey's as one blade of corn is like another. So she had at the moment no idea of spying on him.

But she certainly was. For she discovered that Edward Ashburnham was paying a blackmailer of whom she had never heard something like three hundred pounds a year . . . It was a devil of a blow; it was like death; for she imagined that by that time she had really got to the bottom of her husband's liabilities. You see, they were pretty heavy. What had really smashed them up had been a perfectly commonplace affair at Monte Carlo – an affair with a cosmopolitan harpy who passed for the mistress of a Russian Grand Duke. She exacted a twenty thousand pound pearl tiara from him as the price of her favours for a week or so. It would have pipped[79] him a good deal to have found so much, and he was not in the ordinary way a gambler. He might, indeed, just have found the twenty thousand and the not slight charges of a week at an hotel with the fair creature. He must have been worth at that date five hundred thousand dollars and a little over.

Well, he must needs go to the tables and lose forty thousand pounds . . . Forty thousand solid pounds, borrowed from sharks! And even after that he must – it was an imperative passion – enjoy the favours of the lady. He got them, of course, when it was a matter of solid bargaining, for far less than twenty thousand, as he might, no doubt, have done from the first. I daresay ten thousand dollars covered the bill.

Anyhow, there was a pretty solid hole in a fortune of a hundred thousand pounds or so. And Leonora had to fix things up; he would have run from money-lender to money-lender. And that was quite in the early days of her discovery of his infidelities – if you like to call them infidelities. And she discovered that one from public sources. God knows what would have happened if she had not discovered it from public sources. I suppose he would have concealed it from her until they were penniless. But she was able, by the grace of God, to get hold of the actual lenders of the money, to learn the exact sums that were needed. And she went off to England.

Yes, she went right off to England to her attorney and his while he was still in the arms of his Circe – at Antibes,[80] to which place they had retired. He got sick of the lady quite quickly, but not before Leonora had had such lessons in the art of business from her attorney that she had her plan as clearly drawn up as was ever that of General Trochu for keeping the Prussians out of Paris in 1870.[81] It was about as effectual at first, or it seemed so.

That would have been, you know, in 1895, about nine years before the date of which I am talking – the date of Florence's getting her hold over Leonora; for that was what it amounted to . . . Well, Mrs Ashburnham had simply forced Edward to settle all his property upon her. She could force him to do anything; in his clumsy, good-natured, inarticulate way he was as frightened of her as of the devil. And he admired her enormously, and he was as fond of her as any man could be of any woman. She took advantage of it to treat him as if he had been a person whose estates are being managed by the Court of Bankruptcy. I suppose it was the best thing for him.

Anyhow, she had no end of a job for the first three years or so. Unexpected liabilities kept on cropping up – and that afflicted fool did not make it any easier. You see, along with the passion of the chase went a frame of mind that made him be extraordinarily ashamed of himself. You may not believe it, but he really had such a sort of respect for the chastity of Leonora's imagination that he hated – he was positively revolted at the thought that she should know that the sort of thing that he did existed in the world. So he would stick out in an agitated way against the accusation of ever having done anything. He wanted to preserve the virginity of his wife's thoughts. He told me that himself during the long walks we had at the last – while the girl was on the way to Brindisi.

So, of course, for those three years or so, Leonora had many agitations. And it was then that they really quarrelled.

Yes, they quarrelled bitterly. That seems rather extravagant. You might have thought that Leonora would be just calmly loathing and he lachrymosely contrite. But that was not it a bit . . . Along with Edward's passions and his shame for them went the violent conviction of the duties of his station – a conviction that was quite unreasonably expensive. I trust I have not, in talking of his liabilities, given the impression that poor Edward was a promiscuous libertine. He was not; he was a sentimentalist. The servant girl in the Kilsyte case had been pretty, but mournful of appearance. I think that, when he had kissed her, he had desired rather to comfort her. And, if she had succumbed to his blandishments I daresay he would have set her up in a little house in Portsmouth or Winchester and would have been faithful to her for four or five years. He was quite capable of that.

No, the only two of his affairs of the heart that cost him money were that of the Grand Duke's mistress and that which was the subject of the blackmailing letter that Leonora opened. That had been a quite passionate affair with quite a nice woman. It had succeeded the one with the Grand Ducal lady. The lady was the wife of a brother officer and Leonora had known all about the passion, which had been quite a real passion and had lasted for several years. You see, poor Edward's passions were quite logical in their progression upwards. They began with a servant, went on to a courtesan and then to a quite nice woman, very unsuitably mated. For she had a quite nasty husband who, by means of letters and things, went on blackmailing poor Edward to the tune of three or four hundred a year – with threats of the Divorce Court. And after this lady came Maisie Maidan, and after poor Maisie only one more affair and then – the real passion of his life. His marriage with Leonora had been arranged by his parents and, though he always admired her immensely, he had hardly ever pretended to be much more than tender to her, though he desperately needed her moral support, too . . .

But his really trying liabilities were mostly in the nature of generosities proper to his station. He was, according to Leonora, always remitting his tenants' rents and giving the tenants to understand that the reduction would be permanent; he was always redeeming drunkards who came before his magisterial bench; he was always trying to put prostitutes into respectable places – and he was a perfect maniac about children. I don't know how many ill-used people he did not pick up and provide with careers – Leonora has told me, but I daresay she exaggerated and the figure seems so preposterous that I will not put it down. All these things, and the continuance of them seemed to him to be his duty – along with impossible subscriptions to hospitals and Boy Scouts and to provide prizes at cattle shows and anti-vivisection societies . . .

Well, Leonora saw to it that most of these things were not continued. They could not possibly keep up Bramshaw Manor at that rate after the money had gone to the Grand Duke's mistress. She put the rents back at their old figures; discharged the drunkards from their homes, and sent all the societies notice that they were to expect no more subscriptions. To the children, she was more tender; nearly all of them she supported till the age of apprenticeship or domestic service. You see, she was childless herself.

She was childless herself, and she considered herself to be to blame. She had come of a penniless branch of the Powys family, and they had forced upon her poor dear Edward without making the stipulation that the children should be brought up as Catholics. And that, of course, was spiritual death to Leonora. I have given you a wrong impression if I have not made you see that Leonora was a woman of a strong, cold conscience, like all English Catholics. (I cannot, myself, help disliking this religion; there is always, at the bottom of my mind, in spite of Leonora, the feeling of shuddering at the Scarlet Woman, that filtered in upon me in the tranquillity of the little old Friends' Meeting House in Arch Street,[82] Philadephia.) So I do set down a good deal of Leonora's mismanagement of poor dear Edward's case to the peculiarly English form of her religion. Because, of course, the only thing to have done for Edward would have been to let him sink down until he became a tramp of gentlemanly address, having, maybe, chance love affairs upon the highways. He would have done so much less harm; he would have been much less agonized too. At any rate, he would have had fewer chances of ruining and of remorse. For Edward was great at remorse.

But Leonora's English Catholic conscience, her rigid principles, her coldness, even her very patience, were, I cannot help thinking, all wrong in this special case. She quite seriously and naïvely imagined that the Church of Rome disapproves of divorce; she quite seriously and naïvely believed that her church could be such a monstrous and imbecile institution as to expect her to take on the impossible job of making Edward Ashburnham a faithful husband. She had, as the English would say, the Nonconformist temperament. In the United States of North America we call it the New England conscience. For, of course, that frame of mind has been driven in on the English Catholics. The centuries that they have gone through – centuries of blind and malignant oppression, of ostracism from public employment, of being, as it were, a small beleaguered garrison in a hostile country, and therefore having to act with great formality – all these things have combined to perform that conjuring trick. And I suppose that Papists in England are even technically Nonconformists.

Continental Papists are a dirty, jovial and unscrupulous crew. But that, at least, lets them be opportunists. They would have fixed poor dear Edward up all right. (Forgive my writing of these monstrous things in this frivolous manner. If I did not I should break down and cry.) In

Milan, say, or in Paris, Leonora would have had her marriage dissolved in six months for two hundred dollars paid in the right quarter. And Edward would have drifted about until he became a tramp of the kind I have suggested. Or he would have married a barmaid who would have made him such frightful scenes in public places and would so have torn out his moustache and left visible signs upon his face that he would have been faithful to her for the rest of his days. That was what he wanted to redeem him . . .

For, along with his passions and his shames there went the dread of scenes in public places, of outcry, of excited physical violence; of publicity, in short. Yes, the barmaid would have cured him. And it would have been all the better if she drank; he would have been kept busy looking after her.

I know that I am right in this. I know it because of the Kilsyte case. You see, the servant girl that he then kissed was nurse in the family of the Nonconformist head of the county – whatever that post may be called. And that gentleman was so determined to ruin Edward, who was the chairman of the Tory caucus, or whatever it is – that the poor dear sufferer had the very devil of a time. They asked questions about it in the House of Commons; they tried to get the Hampshire magistrates degraded; they suggested to the War Ministry that Edward was not the proper person to hold the King's commission. Yes, he got it hot and strong.

The result you have heard. He was completely cured of philandering amongst the lower classes. And that seemed a real blessing to Leonora. It did not revolt her so much to be connected – it is a sort of connection – with people like Mrs Maidan, instead of with a little kitchenmaid.

In a dim sort of way, Leonora was almost contented when she arrived at Nauheim, that evening . . .

She had got things nearly straight by the long years of scraping in little stations in Chitral and Burma – stations where living is cheap in comparison with the life of a county magnate, and where, moreover, liaisons of one sort or another are normal and inexpensive too. So that, when Mrs Maidan came along – and the Maidan affair might have caused trouble out there because of the youth of the husband – Leonora had just resigned herself to coming home. With pushing and scraping and with letting Bramshaw Teleragh, and with selling a picture and a relic of Charles I or so, she had got – and, poor dear, she had never had a really decent dress to her back in all those years and years – she had got, as she imagined, her poor dear husband back into much the same financial position as had been his before the mistress of the Grand Duke had happened along. And, of course, Edward himself had helped her a little on the financial side. He was a fellow that many men liked. He was so presentable and quite ready to lend you his cigar puncher – that sort of thing. So, every now and then some financier whom he met about would give him a good, sound, profitable tip. And Leonora was never afraid of a bit of a gamble – English Papists seldom are, I do not know why.

So nearly all her investments turned up trumps, and Edward was really in fit case to reopen Bramshaw Manor and once more to assume his position in the county. Thus Leonora had accepted Maisie Maidan almost with resignation – almost with a sigh of relief. She really liked the poor child – she had to like somebody. And, at any rate, she felt she could trust Maisie – she could trust her not to rook Edward for several thousands a week, for Maisie had refused to accept so much as a trinket ring from him. It is true that Edward gurgled and raved about the girl in a way that she had never yet experienced. But that, too, was almost a relief. I think she would really have welcomed it if he could have come across the love of his life. It would have given her a rest.

And there could not have been anyone better than poor little Mrs Maidan; she was so ill she could not want to be taken on expensive jaunts . . . It was Leonora herself who paid Maisie's expenses to Nauheim. She handed over the money to the boy husband, for Maisie would never have allowed it; but the husband was in agonies of fear. Poor devil!

I fancy that, on the voyage from India, Leonora was as happy as ever she had been in her life. Edward was wrapped up, completely, in his girl – he was almost like a father with a child, trotting about with rugs and physic and things, from deck to deck. He behaved, however, with great circumspection, so that nothing leaked through to the other passengers. And Leonora had almost attained to the attitude of a mother towards Mrs Maidan. So it had looked very well – the benevolent, wealthy couple of good people, acting as saviours to the poor, dark-eyed, dying young thing. And that attitude of Leonora's towards Mrs Maidan no doubt partly accounted for the smack in the face. She was hitting a naughty child who had been stealing chocolates at an inopportune moment.

It was certainly an inopportune moment. For, with the opening of that blackmailing letter from that injured brother officer, all the old terrors had redescended upon Leonora. Her road had again seemed to stretch out endless; she imagined that there might be hundreds and hundreds of such things that Edward was concealing from her – that they might necessitate more mortgagings, more pawnings of bracelets, more and always more horrors. She had spent an excruciating afternoon. The matter was one of a divorce case, of course, and she wanted to avoid publicity as much as Edward did, so that she saw the necessity of continuing the payments. And she did not so much mind that. They could find three hundred a year. But it was the horror of there being more such obligations.

· She had had no conversation with Edward for many years – none that went beyond the mere arrangements for taking trains or engaging servants. But that afternoon she had to let him have it. And he had been just the same as ever. It was like opening a book after a decade to find the words the same. He had the same motives. He had not wished to tell her about the case because he had not wished her to sully her mind with the idea that there was such a thing as a brother officer who could be a blackmailer – and he had wanted to protect the credit of his old light of love. That lady was certainly not concerned with her husband. And he swore, and swore, and swore, that there was nothing else in the world against him. She did not believe him.

He had done it once too often – and she was wrong for the first time, so that he acted a rather creditable part in the matter. For he went right straight out to the post office and spent several hours in coding a telegram to his solicitor, bidding that hard-headed man to threaten to take out at once a warrant against the fellow who was on his track. He said afterwards that it was a bit too thick on poor old Leonora to be ballyragged any more. That was really the last of his outstanding accounts, and he was ready to take his personal chance of the Divorce Court if the blackmailer turned nasty. He would face it out – the publicity, the papers, the whole bally show. Those were his simple words . . .

He had made, however, the mistake of not telling Leonora where he was going, so that, having seen him go to his room to fetch the code for the telegram, and seeing, two hours later, Maisie Maidan come out of his room, Leonora imagined that the two hours she had spent in silent agony Edward had spent with Maisie Maidan in his arms. That seemed to her to be too much.

As a matter of fact, Maisie's being in Edward's room had been the result, partly of poverty, partly of pride, partly of sheer innocence. She could not, in the first place, afford a maid; she refrained as much as possible from sending the hotel servants on errands, since every penny was of importance to her, and she feared to have to pay high tips at the end of her stay. Edward had lent her one of his fascinating cases containing fifteen different sizes of scissors, and, having seen, from her window, his departure for the post office, she had taken the opportunity of returning the case. She could not see why she should not, though she felt a certain remorse at the thought that she had kissed the pillows of his bed. That was the way it took her.

But Leonora could see that, without the shadow of a doubt, the incident gave Florence a hold over her. It let Florence into things and Florence was the only created being who had any idea that the Ashburnhams were not just good people with nothing to their tails. She determined at once, not so much to give Florence the privilege of her intimacy – which would have been the payment of a kind of blackmail – as to keep Florence under observation until she could have demonstrated to Florence that she was not in the least jealous of poor Maisie. So that was why she had entered the dining-room arm in arm with my wife, and why she had so markedly planted herself at our table. She never left us, indeed, for a minute that night, except just to run up to Mrs Maidan's room to beg her pardon and to beg her also to let Edward take her very markedly out into the gardens that night. She said herself, when Mrs Maidan came rather wistfully down into the lounge where we were all sitting: 'Now, Edward, get up and take Maisie to the Casino. I want Mrs Dowell to tell me all about the families in Connecticut who came from Fordingbridge.' For it had been discovered that Florence came of a line that had actually owned Bramshaw Teler-agh for two centuries before the Ashburnhams came there. And there she sat with me in that hall, long after Florence had gone to bed, so that I might witness her gay reception of that pair. She could play up.

And that enables me to fix exactly the day of our going to the town of M—. For it was the very day poor Mrs Maidan died. We found her dead when we got back – pretty awful, that, when you come to figure out what it all means . . .

At any rate the measure of my relief when Leonora said that she was an Irish Catholic gives you the measure of my affection for that couple. It was an affection so intense that even to this day I cannot think of Edward without sighing. I do not believe that I could have gone on any more without them. I was getting too tired. And I verily believe, too, that if my suspicion that Leonora was jealous of Florence had been the reason she gave for her outburst I should have turned upon Florence with the maddest kind of rage. Jealousy would have been incurable. But Florence's mere silly jibes at the Irish and at the Catholics could be apologized out of existence. And that I appeared to fix up in two minutes or so.

She looked at me for a long time rather fixedly and queerly while I was doing it. And at last I worked myself up to saying:

'Do accept the situation. I confess that I do not like your religion. But I like you so intensely. I don't mind saying that I have never had anyone to be really fond of, and I do not believe that anyone has ever been fond of me, as I believe you really to be.'

'Oh, I'm fond enough of you,' she said. 'Fond enough to say that I wish every man was like you. But there are others to be considered.' She was thinking, as a matter of fact, of poor Maisie. She picked a little piece of pellitory out of the breast-high wall in front of us. She chafed it for a long minute between her finger and thumb, then she threw it over the coping.

'Oh, I accept the situation,' she said at last, 'if you can.'

VI

I remember laughing at the phrase, 'accept the situation', which she seemed to repeat with a gravity too intense. I said to her something like:

'It's hardly as much as that. I mean, that I must claim the liberty of a free American citizen to think what I please about your co-religionists. And I suppose that Florence must have liberty to think what she pleases and to say what politeness allows her to say.'

'She had better,' Leonora answered, 'not say one single word against my people or my faith.'

It struck me at the time, that there was an unusual, an almost threatening, hardness in her voice. It was almost as if she were trying to convey to Florence, through me, that she would seriously harm my wife if Florence went to something that was an extreme. Yes, I remember thinking at the time that it was almost as if Leonora were saying, through me to Florence:

'You may outrage me as you will; you may take all that I personally possess, but do not you dare to say one single thing in view of the situation that that will set up – against the faith that makes me become the doormat for your feet.'

But obviously, as I saw it, that could not be her meaning. Good people, be they ever so diverse in creed, do not threaten each other. So that I read Leonora's words to mean just no more than:

'It would be better if Florence said nothing at all against my co-religionists, because it is a point that I am touchy about.'

That was the hint that, accordingly, I conveyed to Florence when, shortly afterwards, she and Edward came down from the tower. And I want you to understand that, from that moment until after Edward and the girl and Florence were all dead together, I had never the remotest glimpse, not the shadow of a suspicion, that there was anything wrong, as the saying is. For five minutes, then, I entertained the possibility that Leonora might be jealous; but there was never another flicker in that flame-like personality. How in the world should I get it?

For, all that time, I was just a male sick nurse. And what chance had I against those three hardened gamblers, who were all in league to conceal their hands from me? What earthly chance? They were three to one and they made me happy. Oh God, they made me so happy that I doubt if even paradise, that shall smooth out all temporal wrongs, shall ever give me the like. And what could they have done better, or what could they have done that could have been worse? I don't know . . .

I suppose that, during all that time I was a deceived husband and that Leonora was pimping for Edward. That was the cross that she had to take up during her long Calvary of a life . . .

You ask how it feels to be a deceived husband. Just Heavens, I do not know. It feels just nothing at all. It is not Hell, certainly it is not necessarily Heaven. So I suppose it is the intermediate stage. What do they call it? Limbo. No, I feel nothing at all about that. They are dead; they have gone before their Judge who, I hope, will open to them the springs of His compassion. It is not my business to think about it. It is simply my business to say, as Leonora's people say: '*Requiem aeternam dona eis, Domine; et lux perpetua luceat eis. In memoria aeterna erit.*'[83] But what were they? The just? The unjust? God knows! I think that the pair of them were only poor wretches, creeping over this earth in the shadow of an eternal wrath. It is very terrible. . . .

It is almost too terrible, the picture of that judgement, as it appears to me sometimes, at nights. It is probably the suggestion of some picture that I have seen somewhere. But upon an immense plain, suspended in mid-air, I seem to see three figures, two of them clasped close in an intense embrace, and one intolerably solitary. It is in black and white, my picture of that judgement, an etching, perhaps; only I cannot tell an etching from a photographic reproduction. And the immense plain is the hand of God, stretching out for miles and miles, with great spaces above it and below it. And they are in the sight of God, and it is Florence that is alone . . .

And, do you know, at the thought of that intense solitude I feel an overwhelming desire to rush forward and comfort her. You cannot, you see, have acted as nurse to a person for twelve years without wishing to go on nursing them, even though you hate them with the hatred of the adder, and even in the palm of God. But, in the nights, with that vision of judgement before me, I know that I hold myself back. For I hate Florence. I hate Florence with such a hatred that I would not spare her an eternity of loneliness. She need not have done what she did. She was an American, a New Englander. She had not the hot passions of these Europeans. She cut out that poor imbecile of an Edward – and I pray God that he is really at peace, clasped close in the arms of that poor, poor girl! And, no doubt, Maisie Maidan will find her young husband again, and Leonora will burn, clear and serene, a northern light[84] and one of the archangels of God. And me . . . Well, perhaps, they will find me an elevator to run . . . But Florence . . .

She should not have done it. She should not have done it. It was playing it too low down. She cut out poor dear Edward from sheer vanity; she meddled between him and Leonora from a sheer, imbecile spirit of district visiting. Do you understand that, whilst she was Edward's mistress, she was perpetually trying to reunite him to his wife? She would gabble on to Leonora about forgiveness – treating the subject from the bright, American point of view. And Leonora would treat her like the whore she was. Once she said to Florence in the early morning:

'You come to me straight out of his bed to tell me that that is my proper place. I know it, thank you.'

But even that could not stop Florence. She went on saying that it was her ambition to leave this world a little brighter by the passage of her brief life, and how thankfully she would leave Edward, whom she thought she had brought to a right frame of mind, if Leonora would only give him a chance. He needed, she said, tenderness beyond anything.

And Leonora would answer – for she put up with this outrage for years – Leonora, as I understand, would answer something like:

'Yes, you would give him up. And you would go on writing to each other in secret, and committing adultery in hired rooms. I know the pair of you, you know. No. I prefer the situation as it is.'

Half the time Florence would ignore Leonora's remarks. She would think they were not quite ladylike. The other half of the time she would try to persuade Leonora that her love for Edward was quite spiritual – on account of her heart. Once she said:

'If you can believe that of Maisie Maidan, as you say you do, why cannot you believe it of me?'

Leonora was, I understand, doing her hair at that time in front of the mirror in her bedroom. And she looked round at Florence, to whom she did not usually vouchsafe a glance, – she looked round coolly and calmly, and said:

'Never do you dare to mention Mrs Maidan's name again. You murdered her. You and I murdered her between us. I am as much a scoundrel as you. I don't like to be reminded of it.'

Florence went off at once into a babble of how could she have hurt a person whom she hardly knew, a person whom with the best intentions, in pursuance of her efforts to leave the world a little brighter, she had tried to save from Edward. That was how she figured it out to herself. She really thought that . . . So Leonora said patiently:

'Very well, just put it that I killed her and that it's a painful subject. One does not like to think that one had killed someone. Naturally not. I ought never to have brought her from India.'

And that, indeed, is exactly how Leonora looked at it. It is stated a little baldly, but Leonora was always a great one for bald statements.

What had happened on the day of our jaunt to the ancient city of M— had been this:

Leonora, who had been even then filled with pity and contrition for the poor child, on returning to our hotel had gone straight to Mrs Maidan's room. She had wanted just to pet her. And she had perceived at first only, on the clear, round table covered with red velvet, a letter addressed to her. It ran something like:

'Oh, Mrs Ashburnham, how could you have done it? I trusted you so. You never talked to me about me and Edward, but I trusted you. How could you buy me from my husband? I have just heard how you have – in the hall they were talking about it, Edward and the American lady. You paid the money for me to come here. Oh, how could you? How could you? I am going straight back to Bunny . . .'

Bunny was Mrs Maidan's husband.

And Leonora said that, as she went on reading the letter, she had, without looking round her, a sense that that hotel room was cleared, that there were no papers on the table, that there were no clothes on the hooks, and that there was a strained silence – a silence, she said, as if there were something in the room that drank up such sounds as there were. She had to fight against that feeling, whilst she read the postscript of the letter.

'I did not know you wanted me for an adulteress,' the postscript began. The poor child was hardly literate.[85] 'It was surely not right of you and I never wanted to be one. And I heard Edward call me a poor little rat to the American lady. He always called me a little rat in private, and I did not mind. But, if he called me it to her, I think he does not love me any more. Oh, Mrs Ashburnham, you knew the world and I knew nothing. I thought it would be all right if you thought it could, and I thought you would not have brought me if you did not, too. You should not have done it, and we out of the same convent . . .'

Leonora said that she screamed when she read that.

And then she saw that Maisie's boxes were all packed, and she began a search for Mrs Maidan herself – all over the hotel. The manager said that Mrs Maidan had paid her bill, and had gone up to the station to ask the *Reiseverkehrsbureau*[86] to make her out a plan for her immediate return to Chitral. He imagined that he had seen her come back, but he was not quite certain. No one in the large hotel had bothered his head about the child. And she, wandering solitarily in the hall, had no doubt sat down beside a screen that had Edward and Florence on the other side. I never heard then or after what had passed between that precious couple. I fancy Florence was just about beginning her cutting out of poor dear Edward by addressing to him some words of friendly warning as to the ravages he might be making in the girl's heart. That would be the sort of way she would begin. And Edward would have sentimentally assured her that there was nothing in it; that Maisie was just a poor little rat whose passage to Nauheim his wife had paid out of her own pocket. That would have been enough to do the trick.

For the trick was pretty efficiently done. Leonora, with panic growing and with contrition very large in her heart, visited every one of the public rooms of the hotel – the dining-room, the lounge, the *Schreibzimmer*,[87] the winter garden. God knows what they wanted with a winter garden in an hotel that is only open from May till October. But there it was. And then Leonora ran – yes, she ran up the stairs – to see if Maisie had not returned to her rooms. She had determined to take that child right away from that hideous place. It seemed to her to be all unspeakable. I do not mean to say that she was not quite cool about it. Leonora was always Leonora. But the cold justice of the thing demanded that she should play the part of mother to this child who had come from the same convent. She figured it out to amount to that. She would leave Edward to Florence – and to me – and she would devote all her time to providing that child with an atmosphere of love until she could be returned to her poor young husband. It was naturally too late.

She had not cared to look round Maisie's rooms at first. Now, as soon as she came in, she perceived, sticking out beyond the bed, a small pair of feet in high-heeled shoes. Maisie had died in the effort to strap up a great portmanteau. She had died so grotesquely that her little body had fallen forward into the trunk, and it had closed upon her, like the jaws of a gigantic alligator. The key was in her hand. Her dark hair, like the hair of a Japanese, had come down and covered her body and her face.

Leonora lifted her up – she was the merest featherweight – and laid her on the bed with her hair about her. She was smiling, as if she had just scored a goal in a hockey match. You understand she had not committed suicide. Her heart had just stopped. I saw her, with the long lashes on the cheeks, with the smile about the lips, with the flowers all about her. The stem of a white lily[88] rested in her hand so that the spike of flowers was upon her shoulder. She looked like a bride in the sunlight of the mortuary candles that were all about her, and the white coifs of the two nuns that knelt at her feet with their faces hidden might have been two swans that were to bear her away to kissing-kindness land, or wherever it is. Leonora showed her to me. She would not let either of the others see her. She wanted, you know, to spare poor dear Edward's feelings. He never could bear the sight of a corpse. And, since she never gave him an idea that Maisie had written to her, he imagined that the death had been the most natural thing in the world. He soon got over it. Indeed, it was the one affair of his about which he never felt much remorse.

Part Two

I

The death of Mrs Maidan occurred on the 4th of August, 1904. And then nothing happened until the 4th of August, 1913. There is the curious coincidence of dates, but I do not know whether that is one of those sinister, as if half-jocular and altogether merciless proceedings on the part of a cruel Providence that we call a coincidence. Because it may just as well have been the superstitious mind of Florence that forced her to certain acts, as if she had been hypnotized. It is, however, certain that the 4th of August always proved a significant date for her. To begin with, she was born on the 4th of August. Then, on that date, in the year 1899, she set out with her uncle for the tour round the world in company with a young man called Jimmy. But that was not merely a coincidence. Her kindly old uncle, with the supposedly damaged heart, was in his delicate way, offering her, in this trip, a birthday present to celebrate her coming of age. Then, on the 4th of August, 1900, she yielded to an action that certainly coloured her whole life – as well as mine. She had no luck. She was probably offering herself a birthday present that morning . . .

On the 4th of August, 1901, she married me, and set sail for Europe in a great gale of wind – the gale that affected her heart. And no doubt there, again, she was offering herself a birthday gift – the birthday gift of my miserable life. It occurs to me that I have never told you anything about my marriage. That was like this: I have told you, as I think, that I first met Florence at the Stuyvesants', in Fourteenth Street. And, from that moment, I determined with all the obstinacy of a possibly weak nature, if not to make her mine, at least to marry her. I had no occupation – I had no business affairs. I simply camped down there in Stamford, in a vile hotel, and just passed my days in the house, or on the verandah of the Misses Hurlbird. The Misses Hurlbird, in an odd, obstinate way, did not like my presence. But they were hampered by the national manners of these occasions. Florence had her own sitting-room. She could ask to it whom she liked, and I simply walked into that apartment. I was as timid as you will, but in that matter I was like a chicken that is determined to get across the road in front of an automobile. I would walk into Florence's pretty, little, old-fashioned room, take off my hat, and sit down.

Florence had, of course, several other fellows, too – strapping young New Englanders, who worked during the day in New York and spent only the evenings in the village of their birth. And, in the evenings, they would march in on Florence with almost as much determination as I myself showed. And I am bound to say that they were received with as much disfavour as was my portion – from the Misses Hurlbird . . .

They were curious old creatures, those two. It was almost as if they were members of an ancient family under some curse – they were so gentlewomanly, so proper, and they sighed so. Sometimes I would see tears in their eyes. I do not know that my courtship of Florence made much progress at first. Perhaps that was because it took place almost entirely during the daytime, on hot afternoons, when the clouds of dust hung like fog, right up as high as the tops of the thin-leaved elms. The night, I believe, is the proper season for the gentle feats of love, not a Connecticut July afternoon, when any sort of proximity is an almost appalling thought. But, if I never so much as kissed Florence, she let me discover very easily, in the course of a fortnight, her simple wants. And I could supply those wants . . .

She wanted to marry a gentleman of leisure; she wanted a European establishment. She wanted her husband to have an English accent, an income of fifty thousand dollars a year from real estate and no ambitions to increase that income. And – she faintly hinted – she did not want much physical passion in the affair. Americans, you know, can envisage such unions without blinking.

She gave out this information in floods of bright talk – she would pop a little bit of it into comments over a view of the Rialto, Venice, and, whilst she was brightly describing Balmoral Castle,[89] she would say that her ideal husband would be one who could get her received at the British Court. She had spent, it seemed, two months in Great Britain – seven weeks in touring from Stratford to Strathpeffer, and one as paying guest in an old English family near Ledbury,[90] an impoverished, but still stately family, called Bagshawe. They were to have spent two months more in that tranquil bosom, but inopportune events, apparently in her uncle's business, had caused their rather hurried return to Stamford. The young man called Jimmy had remained in Europe to perfect his knowledge of that continent. He certainly did: he was most useful to us afterwards.

But the point that came out – that there was no mistaking – was that Florence was coldly and calmly determined to take no look at any man who could not give her a European settlement. Her glimpse of English home life had effected this. She meant, on her marriage, to have a year in Paris, and then to have her husband buy some real estate in the neighbourhood of Fordingbridge, from which place the Hurlbirds had come in the year 1688.[91] On the strength of that she was going to take her place in the ranks of English county society. That was fixed.

I used to feel mightily elevated when I considered these details, for I could not figure out that amongst her acquaintances in Stamford there was any fellow that would fill the bill. The most of them were not as wealthy as I, and those that were were not the type to give up the fascinations of Wall Street even for the protracted companionship of Florence. But nothing really happened during the month of July. On the 1st of August Florence apparently told her aunts that she intended to marry me.

She had not told me so, but there was no doubt about the aunts, for, on that afternoon, Miss Florence Hurlbird, Senior, stopped me on my way to Florence's sitting-room and took me, agitatedly, into the parlour. It was a singular interview, in that old-fashioned colonial room, with the spindle-legged furniture, the silhouettes, the miniatures, the portrait of General Braddock,[92] and the smell of lavender. You see, the two poor maiden ladies were in agonies – and they could not say one single thing direct. They would almost wring their hands and ask if I had considered such a thing as different temperaments. I assure you they were almost affectionate, concerned for me even, as if Florence were too bright for my solid and serious virtues.

For they had discovered in me solid and serious virtues. That might have been because I had once dropped the remark that I preferred General Braddock to General Washington. For the Hurlbirds had backed the losing side in the War of Independence,[93] and had been seriously impoverished and quite efficiently oppressed for that reason. The Misses Hurlbird could never forget it.

Nevertheless they shuddered at the thought of a European career for myself and Florence. Each of them really wailed when they heard that that was what I hoped to give their niece. That may have been partly because they regarded Europe as a sink of iniquity, where strange laxities prevailed. They thought the Mother Country as Erastian as any other. And they carried their protests to extraordinary lengths, for them . . .

They even, almost, said that marriage was a sacrament; but neither Miss Florence nor Miss Emily could quite bring herself to utter the word. And they almost brought themselves to say that Florence's early life had been characterized by flirtations – something of that sort.

I know I ended the interview by saying:

'I don't care. If Florence has robbed a bank I am going to marry her and take her to Europe.'

And at that Miss Emily wailed and fainted. But Miss Florence, in spite of the state of her sister, threw herself on my neck and cried out:

'Don't do it, John. Don't do it. You're a good young man,' and she added, whilst I was getting out of the room to send Florence to her aunt's rescue:

'We ought to tell you more. But she's our dear sister's child.'

Florence, I remember, received me with a chalk-pale face and the exclamation:

'Have those old cats been saying anything against me?' But I assured her that they had not and hurried her into the room of her strangely afflicted relatives. I had really forgotten all about that exclamation of Florence's until this moment. She treated me so very well – with such tact – that, if I ever thought of it afterwards, I put it down to her deep affection for me.

And that evening, when I went to fetch her for a buggy-ride, she had disappeared. I did not lose any time. I went into New York and engaged berths on the 'Pocahontas',[94] that was to sail on the evening of the fourth of the month, and then, returning to Stamford, I tracked out, in the course of the day, that Florence had been driven to Rye Station. And there I found that she had taken the cars to Waterbury.[95] She had, of course, gone to her uncle's. The old man received me with a stony, husky face. I was not to see Florence; she was ill; she was keeping her room. And, from something that he let drop – an odd Biblical phrase that I have forgotten – I gathered that all that family simply did not intend her to marry ever in her life.

I procured at once the name of the nearest minister and a rope ladder – you have no idea how primitively these matters were arranged in those days in the United States. I daresay that may be so still. And at one o'clock in the morning of the 4th of August I was standing in Florence's bedroom. I was so one-minded in my purpose that it never struck me there was anything improper in being, at one o'clock in the morning, in Florence's bedroom. I just wanted to wake her up. She was not, however, asleep. She expected me, and her relatives had only just left her. She received me with an embrace of a warmth . . . Well, it was the first time I had ever been embraced by a woman – and it was the last when a woman's embrace has had in it any warmth for me. . . .

I suppose it was my own fault, what followed. At any rate, I was in such a hurry to get the wedding over, and was so afraid of her relatives finding me there, that I must have received her advances with a certain amount of absence of mind. I was out of that room and down the ladder in under half a minute. She kept me waiting at the foot an unconscionable time – it was certainly three in the morning before we knocked up that minister. And I think that that wait was the only sign Florence ever showed of having a conscience as far as I was concerned, unless her lying for some moments in my arms was also a sign of conscience. I fancy that, if I had shown warmth then, she would have acted the proper wife to me, or would have put me back again. But, because I acted like a Philadelphia gentleman, she made me, I suppose, go through with the part of a male nurse. Perhaps she thought that I should not mind.

After that, as I gather, she had not any more remorse. She was only anxious to carry out her plans. For, just before she came down the ladder, she called me to the top of that grotesque implement that I went up and down like a tranquil jumping jack. I was perfectly collected. She said to me with a certain fierceness:

'It is determined that we sail at four this afternoon? You are not lying about having taken berths?'

I understood that she would naturally be anxious to get away from the neighbourhood of her apparently insane relatives, so that I readily excused her for thinking that I should be capable of lying about such a thing. I made it, therefore, plain to her that it was my fixed determination to sail by the 'Pocahontas'. She said then – it was a moonlit morning, and she was whispering in my ear whilst I stood on the ladder. The hills that surround Waterbury showed, extraordinarily tranquil, around the villa. She said, almost coldly:

'I wanted to know, so as to pack my trunks.' And she added: 'I may be ill, you know. I guess my heart is a little like Uncle Hurlbird's. It runs in families.'

I whispered that the 'Pocahontas' was an extraordinarily steady boat . . .

Now I wonder what had passed through Florence's mind during the two hours that she had kept me waiting at the foot of the ladder. I would give not a little to know. Till then, I fancy she had had no settled plan in her mind. She certainly never mentioned her heart till that time. Perhaps the renewed sight of her Uncle Hurlbird had given her the idea. Certainly her Aunt Emily, who had come over with her to Waterbury, would have rubbed into her, for hours and hours, the idea that any accentuated discussions would kill the old gentleman. That would recall to her mind all the safeguards against excitement with which the poor silly old gentleman had been hedged in during their trip round the world. That, perhaps, put it into her head. Still, I believe there was some remorse on my account, too. Leonora told me that Florence said there was – for Leonora knew all about it, and once went so far as to ask her how she could do a thing so infamous. She excused herself on the score of an overmastering passion. Well, I always say that an overmastering passion is a good excuse for feelings. You cannot help them. And it is a good excuse for straight actions – she might have bolted with the fellow, before or after she married me. And, if they had not enough money to get along with, they might have cut their throats, or sponged on her family, though, of course, Florence wanted such a lot that it would have suited her very badly to have for a husband a clerk in a dry-goods store, which was what old Hurlbird would have made of that fellow. He hated him. No, I do not think that there is much excuse for Florence.

God knows. She was a frightened fool, and she was fantastic, and I suppose that, at that time, she really cared for that imbecile. He certainly didn't care for her. Poor thing . . . At any rate, after I had assured her that the 'Pocahontas' was a steady ship, she just said:

'You'll have to look after me in certain ways – like Uncle Hurlbird is looked after. I will tell you how to do it.' And then she stepped over the sill, as if she were stepping on board a boat. I suppose she had burnt hers! I had, no doubt, eye-openers enough. When we re-entered the Hurlbird mansion at eight o'clock the Hurlbirds were just exhausted. Florence had a hard, triumphant air. We had got married about four in the morning and had sat about in the woods above the town till then, listening to a mocking-bird imitate an old tom-cat. So I guess Florence had not found getting married to me a very stimulating process. I had not found anything much more inspiring to say than how glad I was, with variations. I think I was too dazed. Well, the Hurlbirds were too dazed to say much. We had breakfast together, and then Florence went to pack her grips and things. Old Hurlbird took the opportunity to read me a full-blooded lecture, in the style of an American oration, as to the perils for young American girlhood lurking in the European jungle. He said that Paris was full of snakes in the grass, of which he had had bitter experience. He concluded, as they always do, poor, dear old things, with the aspiration that all American women should one day be sexless – though that is not the way they put it . . .

Well, we made the ship all right by one-thirty – and there was a tempest blowing. That helped Florence a good deal. For we were not ten minutes out from Sandy Hook[96] before Florence went down into her cabin and her heart took her. An agitated stewardess came running up to me, and I went running down. I got my directions how to behave to my wife. Most of them came from her, though it was the ship's doctor who discreetly suggested to me that I had better refrain from manifestations of affection. I was ready enough.

I was, of course, full of remorse. It occurred to me that her heart was the reason for the Hurlbirds' mysterious desire to keep their youngest and dearest unmarried. Of course, they would be too refined to put the motive into words. They were old stock New Englanders. They would not want to have to suggest that a husband must not kiss the back of his wife's neck. They would not like to suggest that he might, for the matter of that. I wonder, though, how Florence got the doctor to enter the conspiracy – the several doctors.

Of course her heart squeaked a bit – she had the same configuration of the lungs as her Uncle Hurlbird. And, in his company, she must have heard a great deal of heart talk from specialists. Anyhow, she and they tied me pretty well down – and Jimmy, of course, that dreary boy – what in the world did she see in him? He was lugubrious, silent, morose. He had no talent as a painter. He was very sallow and dark, and he never shaved sufficiently. He met us at Havre, and he proceeded to make himself useful for the next two years, during which he lived in our flat in Paris, whether we were there or not. He studied painting at Julien's,[97] or some such place . . .

That fellow had his hands always in the pockets of his odious, square-shouldered, broad-hipped, American coats, and his dark eyes were always full of ominous appearances. He was, besides, too fat. Why, I was much the better man . . .

And I daresay Florence would have given me the better. She showed signs of it. I think, perhaps, the enigmatic smile with which she used to look back at me over her shoulder when she went into the bathing place was a sort of invitation. I have mentioned that. It was as if she were saying: 'I am going in here. I am going to stand so stripped and white and straight – and you are a man . . .' Perhaps it was that . . .

No, she cannot have liked that fellow long. He looked like sallow putty. I understand that he had been slim and dark and very graceful at the time of her first disgrace. But, loafing about in Paris, on her pocket-money and on the allowance that old Hurlbird made him to keep out of the United States, had given him a stomach like a man of forty, and dyspeptic irritation on top of it.

God, how they worked me! It was those two between them who really elaborated the rules. I have told you something about them – how I had to head conversations, for all those eleven years, off such topics as love, poverty, crime, and so on. But, looking over what I have written, I see that I have unintentionally misled you when I said that Florence was never out of my sight. Yet that was the impression that I really had until just now. When I come to think of it she was out of my sight most of the time.

You see, that fellow impressed upon me that what Florence needed most of all were sleep and privacy. I must never enter her room without knocking, or her poor little heart might flutter away to its doom. He said these things with his lugubrious croak, and his black eyes like a crow's, so that I seemed to see poor Florence die ten times a day – a little, pale, frail corpse. Why, I would as soon have thought of entering her room without her permission as of burgling a church. I would sooner have committed that crime. I would certainly have done it if I had thought the state of her heart demanded the sacrilege. So at ten o'clock at night the door closed upon Florence, who had gently, and, as if reluctantly, backed up that fellow's recommendations; and she would wish me good night as if she were a *cinquecento*[98] Italian lady saying good-bye to her lover. And at ten o'clock of the next morning there she would come out the door of her room as fresh as Venus rising from any of the couches that are mentioned in Greek legends.

Her room door was locked because she was nervous about thieves; but an electric contrivance on a cord was understood to be attached to her little wrist. She had only to press a bulb to raise the house. And I was provided with an axe – an axe! – great gods, with which to break down her door in case she ever failed to answer my knock, after I knocked really loud several times. It was pretty well thought out, you see.

What wasn't so well thought out were the ultimate consequences – our being tied to Europe. For that young man rubbed it so well into me that Florence would die if she crossed the Channel – he impressed it so fully on my mind that, when later Florence wanted to go to Fordingbridge, I cut the proposal short – absolutely short, with a curt no. It fixed her and it frightened her. I was even backed up by all the doctors. I seemed to have had endless interviews with doctor after doctor, cool, quiet men, who would ask, in reasonable tones, whether there was any reason for our going to England – any special reason. And since I could not see any special reason, they would give the verdict: 'Better not, then.' I daresay they were honest enough, as things go. They probably imagined that the mere associations of the steamer might have effects on Florence's nerves. That would be enough, that and a conscientious desire to keep our money on the Continent.

It must have rattled poor Florence pretty considerably, for you see, the main idea – the only main idea of her heart, that was otherwise cold – was to get to Fordingbridge and be a county lady in the home of her ancestors. But Jimmy got her, there: he shut on her the door of the Channel; even on the fairest day of blue sky, with the cliffs of England shining like mother of pearl in full view of Calais, I would not have let her cross the steamer gangway to save her life. I tell you it fixed her.

It fixed her beautifully, because she could not announce herself as cured, since that would have put an end to the locked bedroom arrangements. And, by the time she was sick of Jimmy – which happened in the year 1903 – she had taken on Edward Ashburnham. Yes, it was a bad fix for her, because Edward could have taken her to Fordingbridge, and, though he could not give her Bramshaw Manor, that home of her ancestors being settled on his wife, she could at least have pretty considerably queened it there or thereabouts, what with our money and the support of the Ashburnhams. Her uncle, as soon as he considered that she had really settled down with me – and I sent him only the most glowing accounts of her virtue and constancy – made over to her a very considerable part of his fortune for which he had no use. I suppose that we had, between us, fifteen thousand a year in English money, though I never quite knew how much of hers went to Jimmy. At any rate, we could have shone in Fordingbridge.

I never quite knew, either, how she and Edward got rid of Jimmy. I fancy that fat and disreputable raven must have had his six golden front teeth knocked down his throat by Edward one morning whilst I had gone out to buy some flowers in the Rue de la Paix,[99] leaving Florence and the flat in charge of those two. And serve him very right, is all that

I can say. He was a bad sort of blackmailer; I hope Florence does not have his company in the next world.

As God is my Judge, I do not believe that I would have separated those two if I had known that they really and passionately loved each other. I do not know where the public morality of the case comes in, and, of course, no man really knows what he would have done in any given case. But I truly believe that I would have united them, observing ways and means as decent as I could. I believe that I should have given them money to live upon and that I should have consoled myself somehow. At that date I might have found some young thing, like Maisie Maidan, or the poor girl, and I might have had some peace. For peace I never had with Florence, and hardly believe that I cared for her in the way of love after a year or two of it. She became for me a rare and fragile object, something burdensome, but very frail. Why it was as if I had been given a thin-shelled pullet's egg to carry on my palm from Equatorial Africa to Hoboken.[100] Yes, she became for me, as it were, the subject of a bet – the trophy of an athlete's achievement, a parsley crown that is the symbol of his chastity, his soberness, his abstentions, and of his inflexible will. Of intrinsic value as a wife, I think she had none at all for me. I fancy I was not even proud of the way she dressed.

But her passion for Jimmy was not even a passion, and, mad as the suggestion may appear, she was frightened for her life. Yes, she was afraid of me. I will tell you how that happened.

I had, in the old days, a darky servant, called Julius, who valeted me, and waited on me, and loved me, like the crown of his head. Now, when we left Waterbury to go to the 'Pocahontas', Florence entrusted to me one very special and very precious leather grip. She told me that her life might depend on that grip, which contained her drugs against heart attacks. And, since I was never much of a hand at carrying things, I entrusted this, in turn, to Julius, who was a grey-haired chap of sixty or so, and very picturesque at that. He made so much impression on Florence that she regarded him as a sort of father, and absolutely refused to let me take him to Paris. He would have inconvenienced her.

Well, Julius was so overcome with grief at being left behind that he must needs go and drop the precious grip. I saw red, I saw purple. I flew at Julius. On the ferry, it was, I filled up one of his eyes; I threatened to strangle him. And, since an unresisting negro can make a deplorable noise and a deplorable spectacle, and, since that was Florence's first adventure in the married state, she got a pretty idea of my character. It affirmed in her the desperate resolve to conceal from me the fact that she was not what she would have called 'a pure woman'. For that was really the mainspring of her fantastic actions. She was afraid that I should murder her . . .

So she got up the heart attack, at the earliest possible opportunity, on board the liner. Perhaps she was not so very much to be blamed. You must remember that she was a New Englander, and that New England had not yet come to loathe darkies as it does now. Whereas, if she had come from even so little south as Philadelphia, and had been an oldish family, she would have seen that for me to kick Julius was not so outrageous an act as for her cousin, Reggie Hurlbird, to say – as I have heard him say to his English butler – that for two cents he would bat him on the pants. Besides, the medicine-grip did not bulk as largely in her eyes as it did in mine, where it was the symbol of the existence of an adored wife of a day. To her it was just a useful lie . . .

Well, there you have the position, as clear as I can make it – the husband an ignorant fool, the wife a cold sensualist with imbecile fears – for I was such a fool that I should never have known what she was or was not – and the blackmailing lover. And then the other lover came along . . .

Well, Edward Ashburnham was worth having. Have I conveyed to you the splendid fellow that he was – the fine soldier, the excellent landlord, the extraordinarily kind, careful and industrious magistrate, the upright, honest, fair-dealing, fair-thinking, public character? I suppose I have not conveyed it to you. The truth is, that I never knew it until the poor girl came along – the poor girl who was just as straight, as splendid and as upright as he. I swear she was. I suppose I ought to have known. I suppose that was, really, why I liked him so much – so infinitely much. Come to think of it, I can remember a thousand little acts of kindliness, of thoughtfulness for his inferiors, even on the Continent. Look here, I know of two families of dirty, unpicturesque,

Hessian paupers that that fellow, with an infinite patience, rooted up, got their police reports, set on their feet, or exported to my patient land. And he would do it quite inarticulately, set in motion by seeing a child crying in the street. He would wrestle with dictionaries, in that unfamiliar tongue . . . Well, he could not bear to see a child cry. Perhaps he could not bear to see a woman and not give her the comfort of his physical attractions.

But, although I liked him so intensely, I was rather apt to take these things for granted. They made me feel comfortable with him, good towards him; they made me trust him. But I guess I thought it was part of the character of any English gentleman. Why, one day he got it into his head that the head waiter at the Excelsior had been crying – the fellow with the grey face and grey whiskers. And then he spent the best part of a week, in correspondence and up at the British consul's, in getting the fellow's wife to come back from London and bring back his girl baby. She had bolted with a Swiss scullion. If she had not come inside the week he would have gone to London himself to fetch her. He was like that.

Edward Ashburnham was like that, and I thought it was only the duty of his rank and station. Perhaps that was all that it was – but I pray God to make me discharge mine as well. And, but for the poor girl, I daresay that I should never have seen it, however much the feeling might have been over me. She had for him such enthusiasm that, although even now I do not understand the technicalities of English life, I can gather enough. She was with them during the whole of our last stay at Nauheim.

Nancy Rufford was her name; she was Leonora's only friend's only child, and Leonora was her guardian, if that is the correct term. She had lived with the Ashburnhams ever since she had been of the age of thirteen, when her mother was said to have committed suicide owing to the brutalities of her father. Yes, it is a cheerful story . . .

Edward always called her 'the girl', and it was very pretty, the evident affection he had for her and she for him. And Leonora's feet she would have kissed – those two were for her the best man and the best woman on earth – and in heaven. I think that she had not a thought of evil in her head – the poor girl . . .

Well, anyhow, she chanted Edward's praises to me for the hour together, but, as I have said, I could not make much of it. It appeared that he had the D.S.O.,[101] and that his troop loved him beyond the love of men. You never saw such a troop as his. And he had the Royal Humane Society's[102] medal with a clasp. That meant, apparently, that he had twice jumped off the deck of a troopship to rescue what the girl called 'Tommies', who had fallen overboard in the Red Sea and such places. He had been twice recommended for the V.C.,[103] whatever that might mean, and, although owing to some technicalities he had never received that apparently coveted order, he had some special place about his sovereign at the coronation. Or perhaps it was some post in the Beefeaters.[104] She made him out like a cross between Lohengrin and the Chevalier Bayard.[105] Perhaps he was . . . But he was too silent a fellow to make that side of him really decorative. I remember going to him at about that time and asking him what the D.S.O. was, and he grunted out:

'It's a sort of a thing they give grocers who've honourably supplied the troops with adulterated coffee in war-time' – something of that sort. He did not quite carry conviction to me, so, in the end, I put it directly to Leonora. I asked her fully and squarely – prefacing the question with some remarks, such as those that I have already given you, as to the difficulty one has in really getting to know people when one's intimacy is conducted as an English acquaintanceship – I asked her whether her husband was not really a splendid fellow – along at least the lines of his public functions. She looked at me with a slightly awakened air – with an air that would have been almost startled if Leonora could ever have been startled.

'Didn't you know?' she asked. 'If I come to think of it there is not a more splendid fellow in any three counties, pick them where you will – along those lines.' And she added, after she had looked at me reflectively for what seemed a long time:

'To do my husband justice there could not be a better man on the earth. There would not be room for it – along those lines.'

'Well,' I said, 'then he must really be Lohengrin and the Cid[106] in one body. For there are not any other lines that count.'

Again she looked at me for a long time.

'It's your opinion that there are no other lines that count?' she asked slowly.

'Well,' I answered gaily, 'you're not going to accuse him of not being a good husband, or of not being a good guardian to your ward?'

She spoke then, slowly, like a person who is listening to the sounds in a sea-shell held to her ear – and, would you believe it? – she told me afterwards that, at that speech of mine, for the first time she had a vague inkling of the tragedy that was to follow so soon – although the girl had lived with them for eight years or so:

'Oh, I'm not thinking of saying that he is not the best of husbands, or that he is not very fond of the girl.'

And then I said something like:

'Well, Leonora, a man sees more of these things than even a wife. And, let me tell you, that in all the years I've known Edward he has never, in your absence, paid a moment's attention to any other woman – not by the quivering of an eyelash. I should have noticed. And he talks of you as if you were one of the angels of God.'

'Oh,' she came up to the scratch, as you could be sure Leonora would always come up to the scratch, 'I am perfectly sure that he always speaks nicely of me.'

I daresay she had practice in that sort of scene – people must have been always complimenting her on her husband's fidelity and adoration. For half the world – the whole of the world that knew Edward and Leonora believed that his conviction in the Kilsyte affair had been a miscarriage of justice – a conspiracy of false evidence, got together by Nonconformist adversaries. But think of the fool that I was . . .

II

Let me think where we were. Oh, yes . . . that conversation took place on the 4th of August, 1913. I remember saying to her that, on that day, exactly nine years before, I had made their acquaintance, so that it had seemed quite appropriate and like a birthday speech to utter my little testimonial to my friend Edward. I could quite confidently say that, though we four had been about together in all sorts of places, for all that length of time, I had not, for my part, one single complaint to make of either of them. And I added, that that was an unusual record for people who had been so much together. You are not to imagine that it was only at Nauheim that we met. That would not have suited Florence.

I find, on looking at my diaries, that on the 4th of September, 1904, Edward accompanied Florence and myself to Paris, where we put him up till the twenty-first of that month. He made another short visit to us in December of that year – the first year of our acquaintance. It must have been during this visit that he knocked Mr Jimmy's teeth down his throat. I daresay Florence had asked him to come over for that purpose. In 1905 he was in Paris three times – once with Leonora, who wanted some frocks. In 1906 we spent the best part of six weeks together at Mentone, and Edward stayed with us in Paris on his way back to London. That was how it went.

The fact was that in Florence the poor wretch had got hold of a Tartar, compared with whom Leonora was a sucking kid. He must have had a hell of a time. Leonora wanted to keep him for – what shall I say – for the good of her church, as it were, to show that Catholic women do not lose their men. Let it go at that, for the moment. I will write more about her motives later, perhaps. But Florence was sticking on to the proprietor of the home of her ancestors. No doubt he was also a very passionate lover. But I am convinced that he was sick of Florence within three years of even interrupted companionship and the life that she led him . . .

If ever Leonora so much as mentioned in a letter that they had had a woman staying with them – or, if she so much as mentioned a woman's name in a letter to me – off would go a desperate cable in cipher to that poor wretch at Bramshaw, commanding him on pain of an instant and horrible disclosure to come over and assure her of his fidelity. I daresay he would have faced it out; I daresay he would have thrown over Florence and taken the risk of exposure. But there he had Leonora to deal with. And Leonora assured him that, if the minutest fragment of the real situation ever got through to my senses, she would wreak upon him the most terrible vengeance that she could think of. And he did not have a very easy job. Florence called for more and more attentions from him as the time went on. She would make him kiss her at any moment of the day; and it was only by his making it plain that a divorced lady could never assume a position in the county of Hampshire that he could prevent her from making a bolt of it with him in her train. Oh, yes, it was a difficult job for him.

For Florence, if you please, gaining in time a more composed view of nature, and overcome by her habits of garrulity, arrived at a frame of mind in which she found it almost necessary to tell me all about it – nothing less than that. She said that her situation was too unbearable with regard to me.

She proposed to tell me all, secure a divorce from me, and go with Edward and settle in California . . . I do not suppose that she was really serious in this. It would have meant the extinction of all hopes of Bramshaw Manor for her. Besides she had got it into her head that Leonora, who was as sound as a roach, was consumptive. She was always begging Leonora, before me, to go and see a doctor. But, none the less, poor Edward seems to have believed in her determination to carry him off. He would not have gone; he cared for his wife too much. But, if Florence had put him at it,[107] that would have meant my getting to know of it, and his incurring Leonora's vengeance. And she could have made it pretty hot for him in ten or a dozen different ways. And she assured me that she would have used every one of them. She was determined to spare my feelings. And she was quite aware that, at that date, the hottest she could have made it for him would have been to refuse, herself, ever to see him again . . .

Well, I think I have made it pretty clear. Let me come to the 4th of August, 1913, the last day of my absolute ignorance – and, I assure you, of my perfect happiness. For the coming of that dear girl only added to it all.

On that 4th of August I was sitting in the lounge with a rather odious Englishman called Bagshawe, who had arrived that night, too late for dinner. Leonora had just gone to bed and I was waiting for Florence and Edward and the girl to come back from a concert at the Casino.

They had not gone there all together. Florence, I remember, had said at first that she would remain with Leonora, and me, and Edward and the girl had gone off alone. And then Leonora had said to Florence with perfect calmness:

'I wish you would go with those two. I think the girl ought to have the appearance of being chaperoned with Edward in these places. I think the time has come.' So Florence, with her light step, had slipped out after them. She was all in black for some cousin or other. Americans are particular in those matters.

We had gone on sitting in the lounge till towards ten, when Leonora had gone up to bed. It had been a very hot day, but there it was cool. The man called Bagshawe had been reading *The Times* on the other side of the room, but then he moved over to me with some trifling question as a prelude to suggesting an acquaintance. I fancy he asked me something about the poll-tax on *Kur*-guests, and whether it could not be sneaked out of. He was that sort of person.

Well, he was an unmistakable man, with a military figure, rather exaggerated, with bulbous eyes that avoided your own, and a pallid complexion that suggested vices practised in secret along with an uneasy desire for making acquaintance at whatever cost . . . The filthy toad . . .

He began by telling me that he came from Ludlow Manor, near Ledbury. The name had a slightly familiar sound, though I could not fix it in my mind. Then he began to talk about a duty on hops, about Californian hops, about Los Angeles, where he had been. He was fencing for a topic with which he might gain my affection.

And then, quite suddenly, in the bright light of the street, I saw Florence running. It was like that – Florence running with a face whiter than paper and her hand on the black stuff over her heart. I tell you, my own heart stood still; I tell you I could not move. She rushed in at the swing doors. She looked round that place of rush chairs, cane tables and newspapers. She saw me and opened her lips. She saw the man who was talking to me. She stuck her hands over her face as if she wished to push her eyes out. And she was not there any more.

I could not move; I could not stir a finger. And then that man said:

'By Jove: Florry Hurlbird.' He turned upon me with an oily and uneasy sound meant for a laugh. He was really going to ingratiate himself with me.

'Do you know who that is?' he asked. 'The last time I saw that girl she was coming out of the bedroom of a young man called Jimmy at five o'clock in the morning. In my house at Ledbury. You saw her recognize me.' He was standing on his feet, looking down at me. I don't know what I looked like. At any rate, he gave a sort of gurgle and then stuttered:

'Oh, I say . . .' Those were the last words I ever heard of Mr Bag-shawe's. A long time afterwards I pulled myself out of the lounge and went up to Florence's room. She had not locked the door – for the first time of our married life. She was lying, quite respectably arranged, unlike Mrs Maidan, on her bed. She had a little phial that rightly should have contained nitrate of amyl,[108] in her right hand. That was on the 4th of August, 1913.

Part Three

I

The odd thing is that what sticks out in my recollection of the rest of that evening was Leonora's saying:

'Of course you might marry her,' and, when I asked whom, she answered:

'The girl.'

Now that is to me a very amazing thing – amazing for the light of possibilities that it casts into the human heart. For I had never had the slightest conscious idea of marrying the girl; I never had the slightest idea even of caring for her. I must have talked in an odd way, as people do who are recovering from an anaesthetic. It is as if one had a dual personality, the one I being entirely unconscious of the other. I had thought nothing; I had said such an extraordinary thing.

I don't know that analysis of my own psychology matters at all to this story. I should say that it didn't or, at any rate, that I had given enough of it. But that odd remark of mine had a strong influence upon what came after. I mean, that Leonora would probably never have spoken to me at all about Florence's relations with Edward if I hadn't said, two hours after my wife's death:

'Now I can marry the girl.'

She had, then, taken it for granted that I had been suffering all that she had been suffering, or, at least, that I had permitted all that she had permitted. So that, a month ago, about a week after the funeral of poor Edward, she could say to me in the most natural way in the world – I had been talking about the duration of my stay at Bramshaw – she said with her clear, reflective intonation:

'Oh, stop here for ever and ever if you can.' And then she added, 'You couldn't be more of a brother to me, or more of a counsellor, or more of a support. You are all the consolation I have in the world. And isn't it odd to think that if your wife hadn't been my husband's mistress, you would probably never have been here at all?'

That was how I got the news – full in the face, like that. I didn't say anything and I don't suppose I felt anything, unless maybe it was with that mysterious and unconscious self that underlies most people. Perhaps one day when I am unconscious or walking in my sleep I may go and spit upon poor Edward's grave. It seems about the most unlikely thing I could do; but there it is.

No, I remember no emotion of any sort, but just the clear feeling that one has from time to time when one hears that some Mrs So-and-So is *au mieux*[109] with a certain gentleman. It made things plainer, suddenly, to my curiosity. It was as if I thought, at that moment, of a windy November evening, that, when I came to think it over afterwards, a dozen unexplained things would fit themselves into place. But I wasn't thinking things over then. I remember that distinctly. I was just sitting back, rather stiffly, in a deep arm-chair. That is what I remember. It was twilight.

Bramshaw Manor lies in a little hollow with lawns across it and pine-woods on the fringe of the dip. The immense wind, coming from across the forest, roared overhead. But the view from the window was perfectly quiet and grey. Not a thing stirred, except a couple of rabbits on the extreme edge of the lawn. It was Leonora's own little study that we were in and we were waiting for the tea to be brought. I, as I said, was sitting in the deep chair, Leonora was standing in the window twirling the wooden acorn at the end of the window-blind cord desultorily round and round. She looked across the lawn and said, as far as I can remember:

'Edward has been dead only ten days and yet there are rabbits on the lawn.'

I understand that rabbits do a great deal of harm to the short grass in England. And then she turned round to me and said without any adornment at all, for I remember her exact words:

'I think it was stupid of Florence to commit suicide.'

I cannot tell you the extraordinary sense of leisure that we two seemed to have at that moment. It wasn't as if we were waiting for a train, it wasn't as if we were waiting for a meal – it was just that there was nothing to wait for. Nothing.

There was an extreme stillness with the remote and intermittent sound of the wind. There was the grey light in that brown, small room. And there appeared to be nothing else in the world.

I knew then that Leonora was about to let me into her full confidence. It was as if – or no, it was the actual fact that – Leonora with an odd English sense of decency had determined to wait until Edward had been in his grave for a full week before she spoke. And with some vague motive of giving her an idea of the extent to which she must permit herself to make confidences, I said slowly – and these words too I remember with exactitude –

'Did Florence commit suicide? I didn't know.'

I was just, you understand, trying to let her know that, if she were going to speak she would have to talk about a much wider range of things than she had before thought necessary.

So that that was the first knowledge I had that Florence had committed suicide. It had never entered my head. You may think that I had been singularly lacking in suspiciousness; you may consider me even to have been an imbecile. But consider exactly the position.

In such circumstances of clamour, of outcry, of the crash of many people running together, of the professional reticence of such people as hotel-keepers, the traditional reticence of such 'good people' as the Ashburnhams – in such circumstances it is some little material object, always, that catches the eye and that appeals to the imagination. I had no possible guide to the idea of suicide and the sight of the little flask of nitrate of amyl in Florence's hand suggested instantly to my mind the idea of the failure of her heart. Nitrate of amyl, you understand, is the drug that is given to relieve sufferers from *angina pectoris*.[110]

Seeing Florence, as I had seen her, running with a white face and with one hand held over her heart, and seeing her, as I immediately afterwards saw her, lying upon her bed with the so familiar little brown flask clenched in her fingers, it was natural enough for my mind to frame the idea. As happened now and again, I thought, she had gone out without her remedy and, having felt an attack coming on whilst she was in the gardens, she had run in to get the nitrate in order, as quickly as possible, to obtain relief. And it was equally inevitable my mind should frame the thought that her heart, unable to stand the strain of the running, should have broken in her side. How could I have known that, during all the years of our married life, that little brown flask had contained, not nitrate of amyl, but prussic acid? It was inconceivable.

Why, not even Edward Ashburnham, who was, after all more intimate with her than I was, had an inkling of the truth. He just thought that she had dropped dead of heart disease. Indeed, I fancy that the only people who ever knew that Florence had committed suicide were Leonora, the Grand Duke, the head of the police and the hotel-keeper. I mention these last three because my recollection of that night is only the sort of pinkish effulgence from the electric lamps in the hotel lounge. There seemed to bob into my consciousness, like floating globes, the faces of those three. Now it would be the bearded, monarchical, benevolent head of the Grand Duke; then the sharp-featured, brown, cavalry-moustached features of the chief of police; then the globular, polished and high-collared vacuousness that represented Monsieur Schontz, the proprietor of the hotel. At times one head would be there alone, at another the spiked helmet of the official would be close to the healthy baldness of the prince; then M. Schontz's oiled locks would push in between the two. The sovereign's soft, exquisitely trained voice would say, '*Ja, ja, ja!*' each word dropping out like so many soft pellets of suet; the subdued rasp of the official would come: '*Zum Befehl, Durchlaucht,*'[111] like five revolver-shots; the voice of M. Schontz would go on and on under its breath like that of an unclean priest reciting from his breviary in the corner of a railway-carriage. That was how it presented itself to me.

They seemed to take no notice of me; I don't suppose that I was even addressed by one of them. But, as long as one or the other, or all three of them were there, they stood between me as if I, being the titular possessor of the corpse, had a right to be present at their conferences. Then they all went away and I was left alone for a long time.

And I thought nothing; absolutely nothing. I had no ideas; I had no strength. I felt no sorrow, no desire for action, no inclination to go upstairs and fall upon the body of my wife. I just saw the pink effulgence, the cane tables, the palms, the globular match-holders, the indented ashtrays. And then Leonora came to me and it appears that I addressed to her that singular remark:

'Now I can marry the girl.'

But I have given you absolutely the whole of my recollection of that evening, as it is the whole of my recollection of the succeeding three or four days. I was in a state just simply cataleptic. They put me to bed and I stayed there; they brought me my clothes and I dressed; they led me to an open grave and I stood beside it. If they had taken me to the edge of a river, or if they had flung me beneath a railway train, I should have been drowned or mangled in the same spirit. I was the walking dead.

Well, those are my impressions.

What had actually happened had been this. I pieced it together afterwards. You will remember I said that Edward Ashburnham and the girl had gone off, that night, to a concert at the Casino and that Leonora had asked Florence, almost immediately after their departure, to follow them and to perform the office of chaperone. Florence, you may also remember, was all in black, being the mourning that she wore for a deceased cousin, Jean Hurlbird. It was a very black night and the girl was dressed in cream-coloured muslin, that must have glimmered under the tall trees of the dark park like a phosphorescent fish in a cupboard. You couldn't have had a better beacon.

And it appears that Edward Ashburnham led the girl not up the straight allée that leads to the Casino, but in under the dark trees of the park. Edward Ashburnham told me all this in his final outburst. I have told you that, upon that occasion, he became deucedly vocal. I didn't pump him. I hadn't any motive. At that time I didn't in the least connect him with my wife. But the fellow talked like a cheap novelist. Or like a very good novelist for the matter of that, if it's the business of a novelist to make you see things clearly.[112] And I tell you I see that thing as clearly as if it were a dream that never left me. It appears that, not very far from the Casino, he and the girl sat down in the darkness upon a public bench. The lights from that place of entertainment must have reached them through the tree-trunks, since, Edward said, he could quite plainly see the girl's face – that beloved face with the high forehead, the queer mouth, the tortured eyebrows, and the direct eyes. And to Florence, creeping up behind them, they must have presented the appearance of silhouettes. For I take it that Florence came creeping up behind them over the short grass to a tree that, I quite well remember, was immediately behind that public seat. It was not a very difficult feat for a woman instinct with jealousy. The Casino orchestra was, as Edward remembered to tell me, playing the Rakocsy March,[113] and although it was not loud enough, at that distance, to drown the voice of Edward Ashburnham it was certainly sufficiently audible to efface, amongst the noises of the night, the slight brushings and rustlings that might have been made by the feet of Florence or by her gown in coming over the short grass. And that miserable woman must have got it in the face, good and strong. It must have been horrible for her. Horrible! Well, I suppose she deserved all that she got.

Anyhow, there you have the picture, the immensely tall trees, elms most of them, towering and feathering away up into the black mistiness that trees seem to gather about them at night; the silhouettes of those two upon the seat; the beams of light coming from the Casino, the woman all in black peeping with fear behind the tree-trunk. It is melodrama; but I can't help it.

And then, it appears, something happened to Edward Ashburnham. He assured me – and I see no reason for disbelieving him – that until that moment he had had no idea whatever of caring for the girl. He said that he had regarded her exactly as he would have regarded a daughter. He certainly loved her, but with a very deep, very tender and very tranquil love. He had missed her when she went away to her convent-school; he had been glad when she had returned. But of more than that he had been totally unconscious. Had he been conscious of it, he assured me, he would have fled from it as from a thing accursed. He realized that it was the last outrage upon Leonora. But the real point was his entire unconsciousness. He had gone with her into that dark park with no quickening of the pulse, with no desire for the intimacy of solitude. He had gone, intending to talk about polo-ponies, and tennis-racquets; about the temperament of the rever-end Mother at the convent she had left and about whether her frock for a party when they got home should be white or blue. It hadn't come into his head that they would talk about a single thing that they hadn't always talked about; it had not even come into his head that the tabu which extended around her was not inviolable. And then, suddenly, that –

He was very careful to assure me that at that time there was no physical motive about his declaration. It did not appear to him to be a matter of a dark night and a propinquity and so on. No, it was simply of her effect on the moral side of his life that he appears to have talked. He said that he never had the slightest notion to enfold her in his arms or so much as to touch her hand. He swore that he did not touch her hand. He said that they sat, she at one end of the bench, he at the other; he leaning slightly towards her and she looking straight towards the light of the Casino, her face illuminated by the lamps. The expression upon her face he could only describe as 'queer'.

At another time, indeed, he made it appear that he thought she was glad. It is easy to imagine that she was glad, since at that time she could have had no idea of what was really happening. Frankly, she adored Edward Ashburnham. He was for her, in everything that she said at that time, the model of humanity, the hero, the athlete, the father of his country, the law-giver. So that for her, to be suddenly, intimately and overwhelmingly praised must have been a matter for mere gladness, however overwhelming it were. It must have been as if a god had approved her handiwork or a king her loyalty. She just sat still and listened, smiling.

And it seemed to her that all the bitterness of her childhood, the terrors of her tempestuous father, the bewailings of her cruel-tongued mother were suddenly atoned for. She had her recompense at last. Because, of course, if you come to figure it out, a sudden pouring forth of passion by a man whom you regard as a cross between a pastor and a father might, to a woman, have the aspect of mere praise for good conduct. It wouldn't, I mean, appear at all in the light of an attempt to gain possession. The girl, at least, regarded him as firmly anchored to his Leonora. She had not the slightest inkling of any infidelities. He had always spoken to her of his wife in terms of reverence and deep affection. He had given her the idea that he regarded Leonora as absolutely impeccable and as absolutely satisfying. Their union had appeared to her to be one of those blessed things that are spoken of and contemplated with reverence by her church.

So that, when he spoke of her as being the person he cared most for in the world, she naturally thought that he meant to except Leonora and she was just glad. It was like a father saying that he approved of a marriageable daughter . . . And Edward, when he realized what he was doing, curbed his tongue at once. She was just glad and she went on being just glad.

I suppose that that was the most monstrously wicked thing that Edward Ashburnham ever did in his life. And yet I am so near to all these people that I cannot think any of them wicked. It is impossible of me to think of Edward Ashburnham as anything but straight, upright and honourable. That, I mean, is, in spite of everything, my permanent view of him. I try at times by dwelling on some of the things that he did to push that image of him away, as you might try to push aside a large pendulum. But it always comes back – the memory of his innumerable acts of kindness, of his efficiency, of his unspiteful tongue. He was such a fine fellow.

So I feel myself forced to attempt to excuse him in this as in so many other things. It is, I have no doubt, a most monstrous thing to attempt to corrupt a young girl just out of a convent. But I think Edward had no idea at all of corrupting her. I believe that he simply loved her. He said that that was the way of it and I, at least, believe him and I believe too that she was the only woman he ever really loved. He said that that was so; and he did enough to prove it. And Leonora said that it was so and Leonora knew him to the bottom of his heart.

I have come to be very much of a cynic in these matters; I mean that it is impossible to believe in the permanence of man's or woman's love. Or, at any rate, it is impossible to believe in the permanence of any early passion. As I see it, at least, with regard to men, a love affair, a love for any definite woman – is something in the nature of a widening of the experience. With each new woman that a man is attracted to there appears to come a broadening of the outlook, or, if you like, an acquiring of new territory. A turn of the eyebrow, a tone of the voice, a queer characteristic gesture – all these things, and it is these things that cause to arise the passion of love – all these things are like so many objects on the horizon of the landscape that tempt a man to walk beyond the horizon, to explore. He wants to get, as it were, behind those eyebrows with the peculiar turn, as if he desired to see the world with the eyes that they overshadow. He wants to hear that voice applying itself to every possible proposition, to every possible topic; he wants to see those characteristic gestures against every possible background. Of the question of the sex-instinct I know very little and I do not think that it counts for very much in a really great passion. It can be aroused by such nothings – by an untied shoelace, by a glance of the eye in passing – that I think it might be left out of the calculation. I don't mean to say that any great passion can exist without a desire for consummation. That seems to me to be a commonplace and to be therefore a matter needing no comment at all. It is a thing, with all its accidents, that must be taken for granted, as, in a novel, or a biography, you take it for granted that the characters have their meals with some regularity. But the real fierceness of desire, the real heat of a passion long continued and withering up the soul of a man is the craving for identity with the woman that he loves. He desires to see with the same eyes, to touch with the same sense of touch, to hear with the same ears, to lose his identity, to be enveloped, to be supported. For, whatever may be said of the relation of the sexes, there is no man who loves a woman that does not desire to come to her for the renewal of his courage, for the cutting asunder of his difficulties. And that will be the mainspring of his desire for her. We are all so afraid, we are all so alone, we all so need from the outside the assurance of our own worthiness to exist.

So, for a time, if such a passion come to fruition, the man will get what he wants. He will get the moral support, the encouragement, the relief from the sense of loneliness, the assurance of his own worth. But these things pass away; inevitably they pass away as the shadows pass across sundials. It is sad, but it is so. The pages of the book will become familiar; the beautiful corner of the road will have been turned too many times. Well, this is the saddest story.

And yet I do believe that for every man there comes at last a woman – or no, that is the wrong way of formulating it. For every man there comes at last a time of life when the woman who then sets her seal upon his imagination has set her seal for good. He will travel over no more horizons; he will never again set the knapsack over his shoulders; he will retire from those scenes. He will have gone out of the business.

That at any rate was the case with Edward and the poor girl. It was quite literally the case. It was quite literally the case that his passions – for the mistress of the Grand Duke, for Mrs Basil, for little Mrs Maidan, for Florence, for whom you will – these passions were merely prelimi-nary canters compared to his final race with death for her. I am certain of that. I am not going to be so American as to say that all true love demands some sacrifice. It doesn't. But I think that love will be truer and more permanent in which self-sacrifice has been exacted. And, in the case of the other women, Edward just cut in and cut them out as he did with the polo-ball from under the nose of Count Baron von Lelöffel. I don't mean to say that he didn't wear himself as thin as a lath in the endeavour to capture the other women; but over her he wore himself to rags and tatters and death – in the effort to leave her alone.

And, in speaking to her on that night, he wasn't, I am convinced, committing a baseness. It was as if his passion for her hadn't existed; as if the very words that he spoke, without knowing that he spoke them, created the passion as they went along. Before he spoke, there was nothing; afterwards, it was the integral fact of his life. Well, I must get back to my story.

And my story was concerning itself with Florence – with Florence, who heard those words from behind the tree. That of course is only conjecture, but I think the conjecture is pretty well justified. You have the fact that those two went out, that she followed them almost immediately afterwards through the darkness and, a little later, she came running back to the hotel with that pallid face and the hand clutching her dress over her heart. It can't have been only Bagshawe. Her face was contorted with agony before ever her eyes fell upon me or upon him beside me. But I dare say Bagshawe may have been the determining influence in her suicide. Leonora says that she had that flask, apparently of nitrate of amyl, but actually of prussic acid, for many years and that she was determined to use it if ever I discovered the nature of her relationship with that fellow Jimmy. You see, the mainspring of her nature must have been vanity. There is no reason why it shouldn't have been; I guess it is vanity that makes most of us keep straight, if we do keep straight, in this world.

If it had been merely a matter of Edward's relations with the girl I dare say Florence would have faced it out. She would no doubt have made him scenes, have threatened him, have appealed to his sense of humour, to his promises. But Mr Bagshawe and the fact that the date was the 4th of August must have been too much for her superstitious mind. You see, she had two things that she wanted. She wanted to be a great lady, installed in Bramshaw Teleragh. She wanted also to retain my respect.

She wanted, that is to say, to retain my respect for as long as she lived with me. I suppose, if she had persuaded Edward Ashburnham to bolt with her she would have let the whole thing go with a run. Or perhaps she would have tried to exact from me a new respect for the greatness of her passion on the lines of all for love and the world well lost.[114] That would be just like Florence.

In all matrimonial associations there is, I believe, one constant factor – a desire to deceive the person with whom one lives as to some weak spot in one's character or in one's career. For it is intolerable to live constantly with one human being who perceives one's small meannesses. It is really death to do so – that is why so many marriages turn out unhappily.

I, for instance, am a rather greedy man; I have a taste for good cookery and a watering tooth at the mere sound of the names of certain comestibles. If Florence had discovered this secret of mine I should have found her knowledge of it so unbearable that I never could have supported all the other privations of the régime that she extracted from me. I am bound to say that Florence never discovered this secret.

Certainly she never alluded to it; I dare say she never took sufficient interest in me.

And the secret weakness of Florence – the weakness that she could not bear to have me discover, was just that early escapade with the fellow called Jimmy. Let me, as this is in all probability the last time I shall mention Florence's name, dwell a little upon the change that had taken place in her psychology. She would not, I mean, have minded if I had discovered that she was the mistress of Edward Ashburnham. She would rather have liked it. Indeed, the chief trouble of poor Leonora in those days was to keep Florence from making, before me, theatrical displays, on one line or another, of that very fact. She wanted, in one mood, to come rushing to me, to cast herself on her knees at my feet and to declaim a carefully arranged, frightfully emotional, outpouring as to her passion. That was to show that she was like one of the great erotic women of whom history tells us. In another mood she would desire to come to me disdainfully and to tell me that I was considerably less than a man and that what had happened was what must happen when a real male came along. She wanted to say that in cool, balanced and sarcastic sentences. That was when she wished to appear like the heroine of a French comedy. Because of course she was always play acting.

But what she didn't want me to know was the fact of her first escapade with the fellow called Jimmy. She had arrived at figuring out the sort of low-down Bowery[115] tough that that fellow was. Do you know what it is to shudder, in later life, for some small, stupid action – usually for some small, quite genuine piece of emotionalism – of your early life? Well, it was that sort of shuddering that came over Florence at the thought that she had surrendered to such a low fellow. I don't know that she need have shuddered. It was her footling old uncle's work; he ought never to have taken those two round the world together and shut himself up in his cabin for the greater part of the time. Anyhow, I am convinced that the sight of Mr Bagshawe and the thought that Mr Bagshawe – for she knew that unpleasant and toadlike personality – the thought that Mr Bagshawe would almost certainly reveal to me that he had caught her coming out of Jimmy's bedroom at five o'clock in the morning on the 4th of August, 1900 – that was the determining influence in her suicide. And no doubt the effect of the date was too much for her superstitious personality. She had been born on the 4th of August; she had started to go round the world on the 4th of August; she had become a low fellow's mistress on the 4th of August. On the same day of the year she had married me; on that 4th she had lost Edward's love, and Bagshawe had appeared like a sinister omen – like a grin on the face of Fate. It was the last straw. She ran upstairs, arranged herself decoratively upon her bed – she was a sweetly pretty woman with smooth pink and white cheeks, long hair, the eyelashes falling like a tiny curtain on her cheeks. She drank the little phial of prussic acid and there she lay – oh, extremely charming and clear-cut – looking with a puzzled expression at the electric-light bulb that hung from the ceiling, or perhaps through it, to the stars above. Who knows? Anyhow, there was an end of Florence.

You have no idea how quite extraordinarily for me that was the end of Florence. From that day to this I have never given her another thought; I have not bestowed upon her so much as a sigh. Of course, when it has been necessary to talk about her to Leonora, or when for the purpose of these writings I have tried to figure her out, I have thought about her as I might do about a problem in algebra. But it has always been as a matter for study, not for remembrance. She just went completely out of existence, like yesterday's paper.

I was so deadly tired. And I dare say that my week or ten days of *affaisement*[116] – of what was practically catalepsy – was just the repose that my exhausted nature claimed after twelve years of the repression of my instincts, after twelve years of playing the trained poodle. For that was all that I had been. I suppose that it was the shock that did it – the several shocks. But I am unwilling to attribute my feelings at that time to anything so concrete as a shock. It was a feeling so tranquil. It was as if an immensely heavy – an unbearably heavy knapsack, supported upon my shoulders by straps, had fallen off and left my shoulders themselves that the straps had cut into, numb and without sensation of life. I tell you, I had no regret. What had I to regret? I suppose that my inner soul – my dual personality – had realized long before that Florence was a personality of paper – that she represented a real human being with a heart, with feelings, with sympathies and with emotions only as a banknote represents a certain quantity of gold. I know that sort of feeling came to the surface in me the moment the man Bagshawe told me that he had seen her coming out of that fellow's bedroom. I thought suddenly that she wasn't real; she was just a mass of talk out of guidebooks, of drawings out of fashion-plates. It is even possible that, if that feeling had not possessed me, I should have run up sooner to her room and might have prevented her drinking the prussic acid. But I just couldn't do it; it would have been like chasing a scrap of paper – an occupation ignoble for a grown man.

And, as it began, so that matter has remained. I didn't care whether she had come out of that bedroom or whether she hadn't. It simply didn't interest me. Florence didn't matter.

I suppose you will retort that I was in love with Nancy Rufford and that my indifference was therefore discreditable. Well, I am not seeking to avoid discredit. I was in love with Nancy Rufford as I am in love with the poor child's memory, quietly and quite tenderly in my American sort of way. I had never thought about it until I heard Leonora state that I might now marry her. But, from that moment until her worse than death, I do not suppose that I much thought about anything else. I don't mean to say that I sighed about her or groaned; I just wanted to marry her as some people want to go to Carcassonne.

Do you understand the feeling – the sort of feeling that you must get certain matters out of the way, smooth out certain fairly negligible complications before you can go to a place that has, during all your life, been a sort of dream city? I didn't attach much importance to my superior years. I was forty-five, and she, poor thing, was only just rising twenty-two. But she was older than her years and quieter. She seemed to have an odd quality of sainthood, as if she must inevitably end in a convent with a white coif framing her face. But she had frequently told me that she had no vocation; it just simply wasn't there – the desire to become a nun. Well, I guess that I was a sort of convent myself; it seemed fairly proper that she should make her vows to me.

No, I didn't see any impediment on the score of age. I dare say no man does and I was pretty confident that with a little preparation, I could make a young girl happy. I could spoil her as few young girls have ever been spoiled; and I couldn't regard myself as personally repulsive. No man can, or if he ever comes to do so, that is the end of him. But, as soon as I came out of my catalepsy, I seemed to perceive that my problem – that what I had to do to prepare myself for getting into contact with her, was just to get back into contact with life. I had been kept for twelve years in a rarefied atmosphere; what I then had to do was a little fighting with real life, some wrestling with men of business, some travelling amongst larger cities, something harsh, some-thing masculine. I didn't want to present myself to Nancy Rufford as a sort of an old maid. That was why, just a fortnight after Florence's suicide, I set off for the United States.

II

Immediately after Florence's death Leonora began to put the leash upon Nancy Rufford and Edward. She had guessed what had happened under the trees near the Casino. They stayed at Nauheim some weeks after I went, and Leonora has told me that that was the most deadly time of her existence. It seemed like a long, silent duel with invisible weapons, so she said. And it was rendered all the more difficult by the girl's entire innocence. For Nancy was always trying to go off alone with Edward – as she had been doing all her life, whenever she was home for holidays. She just wanted him to say nice things to her again.

You see, the position was extremely complicated. It was as complicated as it well could be, along delicate lines. There was the complication caused by the fact that Edward and Leonora never spoke to each other except when other people were present. Then, as I have said, their demeanours were quite perfect. There was the complication caused by the girl's entire innocence; there was the further complication that both Edward and Leonora really regarded the girl as their daughter. Or it might be more precise to say that they regarded her as being Leonora's daughter. And Nancy was a queer girl; it is very difficult to describe her to you.

She was tall and strikingly thin; she had a tortured mouth, agonized eyes, and a quite extraordinary sense of fun. You might put it that at times she was exceedingly grotesque and at times extraordinarily beautiful. Why, she had the heaviest head of black hair that I have ever come across; I used to wonder how she could bear the weight of it. She was just over twenty-one and at times she seemed as old as the hills, at times not much more than sixteen. At one moment she would be talking of the lives of the saints and at the next she would be tumbling all over the lawn with the St Bernard puppy. She could ride to hounds like a Maenad[117] and she could sit for hours perfectly still, steeping handkerchief after handkerchief in vinegar when Leonora had one of her headaches. She was, in short, a miracle of patience who could be almost miraculously impatient. It was, no doubt, the convent training that effected that. I remember that one of her letters to me, when she was about sixteen, ran something like:

'On Corpus Christi'[118] – or it may have been some other saint's day, I cannot keep those things in my head – 'our school played Roehampton[119] at hockey. And, seeing that our side was losing, being three goals to one against us at halftime, we retired into the chapel and prayed for victory. We won by five goals to three.' And I remember that she seemed to describe afterwards a sort of saturnalia. Apparently, when the victorious fifteen or eleven came into the refectory for supper, the whole school jumped upon the tables and cheered and broke the chairs on the floor and smashed the crockery – for a given time, until the Reverend Mother rang a hand-bell. That is of course the Catholic tradition – saturnalia that can end in a moment, like the crack of a whip. I don't, of course, like the tradition, but I am bound to say that it gave Nancy – or at any rate Nancy had – a sense of rectitude that I have never seen surpassed. It was a thing like a knife that looked out of her eyes and that spoke with her voice, just now and then. It positively frightened me. I suppose that I was almost afraid to be in a world where there could be so fine a standard. I remember when she was about fifteen or sixteen on going back to the convent I once gave her a couple of English sovereigns as a tip. She thanked me in a peculiarly heartfelt way, saying that it would come in extremely handy. I asked her why and she explained. There was a rule at the school that the pupils were not to speak when they walked through the garden from the chapel to the refectory. And, since this rule appeared to be idiotic and arbitrary, she broke it on purpose day after day. In the evening the children were all asked if they had committed any faults during the day, and every evening Nancy confessed that she had broken this particular rule. It cost her sixpence a time, that being the fine attached to the offence. Just for the information I asked her why she always confessed, and she answered in these exact words:

'Oh, well, the girls of the Holy Child have always been noted for their truthfulness. It's a beastly bore, but I've got to do it.'

I dare say that the miserable nature of her childhood, coming before the mixture of saturnalia and discipline that was her convent life, added something to her queernesses. Her father was a violent madman of a fellow, a major of one of what I believe are called the Highland regiments. He didn't drink, but he had an ungovernable temper, and the first thing that Nancy could remember was seeing her father strike her mother with his clenched fist so that her mother fell over sideways from the breakfast table and lay motionless. The mother was no doubt an irritating woman and the privates of that regiment appeared to have been irritating, too, so that the house was a place of outcries and perpetual disturbances. Mrs Rufford was Leonora's dearest friend and Leonora could be cutting enough at times. But I fancy she was as nothing to Mrs Rufford. The Major would come in to lunch harassed and already spitting out oaths after an unsatisfactory morning's drilling of his stubborn men beneath a hot sun. And then Mrs Rufford would make some cutting remark and pandemonium would break loose. Once, when she had been about twelve, Nancy had tried to intervene between the pair of them. Her father had struck her full upon the forehead a blow so terrible that she had lain unconscious for three days. Nevertheless, Nancy seemed to prefer her father to her mother. She remembered rough kindnesses from him. Once or twice when she had been quite small he had dressed her in a clumsy, impatient, but very tender way. It was nearly always impossible to get a servant to stay in the family and, for days at a time, apparently, Mrs Rufford would be incapable. I fancy she drank. At any rate, she had so cutting a tongue that even Nancy was afraid of her – she so made fun of any tenderness, she so sneered at all emotional displays. Nancy must have been a very emotional child.

Then one day, quite suddenly, on her return from a ride at Fort William,[120] Nancy had been sent, with her governess, who had a white face, right down South to that convent school. She had been expecting to go there in two months' time. Her mother disappeared from her life at that time. A fortnight later Leonora came to the convent and told her that her mother was dead. Perhaps she was. At any rate, I never heard until the very end what became of Mrs Rufford. Leonora never spoke of her.

And then Major Rufford went to India, from which he returned very seldom and only for very short visits; and Nancy lived herself gradually into the life at Bramshaw Teleragh. I think that, from that time onwards, she led a very happy life, till the end. There were dogs and horses and old servants and the Forest. And there were Edward and Leonora, who loved her.

I had known her all the time – I mean, that she always came to the Ashburnhams' at Nauheim for the last fortnight of their stay – and I watched her gradually growing. She was very cheerful with me. She always even kissed me, night and morning, until she was about eighteen. And she would skip about and fetch me things and laugh at my tales of life in Philadelphia. But, beneath her gaiety, I fancy that there lurked some terrors. I remember one day, when she was just eighteen, during one of her father's rare visits to Europe, we were sitting in the gardens, near the iron-stained fountain. Leonora had one of her headaches and we were waiting for Florence and Edward to come from their baths. You have no idea how beautiful Nancy looked that morning.

We were talking about the desirability of taking tickets in lotteries – of the moral side of it, I mean. She was all in white, and so tall and fragile; and she had only just put her hair up, so that the carriage of her neck had that charming touch of youth and of unfamiliarity. Over her throat there played the reflection from a little pool of water, left by a thunderstorm of the night before, and all the rest of her features were in the diffused and luminous shade of her white parasol. Her dark hair just showed beneath her broad, white hat of pierced, chip straw; her throat was very long and leaned forward, and her eyebrows, arching a little as she laughed at some old-fashionedness in my phraseology, had abandoned their tense line. And there was a little colour in her cheeks and light in her deep blue eyes. And to think that that vivid white thing, that saintly and swanlike being – to think that . . . Why, she was like the sail of a ship, so white and so definite in her movements. And to think that she will never . . . Why, she will never do anything again. I can't believe it . . .

Anyhow, we were chattering away about the morality of lotteries.

And then, suddenly, there came from the arcades behind us the over-tones of her father's unmistakable voice; it was as if a modified foghorn had boomed with a reed inside it. I looked round to catch sight of him. A tall, fair, stiffly upright man of fifty, he was walking away with an Italian baron who had had much to do with the Belgian Congo. They must have been talking about the proper treatment of natives, for I heard him say:

'Oh, hang humanity!'[121]

When I looked again at Nancy her eyes were closed and her face was more pallid than her dress, which had at least some pinkish reflections from the gravel. It was dreadful to see her with her eyes closed like that.

'Oh!' she exclaimed, and her hand that had appeared to be groping, settled for a moment on my arm. 'Never speak of it. Promise never to tell my father of it. It brings back those dreadful dreams . . .' And, when she opened her eyes she looked straight into mine. 'The blessed saints,' she said, 'you would think they would spare you such things. I don't believe all the sinning in the world could make one deserve them.'

They say the poor thing was always allowed a light at night, even in her bedroom . . . And yet, no young girl could more archly and lovingly have played with an adored father. She was always holding him by both coat lapels; cross-questioning him as to how he spent his time; kissing the top of his head. Ah, she was well-bred, if ever anyone was.

The poor, wretched man cringed before her – but she could not have done more to put him at his ease. Perhaps she had had lessons in it at her convent. It was only that peculiar note of his voice, used when he was overbearing or dogmatic, that could unman her – and that was only visible when it came unexpectedly. That was because the bad dreams that the blessed saints allowed her to have for her sins always seemed to her to herald themselves by the booming sound of her father's voice. It was that sound that had always preceded his entrance for the terrible lunches of her childhood . . .

I have reported, earlier in this chapter, that Leonora said, during that remainder of their stay at Nauheim, after I had left, it had seemed to her that she was fighting a long duel with unseen weapons against silent adversaries. Nancy, as I have also said, was always trying to go off with

Edward alone. That had been her habit for years. And Leonora found it to be her duty to stop that. It was very difficult. Nancy was used to having her own way, and for years she had been used to going off with Edward, ratting, rabbiting, catching salmon down at Fordingbridge, district-visiting of the sort that Edward indulged in, or calling on the tenants. And at Nauheim she and Edward had always gone up to the Casino alone in the evenings – at any rate, whenever Florence did not call for his attendance. It shows the obviously innocent nature of the regard of those two that even Florence had never had any idea of jealousy. Leonora had cultivated the habit of going to bed at ten o'clock.

I don't know how she managed it, but, for all the time they were at Nauheim, she contrived never to let those two be alone together, except in broad daylight, in very crowded places. If a Protestant had done that it would no doubt have awakened a self-consciousness in the girl. But Catholics, who have always reservations and queer spots of secrecy, can manage these things better. And I dare say that two things made this easier – the death of Florence and the fact that Edward was obviously sickening. He appeared, indeed, to be very ill; his shoulders began to be bowed; there were pockets under his eyes; he had extraordinary moments of inattention.

And Leonora describes herself as watching him as a fierce cat watches an unconscious pigeon in a roadway. In that silent watching, again, I think she was a Catholic – of a people that can think thoughts alien to ours and keep them to themselves. And the thoughts passed through her mind; some of them even got through to Edward with never a word spoken. At first she thought that it might be remorse, or grief, for the death of Florence that was oppressing him. But she watched and watched, and uttered apparently random sentences about Florence before the girl, and she perceived that he had no grief and no remorse. He had not any idea that Florence could have committed suicide without writing at least a tirade to him. The absence of that made him certain that it had been heart disease. For Florence had never undeceived him on that point. She thought it made her seem more romantic.

No, Edward had no remorse. He was able to say to himself that he had treated Florence with gallant attentiveness of the kind that she desired until two hours before her death. Leonora gathered that from the look in his eyes, and from the way he straightened his shoulders over her as she lay in her coffin – from that and a thousand other little things. She would speak suddenly about Florence to the girl and he would not start in the least; he would not even pay attention, but would sit with bloodshot eyes gazing at the tablecloth. He drank a good deal, at that time – a steady soaking of drink every evening till long after they had gone to bed.

For Leonora made the girl go to bed at ten, unreasonable though that seemed to Nancy. She would understand that, whilst they were in a sort of half mourning for Florence, she ought not to be seen at public places, like the Casino; but she could not see why she should not accompany her uncle upon his evening strolls through the park. I don't know what Leonora put up as an excuse – something, I fancy, in the nature of a nightly orison that she made the girl and herself perform for the soul of Florence. And then, one evening, about a fortnight later, when the girl, growing restive at even devotional exercises, clamoured once more to be allowed to go for a walk with Edward, and when Leonora was really at her wits' end, Edward gave himself into her hands. He was just standing up from dinner and had his face averted.

But he turned his heavy head and his bloodshot eyes upon his wife and looked full at her.

'Doctor von Hauptmann,' he said, 'has ordered me to go to bed immediately after dinner. My heart's much worse.'

He continued to look at Leonora for a long minute – with a sort of heavy contempt. And Leonora understood that, with his speech, he was giving her the excuse that she needed for separating him from the girl, and with his eyes he was reproaching her for thinking that he would try to corrupt Nancy.

He went silently up to his room and sat there for a long time – until the girl was well in bed – reading in the Anglican prayer-book. And about half-past ten she heard his footsteps pass her door, going outwards. Two and a half hours later they came back, stumbling heavily.

She remained, reflecting upon this position until the last night of their stay at Nauheim. Then she suddenly acted. For, just in the same way, suddenly after dinner, she looked at him and said:

'Teddy, don't you think you could take a night off from your doctor's orders and go with Nancy to the Casino. The poor child has had her visit so spoiled.'

He looked at her in turn for a long, balancing minute.

'Why, yes,' he said at last.

Nancy jumped out of her chair and kissed him.

Those two words, Leonora said, gave her the greatest relief of any two syllables she had ever heard in her life. For she realized that Edward was breaking up, not under the desire for possession, but from the dogged determination to hold his hand. She could relax some of her vigilance.

Nevertheless, she sat in the darkness behind her half-closed jalousies, looking over the street and the night and the trees until, very late, she could hear Nancy's clear voice coming closer and saying:

'You did look an old guy with that false nose.'

There had been some sort of celebration of a local holiday up in the *Kursaal*. And Edward replied with his sort of sulky good nature:

'As for you, you looked like old Mother Sideacher.'

The girl came swinging along, a silhouette beneath a gas-lamp; Edward, another, slouched at her side. They were talking just as they had talked any time since the girl had been seventeen; with the same tones, the same joke about an old beggar woman who always amused them at Bramshaw. The girl, a little later, opened Leonora's door whilst she was still kissing Edward on the forehead as she had done every night.

'We've had a most glorious time,' she said. 'He's ever so much better. He raced me for twenty yards home. Why are you all in the dark?'

Leonora could hear Edward going about in his room, but, owing to the girl's chatter, she could not tell whether he went out again or not. And then, very much later, because she thought that if he were drinking again something must be done to stop it, she opened for the first time, and very softly, the never-opened door between their rooms. She wanted to see if he had gone out again. Edward was kneeling beside his bed with his head hidden in the counterpane. His arms, outstretched, held out before him a little image of the Blessed Virgin – a tawdry, scarlet and Prussian blue affair that the girl had given him on her first return from the convent. His shoulders heaved convulsively three times, and heavy sobs came from him before she could close the door. He was not a Catholic; but that was the way it took him.

Leonora slept for the first time that night with a sleep from which she never once started.

III

And then Leonora completely broke down – on the day that they returned to Bramshaw Teleragh. It is the infliction of our miserable minds – it is the scourge of atrocious but probably just destiny that no grief comes by itself. No, any great grief, though the grief itself may have gone, leaves in its place a train of horrors, of misery, and despair. For Leonora was, in herself, relieved. She felt that she could trust Edward with the girl and she knew that Nancy could be absolutely trusted. And then, with the slackening of her vigilance, came the slackening of her entire mind. This is perhaps the most miserable part of the entire story. For it is miserable to see a clean intelligence waver; and Leonora wavered.

You are to understand that Leonora loved Edward with a passion that was yet like an agony of hatred. And she had lived with him for years and years without addressing to him one word of tenderness. I don't know how she could do it. At the beginning of that relationship she had been just married off to him. She had been one of seven daughters in a bare, untidy Irish manor-house to which she had returned from the convent I have so often spoken of. She had left it just a year and she was just nineteen. It is impossible to imagine such inexperience as was hers. You might almost say that she had never spoken to a man except a priest. Coming straight from the convent, she had gone in behind the high walls of the manor-house that was almost more cloistral than any convent could have been. There were the seven girls, there was the strained mother, there was the worried father at whom, three times in the course of that year, the tenants took pot-shots from behind a hedge. The women-folk, upon the whole, the tenants respected. Once a week each of the girls, since there were seven of them, took a drive with the mother in the old basketwork chaise drawn by a very fat, very lumbering pony. They paid occasionally a call, but even these were so rare that, Leonora has assured me, only three times in the year that succeeded her coming home from the convent did she enter another person's house. For the rest of the time the seven sisters ran about in the neglected gardens between the unpruned espaliers. Or they played lawn-tennis or fives in an angle of a great wall that surrounded the garden – an angle from which the fruit trees had long died away. They painted in water-colour; they embroidered; they copied verses into albums. Once a week they went to Mass; once a week to the confessional, accompanied by an old nurse. They were happy since they had known no other life.

It appeared to them a singular extravagance when, one day, a photographer was brought over from the county town and photographed them standing, all seven, in the shadow of an old apple tree with the grey lichen on the raddled trunk.

But it wasn't an extravagance.

Three weeks before Colonel Powys had written to Colonel Ashburnham:

'I say, Harry, couldn't your Edward marry one of my girls? It would be a godsend to me, for I'm at the end of my tether and, once one girl begins to go off, the rest of them will follow.'

He went on to say that all his daughters were tall, upstanding, clean-limbed and absolutely pure, and he reminded Colonel Ashburnham that, they having been married on the same day, though in different churches, since the one was a Catholic and the other an Anglican – they had said to each other, the night before, that, when the time came, one of their sons should marry one of their daughters. Mrs Ashburnham had been a Powys and remained Mrs Powys' dearest friend. They had drifted about the world as English soldiers do, seldom meeting, but their women always in correspondence one with another. They wrote about minute things such as the teething of Edward and of the earlier daughters or the best way to repair a Jacob's ladder in a stocking. And, if they met seldom, yet it was often enough to keep each other's personalities fresh in their minds, gradually growing a little stiff in the joints, but always with enough to talk about and with a store of reminiscences. Then, as his girls began to come of an age when they must leave the convent in which they were regularly interned during his years of active service, Colonel Powys retired from the army with the necessity of making a home for them. It happened that the Ashburnhams had never seen any of the Powys girls, though, whenever the four parents met in London, Edward Ashburnham was always of the party. He was at that time twenty-two and, I believe, almost as pure in mind as Leonora herself. It is odd how a boy can have his virgin intelligence untouched in this world.

That was partly due to the careful handling of his mother, partly to the fact that the house to which he went at Winchester[122] had a particularly pure tone and partly to Edward's own peculiar aversion from anything like coarse language or gross stories. At Sandhurst[123] he had just kept out of the way of that sort of thing. He was keen on soldiering, keen on mathematics, on land-surveying, on politics and, by a queer warp of his mind, on literature. Even when he was twenty-two he would pass hours reading one of Scott's novels or the *Chronicles of Froissart*.[124]

Mrs Ashburnham considered that she was to be congratulated, and almost every week she wrote to Mrs Powys, dilating upon her satisfaction.

Then, one day, taking a walk down Bond Street with her son, after having been at Lord's,[125] she noticed Edward suddenly turn his head round to take a second look at a well-dressed girl who had passed them. She wrote about that, too, to Mrs Powys, and expressed some alarm. It had been, on Edward's part, the merest reflex action. He was so very abstracted at that time owing to the pressure his crammer was putting upon him that he certainly hadn't known what he was doing.

It was this letter of Mrs Ashburnham's to Mrs Powys that had caused the letter from Colonel Powys to Colonel Ashburnham – a letter that was half-humorous, half longing. Mrs Ashburnham caused her husband to reply, with a letter a little more jocular – something to the effect that Colonel Powys ought to give them some idea of the goods that he was marketing. That was the cause of the photograph. I have seen it, the seven girls, all in white dresses, all very much alike in feature – all, except Leonora, a little heavy about the chins and a little stupid about the eyes. I dare say it would have made Leonora, too, look a little heavy and a little stupid, for it was not a good photograph. But the black shadow from one of the branches of the apple tree cut right across her face, which is all but invisible.

There followed an extremely harassing time for Colonel and Mrs Powys. Mrs Ashburnham had written to say that, quite sincerely, nothing would give greater ease to her maternal anxieties than to have her son marry one of Mrs Powys' daughters if only he showed some inclination to do so. For, she added, nothing but a love-match was to be thought of in her Edward's case. But the poor Powys couple had to run things so very fine that even the bringing together of the young people was a desperate hazard.

The mere expenditure upon sending one of the girls over from Ireland to Bramshaw was terrifying to them; and whichever girl they selected might not be the one to ring Edward's bell. On the other hand, the expenditure upon mere food and extra sheets for a visit from the Ashburnhams to them was terrifying, too. It would mean, mathematically, going short in so many meals themselves, afterwards. Nevertheless, they chanced it, and all the three Ashburnhams came on a visit to the lonely manor-house. They could give Edward some rough shooting, some rough fishing and a whirl of femininity; but I should say the girls made really more impression upon Mrs Ashburnham than upon Edward himself. They appeared to her to be so clean run and so safe. They were indeed so clean run that, in a faint sort of way, Edward seems to have regarded them rather as boys than as girls. And then, one evening, Mrs Ashburnham had with her boy one of those conversations that English mothers have with English sons. It seems to have been a criminal sort of proceeding, though I don't know what took place at it. Anyhow, next morning Colonel Ashburnham asked on behalf of his son for the hand of Leonora. This caused some consternation to the Powys couple, since Leonora was the third daughter and Edward ought to have married the eldest. Mrs Powys, with her rigid sense of the proprieties, almost wished to reject the proposal. But the Colonel, her husband, pointed out that the visit would have cost them sixty pounds, what with the hire of an extra servant, of a horse and car, and with the purchase of beds and bedding and extra tablecloths. There was nothing else for it but the marriage. In that way Edward and Leonora became man and wife.

I don't know that a very minute study of their progress towards complete disunion is necessary. Perhaps it is. But there are many things that I cannot well make out, about which I cannot well question Leonora, or about which Edward did not tell me. I do not know that there was ever any question of love from Edward to her. He regarded her, certainly, as desirable amongst her sisters. He was obstinate to the extent of saying that if he could not have her he would not have any of them. And, no doubt, before the marriage, he made her pretty speeches out of books that he had read. But, as far as he could describe his feelings at all, later, it seems that, calmly and without any quickening of the pulse, he just carried the girl off, there being no opposition. It had, however, been all so long ago that it seemed to him, at the end of his poor life, a dim and misty affair. He had the greatest admiration for Leonora.

He had the very greatest admiration. He admired her for her truthfulness, for her cleanness of mind, and the clean-run-ness of her limbs, for her efficiency, for the fairness of her skin, for the gold of her hair, for her religion, for her sense of duty. It was a satisfaction to take her about with him.

But she had not for him a touch of magnetism. I suppose, really, he did not love her because she was never mournful; what really made him feel good in life was to comfort somebody who would be darkly and mysteriously mournful. That he had never had to do for Leonora. Perhaps, also, she was at first too obedient. I do not mean to say that she was submissive – that she deferred, in her judgements, to his. She did not. But she had been handed over to him, like some patient medieval virgin; she had been taught all her life that the first duty of a woman is to obey. And there she was.

In her, at least, admiration for his qualities very soon became love of the deepest description. If his pulses never quickened she, so I have been told, became what is called an altered being when he approached her from the other side of a dancing-floor. Her eyes followed him about full of trustfulness, of admiration, of gratitude, and of love. He was also, in a great sense, her pastor and guide – and he guided her into what, for a girl straight out of a convent, was almost heaven. I have not the least idea of what an English officer's wife's existence may be like. At any rate, there were feasts, and chatterings, and nice men who gave her the right sort of admiration, and nice women who treated her as if she had been a baby. And her confessor approved of her life, and Edward let her give little treats to the girls of the convent she had left, and the Reverend Mother approved of him. There could not have been a happier girl for five or six years.

For it was only at the end of that time that clouds began, as the saying is, to arise. She was then about twenty-three, and her purposeful efficiency made her perhaps have a desire for mastery. She began to perceive that Edward was extravagant in his largesses. His parents died just about that time, and Edward, though they both decided that he should continue his soldiering, gave a great deal of attention to the management of Bramshaw through a steward. Aldershot[126] was not very far away, and they spent all his leaves there.

And, suddenly, she seemed to begin to perceive that his generosities were almost fantastic. He subscribed much too much to things connected with his mess, he pensioned off his father's servants, old or new, much too generously. They had a large income, but every now and then they would find themselves hard up. He began to talk of mortgaging a farm or two, though it never actually came to that.

She made tentative efforts at remonstrating with him. Her father, whom she saw now and then, said that Edward was much too generous to his tenants; the wives of his brother officers remonstrated with her in private; his large subscriptions made it difficult for their husbands to keep up with them. Ironically enough, the first real trouble between them came from his desire to build a Roman Catholic chapel at Bramshaw. He wanted to do it to honour Leonora, and he proposed to do it very expensively. Leonora did not want it; she could perfectly well drive from Bramshaw to the nearest Catholic Church as often as she liked. There were no Roman Catholic tenants and no Roman Catholic servants except her old nurse who could always drive with her. She had as many priests to stay with her as could be needed – and even the priests did not want a gorgeous chapel in that place where it would have merely seemed an invidious instance of ostentation. They were perfectly ready to celebrate Mass for Leonora and her nurse, when they stayed at Bramshaw, in a cleaned-up outhouse. But Edward was as obstinate as a hog about it.

He was truly grieved at his wife's want of sentiment – at her refusal to receive that amount of public homage from him. She appeared to him to be wanting in imagination – to be cold and hard. I don't exactly know what part her priests played in the tragedy that it all became; I dare say they behaved quite creditably but mistakenly. But then, who would not have been mistaken with Edward? I believe he was even hurt that Leonora's confessor did not make strenuous efforts to convert him. There was a period when he was quite ready to become an emotional Catholic.

I don't know why they did not take him on the hop; but they have queer sorts of wisdoms, those people, and queer sorts of tact. Perhaps they thought that Edward's too early conversion would frighten off other Protestant desirables from marrying Catholic girls. Perhaps they saw deeper into Edward than he saw himself and thought that he would make a not very creditable convert. At any rate they – and Leonora – left him very much alone. It mortified him very considerably. He has told me that if Leonora had then taken his aspirations seriously everything would have been different. But I dare say that was nonsense.

At any rate, it was over the question of the chapel that they had their first and really disastrous quarrel. Edward at that time was not well; he supposed himself to be overworked with his regimental affairs – he was managing the mess at the time. And Leonora was not well – she was beginning to fear that their union might be sterile. And then her father came over from Glasmoyle[127] to stay with them.

Those were troublesome times in Ireland, I understand. At any rate, Colonel Powys had tenants on the brain – his own tenants having shot at him with shot-guns. And, in conversation with Edward's land-steward, he got it into his head that Edward managed his estates with a mad generosity towards his tenants. I understand, also, that those years – the 'nineties – were very bad for farming.[128] Wheat was fetching only a few shillings the hundred; the price of meat was so low that cattle hardly paid for raising; whole English counties were ruined. And Edward allowed his tenants very high rebates.

To do both justice Leonora has since acknowledged that she was in the wrong at that time and that Edward was following out a more far-seeing policy in nursing his really very good tenants over a bad period. It was not as if the whole of his money came from the land; a good deal of it was in rails. But old Colonel Powys had that bee in his bonnet and, if he never directly approached Edward himself on the subject, he preached unceasingly, whenever he had the opportunity, to Leonora. His pet idea was that Edward ought to sack all his own tenants and import a set of farmers from Scotland. That was what they were doing in Essex. He was of opinion that Edward was riding hotfoot to ruin.

That worried Leonora very much – it worried her dreadfully; she lay awake nights; she had an anxious line round her mouth. And that, again, worried Edward. I do not mean to say that Leonora actually spoke to Edward about his tenants – but he got to know that someone, probably her father, had been talking to her about the matter. He got to know it because it was the habit of his steward to look in on them every morning about breakfast-time to report any little happenings. And there was a farmer called Mumford who had only paid half his rent for the last three years. One morning the land-steward reported that Mumford would be unable to pay his rent at all that year. Edward reflected for a moment and then he said something like:

'Oh well, he's an old fellow and his family have been our tenants for over two hundred years. Let him off altogether.'

And then Leonora – you must remember that she had reason for being very nervous and unhappy at that time – let out a sound that was very like a groan. It startled Edward, who more than suspected what was passing in her mind – it startled him into a state of anger. He said sharply:

'You wouldn't have me turn out people who've been earning money for us for centuries – people to whom we have responsibilities – and let in a pack of Scotch farmers?'

He looked at her, Leonora said, with what was practically a glance of hatred and then, precipitately, he left the breakfast-table. Leonora knew that it probably made it all the worse that he had been betrayed into a manifestation of anger before a third party. It was the first and last time that he ever was betrayed into such a manifestation of anger. The land-steward, a moderate and well-balanced man whose family also had been with the Ashburnhams for over a century, took it upon himself to explain that he considered Edward was pursuing a perfectly proper course with his tenants. He erred perhaps a little on the side of generosity, but hard times were hard times, and every one had to feel the pinch, landlord as well as tenants. The great thing was not to let the land get into a poor state of cultivation. Scotch farmers just skinned your fields and let them go down and down. But Edward had a very good set of tenants who did their best for him and for themselves. These arguments at that time carried very little conviction to Leonora. She was, nevertheless, much concerned by Edward's outburst of anger.

The fact is that Leonora had been practising economies in her department. Two of the under-housemaids had gone and she had not replaced them; she had spent much less that year upon dress. The fare she had provided at the dinners they gave had been much less bountiful and not nearly so costly as had been the case in preceding years, and Edward began to perceive a hardness and determination in his wife's character. He seemed to see a net closing round him – a net in which they would be forced to live like one of the comparatively poor county families of the neighbourhood. And, in the mysterious way in which two people, living together, get to know each other's thoughts without a word spoken, he had known, even before his outbreak, that Leonora was worrying about his managing of the estates. This appeared to him to be intolerable. He had, too, a great feeling of self-contempt because he had been betrayed into speaking harshly to Leonora before that land-steward. She imagined that his nerve must be deserting him, and there can have been few men more miserable than Edward was at that period.

You see, he was really a very simple soul – very simple. He imagined that no man can satisfactorily accomplish his life's work without the loyal and wholehearted co-operation of the woman he lives with. And he was beginning to perceive dimly that, whereas his own traditions were entirely collective, his wife was a sheer individualist. His own theory – the feudal theory of an overlord doing his best by his dependents, the dependents meanwhile doing their best for the overlord – this theory was entirely foreign to Leonora's nature. She came of a family of small Irish landlords – that hostile garrison in a plundered country. And she was thinking unceasingly of the children she wished to have.

I don't know why they never had any children – not that I really believe that children would have made any difference. The dissimilarity of Edward and Leonora was too profound. It will give you some idea of the extraordinary naïveté of Edward Ashburnham that, at the time of his marriage and for perhaps a couple of years after, he did not really know how children are produced. Neither did Leonora. I don't mean to say that this state of things continued, but there it was. I dare say it had a good deal of influence on their mentalities. At any rate, they never had a child. It was the Will of God.

It certainly presented itself to Leonora as being the Will of God – as being a mysterious and awful chastisement of the Almighty. For she had discovered shortly before this period that her parents had not exacted from Edward's family the promise that any children she should bear should be brought up as Catholics. She herself had never talked of the matter with either her father, her mother, or her husband. When at last her father had let drop some words leading her to believe that that was the fact, she tried desperately to extort the promise from Edward. She encountered an unexpected obstinacy. Edward was perfectly willing that the girls should be Catholic; the boys must be Anglican. I don't understand the bearing of these things in English society. Indeed, Englishmen seem to me to be a little mad in matters of politics or of religion. In Edward it was particularly queer because he himself was perfectly ready to become a Romanist. He seemed, however, to contemplate going over to Rome himself and yet letting his boys be educated in the religion of their immediate ancestors. This may appear illogical, but I dare say it is not so illogical as it looks. Edward, that is to say, regarded himself as having his own body and soul at his own disposal. But his loyalty to the traditions of his family would not permit him to bind any future inheritors of his name or beneficiaries by the death of his ancestors. About the girls it did not so much matter. They would know other homes and other circumstances. Besides, it was the usual thing. But the boys must be given the opportunity of choosing – and they must have first of all the Anglican teaching. He was perfectly unshakeable about this.

Leonora was in an agony during all this time. You will have to remember she seriously believed that children who might be born to her went in danger, if not absolutely of damnation, at any rate of receiving false doctrine. It was an agony more terrible than she could describe. She didn't indeed attempt to describe it, but I could tell from her voice when she said, almost negligently, 'I used to lie awake whole nights. It was no good my spiritual advisers trying to console me.' I knew from her voice how terrible and how long those nights must have seemed and of how little avail were the consolations of her spiritual advisers. Her spiritual advisers seemed to have taken the matter a little more calmly. They certainly told her that she must not consider herself in any way to have sinned. Nay, they seem even to have extorted, to have threatened her, with a view to getting her out of what they considered to be a morbid frame of mind. She would just have to make the best of things, to influence the children when they came, not by propaganda, but by personality. And they warned her that she would be committing a sin if she continued to think that she had sinned. Nevertheless, she continued to think that she had sinned.

Leonora could not be aware that the man whom she loved passionately and whom, nevertheless, she was beginning to try to rule with a rod of iron – that this man was becoming more and more estranged from her. He seemed to regard her as being not only physically and mentally cold, but even as being actually wicked and mean. There were times when he would almost shudder if she spoke to him. And she could not understand how he could consider her wicked or mean. It only seemed to her a sort of madness in him that he should try to take upon his own shoulders the burden of his troop, of his regiment, of his estate and of half of his county. She could not see that in trying to curb what she regarded as megalomania she was doing anything wicked. She was just trying to keep things together for the sake of the children who did not come. And, little by little, the whole of their intercourse became simply one of agonized discussion as to whether Edward should subscribe to this or that institution or should try to reclaim this or that drunkard. She simply could not see it.

Into this really terrible position of strain, from which there appeared to be no issue, the Kilsyte case came almost as a relief. It is part of the peculiar irony of things that Edward would certainly never have kissed that nursemaid if he had not been trying to please Leonora. Nursemaids do not travel first-class, and, that day, Edward travelled in a third-class carriage in order to prove to Leonora that he was capable of economies. I have said that the Kilsyte case came almost as a relief to the strained situation that then existed between them. It gave Leonora an opportunity of backing him up in a wholehearted and absolutely loyal manner. It gave her the opportunity of behaving to him as he considered a wife should behave to her husband.

You see, Edward found himself in a railway carriage with a quite pretty girl of about nineteen. And the quite pretty girl of about nineteen, with dark hair and red cheeks and blue eyes, was quietly weeping. Edward had been sitting in his corner thinking about nothing at all. He had chanced to look at the nursemaid; two large, pretty tears came out of her eyes and dropped into her lap. He immediately felt that he had got to do something to comfort her. That was his job in life. He was desperately unhappy himself and it seemed to him the most natural thing in the world that they should pool their sorrows. He was quite democratic; the idea of the difference in their station never seems to have occurred to him. He began to talk to her. He discovered that her young man had been seen walking out with Annie of Number 54. He moved over to her side of the carriage. He told her that the report probably wasn't true; that, after all, a young man might take a walk with Annie from Number 54 without its denoting anything very serious. And he assured me that he felt at least quite half-fatherly when he put his arm around her waist and kissed her. The girl, however, had not forgotten the difference of her station.

All her life, by her mother, by other girls, by schoolteachers, by the whole tradition of her class she had been warned against gentlemen. She was being kissed by a gentleman. She screamed, tore herself away; sprang up and pulled a communication cord.

Edward came fairly well out of the affair in the public estimation; but it did him, mentally, a good deal of harm.

IV

It is very difficult to give an all-round impression of any man. I wonder how far I have succeeded with Edward Ashburnham. I dare say I haven't succeeded at all. It is even very difficult to see how such things matter. Was it the important point about poor Edward that he was very well built, carried himself well, was moderate at the table and led a regular life – that he had, in fact, all the virtues that are usually accounted English? Or have I in the least succeeded in conveying that he was all those things and had all those virtues? He certainly was them and had them up to the last months of his life. They were the things that one would set upon his tombstone. They will, indeed, be set upon his tombstone by his widow.

And have I, I wonder, given the due impression of how his life was portioned and his time laid out? Because, until the very last, the amount of time taken up by his various passions was relatively small. I have been forced to write very much about his passions, but you have to consider – I should like to be able to make you consider – that he rose every morning at seven, took a cold bath, breakfasted at eight, was occupied with his regiment from nine until one; played polo or cricket with the men when it was the season for cricket, till tea-time. Afterwards he would occupy himself with the letters from his land-steward or with the affairs of his mess, till dinner-time. He would dine and pass the evening playing cards, or playing billiards with Leonora or at social functions of one kind or another. And the greater part of his life was taken up by that – by far the greater part of his life. His love-affairs, until the very end, were sandwiched in at odd moments or took place during the social evenings, the dances and dinners. But I guess I have made it hard for you, O silent listener, to get that impression. Anyhow, I hope I have not given you the idea that Edward Ashburnham was a pathological case. He wasn't. He was just a normal man and very much of a sentimentalist. I dare say the quality of his youth, the nature of his mother's influence, his ignorances, the crammings that he received at the hands of army coaches – I dare say that all these excellent influences upon his adolescence were very bad for him. But we all have to put up with that sort of thing and no doubt it is very bad for all of us. Nevertheless, the outline of Edward's life was an outline perfectly normal of the life of a hard-working, sentimental and efficient professional man.

That question of first impressions has always bothered me a good deal – but quite academically. I mean that, from time to time I have wondered whether it were or were not best to trust to one's first impressions in dealing with people. But I never had anybody to deal with except waiters and chambermaids and the Ashburnhams, with whom I didn't know that I was having any dealings. And, as far as waiters and chambermaids were concerned, I have generally found that my first impressions were correct enough. If my first idea of a man was that he was civil, obliging, and attentive, he generally seemed to go on being all those things. Once, however, at our Paris flat we had a maid who appeared to be charming and transparently honest. She stole, nevertheless, one of Florence's diamond rings. She did it, however, to save her young man from going to prison. So here, as somebody says somewhere, was a special case.

And, even in my short incursion into American business life – an incursion that lasted during part of August and nearly the whole of September – I found that to rely upon first impressions was the best thing I could do. I found myself automatically docketing and labelling each man as he was introduced to me, by the run of his features and by the first words that he spoke. I can't, however, be regarded as really doing business during the time that I spent in the United States. I was just winding things up. If it hadn't been for my idea of marrying the girl I might possibly have looked for something to do in my own country. For my experiences there were vivid and amusing. It was exactly as if I had come out of a museum into a riotous fancy-dress ball. During my life with Florence I had almost come to forget that there were such things as fashions or occupations or the greed of gain. I had, in fact, forgotten that there was such a thing as a dollar and that a dollar can be extremely desirable if you don't happen to possess one. And I had forgotten, too, that there was such a thing as gossip that mattered. In that particular, Philadelphia was the most amazing place I have ever been in my life. I was not in that city for more than a week or ten days and I didn't there transact anything much in the way of business; nevertheless, the number of times that I was warned by everybody against everybody else was simply amazing. A man I didn't know would come up behind my lounge chair in the hotel, and, whispering cautiously beside my ear, would warn me against some other man that I equally didn't know but who would be standing by the bar. I don't know what they thought I was there to do – perhaps to buy out the city's debt or get a controlling hold of some railway interest. Or, perhaps, they imagined that I wanted to buy a newspaper, for they were either politicians or reporters, which, of course, comes to the same thing. As a matter of fact, my property in Philadelphia was mostly real estate in the old-fashioned part of the city and all I wanted to do there was just to satisfy myself that the houses were in good repair and the doors kept properly painted. I wanted also to see my relations, of whom I had a few. These were mostly professional people and they were mostly rather hard up because of the big bank failure in 1907 or thereabouts.[129] Still, they were very nice. They would have been nicer still if they hadn't, all of them, had what appeared to me to be the mania that what they called influences were working against them. At any rate, the impression of that city was one of old-fashioned rooms, rather English than American in type, in which handsome but careworn ladies, cousins of my own, talked principally about mysterious movements that were going on against them. I never got to know what it was all about; perhaps they thought I knew or perhaps there weren't any movements at all. It was all very secret and subtle and subterranean. But there was a nice young fellow called Carter who was a sort of second-nephew of mine, twice removed. He was handsome and dark and gentle and tall and modest. I understand also that he was a good cricketer. He was employed by the real-estate agents who collected my rents. It was he, therefore, who took me over my own property and I saw a good deal of him and of a nice girl called Mary, to whom he was engaged. At that time I did, what I certainly shouldn't do now – I made some careful inquiries as to his character. I discovered from his employers that he was just all that he appeared, honest, industrious, high-spirited, friendly and ready to do anyone a good turn. His relatives, however, as they were mine, too – seemed to have something darkly mysterious against him. I imagined that he must have been mixed up in some case of graft or that he had at least betrayed several innocent and trusting maidens. I pushed, however, that particular mystery home and discovered it was only that he was a Democrat. My own people were mostly Republicans. It seemed to make it worse and more darkly mysterious to them that young Carter was what they called a sort of a Vermont Democrat[130] which was the whole ticket and no mistake. But I don't know what it means. Anyhow, I suppose that my money will go to him when I die – I like the recollection of his friendly image and of the nice girl he was engaged to. May Fate deal very kindly with them.

I have said just now that in my present frame of mind, nothing would ever make me make inquiries as to the character of any man that I liked at first sight. (The little digression as to my Philadelphia experiences was really meant to lead around to this.) For who in this world can give anyone a character? Who in this world knows anything of any other heart – or of his own? I don't mean to say that one cannot form an average estimate of the way a person will behave. But one cannot be certain of the way any man will behave in every case – and until one can do that a 'character' is of no use to anyone. That, for instance, was the way with Florence's maid in Paris. We used to trust that girl with blank cheques for the payment of the tradesmen. For quite a time she was so trusted by us. Then, suddenly, she stole a ring. We should not have believed her capable of it; she would not have believed herself capable of it. It was nothing in her character. So, perhaps, it was with Edward Ashburnham.

Or, perhaps, it wasn't. No, I rather think it wasn't. It is difficult to figure out. I have said that the Kilsyte case eased the immediate tension for him and Leonora. It let him see that she was capable of loyalty to him; it gave her her chance to show that she believed in him. She accepted without question his statement that, in kissing the girl, he wasn't trying to do more than administer fatherly comfort to a weeping child. And, indeed, his own world – including the magistrates – took that view of the case. Whatever people say, one's world can be perfectly charitable at times . . . But, again, as I have said, it did Edward a great deal of harm.

That, at least, was his view of it. He assured me that, before that case came on and was wrangled about by counsel with all sorts of dirty-mindedness that counsel in that sort of case can impute, he had not had the least idea that he was capable of being unfaithful to Leonora. But, in the midst of that tumult – he says that it came suddenly into his head whilst he was in the witness-box – in the midst of those august ceremonies of the law there came suddenly into his mind the recollection of the softness of the girl's body as he had pressed her to him. And, from that moment, that girl appeared desirable to him – and Leonora completely unattractive.

He began to indulge in daydreams in which he approached the nursemaid more tactfully and carried the matter much further. Occasionally he thought of other women in terms of wary courtship – or, perhaps, it would be more exact to say that he thought of them in terms of tactful comforting, ending in absorption. That was his own view of the case. He saw himself as the victim of the law. I don't mean to say that he saw himself as a kind of Dreyfus.[131] The law, practically, was quite kind to him. It stated that in its view Captain Ashburnham had been misled by an ill-placed desire to comfort a member of the opposite sex, and it fined him five shillings for his want of tact, or of knowledge of the world. But Edward maintained that it had put ideas into his head.

I don't believe it, though he certainly did. He was twenty-seven then, and his wife was out of sympathy with him – some crash was inevitable. There was between them a momentary *rapprochement*; but it could not last. It made it, probably, all the worse that, in that particular matter, Leonora had come so very well up to the scratch. For, whilst Edward respected her more and was grateful to her, it made her seem by so much the more cold in other matters that were near his heart – his responsibilities, his career, his tradition. It brought his despair of her up to a point of exasperation – and it riveted on him the idea that he might find some other woman who would give him the moral support that he needed. He wanted to be looked upon as a sort of Lohengrin.

At that time, he says, he went about deliberately looking for some woman who could help him. He found several – for there were quite a number of ladies in his set who were capable of agreeing with this handsome and fine fellow that the duties of a feudal gentleman were feudal. He would have liked to pass his days talking to one or other of these ladies. But there was always an obstacle – if the lady were married there would be a husband who claimed the greater part of her time and attention. If, on the other hand, it were an unmarried girl, he could not see very much of her for fear of compromising her. At that date, you understand, he had not the least idea of seducing any one of these ladies. He wanted only moral support at the hands of some female, because he found men difficult to talk to about ideals. Indeed, I do not believe that he had, at any time, any idea of making any one his mistress. That sounds queer; but I believe it is quite true as a statement of character.

It was, I believe, one of Leonora's priests – a man of the world – who suggested that she should take him to Monte Carlo.[132] He had the idea that what Edward needed, in order to fit him for the society of Leonora, was a touch of irresponsibility. For Edward, at that date, had much the aspect of a prig. I mean that, if he played polo and was an excellent dancer he did the one for the sake of keeping himself fit and the other because it was a social duty to show himself at dances, and, when there, to dance well. He did nothing for fun except what he considered to be his work in life. As the priest saw it, this must for ever estrange him from Leonora – not because Leonora set much store by the joy of life, but because she was out of sympathy with Edward's work. On the other hand, Leonora did like to have a good time, now and then, and, as the priest saw it, if Edward could be got to like having a good time now and then, too, there would be a bond of sympathy between them. It was a good idea, but it worked out wrongly.

It worked out, in fact, in the mistress of the Grand Duke. In anyone less sentimental than Edward that would not have mattered. With Edward it was fatal. For, such was his honourable nature, that for him to enjoy a woman's favours made him feel that she had a bond on him for life. That was the way it worked out in practice. Psychologically it meant that he could not have a mistress without falling violently in love with her. He was a serious person – and in this particular case it was very expensive. The mistress of the Grand Duke – a Spanish dancer of passionate appearance – singled out Edward for her glances at a ball that was held in their common hotel. Edward was tall, handsome, blond and very wealthy as she understood – and Leonora went up to bed early. She did not care for public dances, but she was relieved to see that Edward appeared to be having a good time with several amiable girls. And that was the end of Edward – for the Spanish dancer of passionate appearance wanted one night of him for his *beaux yeux*.[133] He took her into to the dark gardens and, remembering suddenly the girl of the Kilsyte case, he kissed her. He kissed her passionately, violently, with a sudden explosion of the passion that had been bridled all his life – for Leonora was cold, or at any rate, well behaved. La Dolciquita liked this reversion, and he passed the night in her bed.

When the palpitating creature was at last asleep in his arms he discovered that he was madly, was passionately, was overwhelmingly in love with her. It was a passion that had arisen like fire in dry corn. He could think of nothing else; he could live for nothing else. But La Dolciquita was a reasonable creature without an ounce of passion in her. She wanted a certain satisfaction of her appetites and Edward had appealed to her the night before. Now that was done with, and, quite coldly, she said that she wanted money if he was to have any more of her. It was a perfectly reasonable commercial transaction. She did not care two buttons for Edward or for any man and he was asking her to risk a very good situation with the Grand Duke. If Edward could put up sufficient money to serve as a kind of insurance against accident she was ready to like Edward for a time that would be covered, as it were, by the policy. She was getting fifty thousand dollars a year from her Grand Duke; Edward would have to pay a premium of two years' hire for a month of her society. There would not be much risk of the Grand Duke's finding it out and it was not certain that he would give her the keys of the street[134] if he did find out. But there was the risk – a twenty per cent risk, as she figured it out. She talked to Edward as if she had been a solicitor with an estate to sell – perfectly quietly and perfectly coldly without any inflections in her voice. She did not want to be unkind to him; but she could see no reason for being kind to him. She was a virtuous business woman with a mother and two sisters and her own old age to be provided comfortably for. She did not expect more than a five years' further run. She was twenty-four and, as she said: 'We

Spanish women are horrors at thirty.' Edward swore that he would provide for her for life if she would come to him and leave off talking so horribly; but she only shrugged one shoulder slowly and contemptuously. He tried to convince this woman, who, as he saw it, had surrendered to him her virtue, that he regarded it as in any case his duty to provide for her, and to cherish her and even to love her – for life. In return for her sacrifice he would do that. In return, again, for his honourable love she would listen for ever to the accounts of his estate. That was how he figured it out.

She shrugged the same shoulder with the same gesture and held out her left hand with the elbow at her side:

'*Enfin, mon ami*,' she said, 'put in this hand the price of that tiara at Forli's[135] or . . .' And she turned her back on him.

Edward went mad; his world stood on its head; the palms in front of the blue sea danced grotesque dances. You see, he believed in the virtue, tenderness and moral support of women. He wanted more than anything to argue with La Dolciquita; to retire with her to an island and point out to her the damnation of her point of view and how salvation can only be found in true love and the feudal system. She had once been his mistress, he reflected, and by all the moral laws she ought to have gone on being his mistress or at the very least his sympathetic confidante. But her rooms were closed to him; she did not appear in the hotel. Nothing: blank silence. To break that down he had to have twenty thousand pounds. You have heard what happened.

He spent a week of madness; he hungered; his eyes sank in; he shuddered at Leonora's touch. I dare say that nine-tenths of what he took to be his passion for La Dolciquita was really discomfort at the thought that he had been unfaithful to Leonora. He felt uncommonly bad, that is to say – oh, unbearably bad, and he took it all to be love. Poor devil, he was incredibly naïve. He drank like a fish after Leonora was in bed and he spread himself over the tables, and this went on for about a fortnight. Heaven knows what would have happened; he would have thrown away every penny that he possessed.

On the night after he had lost about forty thousand pounds and whilst the whole hotel was whispering about it, La Dolciquita walked composedly into his bedroom. He was too drunk to recognize her, and she sat in his armchair, knitting and holding smelling salts to his nose – for he was pretty far gone with alcoholic poisoning – and, as soon as he was able to understand her, she said:

'Look here, *mon ami*, do not go to the tables again. Take a good sleep now and come and see me this afternoon.'

He slept till the lunch-hour. By that time Leonora had heard the news. A Mrs Colonel Whelan had told her. Mrs Colonel Whelan seems to have been the only sensible person who was ever connected with the Ashburnhams. She had argued it out that there must be a woman of the harpy variety connected with Edward's incredible behaviour and mien; and she advised Leonora to go straight off to Town[136] – which might have the effect of bringing Edward to his senses – and to consult her solicitor and her spiritual adviser. She had better go that very morning; it was no good arguing with a man in Edward's condition.

Edward, indeed, did not know that she had gone. As soon as he awoke he went straight to La Dolciquita's room and she stood him his lunch in her own apartments. He fell on her neck and wept, and she put up with it for a time. She was quite a good-natured woman. And, when she had calmed him down with *eau de mélisse*,[137] she said:

'Look here, my friend, how much money have you left? Five thousand dollars? Ten?' For the rumour went that Edward had lost two kings' ransoms a night for fourteen nights and she imagined that he must be near the end of his resources.

The *eau de mélisse* had calmed Edward to such an extent that, for the moment, he really had a head on his shoulders. He did nothing more than grunt:

'And then?'

'Why,' she answered, 'I may just as well have the ten thousand dollars as the tables. I will go with you to Antibes for a week for that sum.'

Edward grunted: 'Five.' She tried to get seven thousand five hundred; but he stuck to his five thousand and the hotel expenses at Antibes. The sedative carried him just as far as that and then he collapsed again. He had to leave for Antibes at three; he could not do without it. He left a note for Leonora saying that he had gone off for a week with the Clinton Morleys, yachting.

He did not enjoy himself very much at Antibes. La Dolciquita could talk of nothing with any enthusiasm except money, and she tired him unceasingly, during every waking hour, for presents of the most expensive description. And, at the end of a week, she just quietly kicked him out. He hung about in Antibes for three days. He was cured of the idea that he had any duties towards La Dolciquita – feudal or otherwise. But his sentimentalism required of him an attitude of Byronic gloom – as if his court had gone into half-mourning. Then his appetite suddenly returned, and he remembered Leonora. He found at his hotel at Monte Carlo a telegram from Leonora, dispatched from London, saying: 'Please return as soon as convenient.' He could not understand why Leonora should have abandoned him so precipitately when she only thought that he had gone yachting with the Clinton Morleys. Then he discovered that she had left the hotel before he had written the note. He had a pretty rocky journey back to town; he was frightened out of his life – and Leonora had never seemed so desirable to him.

V

I call this the Saddest Story, rather than 'The Ashburnham Tragedy', just because it is so sad, just because there was no current to draw things along to a swift and inevitable end. There is about it none of the elevation that accompanies tragedy; there is about it no nemesis, no destiny. Here were two noble people – for I am convinced that both Edward and Leonora had noble natures – here, then, were two noble natures, drifting down life, like fire-ships afloat on a lagoon and causing miseries, heartaches, agony of the mind and death. And they themselves steadily deteriorated. And why? For what purpose? To point what lesson? It is all a darkness.

There is not even any villain in the story – for even Major Basil, the husband of the lady who next, and really, comforted the unfortunate Edward – even Major Basil was not a villain in this piece. He was a

slack, loose, shiftless sort of fellow – but he did not do anything to
Edward. Whilst they were in the same station in Burma he borrowed
a good deal of money – though, really, since Major Basil had no
particular vices, it was difficult to know why he wanted it. He collected
– different types of horses' bits from the earliest times to the present
day – but, since he did not prosecute even this occupation with any
vigour, he cannot have needed much money for the acquirement, say,
of the bit of Genghis Khan's charger[138] – if Genghis Khan had a charger.
And when I say that he borrowed a good deal of money from Edward
I do not mean to say that he had more than a thousand pounds from
him during the five years that the connection lasted. Edward, of course,
did not have a great deal of money; Leonora was seeing to that. Still,
he may have had five hundred pounds a year English, for his *menus
plaisirs*[139] – for his regimental subscriptions and for keeping his men
smart. Leonora hated that; she would have preferred to buy dresses
for herself or to have devoted the money to paying off a mortgage.
Still, with her sense of justice, she saw that, since she was managing a
property bringing in three thousand a year with a view to re-establishing
it as a property of five thousand a year and since the property really, if
not legally, belonged to Edward, it was reasonable and just that Edward
should get a slice of his own. Of course she had the devil of a job.

I don't know that I have got the financial details exactly right. I am a
pretty good head at figures, but my mind, still, sometimes mixes up
pounds with dollars and I get a figure wrong. Anyhow, the proposition
was something like this: Properly worked and without rebates to the
tenants and keeping up schools and things, the Bramshaw estate should
have brought in about five thousand a year when Edward had it. It
brought in actually about four. (I am talking in pounds, not dollars.)
Edward's excesses with the Spanish Lady had reduced its value to about
three – as the maximum figure, without reductions. Leonora wanted
to get it back to five.

She was, of course, very young to be faced with such a proposition
– twenty-four is not a very advanced age. So she did things with a
youthful vigour that she would, very likely, have made more merciful,
if she had known more about life. She got Edward remarkably on the
hop. He had to face her in a London hotel, when he crept back from

Monte Carlo with his poor tail between his poor legs. As far as I can make out she cut short his first mumblings and his first attempts at affectionate speech with words something like:

'We're on the verge of ruin. Do you intend to let me pull things together? If not I shall retire to Hendon on my jointure.' (Hendon represented a convent to which she occasionally went for what is called a 'retreat' in Catholic circles.)

And poor dear Edward knew nothing – absolutely nothing. He did not know how much money he had, as he put it, 'blued' at the tables. It might have been a quarter of a million for all he remembered. He did not know whether she knew about La Dolciquita or whether she imagined that he had gone off yachting or had stayed at Monte Carlo. He was just dumb and he just wanted to get into a hole and not have to talk. Leonora did not make him talk and she said nothing herself.

I do not know much about English legal procedure – I cannot, I mean, give technical details of how they tied him up. But I know that, two days later, without her having said more than I have reported to you, Leonora and her attorney had become the trustees, as I believe it is called, of all Edward's property, and there was an end of Edward as the good landlord and father of his people. He went out.

Leonora then had three thousand a year at her disposal. She occupied Edward with getting himself transferred to a part of his regiment that was in Burma – if that is the right way to put it. She herself had an interview, lasting a week or so – with Edward's land-steward. She made him understand that the estate would have to yield up to its last penny. Before they left for India she had let Bramshaw for seven years at a thousand a year. She sold two Vandykes[140] and a little silver for eleven thousand pounds and she raised, on mortgage, twenty-nine thousand. That went to Edward's money-lending friends in Monte Carlo. So she had to get the twenty-nine thousand back, for she did not regard the Vandykes and the silver as things she would have to replace. They were just frills to the Ashburnham vanity. Edward cried for two days over the disappearance of his ancestors and then she wished she had not done it; but it did not teach her anything and it lessened such esteem as she had for him. She did not also understand that to let Bramshaw affected him with a feeling of physical soiling – that it was almost as bad for him as if a woman belonging to him had become a prostitute. That was how it did affect him; but I dare say she felt just as bad about the Spanish dancer.

So she went at it. They were eight years in India, and during the whole of that time she insisted that they must be self-supporting – they had to live on his Captain's pay, plus the extra allowance for being at the front. She gave him the five hundred a year for Ashburnham frills, as she called it to herself – and she considered she was doing him very well.

Indeed, in a way, she did him very well – but it was not his way. She was always buying him expensive things which, as it were, she took off her own back. I have, for instance, spoken of Edward's leather cases. Well, they were not Edward's at all; they were Leonora's manifestations. He liked to be clean, but he preferred, as it were, to be threadbare. She never understood that, and all that pigskin was her idea of a reward to him for putting her up to a little speculation by which she made eleven hundred pounds. She did, herself, the threadbare business. When they went up to a place called Simla,[141] where, as I understand, it is cool in the summer and very social – when they went up to Simla for their healths it was she who had him prancing around, as we should say in the United States, on a thousand-dollar horse with the gladdest of glad rags all over him. She herself used to go into 'retreat'. I believe that was very good for her health and it was also very inexpensive.

It was probably also very good for Edward's health, because he pranced about mostly with Mrs Basil, who was a nice woman and very, very kind to him. I suppose she was his mistress, but I never heard it from Edward, of course. I seem to gather that they carried it on in a high romantic fashion, very proper to both of them – or, at any rate, for Edward; she seems to have been a tender and gentle soul who did what he wanted. I do not mean to say that she was without character; that was her job, to do what Edward wanted. So I figured it out, that for those five years, Edward wanted long passages of deep affection kept up in long, long talks and that every now and then they 'fell,' which would give Edward an opportunity for remorse and an excuse to lend the Major another fifty. I don't think that Mrs Basil considered it to be 'falling'; she just pitied him and loved him.

You see, Leonora and Edward had to talk about something during all these years. You cannot be absolutely dumb when you live with a person unless you are an inhabitant of the North of England or the State of Maine. So Leonora imagined the cheerful device of letting him see the accounts of his estate and discussing them with him. He did not discuss them much; he was trying to behave prettily. But it was old Mr Mumford – the farmer who did not pay his rent – that threw Edward into Mrs Basil's arms. Mrs Basil came upon Edward in the dusk, in the Burmese garden, with all sorts of flowers and things. And he was cutting up that crop – with his sword, not a walking-stick. He was also carrying on and cursing in a way you would not believe.

She ascertained that an old gentleman called Mumford had been ejected from his farm and had been given a little cottage rent-free, where he lived on ten shillings a week from a farmers' benevolent society, supplemented by seven that was being allowed him by the Ashburnham trustees. Edward had just discovered that fact from the estate accounts. Leonora had left them in his dressing-room and he had begun to read them before taking off his marching-kit. That was how he came to have a sword. Leonora considered that she had been unusually generous to old Mr Mumford in allowing him to inhabit a cottage, rent-free, and in giving him seven shillings a week. Anyhow, Mrs Basil had never seen a man in such a state as Edward was. She had been passionately in love with him for quite a time, and he had been longing for her sympathy and admiration with a passion as deep. That was how they came to speak about it, in the Burmese garden, under the pale sky, with sheaves of severed vegetation, misty and odorous, in the night around their feet. I think they behaved themselves with decorum for quite a time after that, though Mrs Basil spent so many hours over the accounts of the Ashburnham estate that she got the name of every field by heart. Edward had a huge map of his lands in his harness-room and Major Basil did not seem to mind. I believe that people do not mind much in lonely stations.

It might have lasted for ever if the Major had not been made what is called a brevet-colonel during the shuffling of troops that went on just before the South African War.[142] He was sent off somewhere else and, of course, Mrs Basil could not stay with Edward. Edward ought, I suppose, to have gone to the Transvaal. It would have done him a great deal of good to get killed. But Leonora would not let him; she had heard awful stories of the extravagance of the hussar regiment in wartime – how they left hundred-bottle cases of champagne, at five guineas a bottle, on the veldt and so on. Besides, she preferred to see how Edward was spending his five hundred a year. I don't mean to say that Edward had any grievance in that. He was never a man of the deeds of heroism sort and it was just as good for him to be sniped at up in the hills of the North Western frontier, as to be shot at by an old gentleman in a top-hat at the bottom of some spruit.[143] Those are more or less his words about it. I believe he quite distinguished himself over there. At any rate, he had had his D.S.O. and was made a brevet-major.

Leonora, however, was not in the least keen on his soldiering. She hated also his deeds of heroism. One of their bitterest quarrels came after he had, for the second time, in the Red Sea, jumped overboard from the troopship and rescued a private soldier. She stood it the first time and even complimented him. But the Red Sea was awful, that trip, and the private soldiers seemed to develop a suicidal craze. It got on Leonora's nerves; she figured Edward, for the rest of that trip, jumping overboard every ten minutes. And the mere cry of 'Man overboard' is a disagreeable, alarming and disturbing thing. The ship gets stopped and there are all sorts of shouts. And Edward would not promise not to do it again, though, fortunately, they struck a streak of cooler weather when they were in the Persian Gulf. Leonora had got it into her head that Edward was trying to commit suicide, so I guess it was pretty awful for her when he would not give the promise. Leonora ought never to have been on that troopship; but she got there somehow, as an economy.

Major Basil discovered his wife's relation with Edward just before he was sent to his other station. I don't know whether that was a blackmailer's adroitness or just a trick of destiny. He may have known of it all the time or he may not. At any rate, he got hold of, just about then, some letters and things. It cost Edward three hundred pounds immediately. I do not know how it was arranged; I cannot imagine how even a blackmailer can make his demands. I suppose there is some sort of way of saving your face. I figure the Major as disclosing the letters to Edward with furious oaths, then accepting his explanations that the letters were perfectly innocent if the wrong construction were not put upon them. Then the Major would say: 'I say, old chap, I'm deuced hard up. Couldn't you lend me three hundred or so?' I fancy that was how it was. And, year by year, after that there would come a letter from the Major, saying that he was deuced hard up and couldn't Edward lend him three hundred or so?

Edward was pretty hard hit when Mrs Basil had to go away. He really had been very fond of her, and he remained faithful to her memory for quite a long time. And Mrs Basil had loved him very much and continued to cherish a hope of reunion with him. Three days ago there came a quite proper but very lamentable letter from her to Leonora, asking to be given particulars as to Edward's death. She had read the advertisement of it in an Indian paper. I think she must have been a very nice woman . . .

And then the Ashburnhams were moved somewhere up towards a place or a district called Chitral. I am no good at geography of the Indian Empire. By that time they had settled down into a model couple and they never spoke in private to each other. Leonora had given up even showing the accounts of the Ashburnham estate to Edward. He thought that that was because she had piled up such a lot of money that she did not want him to know how she was getting on any more. But, as a matter of fact, after five or six years it had penetrated to her mind that it was painful to Edward to have to look on at the accounts of his estate and have no hand in the management of it. She was trying to do him a kindness. And, up in Chitral, poor dear little Maisie Maidan came along . . .

That was the most unsettling to Edward of all his affairs. It made him suspect that he was inconstant. The affair with the Dolciquita he had sized up as a short attack of madness like hydrophobia. His relations with Mrs Basil had not seemed to him to imply moral turpitude of a gross kind. The husband had been complaisant; they had really loved each other; his wife was very cruel to him and had long ceased to be a wife to him. He thought that Mrs Basil had been his soul mate, separated from him by an unkind fate – something sentimental of that sort.

But he discovered that, whilst he was still writing long weekly letters to Mrs Basil, he was beginning to be furiously impatient if he missed seeing Maisie Maidan during the course of the day. He discovered himself watching the doorways with impatience; he discovered that he disliked her boy husband very much for hours at a time. He discovered that he was getting up at unearthly hours in order to have time, later in the morning, to go for a walk with Maisie Maidan. He discovered himself using little slang words that she used and attaching a sentimental value to those words. These, you understand, were discoveries that came so late that he could do nothing but drift. He was losing weight; his eyes were beginning to fall in; he had touches of bad fever. He was, as he described it, pipped.

And, one ghastly hot day, he suddenly heard himself say to Leonora:

'I say, couldn't we take Mrs Maidan with us to Europe and drop her at Nauheim?'

He hadn't had the least idea of saying that to Leonora. He had merely been standing, looking at an illustrated paper, waiting for dinner. Dinner was twenty minutes late or the Ashburnhams would not have been alone together. No, he hadn't had the least idea of framing that speech. He had just been standing in a silent agony of fear, of longing, of heat, of fever. He was thinking that they were going back to Bramshaw in a month and that Maisie Maidan was going to remain behind and die. And then, that had come out.

The punkah swished in the darkened room; Leonora lay exhausted and motionless in her cane lounge; neither of them stirred. They were both at that time very ill in indefinite ways.

And then Leonora said:

'Yes. I promised it to Charlie Maidan this afternoon. I have offered to pay her ex's[144] myself.'

Edward just saved himself from saying: 'Good God!' You see, he had not the least idea of what Leonora knew – about Maisie, about Mrs Basil, even about La Dolciquita. It was a pretty enigmatic situation for him. It struck him that Leonora must be intending to manage his loves as she managed his money affairs and it made her more hateful to him – and more worthy of respect.

Leonora, at any rate, had managed his money to some purpose. She had spoken to him, a week before, for the first time in several years – about money. She had made twenty-two thousand pounds out of the Bramshaw land and seven by the letting of Bramshaw furnished. By fortunate investments – in which Edward had helped her – she had made another six or seven thousand that might well become more. The mortgages were all paid off, so that, except for the departure of the two Vandykes and the silver, they were as well off as they had been before the Dolciquita had acted the locust. It was Leonora's great achievement. She laid the figures before Edward, who maintained an unbroken silence.

'I propose,' she said, 'that you should resign from the Army and that we should go back to Bramshaw. We are both too ill to stay here any longer.'

Edward said nothing at all.

'This,' Leonora continued passionlessly, 'is the great day of my life.'

Edward said:

'You have managed the job amazingly. You are a wonderful woman.' He was thinking that if they went back to Bramshaw they would leave Maisie Maidan behind. That thought occupied him exclusively. They must, undoubtedly, return to Bramshaw; there could be no doubt that Leonora was too ill to stay in that place. She said:

'You understand that the management of the whole of the expenditure of the income will be in your hands. There will be five thousand a year.'

She thought that he cared very much about the expenditure of an income of five thousand a year and that the fact that she had done so much for him would rouse in him some affection for her. But he was thinking exclusively of Maisie Maidan – of Maisie, thousands of miles away from him. He was seeing the mountains between them – blue mountains and the sea and sunlit plains. He said:

'That is very generous of you.' And she did not know whether that were praise or a sneer. That had been a week before. And all that week he had passed in an increasing agony at the thought that those mountains, that sea, and those sunlit plains would be between him and Maisie Maidan. That thought shook him in the burning nights: the sweat poured from him and he trembled with cold, in the burning noons – at that thought. He had no minute's rest; his bowels turned round and round within him: his tongue was perpetually dry and it seemed to him that the breath between his teeth was like air from a pest-house.

He gave no thought to Leonora at all; he had sent in his papers.[145]

They were to leave in a month. It seemed to him to be his duty to leave that place and to go away, to support Leonora. He did his duty.

It was horrible, in their relationship at that time, that whatever she did caused him to hate her. He hated her when he found that she proposed to set him up as the Lord of Bramshaw again – as a sort of dummy lord, in swaddling clothes. He imagined that she had done this in order to separate him from Maisie Maidan. Hatred hung in all the heavy nights and filled the shadowy corners of the room. So when he heard that she had offered to the Maidan boy to take his wife to Europe with him, automatically he hated her since he hated all that she did. It seemed to him, at that time, that she could never be other than cruel even if, by accident, an act of hers were kind . . . Yes, it was a horrible situation.

But the cool breezes of the ocean seemed to clear up that hatred as if it had been a curtain. They seemed to give him back admiration for her, and respect. The agreeableness of having money lavishly at command, the fact that it had bought for him the companionship of Maisie Maidan – these things began to make him see that his wife might have been right in the starving and scraping upon which she had insisted. He was at ease; he was even radiantly happy when he carried cups of bouillon for Maisie Maidan along the deck. One night, when he was leaning beside Leonora, over the ship's side, he said suddenly:

'By Jove, you're the finest woman in the world. I wish we could be better friends.'

She just turned away without a word and went to her cabin. Still, she was very much better in health.

And now, I suppose, I must give you Leonora's side of the case . . .

That is very difficult. For Leonora, if she preserved an unchanged front, changed very frequently her point of view. She had been drilled – in her tradition, in her upbringing – to keep her mouth shut. But there were times, she said, when she was so near yielding to the temptation of speaking that afterwards she shuddered to think of those times. You must postulate that what she desired above all things was to keep a shut mouth to the world, to Edward and to the women that he loved. If he spoke she would despise herself.

From the moment of his unfaithfulness with La Dolciquita she never acted the part of wife to Edward. It was not that she intended to keep herself from him as a principle, for ever. Her spiritual advisers, I believe, forbade that. But she stipulated that he must, in some way, perhaps symbolical, come back to her. She was not very clear as to what she meant; probably she did not know herself. Or perhaps she did.

There were moments when he seemed to be coming back to her; there were moments when she was within a hair of yielding to her physical passion for him. In just the same way, at moments, she almost yielded to the temptation to denounce Mrs Basil to her husband or Maisie Maidan to hers. She desired then to cause the horrors and pains of public scandals. For, watching Edward more intently and with more straining of ears than that which a cat bestows upon a bird overhead, she was aware of the progress of his passion for each of these ladies. She was aware of it from the way in which his eyes returned to doors and gateways; she knew from his tranquillities when he had received satisfactions.

At times she imagined herself to see more than was warranted. She imagined that Edward was carrying on intrigues with other women – with two at once; with three. For whole periods she imagined him to be a monster of libertinage and she could not see that he could have anything against her. She left him his liberty; she was starving herself to build up his fortunes; she allowed herself none of the joys of femininity – no dresses, no jewels – hardly even friendships, for fear they should cost money.

And yet, oddly, she could not but be aware that both Mrs Basil and Maisie Maidan were nice women. The curious, discounting eye which one woman can turn on another did not prevent her seeing that Mrs Basil was very good to Edward and Mrs Maidan very good for him. That seemed to her to be a monstrous and incomprehensible working of Fate's. Incomprehensible! Why, she asked herself again and again, did none of the good deeds that she did for her husband ever come through to him, or appear to him as good deeds? By what trick of mania could not he let her be as good to him as Mrs Basil was? Mrs Basil was not so extraordinarily dissimilar to herself. She was, it was true, tall, dark, with soft mournful voice and a great kindness of manner for every created thing, from punkah men to flowers on the trees. But she was not so well read as Leonora, at any rate in learned books. Leonora could not stand novels. But, even with all her differences, Mrs Basil did not appear to Leonora to differ so very much from herself. She was truthful, honest and, for the rest, just a woman. And Leonora had a vague sort of idea that, to a man, all women are the same after three weeks of close intercourse. She thought that the kindness should no longer appeal, the soft and mournful voice no longer thrill, the tall darkness no longer give a man the illusion that he was going into the depths of an unexplored wood. She could not understand how Edward could go on and on maundering over Mrs Basil. She could not see why he should continue to write her long letters after their separation. After that, indeed, she had a very bad time.

She had at that period what I will call the 'monstrous' theory of Edward. She was always imagining him ogling at every woman that he came across. She did not, that year, go into 'retreat' at Simla because she was afraid that he would corrupt her maid in her absence. She imagined him carrying on intrigues with native women or Eurasians. At dances she was in a fever of watchfulness . . .

She persuaded herself that this was because she had a dread of scandals. Edward might get himself mixed up with a marriageable daughter of some man who would make a row or some husband who would matter. But, really, she acknowledged afterwards to herself, she was hoping that, Mrs Basil being out of the way, the time might have come when Edward should return to her. All that period she passed in an agony of jealousy and fear – the fear that Edward might really become promiscuous in his habits.

So that, in an odd way, she was glad when Maisie Maidan came along – and she realized that she had not, before, been afraid of husbands and of scandals, since, then, she did her best to keep Maisie's husband unsuspicious. She wished to appear so trustful of Edward that Maidan could not possibly have any suspicions. It was an evil position for her. But Edward was very ill and she wanted to see him smile again. She thought that if he could smile again through her agency he might return, through gratitude and satisfied love – to her. At that time she thought that Edward was a person of light and fleeting passions. And she could understand Edward's passion for Maisie, since Maisie was one of those women to whom other women will allow magnetism.

She was very pretty; she was very young; in spite of her heart she was very gay and light on her feet. And Leonora was really very fond of Maisie, who was fond enough of Leonora. Leonora, indeed, imagined that she could manage this affair all right. She had no thought of Maisie's being led into adultery; she imagined that if she could take Maisie and Edward to Nauheim, Edward would see enough of her to get tired of her pretty little chatterings, and of the pretty little motions of her hands and feet. And she thought she could trust Edward. For there was not any doubt of Maisie's passion for Edward. She raved about him to Leonora as Leonora had heard girls rave about drawing masters in schools. She was perpetually asking her boy husband why he could not dress, ride, shoot, play polo, or even recite sentimental poems, like their major. And young Maidan had the greatest admiration for Edward, and he adored, was bewildered by and entirely trusted his wife. It appeared to him that Edward was devoted to Leonora. And Leonora imagined that when poor Maisie was cured of her heart and Edward had seen enough of her, he would return to her. She had the vague, passionate idea that when Edward had exhausted a number of other types of women he must turn to her. Why should not her type have its turn in his heart? She imagined that, by now, she understood him better, that she understood better his vanities and that, by making him happier, she could arouse his love.

Florence knocked all that on the head. . . .

Part Four

I

I have, I am aware, told this story in a very rambling way so that it may be difficult for anyone to find their path through what may be a sort of maze. I cannot help it. I have stuck to my idea of being in a country cottage with a silent listener, hearing between the gusts of the wind and amidst the noises of the distant sea, the story as it comes. And, when one discusses an affair – a long, sad affair – one goes back, one goes forward. One remembers points that one has forgotten and one explains them all the more minutely since one recognizes that one has forgotten to mention them in their proper places and that one may have given, by omitting them, a false impression. I console myself with thinking that this is a real story and that, after all, real stories are probably told best in the way a person telling a story would tell them. They will then seem most real.

At any rate, I think I have brought my story up to the date of Maisie Maidan's death. I mean that I have explained everything that went before it from the several points of view that were necessary – from Leonora's, from Edward's and, to some extent, from my own. You have the facts for the trouble of finding them; you have the points of view as far as I could ascertain or put them. Let me imagine myself back, then, at the day of Maisie's death – or rather at the moment of Florence's dissertation on the Protest, up in the old Castle of the town of M—. Let us consider Leonora's point of view with regard to Florence; Edward's, of course, I cannot give you, for Edward naturally never spoke of his affair with my wife. (I may, in what follows, be a little hard on Florence; but you must remember that I have been writing away at this story now for six months and reflecting longer and longer upon these affairs.)

And the longer I think about them the more certain I become that Florence was a contaminating influence – she depressed and deteriorated poor Edward; she deteriorated, hopelessly, the miserable Leonora. There is no doubt that she caused Leonora's character to deteriorate. If there was a fine point about Leonora it was that she was proud and that she was silent. But that pride and that silence broke when she made that extraordinary outburst, in the shadowy room that contained the Protest, and in the little terrace looking over the river. I don't mean to say that she was doing a wrong thing. She was certainly doing right in trying to warn me that Florence was making eyes at her husband. But, if she did the right thing, she was doing it in the wrong way. Perhaps she should have reflected longer; she should have spoken, if she wanted to speak, only after reflection. Or it would have been better if she had acted – if, for instance, she had so chaperoned Florence that private communication between her and Edward became impossible. She should have gone eavesdropping; she should have watched outside bedroom doors. It is odious; but that is the way the job is done. She should have taken Edward away the moment Maisie was dead. No, she acted wrongly . . .

And yet, poor thing, is it for me to condemn her – and what did it matter in the end? If it had not been Florence, it would have been some other . . . Still, it might have been a better woman than my wife. For Florence was vulgar; Florence was a common flirt who would not, at the last, *lâcher prise*,[146] and Florence was an unstoppable talker. You could not stop her; nothing would stop her. Edward and Leonora were at least proud and reserved people. Pride and reserve are not the only things in life; perhaps they are not even the best things. But if they happen to be your particular virtues you will go all to pieces if you let them go. And Leonora let them go. She let them go before poor Edward did even. Consider her position when she burst out over the Luther-Protest . . . Consider her agonies . . .

You are to remember that the main passion of her life was to get Edward back; she had never, till that moment, despaired of getting him back. That may seem ignoble; but you have also to remember that her getting him back represented to her not only a victory for herself. It would, as it appeared to her, have been a victory for all wives and a victory for her Church. That was how it presented itself to her. These things are a little inscrutable. I don't know why the getting back of Edward should have represented to her a victory for all wives, for Society and for her Church. Or, maybe, I have a glimmering of it.

She saw life as a perpetual sex-battle between husbands who desire to be unfaithful to their wives, and wives who desire to recapture their husbands in the end. That was her sad and modest view of matrimony. Man, for her, was a sort of brute who must have his divagations, his moments of excess, his nights out, his, let us say, rutting seasons. She had read few novels, so that the idea of a pure and constant love succeeding the sound of wedding bells had never been very much presented to her. She went, numbed and terrified, to the Mother Superior of her childhood's convent with the tale of Edward's infidelities with the Spanish dancer, and all that the old nun, who appeared to her to be infinitely wise, mystic and reverend, had done had been to shake her head sadly and to say:

'Men are like that. By the blessing of God it will all come right in the end.'

That was what was put before her by her spiritual advisers as her programme in life. Or, at any rate, that was how their teachings came through to her – that was the lesson she told me she had learned of them. I don't know exactly what they taught her. The lot of women was patience and patience and again patience – *ad majorem Dei gloriam*[147] – until upon the appointed day, if God saw fit, she should have her reward. If then, in the end, she should have succeeded in getting Edward back she would have kept her man within the limits that are all that wifehood has to expect. She was even taught that such excesses in men are natural, excusable – as if they had been children.

And the great thing was that there should be no scandal before the congregation. So she had clung to the idea of getting Edward back with a fierce passion that was like an agony. She had looked the other way; she had occupied herself solely with one idea. That was the idea of having Edward appear, when she did get him back, wealthy, glorious as it were, on account of his lands, and upright. She would show, in fact, that in an unfaithful world one Catholic woman had succeeded in retaining the fidelity of her husband. And she thought she had come near her desires.

Her plan with regard to Maisie had appeared to be working admirably. Edward had seemed to be cooling off towards the girl. He did not hunger to pass every minute of the time at Nauheim beside the child's recumbent form; he went out to polo matches; he played auction bridge in the evenings; he was cheerful and bright. She was certain that he was not trying to seduce that poor child; she was beginning to think that he had never tried to do so. He seemed in fact to be dropping back into what he had been for Maisie in the beginning – a kind, attentive, superior officer in the regiment, paying gallant attentions to a bride. They were as open in their little flirtations as the dayspring from on high.[148] And Maisie had not appeared to fret when he went off on excursions with us; she had to lie down for so many hours on her bed every afternoon, and she had not appeared to crave for the attentions of Edward at those times.

And Edward was beginning to make little advances to Leonora. Once or twice, in private – for he often did it before people – he had said: 'How nice you look!' or 'What a pretty dress!' She had gone with Florence to Frankfurt, where they dress as well as in Paris, and had got herself a gown or two. She could afford it, and Florence was an excellent adviser as to dress. She seemed to have got hold of the clue to the riddle.

Yes, Leonora seemed to have got hold of the clue to the riddle. She imagined herself to have been in the wrong to some extent in the past. She should not have kept Edward on such a tight rein with regard to money. She thought she was on the right tack in letting him – as she had done only with fear and irresolution – have again the control of his income. He came even a step towards her and acknowledged, spontaneously, that she had been right in husbanding, for all those years, their resources. He said to her one day:

'You've done right, old girl. There's nothing I like so much as to have a little to chuck away. And I can do it, thanks to you.'

That was really, she said, the happiest moment of her life. And he, seeming to realize it, had ventured to pat her on the shoulder. He had, ostensibly, come in to borrow a safety pin of her.

And the occasion of her boxing Maisie's ears, had, after it was over, riveted in her mind the idea that there was no intrigue between Edward and Mrs Maidan. She imagined that, from henceforward, all that she had to do was to keep him well supplied with money and his mind amused with pretty girls. She was convinced that he was coming back to her. For that month she no longer repelled his timid advances that never went very far. For he certainly made timid advances. He patted her on the shoulder; he whispered into her ear little jokes about the odd figures that they saw up at the Casino. It was not much to make a little joke – but the whispering of it was a precious intimacy . . .

And then – smash – it all went. It went to pieces at the moment when Florence laid her hand upon Edward's wrist, as it lay on the glass sheltering the manuscript of the Protest, up in the high tower with the shutters where the sunlight here and there streamed in. Or, rather, it went when she noticed the look in Edward's eyes as he gazed back into Florence's. She knew that look.

She had known – since the first moment of their meeting, since the moment of our all sitting down to dinner together – that Florence was making eyes at Edward. But she had seen so many women make eyes at Edward – hundreds and hundreds of women, in railway trains, in hotels, aboard liners, at street corners. And she had arrived at thinking that Edward took little stock in women that made eyes at him. She had formed what was, at that time, a fairly correct estimate of the methods of, the reasons for, Edward's loves. She was certain that hitherto they had consisted of the short passion for the Dolciquita, the real sort of love for Mrs Basil, and what she deemed the pretty courtship of Maisie Maidan. Besides she despised Florence so haughtily that she could not imagine Edward's being attracted by her. And she and Maisie were a sort of bulwark round him.

She wanted, besides, to keep her eyes on Florence – for Florence knew that she had boxed Maisie's ears. And Leonora so desperately desired that her union with Edward should appear to be flawless. But all that went . . .

With the answering gaze of Edward into Florence's blue and uplifted eyes, she knew that it had all gone. She knew that that gaze meant that those two had had long conversations of an intimate kind about their likes and dislikes, about their natures, about their views of marriage. She knew what it meant that she, when we all four walked out together, had always been with me ten yards ahead of Florence and Edward. She did not imagine that it had gone further than talks about their likes and dislikes, about their natures or about marriage as an institution. But, having watched Edward all her life, she knew that that laying on of hands, that answering of gaze with gaze, meant that the thing was unavoidable. Edward was such a serious person.

She knew that any attempt on her part to separate those two would be to rivet on Edward an irrevocable passion; that, as I have before told you, it was a trick of Edward's nature to believe that the seducing of a woman gave her an irrevocable hold over him for life. And that touching of hands, she knew, would give that woman an irrevocable claim – to be seduced. And she so despised Florence that she would have preferred it to be a parlour-maid. There are very decent parlour-maids.

And, suddenly, there came into her mind the conviction that Maisie Maidan had a real passion for Edward; that this would break her heart – and that she, Leonora, would be responsible for that. She went, for the moment, mad. She clutched me by the wrist; she dragged me down those stairs and across that whispering *Rittersaal* with the high painted pillars, the high painted chimney-piece. I guess she did not go mad enough.

She ought to have said:

'Your wife is a harlot who is going to be my husband's mistress . . .' That might have done the trick. But, even in her madness, she was afraid to go as far as that. She was afraid that, if she did, Edward and Florence would make a bolt of it, and that, if they did that, she would lose forever all chance of getting him back in the end. She acted very badly to me.

Well, she was a tortured soul who put her Church before the interests of a Philadelphia Quaker. That is all right – I daresay the Church of Rome is the more important of the two.

A week after Maisie Maidan's death she was aware that Florence had become Edward's mistress. She waited outside Florence's door and met Edward as he came away. She said nothing and he only grunted. But I guess he had a bad time.

Yes, the mental deterioration that Florence worked in Leonora was extraordinary; it smashed up her whole life and all her chances. It made her, in the first place, hopeless – for she could not see how, after that, Edward could return to her – after a vulgar intrigue with a vulgar woman. His affair with Mrs Basil, which was now all that she had to bring, in her heart, against him, she could not find it in her to call an intrigue. It was a love affair – a pure enough thing in its way. But this seemed to her to be a horror – a wantonness, all the more detestable to her, because she so detested Florence. And Florence talked . . .

That was what was terrible, because Florence forced Leonora herself to abandon her high reserve – Florence and the situation. It appears that Florence was in two minds whether to confess to me or to Leonora. Confess she had to. And she pitched at last on Leonora, because if it had been me she would have had to confess a great deal more. Or, at least, I might have guessed a great deal more, about her 'heart', and about Jimmy. So she went to Leonora one day and began hinting and hinting. And she enraged Leonora to such an extent that at last Leonora said:

'You want to tell me that you are Edward's mistress. You can be. I have no use for him.'

That was really a calamity for Leonora, because, once started, there was no stopping the talking. She tried to stop – but it was not to be done. She found it necessary to send Edward messages through Florence; for she would not speak to him. She had to give him, for instance, to understand that if I ever came to know of his intrigue she would ruin him beyond repair. And it complicated matters a good deal that Edward, at about this time, was really a little in love with her. He thought that he had treated her so badly; that she was so fine. She was so mournful that he longed to comfort her, and he thought himself such a blackguard that there was nothing he would not have done to make amends. And Florence communicated these items of information to Leonora.

I don't in the least blame Leonora for her coarseness to Florence; it must have done Florence a world of good. But I do blame her for giving way to what was in the end a desire for communicativeness. You see that business cut her off from her Church. She did not want to confess what she was doing because she was afraid that her spiritual advisers would blame her for deceiving me. I rather imagine that she would have preferred damnation to breaking my heart. That is what it works out at. She need not have troubled.

But, having no priests to talk to, she had to talk to someone, and as Florence insisted on talking to her, she talked back, in short, explosive sentences, like one of the damned. Precisely like one of the damned. Well, if a pretty period in hell on this earth can spare her any period of pain in Eternity – where there are not any periods – I guess Leonora will escape hell fire.

Her conversations with Florence would be like this. Florence would happen in on her, whilst she was doing her wonderful hair, with a proposition from Edward, who seems about that time to have conceived the naïve idea that he might become a polygamist. I daresay it was Florence who put it into his head. Anyhow, I am not responsible for the oddities of the human psychology. But it certainly appears that at about that date Edward cared more for Leonora than he had ever done before – or, at any rate, for a long time. And, if Leonora had been a person to play cards and if she had played her cards well, and if she had had no sense of shame and so on, she might then have shared Edward with Florence until the time came for jerking that poor cuckoo out of the nest.

Well, Florence would come to Leonora with some such proposition. I do not mean to say that she put it baldly, like that. She stood out that she was not Edward's mistress until Leonora said that she had seen Edward coming out of her room at an advanced hour of the night. That checked Florence a bit; but she fell back upon her 'heart' and stuck out that she had merely been conversing with Edward in order to bring him to a better frame of mind. Florence had, of course, to stick to that story; for even Florence would not have had the face to implore Leonora to grant her favours to Edward if she had admitted that she was Edward's mistress. That could not be done. At the same time Florence had such a pressing desire to talk about something. There would have been nothing else to talk about but a *rapprochement* between that estranged pair. So Florence would go on babbling and Leonora would go on brushing her hair. And then Leonora would say suddenly something like:

'I should think myself defiled if Edward touched me now that he has touched you.'

That would discourage Florence a bit; but after a week or so, on another morning she would have another try.

And even in other things Leonora deteriorated. She had promised Edward to leave the spending of his own income in his own hands. And she had fully meant to do that. I daresay she would have done it too; though, no doubt, she would have spied upon his banking account in secret. She was not a Roman Catholic for nothing. But she took so serious a view of Edward's unfaithfulness to the memory of poor little Maisie that she could not trust him any more at all.

So when she got back to Bramshaw she started, after less than a month, to worry him about the minutest items of his expenditure. She allowed him to draw his own cheques, but there was hardly a cheque that she did not scrutinize – except for a private account of about five hundred a year which, tacitly, she allowed him to keep for expenditure on his mistress or mistresses. He had to have his jaunts to Paris; he had to send expensive cables in cipher to Florence about twice a week. But she worried him about his expenditure on wines, on fruit trees, on harness, on gates, on the account at his blacksmith's for work done to a new patent Army stirrup that he was trying to invent. She could not see why he should bother to invent a new Army stirrup, and she was really enraged when, after the invention was mature, he made a present to the War Office of the designs and the patent rights. It was a remarkably good stirrup.

I have told you, I think, that Edward spent a great deal of time, and about two hundred pounds for law fees on getting a poor girl, the daughter of one of his gardeners, acquitted of a charge of murdering her baby. That was positively the last act of Edward's life. It came at a time when Nancy Rufford was on her way to India; when the most horrible gloom was over the household; when Edward himself was in an agony and behaving as prettily as he knew how. Yet even then Leonora made him a terrible scene about this expenditure of time and trouble. She sort of had the vague idea that what had passed with the girl and the rest of it ought to have taught Edward a lesson – the lesson of economy. She threatened to take his banking account away from him again. I guess that made him cut his throat. He might have stuck it out otherwise – but the thought that he had lost Nancy and that, in addition, there was nothing left for him but a dreary, dreary succession of days in which he could be of no public service . . . Well, it finished him.

It was during those years that Leonora tried to get up a love affair of her own with a fellow called Bayham – a decent sort of fellow. A really nice man. But the affair was no sort of success. I have told you about it already . . .

I I

Well, that about brings me up to the date of my receiving, in Waterbury, the laconic cable from Edward to the effect that he wanted me to go to Bramshaw and have a chat. I was pretty busy at the time and I was half minded to send him a reply cable to the effect that I would start in a fortnight. But I was having a long interview with old Mr Hurlbird's attorneys and immediately afterwards I had to have a long interview with the Misses Hurlbird, so I delayed cabling.

I had expected to find the Misses Hurlbird excessively old – in the nineties or thereabouts. The time had passed so slowly that I had the impression that it must have been thirty years since I had been in the United States. It was only twelve years. Actually Miss Hurlbird was just sixty-one and Miss Florence Hurlbird fifty-nine, and they were both, mentally and physically, as vigorous as could be desired. They were, indeed, more vigorous, mentally, than suited my purpose, which was to get away from the United States as quickly as I could. The Hurlbirds were an exceedingly united family – exceedingly united except on one set of points. Each of the three of them had a separate doctor, whom they trusted implicity – and each had a separate attorney. And each of them distrusted the other's doctor and the other's attorney. And, naturally, the doctors and the attorneys warned one all the time –

against each other. You cannot imagine how complicated it all became for me. Of course I had an attorney of my own – recommended to me by young Carter, my Philadelphia nephew.

I do not mean to say that there was any unpleasantness of a grasping kind. The problem was quite another one – a moral dilemma. You see, old Mr Hurlbird had left all his property to Florence with the mere request that she would have erected to him in the city of Waterbury, Conn., a memorial that should take the form of some sort of institution for the relief of sufferers from the heart. Florence's money had all come to me – and with it old Mr Hurlbird's. He had died just five days before Florence.

Well, I was quite ready to spend a round million dollars on the relief of sufferers from the heart. The old gentleman had left about a million and a half; Florence had been worth about eight hundred thousand – and as I figured it out, I should cut up at about a million myself. Anyhow, there was ample money. But I naturally wanted to consult the wishes of his surviving relatives and then the trouble really began. You see, it had been discovered that Mr Hurlbird had had nothing whatever the matter with his heart. His lungs had been a little affected all through his life and he had died of bronchitis.

It struck Miss Florence Hurlbird that, since her brother had died of lungs and not of heart, his money ought to go to lung patients. That, she considered, was what her brother would have wished. On the other hand, by a kink, that I could not at the time understand, Miss Hurlbird insisted that I ought to keep the money all to myself. She said that she did not wish for any monuments to the Hurlbird family.

At the time I thought that that was because of a New England dislike for necrological ostentation. But I can figure out now, when I remember certain insistent and continued questions that she put to me, about Edward Ashburnham, that there was another idea in her mind. And Leonora has told me that, on Florence's dressing-table, beside her dead body, there had lain a letter to Miss Hurlbird – a letter which Leonora posted without telling me. I don't know how Florence had time to write to her aunt; but I can quite understand that she would not like to go out of the world without making some comments. So I guess Florence had told Miss Hurlbird a good bit about Edward Ashburnham in a few scrawled words – and that was why the old lady did not wish the name of Hurlbird perpetuated. Perhaps also she thought that I had earned the Hurlbird money.

It meant a pretty tidy lot of discussing, what with the doctors warning each other about the bad effects of discussions on the health of the old ladies, and warning me covertly against each other, and saying that old Mr Hurlbird might have died of heart, after all, in spite of the diagnosis of *his* doctor. And the solicitors all had separate methods of arranging about how the money should be invested and entrusted and bound.

Personally, I wanted to invest the money so that the interest could be used for the relief of sufferers from the heart. If old Mr Hurlbird had not died of any defects in that organ he had considered that it was defective. Moreover, Florence had certainly died of her heart, as I saw it. And when Miss Florence Hurlbird stood out that the money ought to go to chest sufferers I was brought to thinking that there ought to be a chest institution too, and I advanced the sum that I was ready to provide to a million and a half of dollars. That would have given seven hundred and fifty thousand to each class of invalid. I did not want money at all badly. All I wanted it for was to be able to give Nancy Rufford a good time. I did not know much about housekeeping expenses in England where, I presumed, she would wish to live. I knew that her needs at that time were limited to good chocolates, and a good horse or two, and simple, pretty frocks. Probably she would want more than that later on. But even if I gave a million and a half dollars to these institutions I should still have the equivalent of about twenty thousand a year English, and I considered that Nancy could have a pretty good time on that or less.

Anyhow, we had a stiff set of arguments up at the Hurlbird mansion which stands on a bluff over the town. It may strike you, silent listener, as being funny if you happen to be European. But moral problems of that description and the giving of millions to institutions are immensely serious matters in my country. Indeed, they are the staple topics for consideration amongst the wealthy classes. We haven't got peerage and social climbing to occupy us much, and decent people do not take interest in politics or elderly people in sport. So that there were real tears shed by both Miss Hurlbird and Miss Florence before I left that city.

I left it quite abruptly. Four hours after Edward's telegram came another from Leonora, saying: 'Yes, do come. You could be so helpful.' I simply told my attorney that there was the million and a half; that he could invest it as he liked, and that the purposes must be decided by the Misses Hurlbird. I was, anyhow, pretty well worn out by all the discussions. And, as I have never heard yet from the Misses Hurlbird, I rather think that Miss Hurlbird, either by revelations or by moral force, has persuaded Miss Florence that no memorial to their names shall be erected in the city of Waterbury, Conn. Miss Hurlbird wept dreadfully when she heard that I was going to stay with the Ashburnhams, but she did not make any comments. I was aware, at that date, that her niece had been seduced by that fellow Jimmy before I had married her – but I contrived to produce on her the impression that I thought Florence had been a model wife. Why, at that date I still believed that Florence had been perfectly virtuous after her marriage to me. I had not figured it out that she could have played it so low down as to continue her intrigue with that fellow under my roof. Well, I was a fool. But I did not think much about Florence at that date. My mind was occupied with what was happening at Bramshaw.

I had got it into my head that the telegrams had something to do with Nancy. It struck me that she might have shown signs of forming an attachment for some undesirable fellow and that Leonora wanted me to come back and marry her out of harm's way. That was what was pretty firmly in my mind. And it remained in my mind for nearly ten days after my arrival at that beautiful old place. Neither Edward nor Leonora made any motion to talk to me about anything other than the weather and the crops. Yet, although there were several young fellows about, I could not see that any one in particular was distinguished by the girl's preference. She certainly appeared illish and nervous, except when she woke up to talk gay nonsense to me. Oh, the pretty thing that she was . . .

I imagined that what must have happened was that the undesirable young man had been forbidden the place and that Nancy was fretting a little.

What had happened was just Hell. Leonora had spoken to Nancy; Nancy had spoken to Edward; Edward had spoken to Leonora – and they had talked and talked. And talked. You have to imagine horrible pictures of gloom and half lights, and emotions running through silent nights – through whole nights. You have to imagine my beautiful Nancy appearing suddenly to Edward, rising up at the foot of his bed, with her long hair falling, like a split cone of shadow, in the glimmer of a night-light that burned beside him. You have to imagine her, a silent, a no doubt agonized figure, like a spectre, suddenly offering herself to him – to save his reason! And you have to imagine his frantic refusal – and talk. And talk! My God!

And yet, to me, living in the house, enveloped with the charm of the quiet and ordered living, with the silent, skilled servants whose mere laying out of my dress clothes was like a caress – to me who was hourly with them they appeared like tender, ordered and devoted people, smiling, absenting themselves at the proper intervals; driving me to meets – just good people! How the devil – how the devil do they do it?

At dinner one evening Leonora said – she had just opened a telegram: 'Nancy will be going to India, tomorrow, to be with her father.'

No one spoke. Nancy looked at her plate; Edward went on eating his pheasant. I felt very bad; I imagined that it would be up to me to propose to Nancy that evening. It appeared to me to be queer that they had not given me any warning of Nancy's departure – but I thought that that was only English manners – some sort of delicacy that I had not got the hang of. You must remember that at that moment I trusted in Edward and Leonora and in Nancy Rufford, and in the tranquillity of ancient haunts of peace, as I had trusted in my mother's love. And that evening Edward spoke to me.

What in the interval had happened had been this:

Upon her return from Nauheim Leonora had completely broken down – because she knew she could trust Edward. That seems odd but, if you know anything about breakdowns, you will know that by the ingenious torments that fate prepares for us, these things come as soon as, a strain having relaxed, there is nothing more to be done. It is after a husband's long illness and death that a widow goes to pieces; it is at the end of a long rowing contest that a crew collapses and lies forward upon its oars. And that was what happened to Leonora.

From certain tones in Edward's voice; from the long, steady stare that he had given her from his bloodshot eyes on rising from the dinner table in the Nauheim hotel, she knew that, in the affair of the poor girl, this was a case in which Edward's moral scruples, or his social code, or his idea that it would be playing it *too* low down, rendered Nancy perfectly safe. The girl, she felt sure, was in no danger at all from Edward. And in that she was perfectly right. The smash was to come from herself.

She relaxed; she broke; she drifted, at first quickly, then with an increasing momentum, down the stream of destiny. You may put it that, having been cut off from the restraints of her religion, for the first time in her life, she acted along the lines of her instinctive desires. I do not know whether to think that, in that she was no longer herself; or that, having let loose the bonds of her standards, her conventions and her traditions, she was being, for the first time, her own natural self. She was torn between her intense, maternal love for the girl and an intense jealousy of the woman who realizes that the man she loves has met what appears to be the final passion of his life. She was divided between an intense disgust for Edward's weakness in conceiving this passion, an intense pity for the miseries that he was enduring, and a feeling equally intense, but one that she hid from herself – a feeling of respect for Edward's determination to keep himself, in this particular affair, unspotted.

And the human heart is a very mysterious thing. It is impossible to say that Leonora, in acting as she then did, was not filled with a sort of hatred of Edward's final virtue. She wanted, I think, to despise him. He was, she realized, gone from her for good. Then let him suffer, let him agonize; let him, if possible, break and go to that Hell that is the abode of broken resolves. She might have taken a different line. It would have been so easy to send the girl away to stay with some friends; to have taken her away herself upon some pretext or other. That would not have cured things but it would have been the decent line . . . But, at that date, poor Leonora was incapable of taking any line whatever.

She pitied Edward frightfully at one time – and then she acted along the lines of pity; she loathed him at another and then she acted as her loathing dictated. She gasped, as a person dying of tuberculosis gasps for air. She craved madly for communication with some other human soul. And the human soul that she selected was that of the girl.

Perhaps Nancy was the only person that she could have talked to. With her necessity for reticences, with her coldness of manner, Leonora had singularly few intimates. She had none at all, with the exception of the Mrs Colonel Whelan, who had advised her about the affair with La Dolciquita, and the one or two religious, who had guided her through life. The Colonel's wife was at that time in Madeira,[149] the religious she now avoided. Her visitors' book had seven hundred names in it; there was not a soul that she could speak to. She was Mrs Ashburnham of Bramshaw Teleragh.

She was the great Mrs Ashburnham of Bramshaw and she lay all day upon her bed in her marvellous, light, airy bedroom with the chintzes and the Chippendale and the portraits of deceased Ashburnhams by Zoffany and Zucchero.[150] When there was a meet she would struggle up – supposing it were within driving distance – and let Edward drive her and the girl to the crossroads or the country house. She would drive herself back alone; Edward would ride off with the girl. Ride Leonora could not, that season – her head was too bad. Each pace of her mare was an anguish.

But she drove with efficiency and precision; she smiled at the Gimmers and Ffoulkes and the Hedley Seatons. She threw with exactitude pennies to the boys who opened gates for her; she sat upright on the seat of the high dogcart; she waved her hands to Edward and Nancy as they rode off with the hounds, and every one could hear her clear, high voice, in the chilly weather, saying:

'Have a good time!'

Poor forlorn woman! . . .

There was, however, one spark of consolation. It came from the fact that Rodney Bayham, of Bayham, followed her always with his eyes. It had been three years since she had tried her abortive love-affair with him. Yet still, on the winter mornings he would ride up to her shafts and just say: 'Good day,' and look at her with eyes that were not imploring, but seemed to say: 'You see, I am still, as the Germans say, A.D. – at disposition.'

It was a great consolation, not because she proposed ever to take him up again, but because it showed her that there was in the world one faithful soul in riding-breeches. And it showed her that she was not losing her looks.

And, indeed, she was not losing her looks. She was forty, but she was as clean run as on the day she had left the convent – as clear in outline, as clear coloured in the hair, as dark blue in the eyes. She thought that her looking-glass told her this; but there are always the doubts. . . . Rodney Bayham's eyes took them away.

It is very singular that Leonora should not have aged at all. I suppose that there are some types of beauty and even of youth made for the embellishments that come with enduring sorrow. That is too elaborately put. I mean that Leonora, if everything had prospered, might have become too hard and, maybe, overbearing. As it was she was tuned down to appearing efficient – and yet sympathetic. That is the rarest of all blends. And yet I swear that Leonora, in her restrained way, gave the impression of being intensely sympathetic. When she listened to you she appeared also to be listening to some sound that was going on in the distance. But still, she listened to you and took in what you said, which, since the record of humanity is a record of sorrows, was, as a rule, something sad.

I think that she must have taken Nancy through many terrors of the night and many bad places of the day. And that would account for the girl's passionate love for the elder woman. For Nancy's love for Leonora was an admiration that is awakened in Catholics by their feeling for the Virgin Mary and for various of the saints. It is too little to say that the girl would have laid her life at Leonora's feet. Well, she laid there the offer of her virtue – and her reason. Those were sufficient instalments of her life. It would today be much better for Nancy Rufford if she were dead.

Perhaps all these reflections are a nuisance; but they crowd on me. I will try to tell the story.

You see – when she came back from Nauheim Leonora began to have her headaches – headaches lasting through whole days, during which she could speak no word and could bear to hear no sound. And, day after day, Nancy would sit with her, silent and motionless for hours, steeping handkerchiefs in vinegar and water, and thinking her own thoughts. It must have been very bad for her – and her meals alone with Edward must have been bad for her too – and beastly bad for Edward. Edward, of course, wavered in his demeanour. What else could he do? At times he would sit silent and dejected over his untouched food. He would utter nothing but monosyllables when Nancy spoke to him. Then he was simply afraid of the girl falling in love with him. At other times he would take a little wine; pull himself together; attempt to chaff Nancy about a stake and binder hedge that her mare had checked at, or talk about the habits of the Chitralis. That was when he was thinking that it was rough on the poor girl that he should have become a dull companion. He realized that his talking to her in the park at Nauheim had done her no harm.

But all that was doing a great deal of harm to Nancy. It gradually opened her eyes to the fact that Edward was a man with his ups and downs and not an invariably gay uncle like a nice dog, a trustworthy horse or a girl friend. She would find him in attitudes of frightful dejection, sunk into his armchair in the study that was half a gunroom. She would notice through the open door that his face was the face of an old, dead man, when he had no one to talk to. Gradually it forced itself upon her attention that there were profound differences between the pair that she regarded as her uncle and her aunt. It was a conviction that came very slowly.

It began with Edward's giving an oldish horse to a young fellow called Selmes. Selmes' father had been ruined by a fraudulent solicitor and the Selmes family had had to sell their hunters. It was a case that had excited a good deal of sympathy in that part of the county. And Edward, meeting the young man one day, unmounted, and seeing him to be very unhappy, had offered to give him an old Irish cob upon which he was riding. It was a silly sort of thing to do, really. The horse was worth from thirty to forty pounds and Edward might have known that the gift would upset his wife. But Edward just had to comfort that unhappy young man whose father he had known all his life. And what made it all the worse was that young Selmes could not afford to keep the horse even. Edward recollected this, immediately after he had made the offer, and said quickly:

'Of course I mean that you should stable the horse at Bramshaw until you have time to turn round or want to sell him and get a better.'

Nancy went straight home and told all this to Leonora, who was lying down. She regarded it as a splendid instance of Edward's quick consideration for the feelings and the circumstances of the distressed. She thought it would cheer Leonora up – because it ought to cheer any woman up to know that she had such a splendid husband. That was the last girlish thought she ever had. For Leonora, whose headache had left her collected but miserably weak, turned upon her bed and uttered words that were amazing to the girl:

'I wish to God,' she said, 'that he was your husband, and not mine. We shall be ruined. We shall be ruined. Am I *never* to have a chance?' And suddenly Leonora burst into a passion of tears. She pushed herself up from the pillows with one elbow and sat there – crying, crying, crying, with her face hidden in her hands and the tears falling through her fingers.

The girl flushed, stammered and whimpered as if she had been personally insulted.

'But if Uncle Edward . . .' she began.

'That man,' said Leonora, with an extraordinary bitterness, 'would give the shirt off his back and off mine – and off yours to any . . .' She could not finish the sentence.

At that moment she had been feeling an extraordinary hatred and contempt for her husband. All the morning and all the afternoon she had been lying there thinking that Edward and the girl were together – in the field and hacking it home at dusk. She had been digging her sharp nails into her palms.

The house had been very silent in the drooping winter weather. And then, after an eternity of torture, there had invaded it the sound of opening doors, of the girl's gay voice saying:

'Well, it was only under the mistletoe.' . . . And there was Edward's gruff undertone. Then Nancy had come in, with feet that had hastened up the stairs and that tiptoed as they approached the open door of Leonora's room. Bramshaw had a great big hall with oak floors and tiger skins. Round this hall there ran a gallery upon which Leonora's doorway gave. And even when she had the worst of her headaches she liked to have her door open – I suppose so that she might hear the approaching footsteps of ruin and disaster. At any rate she hated to be in a room with a shut door.

At that moment Leonora hated Edward with a hatred that was like hell, and she would have liked to bring her riding-whip down across the girl's face. What right had Nancy to be young and slender and dark, and gay at times, at times mournful? What right had she to be exactly the woman to make Leonora's husband happy? For Leonora knew that Nancy would have made Edward happy.

Yes, Leonora wished to bring her riding-whip down on Nancy's young face. She imagined the pleasure she would feel when the lash fell across those queer features; the pleasure she would feel at drawing the handle at the same moment toward her, so as to cut deep into the flesh and to leave a lasting wheal.

Well, she left a lasting wheal, and her words cut deeply into the girl's mind . . .

They neither of them spoke about that again. A fortnight went by – a fortnight of deep rains, of heavy fields, of bad scent. Leonora's headaches seemed to have gone for good. She hunted once or twice, letting herself be piloted by Bayham, whilst Edward looked after the girl. Then, one evening, when those three were dining alone, Edward said, in the queer, deliberate, heavy tones that came out of him in those days (he was looking at the table):

'I have been thinking that Nancy ought to do more for her father. He is getting an old man. I have written to Colonel Rufford, suggesting that she should go to him.'

Leonora called out:

'How dare you? How dare you?'

The girl put her hand over her heart and cried out: 'Oh, my sweet Saviour, help me!' That was the queer way she thought within her mind, and the words forced themselves to her lips. Edward said nothing.

And that night, by a merciless trick of the devil that pays attention to this sweltering hell of ours, Nancy Rufford had a letter from her mother.

It came whilst Leonora was talking to Edward, or Leonora would have intercepted it as she had intercepted others. It was an amazing and a horrible letter . . .

I don't know what it contained. I just average out from its effects on Nancy that her mother, having eloped with some worthless sort of fellow, had done what is called 'sinking lower and lower'. Whether she was actually on the streets I do not know, but I rather think that she eked out a small allowance that she had from her husband by that means of livelihood. And I think that she stated as much in her letter to Nancy and upbraided the girl with living in luxury whilst her mother starved. And it must have been horrible in tone, for Mrs Rufford was a cruel sort of woman at the best of times. It must have seemed to that poor girl, opening her letter, for distraction from another grief, up in her bedroom, like the laughter of a devil.

I just cannot bear to think of my poor dear girl at that moment . . .

And, at the same time, Leonora was lashing, like a cold fiend, into the unfortunate Edward. Or, perhaps, he was not so unfortunate; because he had done what he knew to be the right thing, he may be deemed happy. I leave it to you. At any rate, he was sitting in his deep chair, and Leonora came into his room – for the first time in nine years. She said:

'This is the most atrocious thing you have done in your atrocious life.' He never moved and he never looked at her. God knows what was in Leonora's mind exactly.

I like to think that, uppermost in it was concern and horror at the thought of the poor girl's going back to a father whose voice made her shriek in the night. And, indeed, that motive was very strong with Leonora. But I think there was also present the thought that she wanted to go on torturing Edward with the girl's presence. She was, at that time, capable of that.

Edward was sunk in his chair; there were in the room two candles, hidden by green glass shades. The green shades were reflected in the glasses of the bookcases that contained not books but guns with gleaming brown barrels and fishing-rods in green baize over-covers. There was dimly to be seen, above a mantelpiece encumbered with spurs, hooves and bronze models of horses, a dark-brown picture of a white horse.

'If you think,' Leonora said, 'that I do not know that you are in love with the girl . . .' She began spiritedly, but she could not find any ending for the sentence. Edward did not stir; he never spoke. And then Leonora said:

'If you want me to divorce you, I will. You can marry her then. She's in love with you.'

He groaned at that, a little, Leonora said. Then she went away.

Heaven knows what happened in Leonora after that. She certainly does not herself know. She probably said a good deal more to Edward than I have been able to report; but that is all that she has told me and I am not going to make up speeches. To follow her psychological development of that moment I think we must allow that she up-braided him for a great deal of their past life, whilst Edward sat absolutely silent. And, indeed, in speaking of it afterwards, she has said several times: 'I said a great deal more to him than I wanted to, just because he was so silent.' She talked, in fact, in the endeavour to sting him into speech.

She must have said so much that, with the expression of her grievance, her mood changed. She went back to her own room in the gallery, and sat there for a long time thinking. And she thought herself into a mood of absolute unselfishness, of absolute self-contempt, too. She said to herself that she was no good; that she had failed in all her efforts – in her efforts to get Edward back as in her efforts to make him curb his expenditure. She imagined herself to be exhausted; she imagined herself to be done. Then a great fear came over her.

She thought that Edward, after what she had said to him, must have committed suicide. She went out on to the gallery and listened; there was no sound in all the house except the regular beat of the great clock in the hall. But, even in her debased condition, she was not the person to hang about. She acted. She went straight to Edward's room, opened the door, and looked in.

He was oiling the breech action of a gun. It was an unusual thing for him to do, at that time of night, in his evening clothes. It never occurred to her, nevertheless, that he was going to shoot himself with that implement. She knew that he was doing it just for occupation – to keep himself from thinking. He looked up when she opened the door, his face illuminated by the light cast upwards from the round orifices in the green candle shades.

She said:

'I didn't imagine that I should find Nancy here.' She thought that she owed that to him. He answered then:

'I don't imagine that you did imagine it.' Those were the only words he spoke that night. She went, like a lame duck, back through the long corridors; she stumbled over the familiar tiger skins in the dark hall. She could hardly drag one limb after the other. In the gallery she perceived that Nancy's door was half open and that there was a light in the girl's room. A sudden madness possessed her, a desire for action, a thirst for self-explanation.

Their rooms all gave on to the gallery; Leonora's to the east, the girl's next, then Edward's. The sight of those three open doors, side by side, gaping to receive whom the chances of the black night might bring, made Leonora shudder all over her body. She went into Nancy's room.

The girl was sitting perfectly still in an armchair, very upright, as she had been taught to sit at the convent. She appeared to be as calm as a church; her hair fell, black and like a pall, down over both her shoulders. The fire beside her was burning brightly; she must have just put coals on. She was in a white silk kimono that covered her to the feet. The clothes that she had taken off were exactly folded upon the proper seats. Her long hands were one upon each arm of the chair that had a pink and white chintz back.

Leonora told me these things. She seemed to think it extraordinary that the girl could have done such orderly things as fold up the clothes she had taken off upon such a night – when Edward had announced that he was going to send her to her father, and when, from her mother, she had received that letter. The letter, in its envelope, was in her right hand.

Leonora did not at first perceive it. She said:

'What are you doing so late?'

The girl answered: 'Just thinking.'

They seemed to think in whispers and to speak below their breaths. Then Leonora's eyes fell on the envelope, and she recognized Mrs Rufford's handwriting.

It was one of those moments when thinking was impossible, Leonora said. It was as if stones were being thrown at her from every direction and she could only run. She heard herself exclaim:

'Edward's dying – because of you. He's dying. He's worth more than either of us . . .'

The girl looked past her at the panels of the half-closed door.

'My poor father,' she said, 'my poor father.'

'You must stay here,' Leonora answered fiercely. 'You must stay here. I tell you you must stay here.'

'I am going to Glasgow,' Nancy answered. 'I shall go to Glasgow tomorrow morning. My mother is in Glasgow.'

It appears that it was in Glasgow that Mrs Rufford pursued her disorderly life. She had selected that city, not because it was more profitable but because it was the natal home of her husband to whom she desired to cause as much pain as possible.

'You must stay here,' Leonora began, 'to save Edward. He's dying for love of you.'

The girl turned her calm eyes upon Leonora.

'I know it,' she said. 'And I am dying for love of him.'

Leonora uttered an 'Ah,' that, in spite of herself, was an 'Ah' of horror and of grief.

'That is why,' the girl continued, 'I am going to Glasgow – to take my mother away from there.' She added, 'To the ends of the earth,' for, if the last months had made her nature that of a woman, her phrases were still romantically those of a schoolgirl. It was as if she had grown up so quickly that there had not been time to put her hair up. But she added: 'We're no good – my mother and I.'

Leonora said, with her fierce calmness:

'No. No. You're not no good. It's I that am no good. You can't let that man go on to ruin for want of you. You must belong to him.'

The girl, she said, smiled at her with a queer, far-away smile – as if she were a thousand years old, as if Leonora were a tiny child.

'I knew you would come to that,' she said, very slowly. 'But we are not worth it – Edward and I.'

III

Nancy had, in fact, been thinking ever since Leonora had made that comment over the giving of the horse to young Selmes. She had been thinking and thinking, because she had had to sit for many days silent beside her aunt's bed. (She had always thought of Leonora as her aunt.) And she had had to sit thinking during many silent meals with Edward. And then, at times, with his bloodshot eyes and creased, heavy mouth, he would smile at her. And gradually the knowledge had come to her that Edward did not love Leonora and that Leonora hated Edward. Several things contributed to form and to harden this conviction.

She was allowed to read the papers in those days – or, rather, since Leonora was always on her bed and Edward breakfasted alone and went out early, over the estate, she was left alone with the papers. One day, in the papers, she saw the portrait of a woman she knew very well. Beneath it she read the words: 'The Hon. Mrs Brand, plaintiff in the remarkable divorce case reported on p. 8.' Nancy hardly knew what a divorce case was. She had been so remarkably well brought up, and Roman Catholics do not practise divorce. I don't know how Leonora had done it exactly. I suppose she had always impressed it on Nancy's mind that nice women did not read these things, and that would have been enough to make Nancy skip those pages.

She read, at any rate, the account of the Brand divorce case – principally because she wanted to tell Leonora about it. She imagined that Leonora, when her headache left her, would like to know what was happening to Mrs Brand, who lived at Christchurch[151] and whom they both liked very well. The case occupied three days, and the report that Nancy first came upon was that of the third day. Edward, however, kept the papers of the week, after his methodical fashion, in a rack in his gunroom, and when she had finished her breakfast Nancy went to that quiet apartment and had what she would have called a good read. It seemed to her to be a queer affair. She could not understand why one counsel should be so anxious to know all about the movements of Mr Brand upon a certain day; she could not understand why a chart of the bedroom accommodation at Christchurch Old Hall should be produced in court. She did not even see why they should want to know that, upon a certain occasion, the drawing-room door was locked. It made her laugh; it appeared to be all so senseless that grown people should occupy themselves with such matters. It struck her, nevertheless, as odd that one of the counsel should cross-question Mr Brand so insistently and so impertinently as to his feelings for Miss Lupton. Nancy knew Miss Lupton of Ringwood[152] very well – a jolly girl, who rode a horse with two white fetlocks. Mr Brand persisted that he did not love Miss Lupton . . . Well, of course he did not love Miss Lupton; he was a married man. You might as well think of Uncle Edward loving . . . loving anybody but Leonora. When people were married there was an end of loving. There were, no doubt, people who misbehaved – but they were poor people – or people not like those she knew.

So these matters presented themselves to Nancy's mind.

But later on in the case she found that Mr Brand had to confess to a 'guilty intimacy' with some one or other. Nancy imagined that he must have been telling some one his wife's secrets; she could not understand why that was a serious offence. Of course it was not very gentlemanly – it lessened her opinion of Mr Brand. But since she found that Mrs Brand had condoned that offence, she imagined that they could not have been very serious secrets that Mr Brand had told. And then, suddenly, it was forced on her conviction that Mr Brand – the mild Mr Brand that she had seen a month or two before their departure to Nauheim, playing 'Blind Man's Buff' with his children and kissing his wife when he caught her – Mr Brand and Mrs Brand had been on the worst possible terms. That was incredible.

Yet there it was – in black and white. Mr Brand drank; Mr Brand had struck Mrs Brand to the ground when he was drunk. Mr Brand was adjudged, in two or three abrupt words, at the end of columns and columns of paper, to have been guilty of cruelty to his wife and to have committed adultery with Miss Lupton. The last words conveyed nothing to Nancy – nothing real, that is to say. She knew that one was commanded not to commit adultery – but why, she thought, should one? It was probably something like catching salmon out of season – a thing one did not do. She gathered it had something to do with kissing, or holding someone in your arms. . . .

And yet the whole effect of that reading upon Nancy was mysterious, terrifying and evil. She felt a sickness – a sickness that grew as she read. Her heart beat painfully; she began to cry. She asked God how He could permit such things to be. And she was more certain that Edward did not love Leonora and that Leonora hated Edward. Perhaps, then, Edward loved someone else. It was unthinkable.

If he could love someone else than Leonora, her fierce unknown heart suddenly spoke in her side, why could it not be herself? And he did not love her . . . This had occurred about a month before she got the letter from her mother. She let the matter rest until the sick feeling went off; it did that in a day or two. Then, finding that Leonora's headaches had gone, she suddenly told Leonora that Mrs Brand had divorced her husband. She asked what, exactly, it all meant.

Leonora was lying on the sofa in the hall; she was feeling so weak that she could hardly find the words. She answered just:

'It means that Mr Brand will be able to marry again.'

Nancy said:

'But . . . but . . .' and then: 'He will be able to marry Miss Lupton.' Leonora just moved a hand in assent. Her eyes were shut.

'Then . . .' Nancy began. Her blue eyes were full of horror: her brows were tight above them; the lines of pain about her mouth were very distinct. In her eyes the whole of that familiar, great hall had a changed aspect. The andirons with the brass flowers at the ends appeared unreal; the burning logs were just logs that were burning and not the comfortable symbols of an indestructible mode of life. The flame fluttered before the high fireback; the St Bernard sighed in his sleep. Outside the winter rain fell and fell. And suddenly she thought that Edward might marry some one else; and she nearly screamed.

Leonora opened her eyes, lying sideways, with her face upon the black and gold pillow of the sofa that was drawn half across the great fireplace.

'I thought,' Nancy said, 'I never imagined . . . Aren't marriages sacraments? Aren't they indissoluble? I thought you were married . . .

and . . .' She was sobbing. 'I thought you were married or not married as you are alive or dead.'

'That,' Leonora said, 'is the law of the Church. It is not the law of the land . . .'

'Oh yes,' Nancy said, 'the Brands are Protestants.'

She felt a sudden safeness descend upon her, and for an hour or so her mind was at rest. It seemed to her idiotic not to have remembered Henry VIII and the basis upon which Protestantism rests.[153] She almost laughed at herself.

The long afternoon wore on; the flames still fluttered when the maid made up the fire; the St Bernard awoke and lolloped away towards the kitchen. And then Leonora opened her eyes and said almost coldly:

'And you? Don't you think you will get married?'

It was so unlike Leonora that, for the moment, the girl was frightened in the dusk. But then, again, it seemed a perfectly reasonable question.

'I don't know,' she answered. 'I don't know that anyone wants to marry me.'

'Several people want to marry you,' Leonora said.

'But I don't want to marry,' Nancy answered. 'I should like to go on living with you and Edward. I don't think I am in the way or that I am really an expense. If I went you would have to have a companion. Or, perhaps, I ought to earn my living . . .'

'I wasn't thinking of that,' Leonora answered in the same dull tone. 'You will have money enough from your father. But most people want to be married.'

I believe that she then asked the girl if she would not like to marry me, and that Nancy answered that she would marry me if she were told to; but that she wanted to go on living there. She added:

'If I married anyone I should want him to be like Edward.'

She was frightened out of her life. Leonora writhed on her couch and called out: 'Oh, God! . . .'

Nancy ran for the maid; for tablets of aspirin; for wet handkerchiefs. It never occurred to her that Leonora's expression of agony was for anything else than physical pain.

You are to remember that all this happened a month before Leonora went into the girl's room at night. I have been casting back again; but

I cannot help it. It is so difficult to keep all these people going. I tell you about Leonora and bring her up to date; then about Edward, who has fallen behind. And then the girl gets hopelessly left behind. I wish I could put it down in diary form. Thus: On the 1st of September they returned from Nauheim. Leonora at once took to her bed. By the 1st of October they were all going to meets together. Nancy had already observed very fully that Edward was strange in his manner. About the 6th of that month Edward gave the horse to young Selmes, and Nancy had cause to believe that her aunt did not love her uncle. On the 20th she read the account of the divorce case, which is reported in the papers of the 18th and the two following days. On the 23rd she had the conversation with her aunt in the hall – about marriage in general and about her own possible marriage. Her aunt's coming to her bedroom did not occur until the 12th of November . . .

Thus she had three weeks for introspection – for introspection beneath gloomy skies, in that old house, rendered darker by the fact that it lay in a hollow crowned by fir trees with their black shadows. It was not a good situation for a girl. She began thinking about love, she who had never before considered it as anything other than a rather humorous, rather nonsensical matter. She remembered chance passages in chance books – things that had not really affected her at all at the time. She remembered someone's love for the Princess Badrulbadour.[154] She remembered to have heard that love was a flame, a thirst, a withering up of the vitals – though she did nor know what the vitals were. She had a vague recollection that love was said to render a hopeless lover's eyes hopeless; she remembered a character in a book who was said to have taken to drink through love; she remembered that lovers' existences were said to be punctuated with heavy sighs. Once she went to the little cottage piano that was in the corner of the hall and began to play. It was a tinkly, reedy instrument, for none of that household had any turn for music. Nancy herself could play a few simple songs, and she found herself playing. She had been sitting on the window seat, looking out on the fading day. Leonora had gone to pay some calls; Edward was looking after some planting up in the new spinney. Thus she found herself playing on the old piano. She did not know how she came to be doing it. A silly lilting wavering tune came from before her in the dusk – a tune in which major notes with their cheerful insistence wavered and melted into minor sounds, as, beneath a bridge, the high-lights on dark waters melt and waver and disappear into black depths. Well, it was a silly old tune . . .

It goes with the words – they are about a willow tree, I think:

> *Thou art to all lost loves the best*
> *The only true plant found.*

– That sort of thing. It is Herrick,[155] I believe, and the music with the reedy, irregular, lilting sound that goes with Herrick. And it was dusk; the heavy, hewn, dark pillars that supported the gallery were like mourning presences; the fire had sunk to nothing – a mere glow amongst white ashes . . . It was a sentimental sort of place and light and hour . . .

And suddenly Nancy found that she was crying. She was crying quietly; she went on to cry with long convulsive sobs. It seemed to her that everything gay, everything charming, all light, all sweetness, had gone out of life. Unhappiness; unhappiness; unhappiness was all around her. She seemed to know no happy being and she herself was agonizing. . . .

She remembered that Edward's eyes were hopeless; she was certain that he was drinking too much; at times he sighed deeply. He appeared as a man who was burning with inward flame; drying up in the soul with thirst; withering up in the vitals. Then, the torturing conviction came to her – the conviction that had visited her again and again – that Edward must love some one other than Leonora. With her little, pedagogic sectarianism she remembered that Catholics do not do this thing. But Edward was a Protestant. Then Edward loved somebody . . .

And, after that thought, her eyes grew hopeless; she sighed as the old St Bernard beside her did. At meals she would feel an intolerable desire to drink a glass of wine, and then another and then a third. Then she would find herself grow gay . . . But in half an hour the gaiety went; she felt like a person who is burning up with an inward flame; desiccating at the soul with thirst; withering up in the vitals. One evening she went into Edward's gunroom – he had gone to a meeting of the National Reserve Committee.[156] On the table beside his chair was a decanter of whisky. She poured out a wine-glassful and drank it off.

Flame then really seemed to fill her body; her legs swelled; her face grew feverish. She dragged her tall height up to her room and lay in the dark. The bed reeled beneath her; she gave way to the thought that she was in Edward's arms; that he was kissing her on her face that burned; on her shoulders that burned, and on her neck that was on fire.

She never touched alcohol again. Not once after that did she have such thoughts. They died out of her mind; they left only a feeling of shame so insupportable that her brain could not take it in and they vanished. She imagined that her anguish at the thought of Edward's love for another person was solely sympathy for Leonora; she determined that the rest of her life must be spent in acting as Leonora's handmaiden – sweeping, tending, embroidering, like some Deborah, some medieval saint – I am not, unfortunately, up in the Catholic hagiology.[157] But I know that she pictured herself as some personage with a depressed, earnest face and tightly closed lips, in a clear white room, watering flowers or tending an embroidery frame. Or, she desired to go with Edward to Africa and to throw herself in the path of a charging lion so that Edward might be saved for Leonora at the cost of her life. Well, along with her sad thoughts she had her childish ones.

She knew nothing – nothing of life, except that one must live sadly. That she now knew. What happened to her on the night when she received at once the blow that Edward wished her to go to her father in India and the blow of the letter from her mother was this. She called first upon her sweet Saviour – and she thought of Our Lord as her sweet Saviour! – that He might make it impossible that she should go to India. Then she realized from Edward's demeanour that he was determined that she should go to India. It must then be right that she should go. Edward was always right in his determinations. He was the Cid; he was Lohengrin; he was the Chevalier Bayard.

Nevertheless her mind mutinied and revolted. She could not leave that house. She imagined that he wished her gone that she might not witness his amours with another girl. Well, she was prepared to tell him that she was ready to witness his amours with another young girl. She would stay there – to comfort Leonora.

Then came the desperate shock of the letter from her mother. Her mother said, I believe, something like: 'You have no right to go on living your life of prosperity and respect. You ought to be on the streets with me. How do you know that you are even Colonel Rufford's daughter?' She did not know what these words meant. She thought of her mother as sleeping beneath the arches whilst the snow fell. That was the impression conveyed to her mind by the words 'on the streets'. A Platonic sense of duty gave her the idea that she ought to go to comfort her mother – the mother that bore her, though she hardly knew what the words meant. At the same time she knew that her mother had left her father with another man – therefore she pitied her father, and thought it terrible in herself that she trembled at the sound of her father's voice. If her mother was that sort of woman it was natural that her father should have had accesses of madness in which he had struck herself to the ground. And the voice of her conscience said to her that her first duty was to her parents. It was in accord with this awakened sense of duty that she undressed with great care and meticulously folded the clothes that she took off. Sometimes, but not very often, she threw them helter-skelter about the room.

And that sense of duty was her prevailing mood when Leonora, tall, clean-run, golden-haired, all in black, appeared in her doorway, and told her that Edward was dying of love for her. She knew then with her conscious mind what she had known within herself for months – that Edward was dying – actually and physically dying – of love for her. It seemed to her that for one short moment her spirit could say: '*Domine, nunc dimittis* . . . Lord, now lettest thou thy servant depart in peace.'[158] She imagined that she could cheerfully go away to Glasgow and rescue her fallen mother.

IV

And it seemed to her to be in tune with the mood, with the hour, and with the woman in front of her to say that she knew Edward was dying of love for her and that she was dying of love for Edward. For that fact had suddenly slipped into place and become real for her as the niched marker on a whist tablet slips round with the pressure of your thumb. That rubber at least was made.

And suddenly Leonora seemed to have become different and she seemed to have become different in her attitude towards Leonora. It was as if she, in her frail, white, silken kimono, sat beside her fire, but upon a throne. It was as if Leonora, in her close dress of black lace, with the gleaming white shoulders and the coiled yellow hair that the girl had always considered the most beautiful thing in the world – it was as if Leonora had become pinched, shrivelled, blue with cold, shivering, suppliant. Yet Leonora was commanding her. It was no good commanding her. She was going on the morrow to her mother who was in Glasgow.

Leonora went on saying that she must stay there to save Edward, who was dying of love for her. And, proud and happy in the thought that Edward loved her, and that she loved him, she did not even listen to what Leonora said. It appeared to her that it was Leonora's business to save her husband's body; she, Nancy, possessed his soul – a precious thing that she would shield and bear away up in her arms – as if Leonora were a hungry dog, trying to spring up at a lamb that she was carrying. Yes, she felt as if Edward's love were a precious lamb that she were bearing away from a cruel and predatory beast. For, at that time, Leonora appeared to her as a cruel and predatory beast. Leonora, Leonora with her hunger, with her cruelty had driven Edward to madness. He must be sheltered by his love for her and by her love – her love from a great distance and unspoken, enveloping him, surrounding him, upholding him; by her voice speaking from Glasgow, saying that she loved, that she adored, that she passed no moment without longing, loving, quivering at the thought of him.

Leonora said loudly, insistently, with a bitterly imperative tone:

'You must stay here; you must belong to Edward. I will divorce him.'

The girl answered:

'The Church does not allow of divorce. I cannot belong to your husband. I am going to Glasgow to rescue my mother.'

The half-opened door opened noiselessly to the full. Edward was there. His devouring, doomed eyes were fixed on the girl's face; his shoulders slouched forward; he was undoubtedly half drunk and he had the whisky decanter in one hand, a slanting candlestick in the other. He said, with a heavy ferocity, to Nancy:

'I forbid you to talk about these things. You are to stay here until I hear from your father. Then you will go to your father.'

The two women, looking at each other, like beasts about to spring, hardly gave a glance to him. He leaned against the doorpost. He said again:

'Nancy, I forbid you to talk about these things. I am the master of this house.' And, at the sound of his voice, heavy, male, coming from a deep chest, in the night with the blackness behind him, Nancy felt as if her spirit bowed before him, with folded hands. She felt that she would go to India, and that she desired never again to talk of these things.

Leonora said:

'You see that it is your duty to belong to him. He must not be allowed to go on drinking.'

Nancy did not answer. Edward was gone; they heard him slipping and shambling on the polished oak of the stairs. Nancy screamed when there came the sound of a heavy fall. Leonora said again:

'You see!'

The sounds went on from the hall below; the light of the candle Edward held flickered up between the hand rails of the gallery. Then they heard his voice:

'Give me Glasgow . . . Glasgow, in Scotland . . . I want the number of a man called White, of Simrock Park, Glasgow . . . Edward White, Simrock Park, Glasgow . . . ten minutes . . . at this time of night . . .' His voice was quite level, normal, and patient. Alcohol took him in the legs, not the speech. 'I can wait,' his voice came again. 'Yes, I know they have a number. I have been in communication with them before.'

'He is going to telephone to your mother,' Leonora said. 'He will make it all right for her.' She got up and closed the door. She came back to the fire, and added bitterly: 'He can always make it all right for everybody, except me – excepting me!'

The girl said nothing. She sat there in a blissful dream. She seemed to see her lover sitting as he always sat, in a round-backed chair, in the dark hall – sitting low, with the receiver at his ear, talking in a gentle, slow voice, that he reserved for the telephone – and saving the world and her, in the black darkness. She moved her hand over the bareness of the base of her throat, to have the warmth of flesh upon it and upon her bosom.

She said nothing; Leonora went on talking . . .

God knows what Leonora said. She repeated that the girl must belong to her husband. She said that she used that phrase because, though she might have a divorce, or even a dissolution of the marriage by the Church, it would still be adultery that the girl and Edward would be committing. But she said that that was necessary; it was the price that the girl must pay for the sin of having made Edward love her, for the sin of loving her husband. She talked on and on, beside the fire. The girl must become an adulteress; she had wronged Edward by being so beautiful, so gracious, so good. It was sinful to be so good. She must pay the price so as to save the man she had wronged.

In between her pauses the girl could hear the voice of Edward, droning on, indistinguishably, with jerky pauses for replies. It made her glow with pride; the man she loved was working for her. He at least was resolved; was malely determined; knew the right thing. Leonora talked on with her eyes boring into Nancy's. The girl hardly looked at her and hardly heard her. After a long time Nancy said – after hours and hours:

'I shall go to India as soon as Edward hears from my father. I cannot talk about these things, because Edward does not wish it.'

At that Leonora screamed out and wavered swiftly towards the closed door. And Nancy found that she was springing out of her chair with her white arms stretched wide. She was clasping the other woman to her breast; she was saying:

'Oh, my poor dear; oh, my poor dear.' And they sat, crouching together in each other's arms, and crying and crying; and they lay down in the same bed, talking and talking, all through the night. And all through the night Edward could hear their voices through the wall. That was how it went . . .

Next morning they were all three as if nothing had happened. Towards eleven Edward came to Nancy, who was arranging some Christmas roses in a silver bowl. He put a telegram beside her on the table. 'You can uncode it for yourself,' he said. Then, as he went out of the door, he said:

'You can tell your aunt I have cabled to Mr Dowell to come over. He will make things easier till you leave.'

The telegram, when it was uncoded, read, as far as I can remember:

'Will take Mrs Rufford to Italy. Undertake to do this for certain. Am devotedly attached to Mrs Rufford. Have no need of financial assistance. Did not know there was a daughter, and am much obliged to you for pointing out my duty. – White.' It was something like that.

Then the household resumed its wonted course of days until my arrival.

V

It is this part of the story that makes me saddest of all. For I ask myself unceasingly, my mind going round and round in a weary, baffled space of pain – what should these people have done? What, in the name of God, should they have done?

The end was perfectly plain to each of them – it was perfectly manifest at this stage that, if the girl did not, in Leonora's phrase, 'belong to Edward,' Edward must die, the girl must lose her reason because Edward died – and, that after a time, Leonora, who was the coldest and the strongest of the three, would console herself by marrying Rodney Bayham and have a quiet, comfortable, good time. That end, on that night, whilst Leonora sat in the girl's bedroom and Edward telephoned down below – that end was plainly manifest. The girl, plainly, was half mad already; Edward was half dead; only Leonora, active, persistent, instinct with her cold passion of energy, was 'doing things'. What, then, should they have done? It worked out in the extinction of two very splendid personalities – for Edward and the girl *were* splendid personalities, in order that a third personality, more normal, should have, after a long period of trouble, a quiet, comfortable, good time.

I am writing this, now, I should say, a full eighteen months after the words that end my last chapter. Since writing the words 'until my arrival', which I see end that paragraph, I have seen again for a glimpse, from a swift train, Beaucaire with the beautiful white tower, Tarascon with the square castle, the great Rhone, the immense stretches of the Crau.[159] I have rushed through all Provence – and all Provence no longer matters. It is no longer in the olive hills that I shall find my Heaven; because there is only Hell . . .

Edward is dead; the girl is gone – oh, utterly gone; Leonora is having a good time with Rodney Bayham, and I sit alone in Bramshaw Teleragh. I have been through Provence; I have seen Africa; I have visited Asia to see, in Ceylon, in a darkened room, my poor girl, sitting motionless, with her wonderful hair about her, looking at me with eyes that did not see me, and saying distinctly: '*Credo in unum Deum Omnipotentem*[160] . . . *Credo in unum Deum Omnipotentem.*' Those are the only reasonable words she uttered; those are the only words, it appears, that she ever will utter. I suppose that they are reasonable words; it must be extraordinarily reasonable for her, if she can say that she believes in an Omnipotent Deity. Well, there it is. I am very tired of it all . . .

For, I daresay, all this may sound romantic, but it is tiring, tiring, tiring to have been in the midst of it; to have taken the tickets; to have caught the trains; to have chosen the cabins; to have consulted the purser and the stewards as to diet for the quiescent patient who did nothing but announce her belief in an Omnipotent Deity. That may sound romantic – but it is just a record of fatigue.

I don't know why I should always be selected to be serviceable. I don't resent it – but I have never been the least good. Florence selected me for her own purposes, and I was no good to her; Edward called me to come and have a chat with him, and I couldn't stop him cutting his throat.

And then, one day eighteen months ago, I was quietly writing in my room at Bramshaw when Leonora came to me with a letter. It was a very pathetic letter from Colonel Rufford about Nancy. Colonel Rufford had left the army and had taken up an appointment at a tea-planting estate in Ceylon. His letter was pathetic because it was so brief, so inarticulate, and so business-like. He had gone down to the boat to meet his daughter, and had found his daughter quite mad. It appears that at Aden,[161] Nancy had seen in a local paper the news of Edward's suicide. In the Red Sea she had gone mad. She had remarked to Mrs Colonel Luton, who was chaperoning her, that she believed in an Omnipotent Deity. She hadn't made any fuss; her eyes were quite dry and glassy. Even when she was mad Nancy could behave herself.

Colonel Rufford said the doctor did not anticipate that there was any chance of his child's recovery. It was, nevertheless, possible that if she could see someone from Bramshaw it might soothe her and it might have a good effect. And he just simply wrote to Leonora: 'Please come and see if you can do it.'

I seem to have lost all sense of the pathetic; but still, that simple, enormous request of the old colonel strikes me as pathetic. He was cursed by his atrocious temper; he had been cursed by a half-mad wife, who drank and went on the streets. His daughter was totally mad – and yet he believed in the goodness of human nature. He believed that Leonora would take the trouble to go all the way to Ceylon in order to soothe his daughter. Leonora wouldn't. Leonora didn't ever want to see Nancy again. I daresay that that, in the circumstances, was natural enough. At the same time she agreed, as it were, on public grounds, that someone soothing ought to go from Bramshaw to Ceylon. She sent me and her old nurse, who had looked after Nancy from the time when the girl, a child of thirteen, had first come to Bramshaw. So off I go, rushing through Provence, to catch the steamer at Marseilles. And I wasn't the least good when I got to Ceylon; and the nurse wasn't the least good. Nothing has been the least good.

The doctors said, at Kandy,[162] that if Nancy could be brought to England, the sea air, the change of climate, the voyage, and all the usual sort of things, might restore her reason. Of course, they haven't restored her reason. She is, I am aware, sitting in the hall, forty paces from where I am now writing. I don't want to be in the least romantic about it. She is very well dressed; she is quite quiet; she is very beautiful. The old nurse looks after her very efficiently.

Of course you have the makings of a situation here, but it is all very humdrum, as far as I am concerned. I should marry Nancy if her reason were ever sufficiently restored to let her appreciate the meaning of the Anglican marriage service. But it is probable that her reason will never be sufficiently restored to let her appreciate the meaning of the Anglican marriage service. Therefore I cannot marry her, according to the law of the land.

So here I am very much where I started thirteen years ago. I am the attendant, not the husband, of a beautiful girl, who pays no attention to me. I am estranged from Leonora, who married Rodney Bayham in my absence and went to live at Bayham. Leonora rather dislikes me, because she has got it into her head that I disapprove of her marriage with Rodney Bayham. Well, I disapprove of her marriage. Possibly I am jealous.

Yes, no doubt I am jealous. In my fainter sort of way I seem to perceive myself following the lines of Edward Ashburnham. I suppose that I should really like to be a polygamist; with Nancy, and with Leonora, and with Maisie Maidan and possibly even with Florence. I am no doubt like every other man; only, probably because of my American origin I am fainter. At the same time I am able to assure you that I am a strictly respectable person. I have never done anything that the most anxious mother of a daughter or the most careful dean of a cathedral would object to. I have only followed, faintly, and in my unconscious desires, Edward Ashburnham. Well, it is all over. Not one of us has got what he really wanted. Leonora wanted Edward, and she has got Rodney Bayham, a pleasant enough sort of sheep. Florence wanted Bramshaw, and it is I who have bought it from Leonora. I didn't really want it; what I wanted mostly was to cease being a nurse-attendant. Well, I am a nurse-attendant. Edward wanted Nancy Rufford, and I have got her. Only she is mad. It is a queer and fantastic world. Why can't people have what they want? The things were all there to content everybody; yet everybody has the wrong thing. Perhaps you can make head or tail of it; it is beyond me.

Is there any terrestrial paradise where, amidst the whispering of the olive-leaves, people can be with whom they like and have what they like and take their ease in shadows and in coolness? Or are all men's lives like the lives of us good people – like the lives of the Ashburnhams, of the Dowells, of the Ruffords – broken, tumultuous, agonized, and unromantic lives, periods punctuated by screams, by imbecilities, by deaths, by agonies? Who the devil knows?

For there was a great deal of imbecility about the closing scenes of the Ashburnham tragedy. Neither of those two women knew what they wanted. It was only Edward who took a perfectly clear line, and he was drunk most of the time. But, drunk or sober, he stuck to what was demanded by convention and by the traditions of his house. Nancy Rufford had to be exported to India, and Nancy Rufford hadn't to hear a word of love from him. She was exported to India and she never heard a word from Edward Ashburnham.

It was the conventional line; it was in tune with the tradition of Edward's house. I daresay it worked out for the greatest good of the body politic. Conventions and traditions, I suppose, work blindly but surely for the preservation of the normal type; for the extinction of proud, resolute and unusual individuals.

Edward was the normal man, but there was too much of the sentimentalist about him; and society does not need too many sentimentalists. Nancy was a splendid creature, but she had about her a touch of madness. Society does not need individuals with touches of madness about them. So Edward and Nancy found themselves steamrolled out and Leonora survives, the perfectly normal type, married to a man who is rather like a rabbit. For Rodney Bayham is rather like a rabbit, and I hear that Leonora is expected to have a baby in three months' time.

So those splendid and tumultuous creatures with their magnetism and their passions – those two that I really loved – have gone from this earth. It is no doubt best for them. What would Nancy have made of Edward if she had succeeded in living with him; what would Edward have made of her? For there was about Nancy a touch of cruelty – a touch of definite actual cruelty that made her desire to see people suffer. Yes, she desired to see Edward suffer. And, by God, she gave him hell.

She gave him an unimaginable hell. Those two women pursued that poor devil and flayed the skin off him as if they had done it with whips. I tell you his mind bled almost visibly. I seem to see him stand, naked to the waist, his forearms shielding his eyes, and flesh hanging from him in rags. I tell you that is no exaggeration of what I feel. It was as if Leonora and Nancy banded themselves together to do execution, for the sake of humanity, upon the body of a man who was at their disposal. They were like a couple of Sioux who had got hold of an Apache and had him well tied to a stake. I tell you there was no end to the tortures they inflicted upon him.

Night after night he would hear them talking; talking; maddened, sweating, seeking oblivion in drink, he would lie there and hear the voices going on and on. And day after day Leonora would come to him and would announce the results of their deliberations.

They were like judges debating over the sentence upon a criminal; they were like ghouls with an immobile corpse in a tomb beside them.

I don't think that Leonora was any more to blame than the girl – though Leonora was the more active of the two. Leonora, as I have said, was the perfectly normal woman. I mean to say that in normal circumstances her desires were those of the woman who is needed by society. She desired children, decorum, an establishment; she desired to avoid waste, she desired to keep up appearances. She was utterly and entirely normal even in her utterly undeniable beauty. But I don't mean to say that she acted perfectly normally in this perfectly abnormal situation. All the world was mad around her and she herself, agonized, took on the complexion of a mad woman; of a woman very wicked; of the villain of the piece. What would you have? Steel is a normal, hard, polished substance. But, if you put it in a hot fire it will become red, soft, and not to be handled. If you put it in a fire still more hot it will drip away. It was like that with Leonora. She was made for normal circumstances – for Mr Rodney Bayham, who will keep a separate establishment, secretly, in Portsmouth, and make occasional trips to Paris and to Budapest.

In the case of Edward and the girl, Leonora broke and simply went all over the place. She adopted unfamiliar and therefore extraordinary and ungraceful attitudes of mind. At one moment she was all for revenge. After haranguing the girl for hours through the night she harangued for hours of the day the silent Edward. And Edward just once tripped up, and that was his undoing. Perhaps he had had too much whisky that afternoon.

She asked him perpetually what he wanted. What did he want? What did he want? And all he ever answered was: 'I have told you'. He meant that he wanted the girl to go to her father in India as soon as her father should cable that he was ready to receive her. But just once he tripped up. To Leonora's eternal question he answered that all he desired in life was that – that he could pick himself together again and go on with his daily occupations if – the girl, being five thousand miles away, would continue to love him. He wanted nothing more. He prayed his God for nothing more. Well, he was a sentimentalist.

And the moment that she heard that, Leonora determined that the girl should not go five thousand miles away and that she should not continue to love Edward. The way she worked it was this:

She continued to tell the girl that she must belong to Edward; she was going to get a divorce; she was going to get a dissolution of marriage from Rome. But she considered it to be her duty to warn the girl of the sort of monster that Edward was. She told the girl of La Dolciquita, of Mrs Basil, of Maisie Maidan, of Florence. She spoke of the agonies that she had endured during her life with the man, who was violent, overbearing, vain, drunken, arrogant, and monstrously a prey to his sexual necessities. And, at hearing of the miseries her aunt had suffered – for Leonora once more had the aspect of an aunt to the girl – with the swift cruelty of youth and, with the swift solidarity that attaches woman to woman, the girl made her resolves. Her aunt said incessantly: 'You must save Edward's life; you must save his life. All that he needs is a little period of satisfaction from you. Then he will tire of you as he has of the others. But you must save his life.'

And, all the while, that wretched fellow knew – by a curious instinct that runs between human beings living together – exactly what was going on. And he remained dumb; he stretched out no finger to help himself. All that he required to keep himself a decent member of society was, that the girl, five thousand miles away, should continue to love him. They were putting a stopper upon that.

I have told you that the girl came one night to his room. And that was the real hell for him. That was the picture that never left his imagination – the girl, in the dim light, rising up at the foot of his bed. He said that it seemed to have a greenish sort of effect as if there were a greenish tinge in the shadows of the tall bedposts that framed her body. And she looked at him with her straight eyes of an unflinching cruelty and she said: 'I am ready to belong to you – to save your life.'

He answered: 'I don't want it; I don't want it; I don't want it.'

And he says that he didn't want it; that he would have hated himself; that it was unthinkable. And all the while he had the immense temptation to do the unthinkable thing, not from the physical desire but because of a mental certitude. He was certain that if she had once submitted to him she would remain his for ever. He knew that.

She was thinking that her aunt had said he had desired her to love him from a distance of five thousand miles. She said: 'I can never love you now I know the kind of man you are. I will belong to you to save your life. But I can never love you.'

It was a fantastic display of cruelty. She didn't in the least know what it meant – to belong to a man. But, at that Edward pulled himself together. He spoke in his normal tones; gruff, husky, overbearing, as he would have done to a servant or to a horse.

'Go back to your room,' he said. 'Go back to your room and go to sleep. This is all nonsense.'

They were baffled, those two women.

And then I came on the scene.

VI

My coming on the scene certainly calmed things down – for the whole fortnight that intervened between my arrival and the girl's departure. I don't mean to say that the endless talking did not go on at night or that Leonora did not send me out with the girl and, in the interval, give Edward a hell of a time. Having discovered what he wanted – that the girl should go five thousand miles away and love him steadfastly as people do in sentimental novels, she was determined to smash that aspiration. And she repeated to Edward in every possible tone that the girl did not love him; that the girl detested him for his brutality, his overbearingness, his drinking habits. She pointed out that Edward in the girl's eyes, was already pledged three or four deep. He was pledged to Leonora herself, to Mrs Basil, and to the memories of Maisie Maidan and to Florence. Edward never said anything.

Did the girl love Edward, or didn't she? I don't know. At that time I daresay she didn't, though she certainly had done so before Leonora had got to work upon his reputation. She certainly had loved him for what I call the public side of his record – for his good soldiering, for his saving lives at sea, for the excellent landlord that he was and the good sportsman. But it is quite possible that all those things came to appear as nothing in her eyes when she discovered that he wasn't a good husband. For, though women, as I see them, have little or no feeling of responsibility towards a county or a country or a career – although they may be entirely lacking in any kind of communal solidarity – they have an immense and automatically working instinct that attaches them to the interest of womanhood. It is, of course, possible for any woman to cut out and to carry off any other woman's husband or lover. But I rather think that a woman will only do this if she has reason to believe that the other woman has given her husband a bad time. I am certain that if she thinks the man has been a brute to his wife she will, with her instinctive feeling for suffering femininity, 'put him back', as the saying is. I don't attach any particular importance to these generalizations of mine. They may be right, they may be wrong; I am only an ageing American with very little knowledge of life. You may take my generalizations or leave them. But I am pretty certain that I am right in the case of Nancy Rufford – that she had loved Edward Ashburnham very deeply and tenderly.

It is nothing to the point that she let him have it good and strong as soon as she discovered that he had been unfaithful to Leonora and that his public services had cost more than Leonora thought they ought to have cost. Nancy would be bound to let him have it good and strong then. She would owe that to feminine public opinion; she would be driven to it by the instinct for self-preservation, since she might well imagine that if Edward had been unfaithful to Leonora, to Mrs Basil and to the memories of the other two, he might be unfaithful to herself. And, no doubt, she had her share of the sex instinct that makes women be intolerably cruel to the beloved person. Anyhow, I don't know whether, at this point. Nancy Rufford loved Edward Ashburnham. I don't know whether she even loved him when, on getting, at Aden, the news of his suicide she went mad. Because that may just as well have been for the sake of Leonora as for the sake of Edward. Or it may have been for the sake of both of them. I don't know. I know nothing. I am very tired.

Leonora held passionately the doctrine that the girl didn't love Edward. She wanted desperately to believe that. It was a doctrine as necessary to her existence as a belief in the personal immortality of the soul. She said that it was impossible that Nancy could have loved Edward after she had given the girl her view of Edward's career and character. Edward, on the other hand, believed maunderingly that some essential attractiveness in himself must have made the girl continue to go on loving him – to go on loving him, as it were, in underneath her official aspect of hatred. He thought she only pretended to hate him in order to save her face and he thought that her quite atrocious telegram from Brindisi was only another attempt to do that – to prove that she had feelings creditable to a member of the feminine commonweal. I don't know. I leave it to you.

There is another point that worries me a good deal in the aspects of this sad affair. Leonora says that, in desiring that the girl should go five thousand miles away and yet continue to love him, Edward was a monster of selfishness. He was desiring the ruin of a young life. Edward on the other hand put it to me that, supposing that the girl's love was a necessity to his existence, and, if he did nothing by word or by action to keep Nancy's love alive, he couldn't be called selfish. Leonora replied that showed he had an abominably selfish nature even though his actions might be perfectly correct. I can't make out which of them was right. I leave it to you.

It is, at any rate, certain that Edward's actions were perfectly – were monstrously, were cruelly – correct. He sat still and let Leonora take away his character, and let Leonora damn him to deepest hell, without stirring a finger. I daresay he was a fool; I don't see what object there was in letting the girl think worse of him than was necessary. Still there it is. And there it is also that all those three presented to the world the spectacle of being the best of good people. I assure you that during my stay for that fortnight in that fine old house, I never so much as noticed a single thing that could have affected that good opinion. And even when I look back, knowing the circumstances, I can't remember a single thing any of them said that could have betrayed them. I can't remember, right up to the dinner, when Leonora read out that telegram – not the tremor of an eyelash, not the shaking of a hand. It was just a pleasant country house-party.

And Leonora kept it up jolly well, for even longer than that – she kept it up as far as I was concerned until eight days after Edward's funeral. Immediately after that particular dinner – the dinner at which I received the announcement that Nancy was going to leave for India on the following day – I asked Leonora to let me have a word with her. She took me into her little sitting-room and I then said – I spare you the record of my emotions – that she was aware that I wished to marry Nancy; that she had seemed to favour my suit and that it appeared to be rather a waste of money upon tickets and rather a waste of time upon travel to let the girl go to India if Leonora thought that there was any chance of her marrying me.

And Leonora, I assure you, was the absolutely perfect British matron. She said that she quite favoured my suit; that she could not desire for the girl a better husband; but that she considered that the girl ought to see a little more of life before taking such an important step. Yes, Leonora used the words 'taking such an important step'. She was perfect. Actually, I think she would have liked the girl to marry me enough but my programme included the buying of the Kershaws' house about a mile and a half away upon the Fordingbridge road, and settling down there with the girl. That didn't at all suit Leonora. She didn't want to have the girl within a mile and a half of Edward for the rest of their lives. Still, I think she might have managed to let me know, in some periphrasis or other, that I might have the girl if I would take her to Philadelphia or Timbuctoo.[163] I loved Nancy very much – and Leonora knew it.

However, I left it at that. I left it with the understanding that Nancy was going away to India on probation. It seemed to me a perfectly reasonable arrangement and I am a reasonable sort of man. I simply said that I should follow Nancy out to India after six months' time or so. Or, perhaps, after a year. Well, you see, I did follow Nancy out to India after a year . . .

I must confess to having felt a little angry with Leonora for not having warned me earlier that the girl would be going. I took it as one of the queer, not very straight methods that Roman Catholics seem to adopt in dealing with matters of this world. I took it that Leonora had been afraid I should propose to the girl or, at any rate, have made considerably greater advances to her than I did, if I had known earlier that she was going away so soon. Perhaps Leonora was right; perhaps Roman Catholics, with their queer, shifty ways, are always right. They are dealing with the queer, shifty thing that is human nature. For it is quite possible that, if I had known Nancy was going away so soon, I should have tried making love to her.[164] And that would have produced another complication. It may have been just as well.

It is queer the fantastic things that quite good people will do in order to keep up their appearance of calm pococurantism. For Edward Ashburnham and his wife called me half the world over in order to sit on the back seat of a dogcart whilst Edward drove the girl to the railway station from which she was to take her departure to India. They wanted, I suppose, to have a witness of the calmness of that function. The girl's luggage had been already packed and sent off before. Her berth on the steamer had been taken. They had timed it all so exactly that it went like clockwork. They had known the date upon which Colonel Rufford would get Edward's letter and they had known almost exactly the hour at which they would receive his telegram asking his daughter to come to him. It had all been quite beautifully and quite mercilessly arranged, by Edward himself. They gave Colonel Rufford, as a reason for telegraphing, the fact that Mrs Colonel Somebody or Other would be travelling by that ship and that she would serve as an efficient chaperon for the girl. It was a most amazing business, and I think that it would have been better in the eyes of God if they had all attempted to gouge out each other's eyes with carving knives. But they were 'good people'.

After my interview with Leonora I went desultorily into Edward's gunroom. I didn't know where the girl was and I thought I might find her there. I suppose I had a vague idea of proposing to her in spite of Leonora. So, I presume, I don't come of quite such good people as the Ashburnhams. Edward was lounging in his chair smoking a cigar and he said nothing for quite five minutes. The candles glowed in the green shades; the reflections were green in the glasses of the bookcases that held guns and fishing-rods. Over the mantelpiece was the brownish picture of the white horse. Those were the quietest moments that I have ever known. Then, suddenly, Edward looked me straight in the eyes and said:

'Look here, old man, I wish you would drive with Nancy and me to the station tomorrow.'

I said that of course I would drive with him and Nancy to the station on the morrow. He lay there for a long time, looking along the line of his knees at the fluttering fire, and then suddenly, in a perfectly calm voice, and without lifting his eyes, he said:

'I am so desperately in love with Nancy Rufford that I am dying of it.'

Poor devil – he hadn't meant to speak of it. But I guess he just had to speak to somebody and I appeared to be like a woman or a solicitor. He talked all night.

Well, he carried out the programme to the last breath.

It was a very clear winter morning, with a good deal of frost in it. The sun was quite bright, the winding road between the heather and the bracken was very hard. I sat on the back seat of the dogcart; Nancy was beside Edward. They talked about the way the cob went; Edward pointed out with the whip a cluster of deer upon a coomb three-quarters of a mile away. We passed the hounds in the level bit of road beside the high trees going into Fordingbridge and Edward pulled up the dogcart so that Nancy might say goodbye to the huntsman and cap him a last sovereign. She had ridden with those hounds ever since she had been thirteen.

The train was five minutes late and they imagined that that was because it was market-day at Swindon or wherever the train came from. That was the sort of thing they talked about. The train came in;

Edward found her a first-class carriage with an elderly woman in it. The girl entered the carriage, Edward closed the door and then she put out her hand to shake mine. There was upon those people's faces no expression of any kind whatever. The signal for the train's departure was a very bright red; that is about as passionate a statement as I can get into that scene. She was not looking her best; she had on a cap of brown fur that did not very well match her hair. She said:

'So long,' to Edward.

Edward answered: 'So long.'

He swung round on his heel and, large, slouching, and walking with a heavy deliberate pace, he went out of the station. I followed him and got up beside him in the high dogcart. It was the most horrible performance I have ever seen.

And, after that, a holy peace, like the peace of God which passes all understanding,[165] descended upon Bramshaw Teleragh. Leonora went about her daily duties with a sort of triumphant smile – a very faint smile, but quite triumphant. I guess she had so long since given up any idea of getting her man back that it was enough for her to have got the girl out of the house and well cured of her infatuation. Once, in the hall, when Leonora was going out, Edward said, beneath his breath – but I just caught the words:

> Thou hast conquered, O pale Galilean.[166]

It was like his sentimentality to quote Swinburne.

But he was perfectly quiet and he had given up drinking. The only thing that he ever said me after that drive to the station was:

'It's very odd. I think I ought to tell you, Dowell, that I haven't any feelings at all about the girl now it's all over. Don't you worry about me. I'm all right.' A long time afterwards he said: 'I guess it was only a flash in the pan.' He began to look after the estates again; he took all that trouble over getting off the gardener's daughter who had murdered her baby. He shook hands smilingly with every farmer in the market-place. He addressed two political meetings; he hunted twice. Leonora made him a frightful scene about spending the two hundred pounds on getting the gardener's daughter acquitted. Everything went on as if the girl had never existed. It was very still weather.

Well, that is the end of the story. And, when I come to look at it I see that it is a happy ending with wedding bells and all. The villains – for obviously Edward and the girl were villains – have been punished by suicide and madness. The heroine – the perfectly normal, virtuous and slightly deceitful heroine – has become the happy wife of a perfectly normal, virtuous and slightly deceitful husband. She will shortly become a mother of a perfectly normal, virtuous, slightly deceitful son or daughter. A happy ending, that is what it works out at.

I cannot conceal from myself the fact that I now dislike Leonora. Without doubt I am jealous of Rodney Bayham. But I don't know whether it is merely a jealousy arising from the fact that I desired myself to possess Leonora or whether it is because to her were sacrificed the only two persons that I have ever really loved – Edward Ashburnham and Nancy Rufford. In order to set her up in a modern mansion, replete with every convenience and dominated by a quite respectable and eminently economical master of the house, it was necessary that Edward and Nancy Rufford should become, for me at least, no more than tragic shades.

I seem to see poor Edward, naked and reclining amidst darkness, upon cold rocks, like one of the ancient Greek damned, in Tartarus[167] or wherever it was.

And as for Nancy . . . Well, yesterday at lunch she said suddenly: 'Shuttlecocks!'

And she repeated the word 'shuttlecocks' three times. I know what was passing in her mind, if she can be said to have a mind, for Leonora has told me that, once, the poor girl said she felt like a shuttlecock being tossed backwards and forwards between the violent personalities of Edward and his wife. Leonora, she said, was always trying to deliver her over to Edward, and Edward tacitly and silently forced her back again. And the odd thing was that Edward himself considered that those two women used *him* like a shuttlecock. Or, rather, he said that they sent him backwards and forwards like a blooming parcel that someone didn't want to pay the postage on. And Leonora also imagined that Edward and Nancy picked her up and threw her down as suited their purely vagrant moods. So there you have the pretty picture. Mind, I am not preaching anything contrary to accepted morality. I am not advocating free love in this or any other case. Society must go on, I suppose, and society can only exist if the normal, if the virtuous, and the slightly deceitful flourish, and if the passionate, the headstrong, and the too-truthful are condemned to suicide and to madness. But I guess that I myself, in my fainter way, come into the category of the passionate, of the headstrong, and the too-truthful. For I can't conceal from myself the fact that I loved Edward Ashburnham – and that I love him because he was just myself. If I had had the courage and virility and possibly also the physique of Edward Ashburnham I should, I fancy, have done much what he did. He seems to me like a large elder brother who took me out on several excursions and did many dashing things whilst I just watched him robbing the orchards, from a distance. And, you see, I am just as much of a sentimentalist as he was . . .

Yes, society must go on; it must breed, like rabbits. That is what we are here for. But then, I don't like society – much. I am that absurd figure, an American millionaire, who has bought one of the ancient haunts of English peace. I sit here, in Edward's gunroom, all day and all day in a house that is absolutely quiet. No one visits me, for I visit no one. No one is interested in me, for I have no interests. In twenty minutes or so I shall walk down to the village, beneath my own oaks, alongside my own clumps of gorse, to get the American mail. My tenants, the village boys and the tradesmen will touch their hats to me. So life peters out. I shall return to dine and Nancy will sit opposite me with the old nurse standing behind her. Enigmatic, silent, utterly well-behaved as far as her knife and fork go, Nancy will stare in front of her with the blue eyes that have over them strained, stretched brows. Once, or perhaps twice, during the meal her knife and fork will be suspended in mid-air as if she were trying to think of something that she had forgotten. Then she will say that she believes in an Omnipotent Deity or she will utter the one word 'shuttlecocks', perhaps. It is very extraordinary to see the perfect flush of health on her cheeks, to see the lustre of her coiled black hair, the poise of the head upon the neck, the grace of the white hands – and to think that it all means nothing – that it is a picture without a meaning. Yes, it is queer.

But, at any rate, there is always Leonora to cheer you up; I don't want to sadden you. Her husband is quite an economical person of so normal a figure that he can get quite a large proportion of his clothes ready-made. That is the great desideratum of life, and that is the end of my story. The child is to be brought up as a Romanist.

It suddenly occurs to me that I have forgotten to say how Edward met his death. You remember that peace had descended upon the house; that Leonora was quietly triumphant and that Edward said his love for the girl had been merely a passing phase. Well, one afternoon we were in the stables together, looking at a new kind of flooring that Edward was trying in a loose box. Edward was talking with a good deal of animation about the necessity of getting the numbers of the Hampshire territorials[168] up to the proper standard. He was quite sober, quite quiet, his skin was clear-coloured; his hair was golden and perfectly brushed; the level brick-dust red of his complexion went clean up to the rims of his eyelids; his eyes were porcelain blue and they regarded me frankly and directly. His face was perfectly expressionless; his voice was deep and rough. He stood well back upon his legs and said:

'We ought to get them up to two thousand three hundred and fifty.'

A stable-boy brought him a telegram and went away. He opened it negligently, regarded it without emotion, and, in complete silence, handed it to me. On the pinkish paper in a sprawled handwriting I read: 'Safe Brindisi. Having rattling good time. Nancy.'

Well, Edward was the English gentleman; but he was also, to the last, a sentimentalist, whose mind was compounded of indifferent poems and novels. He just looked up to the roof of the stable, as if he were looking to Heaven, and whispered something that I did not catch.

Then he put two fingers into the waistcoat pocket of his grey, frieze suit; they came out with a little neat penknife – quite a small penknife. He said to me:

'You might just take that wire to Leonora.' And he looked at me with a direct, challenging, brow-beating glare. I guess he could see in my eyes that I didn't intend to hinder him. Why should I hinder him?

I didn't think he was wanted in the world, let his confounded tenants, his rifle-associations, his drunkards, reclaimed and unreclaimed, get on as they liked. Not all the hundreds and hundreds of them deserved that that poor devil should go on suffering for their sakes.

When he saw that I did not intend to interfere with him his eyes became soft and almost affectionate. He remarked:

'So long, old man, I must have a bit of a rest, you know.'

I didn't know what to say. I wanted to say, 'God bless you', for I also am a sentimentalist. But I thought that perhaps that would not be quite English good form, so I trotted off with the telegram to Leonora. She was quite pleased with it.

Notes

NSOED refers to *The New Shorter Oxford English Dictionary* (Oxford: Clarendon Press, 1993).

1. *'Beati Immaculati'*: 'Blessed are the undefiled' (Latin). 'Blessed are the undefiled in the way, who walk in the law of the Lord' (Psalm 119:1; 118:1 in the Vulgate, the official Roman Catholic Latin text of the Bible, 1592).

2. *the town of Nauheim*: Bad Nauheim is a spa on the northeastern slopes of the Taunus Mountains, twenty-four miles north of Frankfurt-am-Main, central Germany. In 1915 it was in the grand duchy of Hesse-Darmstadt and has long been noted for its salt springs, which are used to treat nerve and heart disorders. Ford visited Nauheim in 1910 with Violet Hunt.

3. *the Ashburnham who accompanied . . . scaffold*: Sir John Ashburnham (1603–71) of Sussex held the position of 'groom of the bedchamber' at the court of Charles I and was also treasurer and paymaster of the Royalist army during the Civil Wars (1642–51). Ford had touched on Sir John in an earlier work, Ford Madox Hueffer, *The Cinque Ports: A Historical and Descriptive Record* (London: William Blackwood, 1900), 36.

4. *Cranford*: the English novelist Elizabeth Gaskell (1810–65) published *Cranford*, a novel loosely based on the Cheshire town of Knutsford, in 1853. It has always been regarded as one of the quintessential portraits of English provincial life.

5. *Chestnut and Walnut Streets*: prime real estate in Philadelphia.

6. *Farnham . . . William Penn*: the founding father of Pennsylvania, William Penn (1644–1718), was an English Quaker. He was born at Tower Hill, London, educated in Essex, and had no connection with Farnham in Surrey.

7. *Fordingbridge*: a small market town in southwest Hampshire on the River Avon and the western edge of the New Forest.

8. *sack of Rome by the Goths*: Rome was sacked by the Visigoths under their king Alaric (*c*. 370–410) in August 410, an event that symbolized the fall of the Roman Empire.

9. *Homburg*: a spa town and watering-place at the southeastern foot of the Taunus Mountains twelve miles north of Frankfurt-am-Main.

10. *the Kur orchestra*: the orchestra which played for the entertainment of patrons of the *Kursaal* ('Cure Hall') at Nauheim.

11. *minuet de la cour*: 'minuet of the court' (French).

12. *mob may sack Versailles; the Trianon*: the baroque Palace of Versailles, twelve miles west of Paris, was the principal residence of the French kings from 1678–1769. In addition to the Grand Château, there are two smaller châteaux, the Grand Trianon and the Petit Trianon. The Palace was stormed by the Paris mob on 6 October 1789 soon after the beginning of the French Revolution. The Petit Trianon was a favourite resort of Marie Antoinette (1755–93), the wife of Louis XVI (1754–93), and she only escaped with difficulty when the mob burst in to her quarters.

13. *Hessian*: 'Of or pertaining to the former grand duchy, or the region or State, of Hesse in Germany' (*NSOED*).

14. *Taunus Wald*: the Taunus Forest, extending northwards over a large area of the Taunus Mountains from Wiesbaden and Bad Homburg.

15. *Swedish exercises*: 'a system of therapeutic muscular exercises' (*NSOED*).

16. *in saecula saeculorum*: 'for ever and ever' (Latin). The words that conclude most prayers in the Tridentine Mass, the eucharistic liturgy used by the Roman Catholic Church from 1570 to 1964.

17. *the Field*: a magazine, founded in 1853, for devotees of field sports and other country pursuits.

18. *Peire Vidal*: the type of the reckless and scatterbrained troubadour (Provençal lyric poets who composed and sang on the theme of courtly love in the Middle Ages), Vidal's biographer called him 'the maddest man in all the world'.

19. *Biarritz . . . mistral*: Biarritz is a coastal town in southwest France on the Bay of Biscay. It became a fashionable resort under the patronage of the Empress Eugénie in the 1850s. Las Tours is situated in the Black Mountains of southwest France, a few miles from Carcassonne. The mistral is a cold, dry, northerly wind that is funnelled down the Rhône Valley in southern France to the Mediterranean.

20. *Poughkeepsie*: a small town in New York State and the location of Vassar College, a non-sectarian institution for the higher education of women, incorporated in 1861 and opened in 1865.

21. *William the Silent . . . Beaucaire*: William the Silent was the name by which William I (1533–84), Prince of Orange, was more widely known. By 'Gustave the Loquacious', Dowell probably has in mind Gustavus Adolphus (1594–1632), King of Sweden (1611–32), whose polyglot accomplishments were legendary.

Henri Fantin Latour (1836–1904) was a French painter of highly detailed, 'Dutch'-style, still-life subjects and group portraits. Tarascon is a largely medieval town near the mouth of the River Rhône. Beaucaire, another medieval town popular with tourists, faces it across the river.

22. *Flatiron . . . Broadway*: the 290-ft-high Fuller or 'Flatiron' Building, completed in 1902, is one of the oldest skyscrapers in New York City.

23. *Mont Majour . . . Carcassonne itself*: Mont Majour is a small town near Tarascon and Beaucaire in Provence, southern France, with a medieval abbey. Carcassonne is a medieval fortified town in the Aude region of southwest France, which was largely rebuilt in the nineteenth century.

24. *Leghorn*: the English name for Livorno, a port in central Italy on the Ligurian sea, south of Pisa and not far from Florence.

25. *modistes and over the plages*: a 'modiste' is a milliner and a 'plage' is a beach. Both words are French.

26. *a Browning tea*: founded in 1881 by F. J. Furnivall and E. H. Hickey and dedicated to examining every aspect of the poetry and life of the English poet Robert Browning (1812–89), the Browning Society is still in existence today (it is now no less concerned with the life and work of Browning's wife, the poet Elizabeth Barratt Browning, 1806–61). A 'Browning tea' would have been a tea party involving either members of the Society or unaffiliated aficionados of Robert Browning's work.

27. *spelling bee*: 'a contest in spelling' (*NSOED*).

28. *Stuyvesant*: the Dutch colonial administrator Peter Stuyvesant (c.1610–72) was Governor of New Netherland until 8 September 1664, when the colony was taken from him by the British and divided into New York and New Jersey. There is a Stuyvesant Square in Manhattan. Dowell probably has in mind a philistine but wealthy crowd of socialites based around a family called Stuyvesant (see p. 67).

29. *Frans Hals . . . Pre-Mycenaic*: Frans Hals (*c*. 1581–1666) was born in Antwerp of Flemish parents, but spent most of his life in Haarlem. His talent was for portraiture and he is best known for the huge and lively groups of archers and musketeers which he painted from 1616. Philips Wouwerman (1619–1668), also a Haarlem painter and a pupil of Hals, painted genre scenes of horsemen, battles and camp life. Mycenaic civilization, the civilization of Bronze Age Greece, flourished between *c*.1650 BC and *c*.1200 BC.

30. *Cnossos . . . Walter Pater*: Cnossos (more commonly Knossos) was the principal city of Minoan Crete. It was excavated between 1899 and 1935 by the British archaeologist Sir Arthur Evans (1851–1941). The most influential and lasting work of the English critic Walter Pater (1839–94) is his *Studies in the*

History of the Renaissance (1873). It had a profound effect on the development of aestheticism in England.

31. *Waterbury*: an industrial city on the River Naugatuck in Connecticut, Waterbury was once famous as the brass centre of the USA.

32. *Democrat . . . Republican*: from 1869, when Ulysses S. Grant took office as the 18th President of the United States, until 1913, when Woodrow Wilson took office as the 28th, the American President had always been a Republican, apart from during Grover Cleveland's two terms of office (1885–9 and 1893–7).

33. *North Cape*: considered to be (though not actually) the most northerly point of the European continent, North Cape is a promontory on a north Norwegian island and a traditional stop for tourist steamers.

34. *Bramshaw*: Bramshaw is situated on the edge of the New Forest, about six miles west of Fordingbridge, in Hampshire.

35. *the Englischer Hof*: the English Hotel.

36. *the Chapeau de Paille of Rubens*: otherwise known as *The Straw Hat* by the Flemish painter Peter Paul Rubens (1577–1640), the most important northern European artist of his day and the greatest exponent of the baroque outside southern Europe. This picture was executed around 1625 and is now in the National Gallery, London.

37. *the Hotel Excelsior*: 'Excelsior' means 'A person who or thing which reaches or aspires to reach higher' (*NSOED*). It is the comparative of the Latin word *excelsus* (lofty).

38. *Fourteenth Hussars*: 'The 14th King's Hussars, later the 14th/20th King's Hussars, who captured Joseph Bonaparte's carriage and retained a silver chamber pot as a trophy after the Battle of Vitoria (1813).' Hence their nickname: 'the Emperor's Chambermaids' (*Brewer's Dictionary of Phrase and Fable*, 1999).

39. *Falls River, N.J.*: there is no such place as 'Falls River, New Jersey' and Dowell almost certainly has in mind the city of Fall River, Massachusetts.

40. *Martingales, Chiffney bits*: a 'martingale' is 'A strap or arrangement of straps fastened at one end to the noseband, bit, or reins of a horse and at the other to its girth, to prevent it from rearing or throwing back its head and to strengthen the action of the bit' (*NSOED*). A 'Chiffney bit' is a special kind of mouthpiece on a bridle invented by the jockey Samuel Chiffney (*c*.1753–1807).

41. *rode a plater down the Khyber cliffs*: a 'plater' is an inferior racehorse, more likely to win one of the runner-up plates than the main prize. The Khyber Pass is a strategic mountain pass, forty-five miles long, in the Safid Kuh range of the Hindu Kush mountains connecting Kabul, capital of Afghanistan, with Peshawar in northern Pakistan, then part of the Northwest Frontier region of the British Indian Empire.

42. *Burlington Arcade*: Burlington Arcade was designed in 1819 but has since been remodelled on a number of occasions, most recently after it was damaged in the Second World War. It runs north off Piccadilly and houses a number of well-known shops.

43. *Gadarene swine*: Matt. 8:28–32 describes how a herd of swine at Gadara in ancient Palestine all rushed violently down a slope and perished in the sea.

44. *Brindisi*: a seaport in Apulia, southeast Italy, on the Adriatic Sea. In the Middle Ages, it was an embarkation port for the Crusaders.

45. *Wiesbaden . . . the Bonner Hussaren*: Wiesbaden is a spa city in central Germany on the River Rhine at the foot of the Taunus Mountains. The Bonner Hussaren were a cavalry regiment based in the Westphalian city of Bonn.

46. *Lelöffel*: Ford and Violet Hunt met a 'Count Lelöffel, one of the "favourite officers of the Kaiser" ', when they stayed at Nauheim in 1910 (Max Saunders, *Ford Madox Ford*, i, 313).

47. *'And so the whole round table is begun' . . . Avanti!*: in Arthurian legend, King Arthur received the Round Table from Leodegraunce of Cameliard when he married his daughter, Guinevere. Her adulterous love for Lancelot led to the break up of the Round Table and Arthur's death. *'Avanti'* means 'forward' in Italian.

48. *Fachingen water*: from the mineral springs of Fachingen, then in the Prussian province of Hesse-Nassau.

49. *Nassau Schwerin*: Nassau was until 1866 an independent and sovereign German duchy, while Schwerin, 129 miles north of Berlin, was capital of the grand duchy of Mecklenburg-Schwerin. 'Nassau Schwerin', however, is one of Dowell's inventions.

50. *bonne bouche*: literally a pleasant taste in the mouth, a treat (French).

51. *his nephew, the Emperor*: that is, Wilhelm II (1859–1941), Emperor of Germany and King of Prussia (1888–1918).

52. *traps*: baggage.

53. *Kümmel*: sweet liqueur from north Germany. It is flavoured with cumin and caraway seeds, which give it digestive qualities.

54. *Episcopalian . . . Quaker*: an Episcopalian is a member of the Protestant Episcopal Church of the USA founded in 1787. A 'Quaker' is a member of what used to be called the Religious Society of Friends, a Christian sect with no ordained ministers, sacraments or formal doctrine. The Quakers were founded by George Fox (1624–91) in the late 1640s and almost immediately suffered persecution in England. In 1682 William Penn led a colony of Quakers to the area of America which would soon take his name, Pennsylvania.

55. *the cock . . . Aesculapius*: Aesculapius (or Asclepius) was the Greek god of

medicine, the son of Apollo and the father of Hygeia. The usual offering to Aesculapius was a cock, hence to 'sacrifice a cock to Aesculapius' means to give thanks – or pay the medical bills – after recovery from illness.

56. *Baedeker*: a series of international guide books, once considered indispensable, published by the German publisher Karl Baedeker (1801–59). Baedeker produced his first guide, to Koblenz, in 1829.

57. *M— . . . like Windsor*: the ancient university town of Marburg has an 11th-century gothic castle containing an important library. It is also home to the oldest Protestant university in Germany (1527). Far from being a square, the site of Windsor Castle in Berkshire, begun by William the Conqueror as a stockaded earthwork, is an irregular parallelogram.

58. *St Elizabeth of Hungary*: (1207–31), lived as a Franciscan nun at Marburg. She built a hospital in the town and the Elisabethkirche was built to contain her tomb. She was canonized by Pope Gregory IX in 1235.

59. *Prussia . . . disagreeable to go into that country*: following Prussia's victory in the Franco-Prussian War of 1870–71, the German Empire was declared under Prussian leadership and her imperial rivalry with Britain began in earnest. Prussian society was highly militarized and widely regarded as unappealingly totalitarian.

60. *the Lahn*: the River Lahn, a tributary of the River Rhine, runs through Marburg.

61. *pour le bon motif!*: with the best intentions! (French).

62. *Ludwig the Courageous . . . one after the other*: Dowell actually has in mind Philip the Magnanimous (1504–67), Landgrave of Hesse (1509 – 67). The German Protestant reformer Martin Luther (1483–1546) allowed Philip to marry a second, but not a third, wife. Henry VIII married six women in succession: Catherine of Aragon, Anne Boleyn, Jane Seymour, Anne of Cleves, Katherine Howard and Catherine Parr.

63. *one of the dark places of the earth*: this phrase had previously been uttered by Charlie Marlow, the principal narrator of *Heart of Darkness* (1902) by Ford's friend Joseph Conrad. Referring to England at the time of the Roman Conquest, Marlow's first words are: 'And this also . . . has been one of the dark places of the earth.'

64. *Arminians and Erastians*: Arminians followed the teachings of the Dutch Protestant theologian Jacobus Arminius (1560–1609), who believed that predestination was conditional, whereas his Calvinist opponents believed it was absolute. 'Erastians' followed the teachings of Thomas Erastus (1524–83), a Swiss theologian who maintained ecclesiastical affairs were always subject to secular authority.

65. *Mrs Markham*: pseudonym of Mrs Elizabeth Penrose (1780–1837), writer of popular, sanitized, historical and other books for children, the best known being *Mrs Markham's History of England* (1823) and *Mrs Markham's History of France* (1828).

66. *Schloss*: castle (German).

67. *Ranke's History of the Popes . . . Table Talk*: the books in question are as follows: Leopold von Ranke, *The Ecclesiastical and Political History of the Popes of Rome During the Sixteenth and Seventeenth Centuries* (1837–9; trans. S. Austin, 1840); John Addington Symonds, *The Renaissance in Italy* (1875–6); J. L. Motley, *The Rise of the Dutch Republic* (1856); and Martin Luther, *The Table Talk or Familiar Discourse of Martin Luther* (1566; trans. W. Hazlitt, 1848).

68. *Droschke*: a four-wheeled carriage (German).

69. *Pennsylvania Duitsch*: the German spoken by German immigrants to Pennsylvania. The word should properly be *Deutsch*, but *Duitsch* is a possible form in the Low German (*Plattdeutsch*) dialect, as spoken in the northern part of Germany.

70. *Trinkgeld*: literally, 'drink money', i.e., a tip (German).

71. *Rittersaal . . . the Reformer*: literally, 'knights' room', i.e., a state room (German). The 'Reformer' was Martin Luther. He instigated the Protestant Reformation when, as a professor of theology at Wittenberg University, he nailed his 95 theses to the doors of Wittenberg Cathedral on 31 October 1517, attacking the sale of papal indulgences. He was excommunicated in 1521. Luther's original intention was reform, not schism, but by 1530 a separate Protestant church had emerged.

72. *the Protest . . . the Courageous . . .*: actually, the document in question is not the 'Protest' itself, but the fifteen-point doctrinal statement drawn up at the Marburg Colloquy of 1529, and signed by, among others, the Swiss Protestant reformer Ulrich Zwingli (1484–1531), Martin Luther, the German Protestant reformer Martin Bucer (1491–1551), a former Dominican friar who was eventually made Regius Professor of Divinity at Cambridge, and Philip the Magnanimous. The statement was not signed by Ludwig the Courageous because he had long been dead.

73. *'thank'ee-marms'*: a 'thank-you-ma'am' is an American colloquialism for 'a hollow or ridge in a road, which causes people passing over it in a vehicle to nod the head involuntarily, as if in acknowledgement of a favour' (*NSOED*).

74. *Free City*: since the Reformation, there had been three sovereign city states within Germany: Bremen, Hamburg and Lübeck.

75. *Spa*: the original health spa, in the Ardennes region of Belgium.

76. *Burma*: in southeast Asia, on the Bay of Bengal and the Andaman Sea, Burma had been ruled as part of British India since 1885. In 1937 it attained a measure of self-government and was separated from India. In 1948 it became an independent republic.

77. *Chitral*: situated about 129 miles north of Peshawar, Chitral was in Ashburnham's time a remote, northwestern outpost of the British Indian Empire close-to the border with Afghanistan. It is now in Pakistan. In 1885, a small British force withstood siege there by local tribes.

78. *Linlithgowshire*: formerly a Scottish county, now part of West Lothian.

79. *pipped*: hurt him financially.

80. *Circe – at Antibes*: Circe is the goddess in Homer's *Odyssey* (Book 10) who turns Odysseus' men into swine on the island of Aeaea. Antibes is a fashionable resort on the Côte d'Azur in the Alpes-Maritimes department of France.

81. *General Trochu . . . in 1870*: the French soldier Jules Louis Trochu (1815–96) was made Military Governor of Paris on 17 August 1870 during the Franco-Prussian War (1870–71). Regarded as timid and too passive, General Trochu resigned his governorship on 22 January 1871. Food shortages forced the Government of National Defence to ask for an armistice with the Prussians the following month.

82. *Scarlet Woman . . . in Arch Street*: the description of the Whore of Babylon in Revelation 17:1–18, 'clothed in purple and scarlet', was often applied to the Roman Catholic Church by its opponents. The largest Quaker Meeting House in the world is on Arch Street, Philadelphia.

83. *'Requiem . . . aeterna erit'*: 'Eternal rest give to them, O Lord; and let perpetual light shine upon them. The just shall be in everlasting remembrance.' From the Gradual of the Tridentine Mass. In Dowell's source, the word *'justus'* follows *'erit'*.

84. *a northern light*: possibly a reference to the *Aurora Borealis* or Northern Lights.

85. *'I did not know you wanted . . . hardly literate*: Maisie's error, presumably, is that she uses 'for', rather than 'as' or 'to be'.

86. *Reiseverkehrsbureau*: travel agency (German).

87. *Schreibzimmer*: writing-room (German).

88. *a white lily*: 'There is a tradition that the lily sprang from the repentant tears of Eve as she went forth from Paradise. In Christian art the lily is an emblem of chastity, innocence and purity' (*Brewer's Dictionary of Phrase and Fable*, 1999).

89. *Balmoral Castle*: in Aberdeenshire is one of the holiday homes of the British Royal Family and its principal country residence in Scotland. The house was bought by Queen Victoria in 1848 and rebuilt for her in 1853–6 by William Smith of Aberdeen.

90. *Stratford to Strathpeffer . . . Ledbury*: Stratford-upon-Avon in Warwickshire is

world famous as the birthplace of Shakespeare; Strathpeffer, a resort town in the Highland region of Scotland, has a noted medicinal spring, and Ledbury is a market town in Herefordshire, twelve miles east of Hereford.

91. *in the year 1688*: suggests the English Hurlbirds may have been Catholics, as the Glorious Revolution of 1688–9 led to the 'abdication' of the unpopular Catholic James II (reigned 1685–8) and the accession to the throne of the Protestant William III and Mary II. The Bill of Rights (1689), among other things, barred Catholics from succeeding to the crown.

92. *General Braddock*: Edward Braddock (1695–1755) was a British general who was killed in an ambush by French troops and native Americans while crossing the River Monongahela in Pennsylvania in July 1755.

93. *General Washington . . . War of Independence*: George Washington (1732–99) was the first President of the United States of America (1783–97) and Commander in Chief of the Congress forces during the American War of Independence (1775–83).

94. *'Pocahontas'*: the daughter of the native American chief Powhatan, Pocahontas (*c.*1595–1617) was brought to England, baptized, and married the English colonist John Rolfe. She died of smallpox at Gravesend as she was about to return to America.

95. *Rye Station . . . cars to Waterbury*: Rye is a suburb of New York City on Long Island Sound. In colonial times, Rye was the first stop on the Boston Post Road after New York City. The 'cars' must refers to railway carriages: for Waterbury, see Note 31.

96. *Sandy Hook*: is a low, sandy peninsula situated in northeast New Jersey, projecting five miles north towards New York City. The Sandy Hook Lighthouse (1763) is the last American landmark before the Atlantic.

97. *Julien's*: Ford has in mind one of the Paris studios which specifically catered for young foreign men (particularly Americans and Britons) who wanted a solid training in drawing and painting without the obstacle of competitive entry.

98. *cinquecento*: sixteenth-century (Italian).

99. *Rue de la Paix*: ironically, Peace Street (French).

100. *Hoboken*: a New Jersey city, lying across the Hudson River from Manhattan, New York City.

101. *D.S.O.*: the Distinguished Service Order is an order of military merit founded on 6 September 1886 by Queen Victoria, its object being to recognize the exceptional service of officers in the army or navy.

102. *Royal Humane Society's*: founded in 1774 'to encourage the saving of human life', the Royal Humane Society is still in existence today.

103. *V.C.*: the Victoria Cross is the highest British decoration for 'conspicuous

bravery or devotion to the country in the presence of the enemy'. It was founded by Queen Victoria in 1856.

104. *the Beefeaters*: the more common name for the Yeomen Warders of the Tower of London, originally appointed by Edward VI (reigned 1547–53). Their uniform is very similar to that of the sovereign's Bodyguard of the Yeomen of the Guard (1485), the oldest royal bodyguard and the oldest military corps in the world. There are six officers and sixty-six men, and it is almost certainly this bodyguard that Dowell has in mind.

105. *Lohengrin and the Chevalier Bayard*: in Arthurian legend, Lohengrin was the courageous son of Percival (Parzifal) and a Knight of the Holy Grail who was drawn on by Richard Wagner (1813–83) in his opera *Lohengrin* (1850). Pierre Terrail, Seigneur de Bayard (c.1473–1524) was a French soldier known as '*le bon chevalier sans peur et sans reproche*' (the good knight without fear and without reproach). He gained particular distinction at the battles of Fornovo (1495) and Marignano (1515).

106. *the Cid*: the Spanish hero Rodrigo (Ruy) Díaz de Vivar (c.1043–99) was better known as El Cid (from the Moorish *Sidi*, 'lord') or El Campeador ('The Warrior'). He survived as a soldier of fortune, fighting for both the Spanish and the Moors, and his greatest achievement was the capture of the kingdom of Valencia (1094). He became its ruler until his death.

107. *put him at it*: a hunting phrase, meaning to make a horse jump a fence.

108. *nitrate of amyl*: a yellow liquid with a penetrating odour used in medicine for *angina pectoris* (see note 110) owing to its power of producing vascular dilation and of stimulating the heart's action. Ironically, amyl nitrate is also abused as an aphrodisiac; it is supposed to extend or intensify orgasm.

109. *au mieux*: on the best of terms (French).

110. *angina pectoris*: 'Severe pain in the chest, and often also the arms and neck, due to inadequate blood supply to the heart muscles' (*NOED*).

111. *'Zum Befehl, Durchlaucht'*: 'At your command, Serene Highness' (German).

112. *it's the business of a novelist . . . things clearly*: recalls Joseph Conrad's Preface to *The Nigger of the 'Narcissus'* (1897): 'My task . . . is, by the power of the written word to make you . . . *see!*'

113. *Rakocsy March*: composed by the Hungarian János Bihari (1764–1827) in c.1810.

114. *all for love and the world well lost*: *All for Love, or The World Well Lost* (1678) is a tragedy by John Dryden (1631–1700).

115. *Bowery*: a street, and by the 1880s a notoriously skid-row neighbourhood, of Lower Manhattan, New York City.

116. *affaisement*: depression or mental breakdown (French).

117. *Maenad*: the Maenads were women inspired to frenzy by Dionysus, the Greek god of wine and ecstasy, son of Zeus and Semele.

118. *Corpus Christi*: in the western Christian Church the Feast of Corpus Christi (Latin: 'Body of Christ') is observed on the first Thursday after Trinity Sunday in honour of the Real Presence of the body of Jesus Christ in the Eucharist. The chief feature of the Feast is the procession of the Blessed Sacrament.

119. *Roehampton*: the Convent of the Sacred Heart, Roehampton, southwest London, was a prestigious boarding school with many of its girls being drawn from the great European Catholic families.

120. *Fort William*: a town in the Highlands region of Scotland at the head of Loch Linnhe and the foot of Ben Nevis.

121. *Belgian Congo . . . hang humanity!'*: the Congo Free State (now called the Democratic Republic of Congo) was established in the 1880s as the private holding of a group of European investors headed by Leopold II (1835–1909, King of the Belgians, 1865–1909). In 1908 it was annexed by Belgium after years of international outcry at the brutality which held sway in the territory (the population of the Congo Free State is said to have declined from between 20 and 30 million to just 8 million before Leopold II was forced to transfer his powers to the Belgian government). The Congo Free State is the setting of Conrad's *Heart of Darkness*, and this passage in *The Good Soldier* clearly picks up the humanitarian concerns of the earlier work.

122. *Winchester*: founded in 1382 by William of Wykeham, Winchester College in Hampshire is England's oldest public school.

123. *Sandhurst*: a village in Berkshire and the location of the Royal Military Academy (1799).

124. *Scott's novels or the Chronicles of Froissart*: Sir Walter Scott (1771–1832) was a prolific novelist and poet. The chronicles of Jean Froissart (*c*.1337 – *c*.1410) record the chivalric exploits of English and French nobles in the 14th century. They were translated into English from French in 1523–5.

125. *Bond Street . . . Lord's*: Bond Street is a premier shopping street in central London extending southwards from Oxford Street to Piccadilly through the exclusive district of Mayfair. Lord's, a cricket ground in the St John's Wood area of north London, has been the home of Middlesex County Cricket Club and the national headquarters of the game in England since the late 19th century.

126. *Aldershot*: in Hampshire is the chief garrison town and army training centre in the United Kingdom.

127. *Glasmoyle*: an imaginary place in Ireland.

128. *the 'nineties . . . very bad for farming*: with the exceptions of 1891 (when unusually heavy autumn rain ruined the next season's corn crops) and 1894, every year from 1891 to 1900 was stricken by drought, and 1893 was especially bad. Moreover, from 1894, there was a disastrous decline in the value of domestic grain and a great increase in the volume of imported grain.

129. *the big bank failure in 1907 or thereabouts*: payment of cheques in currency was suspended in New York on 28 October 1907 and the suspension continued until the beginning of 1908. The crisis was precipitated by overspeculation by a group of American national banks.

130. *a Vermont Democrat*: the key point is that at this time Vermont was an overwhelmingly Republican state, so a Vermont Democrat would have been a rare bird indeed.

131. *Dreyfus*: Alfred Dreyfus (1859–1935) was a French-Jewish army officer who, while serving on the General Staff, was falsely convicted (in 1894) of handing over secrets to the Germans. He was court-martialled and transported to the penal settlement at Devil's Island off the coast of French Guiana in the Caribbean. Intellectual, political and social life was thrown into turmoil by the case, which revealed the degree of anti-Semitism at the heart of French society. After Dreyfus's case was heard again in 1899 he was found guilty a second time, but pardoned. In 1906 the verdict was reversed and in 1930 German military documents proved his innocence.

132. *Monte Carlo*: a fashionable resort in the principality of Monaco on the Riviera famous for its casinos.

133. *beaux yeux*: beautiful eyes (French).

134. *give her the keys of the street*: throw her out.

135. *'Enfin, mon ami . . . Forli's*: 'Well, my friend. . . .' 'Forli's' is an imaginary Monte Carlo jewellery shop.

136. *Town*: i.e. London.

137. *eau de mélisse*: lemon balm water (French).

138. *Genghis Khan's charger*: the Mongol emperor Genghis Khan (*c.*1162–1227), who was more or less continuously at war from the age of thirteen until his death, must have made use of a good many horses or chargers.

139. *menus plaisirs*: entertainments (French).

140. *Vandykes*: portraits by Sir Anthony Van Dyck (1599–1641). Born in Antwerp, from 1632 until his death he lived and worked in England.

141. *Simla*: (now Shimla) from 1865 to 1939, this city in the Himalayan foothills was the summer capital of British India. It is located about 200 miles north of Delhi in the Punjab region.

142. *brevet-colonel . . . South African War*: a brevet-colonel, or any other brevet officer, is one promoted to a rank without the appropriate pay, almost always on a temporary basis. The Boers (Dutch-origin South African farmers), in winning the first Boer War (1880–1) won independence for the Boer republics of the Transvaal and the Orange Free State. Gold was discovered in the Transvaal in 1886 and this led to renewed tension and eventually conflict, with Britain winning the second Boer (or South African) War (1899–1902).

143. *North Western frontier . . . spruit*: the Northwest Frontier, bounded to the north and west by Afghanistan, was the British military district that controlled the strategic Khyber Pass. The British maintained large military forces in the region, which is now a province of northwest Pakistan. A 'spruit' is 'A small watercourse that is usually dry except in the rainy season' (*NSOED*).

144. *ex's*: expenses.

145. *sent in his papers*: i.e., made a formal application to resign his commission.

146. *lâcher prise*: let go (French).

147. *ad majorem Dei gloriam*: for the greater glory of God (Latin). The official motto of the Society of Jesus, otherwise known as the Jesuits.

148. *the dayspring from on high*: Luke 1:76–9. 'Dayspring' means dawn.

149. *Madeira*: a Portuguese island in the Atlantic about 350 miles off the coast of Morocco. Its mild climate has always attracted holiday-makers and the convalescent.

150. *Chippendale . . . Zoffany and Zucchero*: Thomas Chippendale (1718–79) was the pre-eminent British cabinet-maker of his day, especially famed for his elegant chairs. The German-born painter Johann Zoffany (c.1733–1810) worked chiefly in England after about 1761. He was noted for his theatrical scenes and portraits. By 'Zucchero', Dowell means Francesco Zuccarelli (1702–88), an Italian painter who worked in England 1752–62 and 1765–71. He was a founding member of the Royal Academy and a favourite painter of George III.

151. *Christchurch*: Christchurch Old Hall, the Brand family seat, is presumably in or near the Hampshire coastal town of Christchurch. The town is adjacent to Bournemouth, about twenty miles southeast of Bramshaw.

152. *Ringwood*: a Hampshire town on the western edge of the New Forest, about five miles south of Fordingbridge and eight miles southeast of Bramshaw.

153. *Henry VIII . . . Protestantism rests*: Henry VIII broke from the Roman Catholic Church in order to divorce Catherine of Aragon and marry Anne Boleyn.

154. *Princess Badrulbadour*: the heroine of one of the Arabian Nights stories.

155. *Thou art to all . . . Herrick*: lines 1–2 of 'To the Willow Tree' by the English Cavalier poet Robert Herrick (1591–1674).

156. *National Reserve Committee*: an imaginary committee reflecting pre-1914 Anglo-German tensions.

157. *Deborah . . . hagiology*: there has been no St Deborah, indicating that Dowell is not 'up in' hagiology, Catholic or otherwise. In the Bible there are references to Rebekah's nurse Deborah (Gen. 35:8 and 24:.59) and the Deborah who was famed as a military leader (Judges 4 and 5), but neither seems appropriate here.

158. *'Domine, nunc dimittis . . . in peace'*: 'Lord, now lettest thou thy servant depart in peace' (Latin). From the evening prayer, the last monastic office of the day. Its source is the biblical Song of Simeon, Luke 2:29.

159. *the Crau*: La Crau is the name of the flat and featureless plain between Tarascon and Marseilles.

160. *'Credo in unum Deum Omnipotentem'*: 'I believe in one God Almighty' (Latin). Nancy omits the word *Patrem* ('Father') after *Deum*. From the Nicene Creed.

161. *Aden*: now the main port and commercial centre of Yemen, Aden was taken by the British in 1839 and was an important coaling station for steamships on the route to and from India via the Suez Canal (opened 1869).

162. *Kandy*: was an important independent monarchy in Ceylon (now Sri Lanka). It was the last Sinhalese kingdom to be subjugated by a colonial power, the British, in 1818. Kandy is also a town on the Kandy Plateau in central Sri Lanka, and this is where Dowell has in mind. It was the capital of the Sinhalese kings between c.1480 and 1815.

163. *Timbuctoo*: or Timbuktu, is a town in the African republic of Mali (until 1959 the country was known as French Sudan) on the River Niger.

164. *making love to her*: that is, paying suit to her, with not even the faintest hint of the more recent, purely carnal meaning of the phrase.

165. *the peace of God which passes all understanding*: Philippians 4:7: 'And the peace of God, which passeth all understanding, shall keep your hearts and minds through Christ Jesus.'

166. *Thou hast conquered, O pale Galilean*: line 25 of 'Hymn to Proserpine' by Algernon Charles Swinburne (1837–1909). The 'pale Galilean' is Jesus Christ. Swinburne was a friend of Ford's grandfather, the painter Ford Madox Brown (1821–93) and was very kind to Ford when he was a boy.

167. *Tartarus*: in Greek myth, the place in the Underworld where the wicked suffer punishment for their misdeeds on earth.

168. *the Hampshire territorials*: the British Army's Territorial Force (known after 1921 as the Territorial Army) was established following the Territorial and Reserve Forces Act, 1907.